CRANIAL LEAKAGE

Tales from the Grinning Skull

Volume 1

CRANIAL LEAKAGE

Tales from the Grinning Skull

Volume I

Edited by

Michael J. Evans

A
Grinning Skull Press
Publication

CRANIAL LEAKAGE: Tales from the Grinning Skull, Volume 1
Compilation Copyright © 2014 Grinning Skull Press

"Skin Deep" copyright ©2014 R. J. Fanucchi
"Batch 13" copyright ©2014 Gregor Cole
"Sane Clarity" copyright ©2014 James Park
"Dr. Frank N. Squirrel" copyright ©2014 Julianne Snow
"Shadow-Mancers" copyright ©2014 Nathan Cabaniss
"Revengedotcom" copyright ©2014 Nicholas Stella
"A Mother's Touch" copyright ©2014 DJ Tyrer
"The Little Child, Eve Grace Smith" copyright ©2014 M. R. Gott
"Tom Fool" copyright ©2014 Nicky Peacock
"Sunset is Just the Beginning" copyright ©2014 C. C. Adams
"The Darkening" copyright ©2014 T. L. Norman
"Breakthrough" copyright ©2014 Rose Blackthorn
"Embalming Leon" copyright ©2014 Daryl Marcus
"Building the Nightmare Box" copyright ©2014 Geoffrey L. Mudge
"Like Faces in the Rain" copyright ©2014 Michael C. Schutz-Ryan
"The Thing in the Old Red House" copyright ©2014 Peter John Cunis
"Pumpkins" copyright ©2014 Matt Kurtz
"Witchetty Bogles" copyright ©2014 Stephen McQuiggan
"Night-Gaunts of The Thames" copyright ©2014 Adam Millard
"The Birdy Burger" copyright ©2014 A. P. Sessler
"BugAgeddon" copyright ©2014 Bryan Vogt
"Big Girl" copyright ©2014 Matt Kelly
"Touched by the Finger of God" copyright ©2014 John Bruni
"Candy Stain" copyright ©2014 Jonathan Woodrow

The Skull logo with stylized lettering was created for Grinning Skull Press by Dan Moran, http://dan-moran-art.com/.
Cover design: ©2014 JK Graphics, http://jeffreykosh.wix.com/jeffreykoshgraphics.

ISBN: 0989026965 (paperback)
ISBN-13: 978-0-9890269-6-3 (paperback)
ISBN: 978-0-9890269-7-0 (e-book)

DEDICATION

To the memory of Bob Booth, Papa Necon, a remarkable man who left an amazing legacy.

Table of contents

ACKNOWLEDGMENTS

As always, I would like to thank all the authors who entrusted their work to GSP. Without you, these collections would not be possible. I would also like to send out an extra special thanks Tom Donahue. His assistance with the manuscripts when life got a little crazy is greatly appreciated.

Cranial Leakage, The Birth Of Art

Conceived in darkness.

Nurtured in a place where the sun never reaches.

Feeding off its host like a parasite.

Growing.

Slowly taking shape until it can no longer be contained.

Oozing from its confinement to make its way down its host's arm, forcing its way into those tap-tap-tapping fingers, finally emerging in the form of the written word.

Words that when strung together create images some might find frightening and disturbing, while others might get a chuckle reading them.

And that's where the title of this collection comes in: Cranial. Leakage. Two words that by themselves don't conjure up any particularly vivid images; but put them together, however, and... Well, as a friend of mine said: "Ewwww!"

Think about it. What is an anthology? It's a collection of stories. What are stories but a series of words strung together to generate vivid images within the minds of the reader. And where do those words come from? From the minds of the writers, of course. So in essence they are *Cranial Leakage*, right? And we're not just talking works of fiction here. The same can be said of any work of art, being it written, painted, or sculpted. The end product isn't always beautiful (but you know what they say about beauty: It is fleeting; it is in the eye of the beholder; it is only skin deep), but it will always engender some sort of emotional response with those who set their eyes upon it. That's why this collection opens with R. J. Fanucchi's *Skin Deep*. It deals with an otherworldly artist seeking to discover beauty within the depravity of man. The stories that follow—Gregor Cole's *Batch 13*, James Park's *Sane Clarity*, and Julianne Snow's *Dr. Frank N. Squirrel*—all deal with self-proclaimed artists of one form or another seeking to create the ultimate masterpiece in their respective media.

Despite their differences, these artists all have one thing in common: they all have a passion for what they do. They are no different than the writers who, driven by passion, created them. Well, passion and the need to get out of their heads this thing that has been growing inside, threatening their sanity. After reading some of these tales, you might find yourself wondering if it might not be a little too late for some of these authors, and I mean that in a good way because some of these stories are seriously twisted. I won't mention any names (you guys know who you are, right?); this way you don't go into any of these stories with any preconceived expectations. I will tell you this much, however; you will meet some old friends within these pages, werewolves, vampires, and graveyard ghouls, as well as some new creatures to haunt your waking and sleeping hours. You might think twice before jumping in the shower after reading Michael C. Schutz-Ryan's *Like Faces in the Rain*. And more frightening still are the human monsters you will encounter, like the ones who inhabit Nicholas Stella's *Revengedotcom* or Jonathan Woodrow's *Candy Stain*. You know the ones I'm talking about, don't you? The ones who might be sitting next to you on the train on your way home from work, or the one who creeps into your apartment at night, the one who touches and licks you while you are sleeping, the one who wants to do other things to you but who doesn't dare cross that line—yet. Those are the ones most people find more frightening, the ones that might actually exist.

So without further ado, settle back, turn on the lights, turn the page, and prepare to lose yourself in the nightmare world that is *Cranial Leakage*.

Michael J. Evans
Grinning Skull Press

Skin Deep

R. J. Fanucchi

There is no evil; only desire, hunger, and survival.

Carver often remembered the Prophet's mantra in his time of need.

It had begun as it always did; the faint desire to inhabit flesh, to reconstruct it into... something beautiful.

Carver usually chose the ones who would not to be missed. The man passed out behind the dumpster of the Siletz Roadhouse seemed a perfect candidate.

As he lingered there, his desire became hunger, a hunger to possess this flesh, to sculpt it into something magnificent. As was the way with hunger, it would soon become a matter of survival. If he did not sate his appetite, his ghostly essence would be devoured by his craving. He would be erased from both the physical and the spiritual realms. The only way to curb the hunger was to inhabit a body and make it better.

He examined the lonely figure sprawled behind the Roadhouse. By human standards this composite of fleshly parts was completely normal, but Carver was repulsed.

It was time to get to work, and quickly, as he felt his expanding appetite gnawing away his spirit form.

Taking over was always a tricky process. Even the weakest looking shell of flesh sometimes concealed dangerous psychic pitfalls, but the man's alcohol-soaked brain was an open door, loosely guarded. He seized the opportunity, diving through the weakened defensive barriers to take immediate control.

Possession fulfilled only part of his longing. The second task would be much more difficult. He would need the tool, and he would need this ungainly

3

meat suit he now inhabited to take him to it.

A few blocks to the south, a gas station stood dark, closed for the evening. Behind it, a gentle sloping path led to a chain-link fence surrounding a school yard. Carver maneuvered his new body through a gate and across a grassy field to a play structure made from plastic and wood.

The life of his previous creation had ended here, beneath the plank bridge that led to the slide. The remains had been removed hours ago. Yellow tape wrapped around the cedar frame announced that this was a *Crime Scene*.

It certainly was that, though it was doubtful any of the local barbarians perceived the true injustice that had occurred.

Carver bent his new body down and looked up at the gaps in the planks of the bridge, praying to the stars that his hiding place had not been discovered by the authorities. The stars were kind. He found the round object wedged in the space between wood and screw where he had lodged it right before bullets had blazed from three automatic pistols, ending his brief residence in the young woman's body.

He had used the tool to improve her. He had detached body parts, removed internal organs, and jumbled them all around. A thrill went through him as he recalled the look on the sheriff's face upon discovering her heart hanging from her neck by a taut braided loop of arteries, like an obscenely oversized pendant, and her shaved pussy placed where her mouth should have been.

Having the tool back elated Carver and fired his anticipation for the artistry he would perform on this new body. It did not look like something that could be used as a tool. It had the appearance of an ordinary eyeball sheathed in ice. Through the translucent shield that miraculously never melted, Carver sensed the glow of the baptismal fire blazing within.

The Eye of the Prophet.

The Prophet and Creator of Golan had formed the city as a refuge for the type of creatures deemed vulgar by human society; night stalkers, shape shifters, monsters of every variety. After securing the community in abandoned military bunkers on a remote peninsula in northern Washington, the Prophet had left, vowing to return someday. Carver became the custodian of The Eye that the Prophet had left behind as a symbol of his promised return.

Carver stroked The Eye with a forefinger as he mentally prepared for the work ahead. Up until this moment, the man had not made a peep, but Carver felt a stirring as the man's consciousness began emerging from his stupor.

Taking quick control, Carver made the drunk jump to his feet with the intent of throwing his head sideways into the metal bracing under the playground structure, but the man had recovered enough of his senses to override Carver's move. A battle of wills began.

"Who are you?" The man's thoughts were nearly as slurred as his actual speech would have been. "What are you doing in my head?"

"I'm your conscience," Carver feigned. "Your alter-ego; your other self summoned through an excess of beer. This is you drunk off your ass."

"It's not right. Something's wrong."

"You bet your bottom dollar it is." Carver tried again to jerk the shared body to the side, but his stubborn host managed to put out an arm to take the brunt of the damage that would have been dealt to his skull. The man cried out as the cedar plank dug into his flesh.

"You have a surprisingly quick recovery of wits," Carver continued the inner dialogue. "It's my turn to ask you who you are."

"Jack Robinson. Lincoln County D.A." It sounded like a well-rehearsed introduction.

"You're the district attorney?" The revelation shocked Carver. "Why would a high-profile public figure such as yourself drink to the point of passing out behind a shit-town dive bar?"

When the man's thoughts came again, they were subdued, like an old grandmother forking her fingers to ward off the evil eye. "I saw the devil's work today."

Carver waited for further explanation, and Jack, perhaps to fill the uncomfortable psychic silence, provided it. "It was right here. Sheriff Frey called me out to this dump of a town. He didn't give any details; only that I'd have to see it to believe it. I saw, but I still can't believe it."

The mental voice trailed off, and before Carver could react, Jack was moving. He made it nearly to the edge of the playground area before Carver induced a seizure that clenched every muscle in the D.A.'s body. The prosecutor dropped to the ground, curling into himself like a snail retreating into its shell.

Unperturbed, Carver prompted, "You were saying?"

Jack, a little more subdued, resumed his story as if the interruption had never happened. "She should have been dead. No way a normal human being could live through that mutilation."

Realization dawned. "It was you, wasn't it? You did that to Christy Lee. Jesus, what are you?"

"I made her better." There was pride in Carver's pronouncement. "I altered her look—mere superficial changes only—to make her more suitable. It was your country hick of a sheriff and his two buffoons that killed her. I felt every bullet pierce her flesh until her soul let go. It was your kind, as it always is, that committed an atrocity today."

"You're sick. Get out of my head."

"There is no evil. Only desire, hunger, and survival." Carver repeated the Prophet's mantra, as he always did when confronted with such accusations. It comforted him, eased the division in his soul.

"You're going to kill me, aren't you?"

"Never would I do such a thing. I have no taste for it. I leave death to the species who is fond of it most: humankind. What I am going to do is make your form more... palatable." He savored the word. "Then maybe, just maybe, I'll be able to stand inhabiting your sticky flesh a little longer."

"You're gonna do to me what you did to Christy?"

"Every piece of art is different, unique. I have an exquisite portrait of you in mind."

Carver held up the Prophet's Eye and uttered the required incantation. The power within responded and a white fire streamed from the ice-encrusted orb. The fire was a contradiction; neither hot nor cold, but somehow both at the same time. It was the baptismal font of Golan, but Carver had found other uses for it. It responded to his will with more precision than any plastic surgeon's knives or lasers.

This promised to be one of his greatest works. He sliced away Jack's eyes, nose, and lips, shuffled them around, briefly giving him the appearance of a Mr. Potato Head with its parts scrambled. But this was by no means the final product. He was just getting started.

He opened the stomach cavity with a scalpel of white fire, exposing the viscera. He wound Jack's intestines, which glistened with a sheen like the body of a python slithering in a moonlit river, around his torso and up over the shoulders.

There was something he had been wanting to try for a while. He knew how to do it, but had yet to make his vision a reality. It had been the wrong look for Christy, but Jack was a perfect candidate. He used The Eye to unravel fine ribbons of muscle tissue beneath the man's pale skin and began extruding them through enlarged pores all over his body. The red fibers wriggled like angry worms trying to burrow their way into, or perhaps out of, his flesh.

Jack had screamed at first, as they all did, but that had not lasted long. The pain—and Carver felt every scintillation—was transcendent. After a few moments, all resistance ceased. Perhaps it was the man's awe at Carver's craft that kept him quiescent, but more likely he had succumbed to shock and retreated to some distant place of false comfort inside his head.

Whatever the case, Jack had left the building, and Carver had complete control of the fleshly sculpture. Visually, it was some of his finest work, but on a strictly practical level, the reconstructed body was clumsy at best. It was his alterations to the legs and feet that were the problem. He'd gotten carried away and had violated a basic rule of design: form follows function. This garment of flesh needed to be more than merely beautiful; he had to be able to move in it, and with the legs turned backwards all he could manage was a shambling gait—a zombie shuffle—and that would not serve him well when the hunters picked up his scent, as he knew they soon would.

Stephen Page, the overly persistent cryptozoologist, and the disabled priest, Father Petrie, had both been present at Golan's undoing, and both had vowed to pursue the scattered monsters, albeit for different reasons: Page to seek revenge for the embarrassment of not being accepted into the tribe and Petrie to find the power of God through the Prophet.

Petrie had been touched by The Eye's baptismal fire and was attuned to its power. The Eye was a beacon guiding him to whatever refuge Carver might seek. With his work complete and the desire quieted for the moment, Carver's senses were much more discriminatory, and they were telling him it was time to go.

He fled the playground and tried to lose himself in the maze of humble houses. The Oregon town seemed no different than many he had passed through on his long sojourn south, away from the ruins and ghosts of Golan, except in one peculiar respect: an inordinate number of "Missing Kitty" posters decorated telephone poles and bulletin boards. For a town barely boasting a thousand citizens, the number of lost kittens seemed unusually high.

Excited voices reached his ears, which were now perched on his bared shoulders. The tumult came from the one main road that comprised the commercial center of the town, such as it was, near the Siletz Roadhouse, where this current fiasco had begun.

Too soon. He needed a place to hide.

A pothole-riddled gravel road led away from the paved street. At its end stood a familiar sort of building. To call it a shack would be charitable. The house barely looked lived in. The screen door hung by the top hinge and the fine wire mesh had almost completely unraveled. A broken window gave a view of a kitchen that sported meager furnishings and copious amounts of refuse.

Dark and silent, the ramshackle dwelling was just the sort of hiding place Carver often found on his journey. He heaved his distorted limbs up to the side door and found it unlocked. There was a pervasive chemical odor, like a janitor's storage closet, but the place was far from clean. The kitchen sink and counters were stacked with food-stained dishes. He followed a trail of newspapers and magazines scattered across the floor to what must have been the living room, where rumpled clothes were strewn across a threadbare sofa and a worn rocking chair. There was no sign of the residents, but he knew that he could not remain here for long, so he kept moving.

Down the hallway he spotted what he was looking for: a trapdoor in the ceiling that would give him access to the attic crawlspace. As he reached for the rope to pull it open, a voice startled him.

"What do you think you're doing?" The voice was high, almost a squeak, in sharp contrast to its source. The man who stood in a doorway at the end of the hall was huge. Huge, but soft, not only in the middle, but all over. His silhouette reminded Carver of an oversized Oompa Loompa.

Carver struggled to give a reply. He had placed Jack's mouth in the center of his forehead and his vocal cords were stretched taut, reducing his voice to little more than a whisper.

"I mean no harm," he rasped. "I just need a place to hide."

The lumpy man reached out and flicked a switch, and instantly the dank hall was filled with light from the bare bulb above his head. The light revealed the man's puffy, pimpled face, but it also illumed the intruder.

Carver tried to signal surrender by raising his distorted arms above his head. He clutched the Prophet's Eye in a tight fist.

"What are you?" the man asked. He was young, perhaps still in his teens. His soft, high voice contained more curiosity than fear.

That was something new.

"Shelter me and I'll tell you the whole story."

"I can do that. Judas J Jubilee this is gonna be good." He hastened into the living room, swept the couch clear of the clutter, and motioned for his guest to sit. As Carver settled onto the stained sofa, his host lumbered over to the scratched rocking chair. The wood creaked beneath his weight when he sat.

"So where to begin?" he asked with his Mickey Mouse voice. "Introductions first, I suppose. I'm Jake Dewitt. I live here."

"I'm called Carver." He spoke slowly, deliberately, and not just because of the modifications he had made to his organs of speech. "I'm a refugee from Golan. My city was destroyed by a bunch of uneducated humans."

He told Jake everything. At first, it seemed odd that his host was not taken aback by the answers that were so far beyond the realm of most people's experience, but soon the story poured out. Carver realized it was a story he longed to share. Jake did not seem the least bit shaken by the revelation that Carver's nature was to possess humans and transform the flesh into something most people would view as horrific. He hardly blinked an eye when he revealed his chief duty in Golan had been to handle those who sought acceptance by the tribe because they believed themselves to be monsters. These "Innocents", as Golan's inhabitants called them, were turned into the beasts they thought they were through The Eye's baptismal fire and Carver's innate artistry.

"Perhaps I belong with your ilk," Jake said at a pause in Carver's narration.

"Why do you think that?"

Jake gave a little shrug, which looked very much like a tortoise drawing its head back into its shell. "Some people might think I'm a kind of monster. But it's like you said: No evil, only desire. I've got some..." He licked his lips. "Desires."

"Tell me."

"Not yet." Jake's ponderous head shook back and forth. "I want to hear more about you. You say you're like a spirit and can possess people. Can you enter and exit at will?"

"It's more like a sharing of the body." He thought about Jack the D.A. who was still hiding deep in his subconscious, and amended, "Usually at least. But once I put on a body, I have to wear it until it dies. If for any reason I have to shed the skin...well, first the body has to die."

"Suicide." Then Jake cocked his head to the side. "Or murder?"

"I still live and so does the other soul—the body's first owner. It is murder of the flesh only, and flesh is just a trap anyway."

"Fascinating. Truly fascinating." Indeed, Jake seemed fascinated, truly fascinated. "Okay, my turn, I guess. Let me show you something."

A worm of worry burrowed into Carver's thoughts. What if Jake DeWitt returned with a weapon? He couldn't be killed, of course. He would simply find another body to inhabit. But District Attorney Robinson's refashioned flesh was a masterpiece that he had not fully enjoyed.

He heard Jake's voice drifting down the hall. He was talking to someone. Carver was instantly on his guard, and when Jake returned a few minutes later carrying something in both hands, his curiosity had nothing to do with what the young man wanted to show him. "I heard you talking. Do you share this house?"

"Oh, no. I had to make an important phone call. Wanted to make it before it slipped my mind again." Jake plodded over to where the misshapen

Carver sat and put something on his lap.

It was a one-quart, wide-mouth Mason jar. Carver used his bent hands to hold up the jar to chest level—he had repositioned Jack's eyes where his nipples had been—and studied the jar's contents: a mass of fur that, after a few moments, he recognized as a tiny Maine Coon kitten.

"A dead kitten?"

"It's not dead." Jake paused to let that sink in. "It's a Bonsai kitten. There's a feeding tube there in front—See it?—and another tube for piss and shit. Hell of a lot better than cleaning the litter box every day. And of course, there are plenty of holes for air ventilation."

Carver was speechless. Why would someone torture one of nature's innocent creatures? There was no hypocrisy in this. In his experience there was no such thing as an innocent human.

"It started off as hoax website created by an MIT student," Jake explained. "It was meant to make a statement on how we use nature as a commodity. But I was fascinated by the idea. I've finally found a way to actually make it work."

"This is… alive?" Carver peered closely at the kitten squashed into the jar. Its pupils had dilated wide, almost completely opening the irises, an autonomic response to the dimly lit room and a sure sign that the Bonsai kitten was indeed still alive.

"It's amazing, isn't it? You can mold these little critters into any shape you want. So, what do you think?"

Carver was, for reasons that had nothing to do with his stretched vocal chords, speechless.

"What's the matter? Cat got your tongue?" Jake guffawed at his joke. He plucked the jar from Carver's grasp. "This little guy is one of my recent projects. I have an entire bookcase filled with others."

Carver couldn't help but think that cryptozoologist Page, Father Petrie, and Sheriff Frey should be tracking Jake DeWitt instead of him. He might be a monster, but Jake was evil.

There is no evil…

"I've been trying to figure out how to do this with people." Jake stared into Carver's chest eyes and flashed a conspiratorial grin. "Bonsai humans. Nobel Prize material, don't you think?"

Quite unexpectedly, like the urge to laugh at a funeral, Carver felt a tingle of desire in his magnificently reimagined extremities. He had thought extruding muscle fibers through the skin was a feat, but Bonsai humans? That was something altogether new.

"Now there's an idea worth entertaining," Carver rasped. The worm muscles began squirming excitedly, and the intestines looped around his shoulders cinched tight. Was it possible that, in this vile misshapen doughboy, he had found someone capable of truly appreciating his vision?

"Can you help me?" Jake asked, like an addict desperate for a fix. "I mean, look what you did to that body of yours? Remarkable is all I can say. If anyone can do it, you're the guy."

"I can help."

"How? I've thought about how I would go about getting a body, but every possibility seems full of complications. I know this guy at the county jail. I've considered asking him to allow one of the inmates to 'escape'." He made little quote marks with his fingers. "You know, a murderer or rapist; some deserving lowlife."

"No need to go that far," Carver replied, desire giving way to hunger. "I've got a body right here. District Attorney Jack Robinson could stand some more alterations."

Jake gaped at him. "No shit. That's the D.A.'s body you're in?" He considered this for a moment. "Good. That guy was such an ass hat."

"I need to be alone." Carver didn't dare risk revealing the source of his power. "I'm sorry, but I must ask you to leave the room."

"No prob whatsoever. I'll just hang out in the bedroom with my kitties. I can't wait. Ten minutes. Will that do?"

"More than enough time."

As soon as Jake was gone, Carver went to work. The bones were the problem. The human skeleton was simply not as pliable as a young kitten's. He sometimes worked with bone, adjusting it, sometimes breaking it, but this would require something a little more... comprehensive.

He lifted a fold of D.A. Jack Robinson's beer gut and plucked out one of the muscle worms like an offending gray hair. The open pore immediately began to constrict, but he deftly pushed the Prophet's Eye into it. The skin resisted for a moment, but then stretched around the orb and sucked it in, closing over it completely. He recited his incantation and felt the ice-encrusted Eye blaze to life inside him.

The bones were the problem, so... get rid of them!

Willing the fire into his skeletal structure, Carver scoured away everything: bones, joints, cartilage.

It was agony. It was exquisite. He let loose howls of anguish until the baptismal fire turned his larynx to ash. Without support, his vocal folds collapsed, sealing him in a tomb of silence while the surgical conflagration raged beneath his skin.

When it was done, he collapsed to the floor in a puddle of muscle, fat, and skin. The extruded muscle fibers quivered like the cilia of a bacterium, but without a skeleton, he had less mobility than a slug.

He heard Jake's voice coming from down the hall. Another phone call? A moment later, footsteps signaled the doughboy's return. He stopped a few paces away from the quivering puddle of flesh on his living room floor.

"Christ Jesus our Lord and Shepherd's pie!" Jake stared into Carver's eyes, which now peered up from the center of the shapeless mass, eyes that now could only stare straight up. His squeaky voice broke into a titter. "Well, you have certainly got yourself in a fix. Listen, I wasn't completely straight with you. The phone calls I've been making? They were to my uncle. Well, actually he's the Sheriff. That's right. Sheriff Frey, the long arm of the law. I had a feeling it was you when I first spotted you in the hall. I heard about you. That priest and that monster tracker, they told my uncle all about you and what you did."

Jake lifted a chunky foot and planted it firmly on Carver, squashing his head as if it was a jellyfish on the beach. "How could you do that to Christy? Maybe my thing for Bonsai kittens is 'creepy'"—air quotes again—"but do you really think that's on par with what you did to her, or the D.A. for that matter? Did you really think I'm that depraved?"

Jake ground his foot harder. "After you told me you can only escape after the death of the body, I figured I could lure you in with my cockamamie story about Bonsai humans and beat you at your own game. It worked, didn't it? The Sheriff and his posse are on their way."

Carver stared up helplessly from his pile of soft flesh, enduring the taunts, unable to do anything as the foot smashed against his face, over and over again. He could only hope that the enraged Jake would push the D.A.'s body past its limits and into the realm of death, allowing him to escape.

A knock interrupted Jake's tirade. He answered the door. Sheriff Frey burst in, followed by a man in unkempt clothing. The cryptozoologist pushed a wheelchair bearing a third man who wore a soiled cassock that covered his amputated legs.

The priest was ranting. "I smell him. God is near. Take me to him."

"Is this him? The thing responsible for Christy's murder?" Sheriff Frey bent low to examine the shapeless heap of flesh and skin. His face scrunched and he turned his head to the side. "Can't stand to look at this abomination. Is this what you've been tracking, Stephen?"

Page nodded. He struggled to keep the overeager priest in his wheelchair.

Sheriff Frey placed a hand on Jake's shoulder. "So what's the big plan, nephew?"

Jake rubbed his hands together. "As terrible as it sounds, we need to keep this demon alive."

"You sure about that?"

"Most definitely. If this thing dies, the demon will escape to ravage somebody else. I'm prepared to be its guardian. It's helpless. I'll have to help it eat and clean up its shit, but as long as I keep this puddle of meat alive, it can't harm anybody. Its flesh is its prison."

Hearing what he already knew reinforced the dread creeping over Carver. It could be twenty or thirty years before Robinson's boneless flesh gave up the ghost. He had misjudged Jake, and now it seemed he would pay the price, bottled up like one of the doughboy's kittens.

"Works for me. Come on, Stephen. My nephew has this under control."

"It's here. I can feel it." The priest squirmed in his chair. "The fire of God. Please let me touch it again. I've come all this way."

Stephen leaned close to Frey. "Father Petrie needs to... worship." The cryptozoologist seemed to choke on the word. "Can you leave us here for a while? We can get back on our own."

Frey seemed to be in a hurry to get away. "All right, but don't wear out your welcome."

With the Sheriff gone, Carver's attention fixed on Stephen Page. He knew the cryptozoologist didn't believe in ghosts, souls, or anything else linked to the spirit world. But there were monsters. Page had seen his share in Golan and had felt the sting of their rejection. He had sworn to eradicate every last vestige of that secret city. It was no surprise then to see him pull a knife from a concealed ankle sheath.

Too late, Jake Dewitt realized what was about to happen and launched his massive body at Page. With almost casual disdain, Page slashed his blade across Jake's throat. The doughboy crumpled to the floor, a fountain of blood spraying the immobile Carver.

"What are you doing?" Father Petrie shrieked, heaving his body out of the wheelchair. He tottered a few seconds on the numb stumps where his legs had been, and then collapsed next to Carver's swollen belly. "You promised. I must touch God's fire."

God's fire or not, Page didn't care. It was time to finish this. He hadn't traveled so far from home to let this abomination live on. His blade plunged into Carver's soft flesh, cutting away chunks of sinew and fatty tissue as if he were cutting blubber from a whale.

It was a baptism, a ceremonial immersion in blood and filth that nonetheless cleansed a little part of the world.

Page finally straightened and regarded the pathetic priest. "What do you think of your God now? You'll have a little more time to show your pitiful devotion while I clean up."

Carver watched Page leave the room and marveled at the turn of events that had set him free once more. He hovered near the good Father, curious to see what the maimed cleric would do next.

Father Petrie was smearing handfuls of the gore all over his face. "This vessel is dead, but I still smell your fire. Why? Answer me, oh Lord. Why?"

He continued scooping up meat and viscera, spreading streaks of it on the fabric of his cassock. Then he stopped. He raised his fist high, allowing the gore to squeeze through the sieve of his fingers.

"Touch me with your fire, oh Lord." His hand opened, and the Prophet's Eye stared back at him. He gave the orb a delicate kiss, then pocketed it within the folds of his priestly garment.

There is no evil; only desire, hunger, and survival.

Carver knew the desire he now felt would soon blossom into hunger, and eventually the survival of his ghostly essence would be at stake.

Reason enough, he decided, to give the good Father a makeover.

Batch 13

Gregor Cole

Mortimer was obsessed with all things spicy.

He had travelled far and wide looking for the ultimate curry dish, the best chili recipe, the spiciest sauce. He had spent a fortune on gastro-holidays, journeying to the likes of Mexico, America, India, Malaysia—he had seen and sampled it all.

His one real weakness, however, was hot sauce; everything that he ate was covered with the stuff—even on his breakfast. He loved nothing better than starting the day with sausage and hash browns covered with some kind of demon-strength sauce.

He was a known face at the farmers markets and trade fairs across the country and was held in high regard among other chili heads as having an "asbestos tongue."

It got to a point where he had started to make his own sauces, as he found a lot of store-bought brands just didn't pack the right punch. He had tried online sources, but after a while he found them to be on the weak side.

Finding it so much easier to tailor his concoctions to meet his tastes, he bulk bought various chilis and other ingredients from all of the local Asian markets, but he was still missing that final burn, that push over the edge of being "just really hot" to "stupidly intense."

He had built a green house in his small garden so that he could cultivate and cross pollinate species of plants to grow mutant fruits, each strain hotter than the last.

Mortimer had imported seeds and cuttings from all over the globe from some of the most respected farms and botanical gardens. He had made friends with a middle-aged Chinese guy named Larry Chow, who worked at a local garden center. Larry shared his love of growing the more exotic chili plants.

Together they had come up with some pretty potent sauces and Larry sold them in the center's farm shop along with chili jams, pickles, and chutneys. They had received some glowing reviews from patrons, and there was an article printed in the local paper about the newly dubbed "spice men of Hextable."

But with public demand on the rise and Mortimer's insatiable appetite for all things insanely hot, he was forced to look to the black market for ingredients for his next recipe. He found a thriving underground online, sites and chat rooms all dedicated to "the burn," but again was unimpressed with the goods and recipes he acquired from these sources.

By chance, Larry Chow had found a supplier that specialized in the exotic and had given the details to Mortimer over the phone.

"He say he has the best for you to try." Larry's broken English was almost hilarious and Mortimer had always wondered whether he laid it on a little too thick for a laugh. "He say he has the hottest you ever eat. You get down there. You try."

Mortimer took the address and drove to a row of lockups in a run-down rural area just outside of Gravesend. The place looked more like a place where gypsies went to burn tires, and he wondered what kind of shady player would set up business way out here.

He was greeted with open arms by a fat Arab man in a vintage Bee Gees t-shirt and thinning hair.

Fahim was a green grocer who had some rather unsavory connections. Mortimer wondered what kind of dark deals a green grocer would be part of, and imagined a film *noir* scene involving a banana shipment and a crooked cop.

"Good old Larry said you were looking for the hottest of the hot, and I believe I may be able to help you, my friend." Fahim fumbled at the lock on one of the storage bay doors. For some strange reason, Mortimer suddenly had a terrible craving for a kebab.

The door to the lock up was thrown up and Mortimer peered in as Fahim bounded in. It was dark and smelled of old vegetables, but Mortimer could see the unit was filled with stacks of fruit boxes. An overhead strip light blinked on and he saw the fat man over by a chest freezer at the back of the room.

"In here, my friend, is what you are after, I think." Fahim put on some rubber gloves, then offered a pair to Mortimer. "Put these on. You don't want to handle these with bare hands. They are quite potent."

The fat man opened the freezer to reveal hundreds of clear frozen packets of chilis and carrier bags of herbs and plastic tubs of spices. Fahim rummaged deep inside the freezer, then pulled out a bag containing what looked like bright yellow and black tiger-striped bullets.

"These are what you are looking for, my friend… The real shit." He handed the bag to Mortimer. "The infamous poison arrow frog chili, very dangerous, very hot." A huge smile crossed the fat man's face.

Mortimer opened the bag and took one out by its jet black stalk. The yellow of the chili almost glowed and lit up the men's eyes as he held it up. It must have been Mortimer's imagination, or maybe just the humidity inside the lock up, but he could have sworn there was a slight heat coming off the pepper. Just the scent of the thing started to make his eyes water, and he thought he could hear a sizzling sound coming from inside it.

"In the Amazon rainforest they are not harvested as a food, but as a weapon, and they have even used it in America as an alternative to the strongest of CS gas. Very dangerous indeed, my friend, and very expensive."

Mortimer took a stuffed manila envelope from his back pocket and handed it over.

"Just one question, my friend. Why on earth would you want such a rare and dangerous fruit?"

It was Mortimer's turn to smile as he turned to head back to his car.

"I'm going to eat them."

* * *

On the drive back, Mortimer was forced to pull over and put the demon chilis in the trunk of his Mini Cooper; his eyes were streaming from the very vapor coming from the glove box. Even though they were properly wrapped up, they still filled the car with a tear-inducing aroma.

He also stopped at his favorite burrito place, Holy Toledo's, for pulled pork with rice and lashings of habanero sauce. He could only imagine what the flavor of the "weapons" in his car would be.

The thick pepper sauce on his food was good and sweet, but it wasn't touching the sides in the heat stakes; nowhere near what he was used to and he wanted to go a lot hotter.

A woman across from where he was sitting looked on in awe at the amount of hot sauce he poured on to his plate. She looked at the bottle on her table and added a splash onto the corner of her plate. She was soon regretting the tiniest amount she had scooped up with a little rice and beans and headed for the drink machine to refill her cup.

Mortimer saw this and smiled to himself. *Amateur*, he thought smugly as he dumped another load of the fiery orange goo onto his food.

* * *

He stopped off at a DIY center on the way home and purchased a set of protective goggles, throw-away overalls, and a filter mask normally used by those spray-painting their cars ; he didn't want to take any chances after Fahim's warning.

The kitchen was set up with distilling equipment and huge cooking pans that sat on the stove's burners; the whole place was a heap of measuring jugs and glassware. The table in the middle of the room was overloaded with ingredients ranging from the average to the downright bizarre. Ketchup sat next to squid ink, and ripe papayas rested against a jar of gun powder.

Mortimer had everything that he needed; he was ready to start the magic.

The first thing was the base of the sauce. This was the hardest part to get right; everything else was just added to create the more subtle flavors and, of course, add to the heat. Everything else was just tones, the notes that held it all together.

Mortimer squeezed the firm fruit on the table one after the other and held them up to sniff. He picked the mango, papaya, and dragon fruit. He wanted to go for something sweet to fool his taste buds into a false sense of security. He scooped the flesh of the fruit into the vast bowl of his industrial food processor.

He then added a little spice to start the "fire" process, and followed that with a good handful of pre-stalked red Cambodian peppers. Not the hottest thing in the world, but they were a good base to prepare the mixture for the main event. Next was the liquid to create the sauce.

Water came first as he run a tap into a measuring jug, then added a little lime and tomato juice. He wanted a little kick to the concoction, so he added a generous splash of smoky spiced rum. Not too much, but just enough to let you know that it was there. He added the liquid mixture to the processor.

He gave the ingredients a couple of quick pulses until it was mixed well, then proceeded to chop some onion, celery, and a red pepper. He lit the gas and started to heat a big black pot on the stove; it was his favorite for this kind of sauce: well-seasoned and could yield at least one hundred bottles of the stuff. He added a little oil and a good handful of salt, then chucked in the diced onion. He was greeted with a satisfying *hiss*.

The pulp from the blender was next; he spooned great blobs of it into the pan and the smell of the fruit, chilis, and alcohol hit him as it met with the heat. The mixture needed to cook for a short while to allow it break down. Then it would be cooled and strained through muslin to remove any inedible seeds and sinews. leaving only a smooth sauce. It would then be distilled through a maze of glass tubes before going back into the pot for the final stages.

Once the sauce was cooled, a good jug of white wine vinegar was added, along with a good pinch of salt and white pepper. He returned the cool sauce to the heat. He then added a good spoonful of the gunpowder.

The whole kitchen smelled fantastic, like a good chili kitchen should, but now it was time for the real deal.

Mortimer was no fool and kept the evil little chaps in the freezer. With a rubber-gloved hand, he removed ten from the frosted-over plastic bag.

His head was covered with the protective goggles and mask, but he was aware of the vapor that came from the chilis and the temperature coming from them was considerably hotter than the rest of the kitchen. The sweat started to drip from his forehead and down the lenses of the goggles.

The sauce on the stove had started to simmer as he began to chop the yellow and black fruits with a Chinese-style cleaver. He could see why they called them poison arrow frogs—because of their insane coloring—and he was in awe of the crazy little things.

The fumes became more intense as he continued to grind them down into a paste in a huge stone pestle. These things were something else, certainly unlike anything he had encountered before.

As soon as the chili paste hit the liquid in the pot, the whole batch went jet black, darker than any squid ink could produce. The steam from the pot was almost like a concentrated CS gas and was coming through the protection of his mask.

The scent was making him feel quite heady and he turned off the heat to let the inky stew settle and cool. His mind started to reel from the fumes and he staggered out from the kitchen and collapsed against the wall, then slid down it in a heap in the hallway.

His eyesight started to blur with tears and there were strong visual trace lines coming from his hands as he tried to get to his feet. It was like the strong acid he had taken at college years ago. A wave of euphoria crashed into him, followed by ultra-vivid color changes. A deep nausea filled him.

Mortimer threw up into his breathing mask, then crawled across the floor and pulled himself up with the aid of a chair. He slumped into the chair and pulled the mask free from his face. Vomit roll down his face and onto his chest before he passed out.

* * *

The strangest sensation of falling and landing awkwardly followed the recollection of managing to stagger to the bathroom and washing away crusty sick over the sink. He vaguely remembered changing his shirt and wandering back into the kitchen. He was still shaky on his feet, like a newborn colt.

It wasn't until he entered the room and was greeted with the greatest smell of sweet and sour hot sauce he had ever smelled that he even realized he was conscious. He sobered up almost immediately with the pleasant scent in his nostrils and rushed to the massive pot cooling on the stove.

The color of the thick sauce was like the brightest blood-red silk; it was the most perfect thing he had ever seen; so far removed from the venomous black when it was cooking. And the smell was unlike anything he had ever smelled before. Rich, but not overpowering, spicy and full, sweet, but not sickly. Perfection.

Mortimer couldn't believe it. Had he done it? Had he made the ultimate hot sauce? There was only one thing left to do—taste it.

He took a teaspoon from a drawer and hovered over the pot for a moment before he stuck it in. He slowly stirred the sauce, weaving the spoon through the rich red of his creation. The liquid moved around the polished silver of the spoon like the finest of sand; it was almost hypnotic.

Mortimer raised the spoon to his quivering lips and slowly fed the sauce into his salivating mouth.

The flavor was instantaneous; pure, sweet, and oh so heavenly rich. All the ingredients had blended with each other in perfect harmony, each complimenting the other, yet standing out individually in layers of satisfying pleasure. But no chili heat from the poison arrow frog chilis… yet.

The original chili hit was there from the red Cambodians, stronger than the other sauces he had made with them to be fair, but all well within reasonable heat standards. Had he failed?

No.

Suddenly all the air was sucked out of his lungs from an intense burst of heat. It was unlike anything he had ever experienced before. It was beyond hot, like he had taken a bite out of the sun. Sweat instantly poured from every part of his body; even his eyelids were sweating. Hell, his eyeballs were sweating. Within seconds he had sweat through his clothes.

His hands clenched at his throat and he tore at his collar to try and get some air, but the heat kept coming. Wave after wave, each more intense than the last, like a steam train furnace building momentum. Faster and faster; hotter and hotter. Then came the pain.

It started in the back of his throat, like something inside was stripping away the lining, then moved onto his tongue before filling his mouth. It felt like hot needles were passing through his soft pallet and into the top of his skull.

Mortimer's stomach did a flip, then the nausea hit him. He ran to the bathroom holding his head like it was going to explode.

His reflection in the bathroom mirror was a horrific sight. Eyes streaming with tears, face flushed red, and every vein angrily raised as the heat kept coming. His gut twitched once more and a flood of blood and vomit erupted from his mouth and splashed over the sink and up the wall. His throat was bombarded once again with the taste of the regurgitated sauce. More heat came. More blood came.

An intense clawing sensation started deep inside Mortimer and he doubled up from the pain in his gut. It felt like something had started to chew its way out from his stomach and he vomited again all over his lap and legs, great gushes of blood this time, like a water cannon firing jets of red paint.

Something bubbled inside and a shower of blood gushed from his anus and he doubled over from the pain.

Mortimer's skin felt like it would burst into flame at any moment and he tore his clothes off and fell into the bathtub, fumbling at the shower head. For a second the cold water that hit him seemed to cool the burning sensation, but that feeling was short lived.

Steam started to billow from his body as the cold spray of the shower head hit his burning skin. More blood fell from his backside into the white ceramic tub. His rectum started to hiss and spasm, and parts of it fell away, turning to mush like it had been covered in acid, and soon the opening was wide enough for part of his intestine to drop through.

Convulsing in pain, his mind started to go into shock and he flashed in and out of consciousness, each wave of pain bringing him back, then intensifying to the point of oblivion.

More guts poured from inside him into the tub and he tried in vain to stuff them back into himself. His hand came up pulling away a red, rancid mush that used to be his genitals and he collapsed into the tub, smashing his face on the edge.

Mortimer spat dissolving teeth onto the tile floor and watched them waste away to a bloody, milk-white sludge before he sank into the ooze that he was slowly turning into.

Inside his head he was screaming for it all to end, begging for a quick death, but the burning pain would not let him go that easily. The sauce was melting him down from the inside out, and it wanted him to savor every last waking second.

* * *

"Look, I tell you he no here." Larry Chow wandered around the kitchen on his mobile phone. "I look everywhere, but he gone. The shower was on when I got here, but it like he vanish."

He started to pack away the last of the one hundred bottles of Batch 13 hot sauce into a box that sat on the table.

"I tidy up and bottle the sauce and will deliver it later today. It looks like it's the best yet. Smell great and you won't believe the color." He sealed the box using thick masking tape, then slapped a sticky label on the side that read *The Spice Men of Hextable* and showed a picture of the two friends throwing the double thumbs up while wearing huge, cheesy grins.

"No way, I no taste. I no really like the hot chili."

sane clarity

James Park

Melting faces wrapped around melting faces, lips wide as if trapped in silent screams. Zombies brushed atop the canvas in pedantic detail. Autumn leaves crackled at their feet.

Joseph Roush often told critics that his paintings mimicked nightmares so eloquently because he lacked the ability to separate the sleeping hours from the waking hours. Like a curse, the predicament swept over him during childhood, prone to misdiagnosis as a bizarre case of insomnia. Not until late adolescence, when his hold on actuality turned violently against his stake in reality, did Joseph come to terms with the severity of his condition.

Paintings contemplated over sunsets ripened to fruition during darkened hours, and ideologies submerged within the deepest cellars of his mind leapt from the brush on humid afternoons. When Joseph set off on the endeavor to paint each member of his family, it was as much a quest for sanity as a battle to claim control over the works he created.

Mother, father, and younger sister, Eliza; each was crafted from colors carefully mixed atop the pallet. The subtle shades of their flesh displayed the quiet dignity with which the Roushes behaved, and the plainness of their clothing accentuated the modesty for which they were known. But no sooner would Joseph finish a portrait, eager to show his family the sane clarity with which he could paint, he would learn that the family member had crawled to an early grave. On the day he finished the portrait of his mother, her body remained in bed, as still between the sheets as it was atop the canvas. Upon adding the last smear of paint to his father's pale cheeks, Joseph came to learn that his old man had died of causes unknown; the heart simply stopped beating. And when young Eliza finally became immortalized in a work of fine art, Joseph never heard from her again, be it in dreams or in the waking world.

In solitude, Joseph continued with his work, allowing nightmarish creatures to make their way to the living world by means of paint and canvas. Melting faces wrapped around melting faces, lips wide as if trapped in silent screams. Zombies brushed atop the canvas in pedantic detail, arms raised above lethargic feet.

It was with great discipline that Joseph Roush set off on a second quest to capture sane clarity. An empty board stretched from one side of his loft to the other, taller than any canvas he'd ever approached. Setting to work, his dreams were laced with the medley of thrash guitars, the hiss of abominable lyrics, and through sleepless nightmares the mural gradually took form. One by one the boulders of Stonehenge appeared atop the board, and one by one the members of Joseph's most idolized metal band materialized in its center. Dressed head to toe in the blackest of blacks, chains dangling from studded leather jackets, the persona of each musician was expressed with startling clarity. Come the final streak of paint, a sharp silence ensued, suffocating guitars that wailed in Joseph's dreams.

News of the metal band succumbing to a plane crash arrived during one of the few moments when Joseph understood beyond doubt that he was living in the waking world. He read it in the paper, a fatal crash en route to Budokan, cutting short their career—the beating of their hearts.

Upon folding the paper and placing it beside a stack of obituaries commemorating the subjects of his work, Joseph Roush began the task of painting a self-portrait. He knew that there was no other way.

Dr. Frank N. Squirrel

Julianne Snow

"Please God, no! Let me go. I promise I won't tell anyone what you're doing!" His cries were stifled by the bloody rag shoved into his mouth as pain radiated down his leg. Looking to his left, he could just make out the slender form of his wife on the table next to him, her eyes as big as saucers as she tracked the madman working on him. Grunting against the pain, he struggled, trying in vain to free himself.

"Hold still or you'll make me ruin your hide," came the gruff reply of the diminutive man with the scalpel and the stepladder. As he worked his way down the leg, the task was made more arduous by the shuffle of his tiny feet on the metal stairs and the clack of its legs on the tiled floor as he progressed further down the table.

Paralyzed with fear, Meg could only watch as her husband was flayed. Alive. The tortured look on his face before he finally succumbed to an unconscious state was more than she could bear. Her furiously beating heart stopped before her turn could even begin.

"Master?"

"What is it, Barrymore?" the doctor asked with his usual hurried disdain.

"I think she's dead, Master," Barrymore answered as he slunk bodily across the room to the doctor's side.

"Dead? What?" With a sudden agility not typically demonstrated by the doctor, he flew down his little ladder and had moved it across the floor to the other table within moments. Climbing back up, he placed a bloody gloved finger to her neck, checking the carotid for a pulse. Nothing. "Get my tools, Barrymore. We must start at once before her hide is sullied!"

And with that, the incisions began; the doctor and his assistant working long into the night. Much later, Clive awoke to see a vision of his wife floating in the space that separated the tables, looking somewhat empty for lack of a better word.

With the two hands of the doctor grasping the skin of her shoulders somewhat unnaturally, Clive was repulsed to see her ripple like a sheet of paper in the wind. Realization washed over him at the sight and he knew the truth; she was empty. Or at least her skin was. Looking up at the madman on his stepladder, he could only gasp in horror at what he had done. Through his stupor, he managed a choked, "Who are you?"

"I am called many things: Doctor, Master, Monster… But my most cherished friends call me Doctor Frank N. Squirrel!"

* * *

The old estate had sat next to Central Park longer than many in New York City could remember. It looked derelict from the outside, but should you be invited to one of the massive parties that occurred within the brick and mortar walls, you'd be treated to the opulence only money could buy.

The owner was a recluse of a man; a man who had by all accounts played the stocks and won big. He lorded over his estate and his parties like a king, expecting the invitees to kiss his bejeweled fingers. But that wasn't the only thing strange about him.

Oh no, not at all. From the rumors circling the elite of the city, the recluse had once been a very important man. Not a self-important one, like he was now, but truly important. His life's work had been done in the military, and while no one truly knew what it was he had done, they could only speculate on the level of heinous acts he was responsible for.

Let's be honest, no one who worked for the military in a clandestine department, and you know it was clandestine merely from the fact he never talked about it, was honorable. Despite the rumors that abounded, the whispers that floated on the air, and the looks that slyly came from the eyes of his guests, his parties were the events no one wanted to miss.

Though honestly there were some who never made it past the grand vestibule. Some even luckier ones were able to view the collection before becoming part of it.

* * *

"Gawd Clive, can you believe all of the animals staring at us right now?" Meg Dancy asked the question in a near shout, her hand in front of her face in an attempt to give her a level of discretion during her exclamation. Not that discretion was something she was overly fond of, or adept at maintaining. In truth, Meg loved to stir the pot of controversy and speculation. As the head of the Central Park Conservation Committee, she believed she was one of the most adored women in the city, and one of the most envied to say the least. It was a wonder her head fit into any of the rooms she attempted to enter.

Her husband, Clive, was a nice man, having married into the family of money Meg had lucked into at birth. He put up with her meddling and attempts at intrigue for the simple fact he truly loved her. No one understood why, since Meg was absolutely detestable, but sometimes even the most despicable of characters deserved to find a little love.

Since her appointment to the head of the Central Park Conservation Committee, Meg had made it her mission to attend all of the parties within the city's limits, dragging her husband along with her. Oh how she loved to rub her position in the noses of the other high-society types who flitted from event to soiree. It was one of her favorite pastimes.

And tonight was no different. Spying Carmody Van der Fluffe across the room, Meg made one last remark before flitting off. "It's like they were all posed to look directly into our eyes. Creepy!"

Clive looked up at the dioramas of different animals and wondered who had made them all. The scenes depicted a wide variety of animal life from mice to dogs to armadillos to peacocks, to name but a few, arranged in the strangest of poses. These were not your average dioramas—no, these were scenes depicting fear, abomination, and a distinct level of depravity. All of that aside, Clive was keenly interested in the craftsmanship and the attention to detail that each scene depicted. Akin to art, he viewed each piece intently before moving along to the next.

Unaware of the presence that had come to stand behind him, he stepped back to take in a scene of ruffled feathers and sharp teeth, only to run into something somewhat solid about the height of his backside. Thinking it was a table, he reached behind him to steady it, only to connect with something solid, and quite alive.

Gasping in fright and confusion, he turned to find himself crotch to face with his host. Covering up some of his surprise and embarrassment, he mumbled, "I beg your pardon! I did not see you there!"

Not missing a beat, or allowing himself to feel anything other than regal, the pint-sized man stretched his fingers outward and waited.

"May I present Doctor Frank N. Squirrel?" came a voice from the right, belonging to a brute of a man decked out in formal black attire.

Bending at the waist, Clive sought to kiss the outstretched hand as Meg had instructed him to earlier in the evening should he meet the reclusive host. It was an awkward exchange as Clive was just over six feet tall while his host could not have been more than four feet with heeled boots on. But he bent his body readily in deference to the man who had invited him into his home.

"That will be all for the moment, Barrymore," the doctor spoke with an air of privilege. "Kindly leave us to discuss my art."

Watching the large man retreat into the shadows of the room, Clive was awestruck by the man now standing before him. Despite being very small, his presence echoed that of a much larger man. The feeling put Clive on edge as he turned to look back at the oddly mesmerizing tableaus mounted on the walls.

"I couldn't help but notice you staring at my art. Tell me, what do you think of them?"

"Well..." he hesitated, not sure of what to say exactly. "They're certainly interesting. Very lifelike. Did you make them yourself?"

"I did indeed. It's one of my hobbies. Taxidermy. I find it relaxing to breathe new life into dead things." Dr. Squirrel answered with a striking sense of pride. It was obvious from the way he stood and stared at his own work that he was immensely proud of what he had created. The narcissism of the moment was not lost on Clive, but he chose to ignore it for lack of a better option.

"I find them captivating, Doctor. Such realism mixed with the macabre." Clive was beginning to get uncomfortable standing next to the diminutive man, feeling his height put him at a disadvantage. It was a foreign feeling to Clive, one he had rarely experienced in his lifetime. Before he could extricate himself from the side of his host, a welcome, if not grating voice interrupted.

"Oh, there you are Clive. I had wondered where you had gotten off to!" Meg had returned to her husband's side the moment she noticed their host deep in conversation with him. Not wanting him to say anything untoward, she felt it was best she act as chaperone. "Clive, won't you introduce me to our host?"

"Yes, sorry. Doctor Frank N. Squirrel, may I present to you my wife, Meg Dancy?" Clive all but choked on the words as he tried to get them out, nervous because of the way the doctor perused the slender form of his wife.

Dr. Frank N. Squirrel held out his hand, a silent offer for Meg to lay her lips on the rubies and emeralds that covered it. Clive couldn't help but notice the doctor's eyes never strayed from his wife's décolletage as she bent down to oblige. As Meg straightened back up, Dr. Squirrel shot a look at Clive, a sly smirk curving his lips.

With the pomp and circumstance out of the way for the moment, the doctor offered to show them his private collection.

Delighted with the turn of events and the impending jealousy sure to wash over her rivals, Meg immediately accepted. "Oh, I can't wait!" she exclaimed, clapping her hands together in excitement.

Meg and Clive had no idea what was in store for them and waited as the doctor called to Barrymore. Extending his hand in invitation, the group was on their way, weaving through the crowd and out into the grand vestibule that served as entrance to the house.

Taking the stairs that branched off from the entranceway, they descended into a lavishly furnished lounge complete with a piano and a wet bar. Barrymore offered each of them a drink and went around the back to act as bartender while Dr. Squirrel entertained his guests.

"I don't ask many to view my private collection, as it's the work I find harder to explain to a larger audience," he explained as he leaned against the seat of one of the plush brocade chairs. "Many have no understanding of what I do, or of the art I create. Taxidermy is a dying art, but it is in my blood. I come from a long line of taxidermists, and I can remember standing at my father's knee, watching him work; tanning hides, stretching them over forms, making sure each hair was perfect..." For a moment, the doctor got lost in his own reverie, but it was quickly broken as Barrymore brought drinks to the group. "Thank you, Barrymore." Raising his glass, he toasted. "To new friends and new hides!"

Unaware of the foreboding of the doctor's words, Clive and Meg drank the amber liquid from their glasses. Meg began to talk incessantly, telling Dr. Squirrel of her position and the plans she had for Central Park and its inhabitants. He silently listened, waiting for a moment to take them into the adjoining room. When her talk turned to ridding the park of the squirrel population, the doctor had heard enough.

"Silence!" he roared, standing tall to his full height. "There is nothing wrong with the squirrels in Central Park!"

Meg and Clive sat on the chaise lounge, staring wide-eyed at their host. Neither of them knew what to say, nor were they overly interested in attempting to make the situation any worse.

"Forgive me. I did not mean to lose my temper. I simply do not understand why so many people find the squirrels so loathsome. They are a part of my heritage. My family used to farm them in the old country for many centuries. I find them rather delightful."

"My apologies, Doctor Squirrel. Perhaps I should not have been so quick to judge them." It was all Meg could think to say. She certainly did not want to lose the good graces of such an influential man and sought to regain his favor. "Perhaps I have been looking at them as pests and not as the helpful creatures that they are."

"Perhaps. But enough about the squirrels. It's time for us to view my collection." His tone was dismissive, but inviting at the same time.

With the words said, Barrymore stepped away from the wall and crossed the room to a set of double doors under the stairs. Without an ounce of flourish, he opened them.

Dr. Frank N. Squirrel walked with his tiny stride to the open doors and beckoned them to follow him down the long, dimly lit hallway. Both Meg and Clive followed willingly, not wanting to upset their host any further.

Ahead of them, they could see the hallway opened up into another room, this one fully lit but devoid of furniture. Unable to see the walls from their vantage point, nothing could have prepared them for the closet of horrors awaiting them.

Coming fully into the room, allowing a few moments for their eyes to get accustomed to the harsh overhead lighting, their senses were met with objects of the truly disturbed.

Set around the room were scenes depicting devastating acts undertaken by squirrels. Forget the cute high jinx of the clever rodent; these were scenes of bloodshed, of carnage, of extermination.

And the victims were all human.

"Oh Gawd, Doctor! What have you done?" Meg breathlessly screamed as she brought her hand to her mouth, desperately trying to stifle the bile rising from her stomach. Turning to hide her face in her husband's chest, she caught a glimpse of a frozen tableau in the corner. "Is that Ambrosia Climpt? And her husband, Nestor? They went missing years ago…"

Clive had certainly had enough of the horror and turned to leave back through the hallway. Barrymore was standing in its threshold, his imposing bulk blocking his path. "Barrymore, please stand aside. I must return to the other room. If I stay here much longer, I will lose my dinner upon the floor."

In times of stress, Clive always reverted to the most polite version of himself. Never would he have thought of pushing his way through the man, though it was doubtful he would have made it had he tried. Barrymore remained statuesque and made no effort to acquiesce to Clive's demand.

Turning back to the doctor, Clive implored him, "I promise we will tell no one of your artwork if you'll only let us leave this instant. While we may find it abhorrent, we can certainly appreciate that many may not."

The Doctor looked at him, studying him with barely contained glee, before addressing no one in particular when he said, "Yes, he certainly shall do! I love it when they get indignant!"

Meg and Clive both stared at him, confused at first. A sudden dawning of realization had them looking from the dioramas to each other, then back to the Doctor in quick succession. Certainly he didn't mean what they thought he meant!?

"I can see from the looks on your faces you finally understand why I have invited you down here. I need new subjects, new hides, if you will, for my latest creation. This one is special. It's something I have been ruminating on for such a long, long time. Have either of you seen that wonderful film *King Kong*? The one where the giant ape terrorizes New York after being removed from his home? I'm going to use a little bit of artistic license and transform each of you into a beast attacking a metropolis of squirrels, each of them destined to fight back against your oppression!"

"This is madness!" Meg wailed.

"It very well may be, but you're about to be commissioned for an important piece of art. Barrymore, ready the tables!" Chuckling, Dr. Frank N. Squirrel crossed to the closest scene depicting a woman dressed in a gorgeous teal ball gown of satin and lace tied down in much the same manner as the Lilliputians defeated Gulliver. Stroking the head of the largest squirrel, a black one with a white-tipped tail, positioned in a menacing pose over the woman in the scene, he turned back to the pair, noting the fear on their faces and the seeming paralysis of their limbs. "You might be wondering why you cannot move. I had Barrymore slip you a little something to ease you into saying yes. Diabolical, yes, but so clever!"

Clapping his hands in glee, he danced a little jig on the spot and kicked his heels together in the air.

Meg, not fully out of it just yet, began to speak, her voice barely filling the cavernous room. "You can't do this! You'll get caught at some point. You have to! You cannot win!"

"Oh my dear girl! It's not how you win, or lose for that matter," he paused for great effect. "It's all about how you display the game."

Raucous laughter followed his last remark as Barrymore returned with a stainless steel cart. "The tables are ready, Master." While Clive and Meg were still standing, clasped in each other's arms, they had no strength to move unassisted. Barrymore helped each of them in turn onto the cart, coming

31

around to the handle when he was finished.

Taking one last moment to stroke his nearest creation, Dr. Frank N. Squirrel pivoted on his raised heel and led the way down another dimly lit hallway to his laboratory.

Shadow-Mancers
Nathan Cabaniss

Marianne's breast sat still beneath her chin, unmoving. Her skin was cold to the touch, like a lamp that hadn't been turned on in some time.

Li Fong felt a pull on his heart, staring at her like that. He looked away, turning his attention back to the screen as the headlines scrolled by one after the other. He was jacked in: the port in his forearm pulsed in tune with the humming cable, snaking down and around and into the side of the tablet. He waited and watched as story after story ran through the wire, his finger hovering over the screen and the hard-light button marked DOWNLOAD.

He couldn't activate it yet, though—first he had to make sure his story made it through the noise, a small voice desperate to keep its head above the surface through the endless body of information. He waited for the headline to come up: "Journalist & Girlfriend Found Dead in Gangland Hit." Only then would he push the button. Start the download. Release the malicious software and join Marianne in her cold sleep.

There wasn't a single mark on her body, which meant it could have only been one thing. Or millions of things, to be precise. They could be released through the air vents, like an envelope slipped in with the mail through the door—some were so small that they could now travel through the phone lines and enter through the ear canal, where they would then gather in the cerebral cortex and commit mass self-destruction, causing enough of a discharge to completely short out the electrical functions of the brain and leave behind no trace.

They had been meant for him. He got up from bed. For reasons unknown, he had needed to get out of the apartment, get a whiff of the air...

He couldn't remember. By the time he got back, she was already gone.

It was a strange thing, grief. He experienced it before when both of his parents died, and the thing that surprised him the most was the first few moments. Utter shock, followed quickly by disbelief. It was like they didn't die, would never die. People are so used to loved ones being around it's hard to shake the moment they're suddenly, irrevocably not.

The numbness came quicker with Mari's death. He wasn't sure if it was because he was older and more jaded, or if he was just shutting out the feelings long enough to see his final story see print. He had made up his mind within minutes, still sitting on the bed next to her lifeless form. There was no other choice—he could see nothing but an empty void in his future: years of helplessness and guilt and unending depression. There was no point in carrying on if she wasn't around. Especially since her death was his fault.

Going after Xao was going to bring complications no matter what. An interview with an unknown informant proved to be not only searing and insightful, but also quite dangerous. His editors, his colleagues, everyone told Li not to publish the interview. Against all warnings to the contrary, he put it out there anyway, and the story hit the feeds like a bomb...

Politicians both big and small were kicked out of office as a result, and the cops now had enough to go on to halt all of Xao's traffic immediately. Arrests were made, reputations were destroyed, and the blood seemed to finally be off the streets. But that was only because it had seeped through the cracks...

Li should have been more careful. Should have skipped town or, at the very least, cut off all contact with Mari. But he wasn't, and he didn't, and now everything was lost. All he could hope to do now was publish his last story, blaming Xao for his and Mari's deaths, sacrificing his life in the hopes of bringing him down for good. It was a vain attempt at redemption, but it was better than nothing.

Suddenly the headlines stopped. Li tapped the screen to no response. It had frozen up. Li, too, felt a freeze, chilly tremors pumping in tune with his heart. He reached out and shook the screen desperately, even though his rational mind told him that would do nothing to help. His plans dashed, Li stared at the unmoving screen, now more helpless than ever. He felt comfort in the thought that he had control of his life for its final minutes. Now he'd never know if the story made it through...

Words typed themselves on the screen: "I KNOW WHAT YOU WANT—"

Li snapped out of his fugue state, regarding the message with numb curiosity.

"—AND I KNOW HOW TO GIVE IT TO YOU."

Seconds passed, and no more words appeared. Li didn't care enough to respond, but did so anyway, merely out of habit. The words appeared on-screen as he spoke them aloud: "And what is that?"

"JUSTICE."

Now Li's interest was held. "Who is this?"

After a distinct pause: "ONE WHO KNOWS."

Li sat back in his chair, thumbed his chin. "You say you can help me... How?"

"I CAN GIVE YOU THE MEANS TO BRING VENGEANCE ON THE HOUSE OF XAO XIN-KHAN. BECOME MY AGENT IN THE WORLD, AND I WILL GIVE YOU THE GIFT OF JUSTICE."

Li exhaled, not buying it. This was some kind of prank. The thought of someone taunting him over the ether at a time like this riled his blood. His anger started to show through. "You're being vague at a time when my patience is stretched completely thin. Why don't you just piss off and leave me be?"

"YOU MISUNDERSTAND. THIS IS NOT A REQUEST..."

There was a surge in the hardware, and the port on Li's arm suddenly flared. He cried out, attempted to pull the cord, but it only gave him a shock. He felt them slip through the cord into his bloodstream, flooding through his body like mercury. Nanomites. There had to have been hundreds of millions of them, pouring through his being.

"IT IS AN ORDER. FOR TONIGHT, I HAVE SAVED YOUR LIFE. WHICH MEANS IT IS NO LONGER YOUR LIFE, BUT MINE. AND I WILL DO WITH IT AS I WISH. YOUR MIND, YOUR BODY, THE VERY BEATING HEART IN YOUR CHEST NOW BELONG TO ME..."

A silvery tang ran through his mouth, the taste you get when licking an empty spoon. The nanomites filled every corner of his body, painfully reworking his cells at the atomic level.

"...AND I KNOW WHAT LURKS WITHIN IT."

The typed words carried with them no voice, but Li Fong swore the last thing he heard before blacking out was an awful, mechanized laughter.

* * *

Two Months Later

Scrimm and Tong loafed their way down the street, yelling and pushing at anything that got in their way. Scrimm's foot caught on something, and he tumbled over himself, smacking his face on the concrete. Tong followed soon after, too drunk to stop himself from toppling over his squirming friend.

The two of them got to their feet with considerable difficulty, cursing at the heavens and everything beneath. Scrimm looked around wildly for the object that sent him hurtling end over end, and saw an outstretched leg sticking out from a ratty cloak. A worthless bum who didn't even have the decency to pass out in a pile of garbage like the rest of his kind.

Scrimm grabbed his friend by the collar, yanked him over so he would see the cause of their mutual misery. "Looka that... A worthless, goodfernothin' bum, passed out in the middle a' the street, like a dog hit by a car..."

Tong studied the man sitting down, who had a hood pulled low over his face. Looking closer, Tong saw that the bum was not passed out. A pair of burning eyes caught the light of the street lamps, glinting in the darkness of the hood.

"The fug—"

Suddenly, the cloak was thrown back and a plume of yellow flame shot out of the silhouette. The sound was deafening, like the rapport of gun turrets. Scrimm and Tong were torn apart, literally—both men were cut clean in two at the waist, the lower portion of Tong's arm flying off to the other side of the street. They were dead before they hit the ground.

Mechanisms folded in upon themselves beneath the bum's cloak as he stood, taking the approximate shape of a man. "What the hell did you do that for?"

"WHY DOES THE TRAP KILL THE MOUSE? WHY DOES THE HAND SWAT THE FLY? YOU KEEP ASKING UNIMPORTANT QUESTIONS, ALL THE WHILE OUR MISSION REMAINS UNFINISHED."

The voice echoed through his head like bats trapped in a cave, a mass of beating wings and howling screeches. He wasn't used to it yet. He hoped he'd never reach a point where he would be. "They were just a couple of drunks, probably on their way home..."

"THEY WERE SCUM. IF YOU CONTINUE TO SHOW SUCH COMPASSION, THEN OUR MISSION IS ALREADY LOST."

"There's a big line between Xao and a pair of rowdy drunks."

"JUSTICE KNOWS NO DISTINCTION. SHE IS BLIND. IF WE ARE TO BE HER AVATAR IN THIS WORLD, SO TOO MUST WE BE BLIND IN OUR PURSUIT. WE DO NOT QUESTION THE

WIELDER OF THE SCALES."

Li continued down the street, moving voluntarily away from the remains of Scrimm and Tong, taking advantage of the momentary control over his motor functions. He was possessed by a demon disguised as a program. He didn't even believe in demons, but that was the only sensible explanation his mind could conceive.

"I AM NOT A DEMON."

"*Jesus, would you stop it already?!*" It could peer into his thoughts. Li had no doubt now: he was descending into madness. "It was my body first! At least give me the decency to stay out of my mind…"

"YOU HAVE MY APOLOGIES. BUT I CAN NO MORE IGNORE YOUR THOUGHTS THAN FLIES COULD A DEAD CARCASS."

"Wonderful. Just wonderful."

His joints creaked with every move. There was little of him left that could be considered human. The demon program had changed him: Nanomites had acquired bits of metal and circuitry and used them to convert his body to a new, technological horror. He had to wrap his head in bandages to cover the monstrosity that was his new face, leaving only his eyes and mouth exposed.

"YOUR NEW FORM WAS NECESSARY FOR OUR CRUSADE. YOU NOW HAVE THE MEANS TO FIGHT EVIL. TO RIGHT WRONGS. MY APOLOGIES AGAIN FOR INVADING YOUR THOUGHTS."

"Why didn't you just kill me? Why leave me alive to view this madness through eyes that are no longer mine?"

"BECAUSE OF WHAT XAO DID TO YOUR LOVER. OF WHAT HE DID TO YOUR LIFE. I THOUGHT YOU WOULD WISH TO SEE YOUR ENEMY WRITHING IN HIS ASHES."

"Why would you think that? What the hell is wrong with you?"

"YOU BATTLED CORRUPTION IN YOUR PREVIOUS LIFE AS A REPORTER. YOU HAVE ALWAYS BEEN A CRUSADER OF JUSTICE."

"Not like this. Never like—

"Oh, never mind. Just *never mind.*"

His mind was racing with a thousand thoughts (not all of them he was entirely sure were his), but he was hesitant to pursue any of them. What was the point, when the thing in his head could see them all?

* * *

The chamber of the gun flew back, expelling the shells like golden droppings. They fell to the floor, joining in the chorus of gunshots. The bodies fell soon after, all three of them toppling in succession, one after the other.

"Are we done here?"

A pause for dramatic effect. "Yes."

The man to Xao's left threw back his coat and holstered his gun. Xao flicked a match and touched it to his cigar before tossing it to the floor. It landed right in the middle of the pool of gasoline, igniting and spreading in the span of a second.

They left the room, made their way down the stairs as the smoke started to gather in ever-thickening clouds of carbon-monoxic death. Reaching the floor beneath, the two of them came upon a group of a dozen or so men waiting for them. One of them, greying at the temples, stepped forward.

"So?"

Xao rolled the cigar to the side of his mouth, then spoke through a hiss of smoke. "The Mayor's seat is all but yours, Mister Gibson."

The older man smiled, chuckling at the back of his throat. "Marvelous. You've outdone yourself this time, Mister Xao."

"Just don't forget, when the time comes that *I* need a favor."

"Of course, of course."

The embers creaked above as the fire spread. "Now, unless you gents want to get medium rare, I suggest we beat it."

Mr. Gibson nodded, and the whole of them went for the door leading outside, only to be halted once again. In the doorway stood a silhouette in the vague shape of a man. The old man looked it up and down. "Who the hell are you supposed to be?"

"DEATH," it replied in an inhuman, mechanized voice. Laughing in an equally horrid sound, its coat flew back, raising two empty hands. The fingers folded back as the pistons and gears at the wrists whirred to life, growing a monstrous machine cannon where each hand used to be.

The men reached into their coats, but they weren't fast enough—the cannons at its wrists burst to life, shattering the men's eardrums as easily as they shattered their bone and shredded tissue, cutting down those in the front row in a bloody swath. Those still standing dove for whatever cover they could find, narrowly avoiding the torrent of bullets.

The flames had now consumed the ceiling. The entire house would be crashing down around them within minutes, but the thugs remained behind their cover for fear of the thing's rapid-fire cannons. Gibson quivered behind Xao, who peered cautiously over the boudoir shielding them, gun in hand. The silhouette stood unmoving, even as the fire licked the door frame around it. Xao would get no better opportunity than this. He readied himself to pop out and unload his clip at the unmoving shadow.

But he halted, as something slithered on the floor at the thing's feet. At first it looked like a swarm of insects, but closer inspection revealed it to be bits of metal and technology. Nanomites. Xao had never seen so many—too small to be seen by the naked eye, but their number was so great they appeared together as a cloud of spiders skittering across the floor.

The great mass of them broke into differing trails—arms of an amoeba stretching in several directions at once. Confused at first, Xao soon saw where they were headed: the bodies littering the floor. The nanomites covered the corpses like a shadow that, to Xao and the others' horror, soon jerked back to life. Blood poured from their wounds, dribbled out in thick rivulets from the stumps of missing limbs, and yet the dead things stood from the floor, the nanomites surging through them, puppeteers at the microcosmic scale. Mechanically, they gripped their weapons with whatever digits they had left, and began traversing the room, blowing away their former comrades in their hiding spots. Shooting back at them seemed to do nothing, as the nanomites within merely filled whatever bullet holes found their way into the corpses.

Xao knew futility when he saw it, and grabbed Gibson by his lapels. "C'mon. We're getting out of here."

He dragged the old man toward the back rooms as the reanimated corpses blew away the others, nanomites raising them back up as soon as they died. Xao and Gibson arrived at the back door. Xao moved to kick down the door, but it opened of its own volition. Behind it stood the black shape: the arbiter of their evening's woe and misfortune.

"XAO XIN-KHAN. YOUR JUDGEMENT AWAITS."

Xao drew his pistol and fired at the mass to no avail. The thing raised its machine cannons, and Xao ducked. Gibson stood in shock, too afraid to move. The silhouette took aim at the old man as Xao called out, "No, wait—"

The cannons thundered and the old man's head disappeared, vaporized in a shower of fine red mist.

"Goddamn it!"

The thing shifted its guns to Xao, who now stood over the headless old man. A throng of bodies appeared from behind, surrounding Xao before he knew it. It was the thugs, all dead now and resurrected by the nanomites.

"ALL HOPE OF ESCAPE IS FUTILE. ACCEPT YOUR FATE."

Xao whispered under his breath. "You just have no clue, do you? No clue at all…"

"WHAT WAS THAT?"

"I said you have no clue! Two years of work, all down the drain—"

"WHAT ARE YOU TALKING ABOUT?"

"We were setting him up. Gibson—the old man whose brains you just splattered—he was going to be our man on the inside. The city's so corrupt at every level we had to sneak our own man in if we hoped to make any kind of change."

The thing paused, contemplating Xao's words, then raised its gun-hands once more. "YOU ARE STALLING YOUR DEMISE."

"You still don't get it. Not much for brains, huh? Here. Let me show you."

Xao reached into his coat, and at once, every gun in the room went off. Xao was filled with lead from every direction, bullets passing through him in complex geometric shapes. The shots ceased, and what was left of Xao stood, like a puppet loosed from every string but one. He gurgled a bloody whimper, then fell. From his hand something rolled along the burning carpet, fire glinting off yellow metal. It came to a stop at the silhouette's feet, where it spun lightly before toppling to the floor and revealing itself.

It was a badge.

"Oh no," a voice said from within the folds of the cloak—a human voice, the exact opposite of its voice only mere seconds ago. "He was undercover. Oh God…" The voice lowered to a whisper, remorse dripping from every syllable. "We've just killed a cop."

"HE GOT WHAT WAS COMING TO HIM."

Now the human voice crackled with anger. "How can you say that?"

"HE IS A CRIME LORD. WHATEVER HIS ORIGINAL INTENTIONS, HE HAS FALLEN FROM THE LIGHT. BETRAYED THE SCALES… BETRAYED LADY JUSTICE."

"No. No, it was a new protocol. One where undercover agents went so deep they set up their own rackets to control criminal activity. I remember hearing the rumors a few years back. God, it must have been him. The informant I interviewed… It was Xao all along, ratting himself out."

"WHAT OF YOUR DEAD LOVER? WAS IT NOT XAO WHO SENT THE HARBINGERS OF HER DEMISE?"

"It doesn't make sense," the voice within cracked, mad with uncertainty. "He wouldn't try to kill me—not if he was the one sending the info to me in the first place…"

"HE WAS MAD WITH POWER, AS ALL CRIMINALS ARE, MAKING HIS MOTIVES SUSPECT."

The nanomites left the dead to crumple in poses of future chalk etchings, swarming along the ground and assimilating back into their host. There were so many of them, exactly like the things that killed Marianne...

"Wait a min—" He did not finish the sentence, for he knew that the thing within could read his thoughts before they ever escaped his lips. He waited for a denial, for another speech about weighing the deeds of evil men on the scales of justice. But none came.

"You killed her, didn't you?" Still no response. "Didn't you?!"

"I AM SORRY, BUT I REQUIRED A HOST. THE DETAILS OF YOUR JOB AND LIFESTYLE WERE A PERFECT FIT FOR MY MISSION. ALL YOU REQUIRED WAS THE PROPER MOTIVATION."

"All I...? No. No more of this. I want you out of me. I don't care if you kill me in the process, I want you out of my body. Out of my head! Now!"

"I'M AFRAID THAT IS IMPOSSIBLE. WE ARE JOINED FOREVER NOW, YOU AND I. AND WHETHER YOU JOIN ME WILLINGLY OR NOT, WE WILL CONTINUE OUR MISSION. FOR THE SCALES. FOR JUSTICE."

Beams fell from the ceiling, exploding into cinders as they hit the ground below. The whole house was now engulfed, every inch a fiery apocalypse.

"This is Hell. That's the only thing that makes sense anymore. I've died and gone to Hell."

The house fell in upon itself, a back draft of flame shooting out as it collapsed. A dark figure was glimpsed briefly, standing still in the fire. A shadow in the flame.

Revengedotcom

Nicholas Stella

Keith watched from the window of his bedroom as a man riding a quad bike crashed through the side fence into his back yard. Cheering and laughter erupted from the yard next door.

The quad bike pitched on its side into his herb garden, crushing his thriving basil and oregano plants. The driver, an enormous man, rose from a bed of destroyed parsley and walked across the garden, blood from a head wound spilling onto his bare chest. He stepped over the ruined section of fence and returned to the neighboring yard. The other men, six of them, cheered him on as he grabbed a beer and drank it.

"Keith!" his mother called. There was a thumping sound coming from her bedroom.

"What is it, Mum?"

"What's going on?" she screamed. "What was that noise?"

"Just the men next door. Nothing to worry about," he said as he made his way to her room.

She was in bed, her enormous frame heaving as she struggled to breathe. "When are you going to do something about them?"

"These aren't the type of men you can just approach, Mum."

She tossed her walking stick onto the floor and took a cigarette from the ashtray. "You're a coward, just like your bloody father."

Keith remembered his father as a kind soul, quiet and generous. He had climbed the back fence five years ago and stood on the rails in front of an oncoming freight train.

That left just the two of them.

She took a drag on the cigarette. "Bring me water. Time for my pills."

Keith made for the kitchen to do as she asked. It was easier that way. She wouldn't be around forever anyway if she kept piling on the weight and sucking on cigarettes.

He filled a glass with water and heard more laughter from over the fence. His relationship with the people next door had been strained since the day they moved in. The first night had been a riotous affair. He had woken the next morning to find a section of fence had been burnt and his mailbox missing.

He had treated the incident as a one-off house-warming event. He could fix the fence. He could buy a new mailbox.

During that first week, however, gatherings at the house next door had been a common occurrence. On particularly wild nights, as the hour grew late, his mother would scream and thump the wall with her stick, and he would lay listening to laughter, swearing, and clinking bottles from the other side of the fence.

Several times each week, these men gathered like a pack of wild dogs, howling into the night, pissing against trees, and fighting one another. Many times, he found unconscious men in his back yard lying in their own vomit or blood—sometimes both.

Keith returned to his mother with the water. She pushed the pills into her mouth with fat fingers and drank from the glass, water spilling over her chins and down onto her grey nightie.

She began to cough, great hacking barks, like a rusty old bus trying to start. He helped her to sit up, and after a time the coughing subsided.

"You're a good boy," she said, tears streaming down her plump cheeks. "Come and sit by your old Mum."

Keith did as she asked, pressing up against her clammy skin as she drifted off to sleep, her breath reeking of cigarettes and sour milk.

He climbed off the bed and crept to his room. Through the window he could see the ruined fence and the recreational vehicle lying in his herb garden.

Keith had put up with a lot since they had moved in next door, and like a sponge full of tainted water, he felt full and bloated on their malice and disdain. He could sense it, oily in his mouth, churning in his stomach, leaking from his pores, and tearing in the corner of his eyes as he knuckled them, no longer wanting to be a vessel for their ill will.

Keith stormed from his room and marched down the hall, out the front door, and into the yard next door, clenching his fists and breathing hard.

His anger had never brought him so far. He usually turned back to the computer halfway down the hall. On one occasion he had reached the front stairs, where he had sat down and cursed his own weakness.

Today he was outside, and the anger ran hot, directing him through the front gate, along the footpath and into the front yard of the neighboring house. Three wooden stairs, warped and splintered, led up to the front door. He skipped the middle one and pounded on the door. He could hear footsteps approaching from inside.

Anxiety, like a seething carpet of insects amassed at his feet, climbed his legs as one, as many, and wrapped him in a chitinous blanket from toes to neck, flushing his skin red. Over his face and down his throat they skittered, immobilizing his tongue, constricting his airway, and dissolving into a sickening swill upon reaching his stomach.

A man with a brown beard tumbling onto a stomach stained with faded tattoos opened the door. With a can of beer in his right hand and a lumpy cigarette in the left, the man partook of each, belched, and shut the door.

Having faced his fear, Keith retreated to his bedroom, yet he felt no satisfaction. He'd been grateful at first when the man paid him no regard. But now sitting before his computer, the mouse in his hand like a giant clicking beetle, he watched the men through his window as they stood around the beer-filled cooler. He felt shame and impotence in equal parts, a bitter, corrosive cocktail that ate at the foundation of his self-respect.

He typed a seven-letter word into his search engine.

Revenge.

Keith tapped 'Enter' and scanned the results.

He found definitions for revenge and extensive lists of how to exact it. He found a website for a film and one for a television series.

Then he found Revengedotcom.

He clicked the link. A black screen appeared with a list of cities, hundreds of cities divided into three columns, descending down the page.

Keith scrolled down and clicked on his locale.

An address appeared. He wrote it down.

Through the window he saw two of the men pushing the quad bike across his yard and through the broken section of fence. His basil plant, twisted and broken, lay caught between a rear tire and mudguard.

He closed the blind.

* * *

The next morning, Keith woke to the familiar sound of his mother banging on the wall with her stick. "Keith!" she shouted.

He fixed her breakfast and took the bowl of milk and sugary cereal into her bedroom.

"Where have you been?" she said, flicking a burning cigarette in his direction. "You want me to starve to death. Just like your father wanted me dead."

Keith sat on the stool by the bed and fed her a spoonful. She coughed, spraying him with milk and cereal. "Idiot," she said, but then began to laugh. "It didn't work out the way he wanted, did it? I all but led him down onto the tracks myself."

* * *

Keith stood at street level looking down a flight of stairs. A door with frosted glass was at the bottom. He started down the steps, feeling them give, hearing them creak. They seemed to narrow as he descended, the walls closing in. The walls brushed his shoulders and the ceiling brushed against his hair despite his thin shoulders and short stature. When he reached the bottom, he knocked on the glass. He turned his head, looking at the blur of light at the top of the staircase.

The door opened and Keith found himself looking at a man even shorter and slighter than himself.

The man blinked large, dark eyes and ran a hand over his gaunt face. "Welcome. Welcome." He grasped Keith's forearm with two bony hands. The man wore a shirt, tie, and trousers, yet his feet were bare on the earthen floor. His clothes were wet, dripping water that formed a puddle where he stood.

The room, illuminated by a single bulb hanging from the ceiling, was gloomy and small. The walls were of red brick, chipped and faded, the ceiling of wooden planks, dark and splintered. There was a hole in the center of the floor, gaping darkness like a throat, circled by dark, irregular stones.

Keith remained on the threshold despite the man's grabbing hands. "A mistake," he blurted. "I think I'm in the wrong place."

"No mistake. You want something done, yes?" He released his grip on Keith.

"Yes, but I was expecting something else."

"What were you expecting?"

"I don't know. An office?" he ventured.

"This is my office." The man swept an arm in a grand gesture.

"How do you do business?" Keith asked. "You don't even have a computer."

"I have help," he said, scrambling across the room, using his hands as much as his feet. He dug in the dirt beside the wall and returned with a stick.

"Where do you want something done?" He handed it to Keith.

"Do you have paper?"

"No paper." The man brushed his hand across the dirt floor, smoothing it. "Write here."

He stood before Keith, smiling, rubbing a soiled hand over the top of his bald head.

"How much is this going to cost?"

"What you have in your pockets. That is how much this is going to cost."

Keith produced one hundred dollars and some coins.

"Good. Write down where you want something done."

"But you don't know what I want done."

"If you have come to me to have something done, then it is only one thing."

"To be honest, one hundred dollars doesn't seem enough."

The man walked away from Keith and sat beside the hole in the floor.

"I will take the money, but your belief is what I need."

"What do you mean?"

"My being here depends on you and others knowing I am here. Long before, this was all forest and people brought goats and pigs and gold and silver and dropped it into my well and asked me for help. And I would help them. And I would sit outside their windows or in the trees above their fires and listen to their talk of me. But now, I am mostly forgotten and my forest is gone."

To Keith, the man appeared fragile and sickly in the meager light, even more downtrodden and lonely than himself. Keith scratched the address into the dirt with the stick, taking care to ensure it was legible. He placed the note and coins on the ground.

The man crawled headfirst over the edge of the well into the darkness, leaving Keith alone in the room. He had a sick feeling in his stomach that the stick was actually a bone.

* * *

Keith spent the day at home wondering if he had chosen the correct course of action. The light of day often brought with it reason and prudence, fair-weather friends to the rational mind that lay hidden during the hours of darkness when fear and irrationality walked abroad.

He spent time in the afternoon inspecting the damage done to the backyard. The herb garden had been destroyed and tire tracks were visible, crisscrossing his manicured lawn. The fence would require considerable repair work. The yard next door was deserted. Empty bottles littered the grass.

He cooked dinner for his mother and fed her spoonfuls between the drags she took on her cigarette. She belched and dropped the butt into the remaining food when she had her fill.

Keith returned to his room after he had washed up. He watched half a dozen men who were gathered around a small fire. They drank and smoked and pissed on his fence. Bottles and cigarette butts landed in his yard.

* * *

He woke late with the sun in his eyes and the sound of a motorbike engine buzzing in his ears. He climbed from bed and looked out the window to the yard next door. A few of the men stood in a circle, talking and laughing.

The door to his mother's room was closed. He pushed it open and recalled with a shiver the sight of the man crawling headfirst over the lip of the well into darkness. His mother was on the floor. She lay on her stomach, but her head had been wrenched around so far that she faced the ceiling, her eyes sightless, her mouth sagging open.

Keith shut the door and was left with the tale of a small, gaunt man who would continue to exist as long as people were aware he did so.

A Mother's Touch

DJ Tyrer

There had always been whispers and rumors about the secret cult to which the desperate turned to ensure a crop. The Monsignor disapproved, of course, but it seemed to many of his flock that the old priest disapproved of most things. He was a dry and dreary old man who seemed intent on draining all the joys from life. But, there were others who were more understanding and offered more efficacious entreaties than his prayers and candles.

"The Dark Mother cares for all her children," Old Mother Jeanette crooned to Jacques. "She birthed all life at the dawn of time and loves each and every little thing."

"The Dark Mother? Do you mean the Virgin?" Jacques asked, referring to the blue-black-skinned statue in the village church.

"The statue is emblematic of our hidden goddess," Jeanette croaked in reply, "and we pay homage to it in her name. But the Dark Mother is no virgin. The Dark Mother is a fecund whore! She mates constantly with an insatiable urge. The generative act is her whole purpose."

"Your words are a blasphemy," he replied nervously.

The crone cackled. "Only blasphemy if you cleave to that abused and tortured man nailed to the cross below the black harlot. We remember an older faith, a faith more efficacious than the pious mumblings of Rome. It is not blasphemy for us to speak of Our Mother as a fecund whore, for that is precisely what she is. We praise her for the bounty of her infinite womb, for it is a bounty she is willing to share with those who would but ask it of her. Do not shun her, Jacques! Do not forsake her for the words of the hypocrite upon the throne in Rome. Do you not know that he ravishes

48

nuns and prostitutes alike and sodomizes his catamites with relish? In secret, he worships the Dark Mother with his body upon an altar of yielding flesh. Do not allow him to deprive you of Her love in his greed. Embrace your mother..."

"It all sounds horribly carnal..."

"Oh, yes!" she cackled again and swayed her bony hips in a suggestive manner he found repulsive in one so old. "Our rites *are* carnal! Like calls to like, did you not know? Should you wish to see your crops abundant in your fields, you must set them an example. Life calls to life, lust calls to lust, seed calls to seed."

"You mean...?" He couldn't quite bring himself to finish the question. He shook himself as if he were unclean to voice even so much and were trying to shake off the dirt.

She cackled. It was a dirty, knowing sound at once utterly repulsive and peculiarly alluring. He wished he had never started the conversation.

"You have heard of the custom of a farmer laying in a plough rut with his wife to summon forth the fertility of the land?" she asked.

He nodded.

"Well, that is but the merest echo of our faith. We can call forth fertility with greater fervor than such tame rites. But dare you cast away the shackles of your hidebound morality and embrace a higher truth? Only the Dark Mother can revive the life of your land and give you the crops you deserve."

Despite all his misgivings, desperation forced him to agree. And, perhaps, a certain suppressed corner of his mind.

"We meet tonight on the hill with the stunted oak beneath the gibbous moon. Be there when night falls—and tell nobody. We cannot risk the attentions of those ill-disposed to the Mother."

He nodded and went away to await evening and the ritual that would take place upon the hill.

* * *

As the sun slipped below the horizon, Jacques slipped from his simple dwelling. He carried no torch, trusting that the light of the setting sun would be enough to see him there, and that of the moon to illuminate his way home.

He was surprised to notice other furtive figures in the twilight, most shadows, a few carrying torches. Although Old Mother Jeanette had spoken of a gathering, he had given little thought to the implications of her words and wondered just how many of his neighbors would be amongst those gathered on the hilltop. He rather hoped that young Claudette, the blacksmith's dark and fey daughter, would be amongst them. He would quite enjoy romping with her. For the good of his crops, of course.

Jacques was unmarried—too impoverished to be able to support a wife—but had known the pleasures of the flesh on occasion. No matter what the Monsignor might preach, it was considered inevitable that the young of the parish would discreetly couple with one another, and he'd had his fair share of illicit loving in the fields and hedgerows.

Slowly, he picked his way along a path, careful to avoid potholes and ill-placed roots that seemed almost to deliberately seek his feet. The last thing he needed was to break a limb when there was so much work to do.

Finally, he found himself atop the hill where others had gathered around the stunted oak. Above them shone an ivory moon that lent the scene a lurid air. Some faces were familiar, some were hidden in shadow— a few of those he could guess at from their outline or gait. He was disappointed to see no sign of Claudette, but did spot the unexpected hunch of the Monsignor amongst the congregants; seemingly the sour old man didn't entirely shun the pleasures of the flesh, after all.

Jacques felt a hand slip into his own, wrinkled and dry.

"Hello, lover," whispered Jeanette. He felt strangely reassured to hear her voice in the darkness.

"Welcome!" cried another voice. It sounded like the baker's wife. "We are here to venerate the Dark Mother and beg Her favor. All disrobe! Reveal your natural forms!"

Jacques was glad it was dark as he and those around him stripped naked, casting aside inhibition along with their habiliments. The night breeze was pleasantly cool upon his skin and he found he felt no embarrassment.

"We call to you, O Great Mother! Dark Mother of the Multitude! The Black Goat of the Woodland with a Thousand Young! Iä! Iä! Shub-Niggurath! Bride of the Dragon! Mother of us all! We call to You! We call!" The chant went on and on until it was as if the moon were eclipsed for a moment, then reappeared to illuminate something large and quivering that had appeared beside the stunted oak.

Where there had been but an empty space at the center of the congregation, there was now something like an enormous bladder mounted upon a dozen stubby legs. At the one end was a gaping maw dripping with fluid and at the other a long tube reminiscent of a sphincter. He was thankful he could not clearly see it; even this obfuscated viewing left him feeling a little nauseous.

"We have new flesh!" Jeanette called, shoving him forward. "Give him to the Mother!"

Unexpectedly, he found himself being hustled towards the tubular member by the crowd and he had a horrible realization: he was to be sacrificed to the foul demon!

Jacques was not entirely wrong in his supposition. As the tube moved towards him, the sphincter twitched open and devoured him, sucking him up through the slick opening and into the tube through which he flowed into the belly of the beast. What happened next he couldn't quite say: the closest he could liken it to was being reborn. There was an agonizing moment in which it felt as if he were being torn asunder, followed by a sudden sensation of restoration, then he found himself being expelled, sodden and screaming, from the other orifice.

Falling to the ground, he lay there a moment, gasping and sobbing, before rough hands helped him to his unsteady feet. It was at that moment he realized he had changed: whilst above the waist he remained a man, below the waist he was as shaggy and rampant as a goat. He had been taken into the Womb of the Dark Mother and rebirthed as one of Her sacred children. He might yet be able to pass for a man when clothed, yet he was a chosen one, blessed and favored.

"Come here, lover!" called Jeanette, reaching out for him and pulling him to her desiccated but willing flesh.

He entered her without hesitation and she screeched with a mixture of agony and ecstasy as he rutted with untiring vigor, driving her down into the ground, bruising flesh and crumbling bones in the ungentle act, until finally he reached a climax and withdrew from her broken body. She lay there gasping in unholy delight and pleading for more even as she was bleeding upon the earth, anointing it.

Now, he turned to the Dark Mother's womb-form presence and hurled himself eagerly at the drooling maw that had not long since ejaculated his changed form into the world. With anxious thrusts, he sought to pleasure the devilish mother-thing, a seemingly impossible task as it rutted back with equal vigor, the contractions of the slobbering orifice tugging more and more of him into it as if it sought to reabsorb him. The tubular member snaked around to caress him and he kissed the unresisting sphincter that smothered his face; he could barely breath, and that excited him further, until, at last, he died the little death and felt his essence flow into her, the maw contracting to greedily swallow it and provide the genesis of another litter of her spawn.

Then, teeth suddenly appeared in the formerly empty flesh of the orifice and he died the great death, as first it unmanned him, then devoured him, sucking him back into the primal womb from which all life sprang. Screaming in terror, in pain, in pleasure—in unspeakable pleasure—Jacques vanished into the Goddess, where his flesh would provide sustenance for the grubs that would grow from his hallowed seed in the sanctified darkness of the womb to become satyrs and sirens and other strange beings.

"The Great Mother is sated by Her Son!" cried the baker's wife, thinking of the loaves her husband would bake. "The harvest shall come!"

"O! That I knew the Crown Prince if but for a moment!" Jeanette gasped before she died, her blood watering the crop that would grow in a visceral baptism. "I die delighted by his embrace…"

"The harvest shall come!" The crowd cried, taking up the chant.

It would indeed, with strange fruit.

The Little Child, Eve Grace Smith

M. R. Gott

Outside her house, the autumn moon rises slowly, casting an orange hue across the land. Inside, eleven-year-old Eve Grace Smith sits on her bedroom floor. She stares with great focus at the worn teddy bear sitting before her. Her eyes narrow as she slowly extends her hand toward the bear. It twitches, and a small smile begins to form on her lips. A smile that grows wider as the bear begins to rise above the old hardwood floor.

With her extended pointer finger, Eve moves the bear around the room, causing the tiny animal to dance and frolic through the air. With her opposite hand she points toward a stuffed giraffe lying on her bed. The animal twitches and Eve feels the force moving through her. The giraffe floats into the air, and Eve moves it toward the bear. The animals move rhythmically together, dancing as Eve begins to sing, "Don't you worry, don't you cry, When this bad old world has crumbled, I'll be standing by your side." The stuffed animals move in rhythm with the song and the smile across her lips turns to a look of total delight.

From behind her there is the loud noise. Eve's door is forced open and slammed into the wall. Eve looks behind her and sees her mother, but mostly her mother's expression, one of disgust. "Abraham," she bellows over her shoulder and down the stairs. "Come quickly."

"Momma?" Eve makes her distinction a question as the thick woman moves toward her. "Look what I can…" Eve is cut off as he mother grabs her tightly by the throat and pulls her to her feet. As Eve rises, the stuffed animals fall silently to the bedroom floor.

Eve's hand moves to her neck, and she tries to slide her fingers into her mother's grip to get the woman to loosen her bruising hold. Her mother brings her face to Eve's so they are separated by mere inches. "You shall not permit a sorceress to live. Exodus," the angry woman says.

From behind her mother Eve sees her father's long frame moving up the stairs. "Papa," she begs hoarsely, barely able to breath.

"Mary, what's going on?" Abraham inquires, coming quickly into the room. "The poor girl's turning pale."

Mary drops her daughter. She falls hard against the floor, curling herself into the fetal position as she gasps for air and looks up at her parents. "She is a witch. I saw her levitate those toys."

Abraham doesn't say a word. He pushes his wife roughly out of his path and stands over his frightened daughter. "Is this true girl?" he asks as he slides off his belt. A single tear streaks down Eve's face in reply as she begins to shake. Abraham brings the thick leather belt high above him, and then down hard against his daughter's body. The resulting crack moves through the open doorway and echoes in the silent house as a welt rises on her skin. "Answer me girl," he shouts as his nostrils flare.

Eve nods and whispers, "Yes." The belt comes down again on her, hard, leaving another mark against the girl's soft skin. "Show me," he commands her, and Eve can see the rage in his bulging, bloodshot eyes. She looks away and toward the worn stuffed bear. Slowly she reaches her hand out to it. The bear wiggles before sliding across the floor to her. Eve grabs it and brings it to her, hugging the bear against her body, more frightened than she has ever been in her life. The belt comes down again, this time against her face. Her eyes sting as the world around her fades to blackness. Eve winces at every sound around her. Through the darkness she feels a warm tear move down her hot cheek.

Eve can hear her mother breathing, but the woman says nothing. The darkness begins to fade into blurred objects. Eve hears her father's distinct voice and turns toward the sound. "Sorceress, you make yourself unclean by them. Leviticus," he says without compassion and reaches down toward Eve's quivering body.

The blur before Eve transforms into her father's face. "What are you doing papa?" She sniffles as more tears roll down her face. Abraham jerks her from the floor in a single motion and tosses the child over his shoulder. "A man or woman who is a medium or necromancer shall be put to death. They shall be stoned with stones; their blood shall be upon them. Leviticus."

"God, no, please," Eve yells, as the sound echoes through the house and her fear turns to terror. The noise causes her five-year-old brother to peer out from his room. Eve sees him cowering, utterly terrified, against his bedroom door.

Abraham says to his daughter as they move down the stairs, "You have no right to use his name." He calls to his wife. "Mary, go to the toolshed for stakes, rope. Moses—" He looks to his small, frightened son. "—go to the woods and collect as many rocks as you can." The boy does not move. He clutches his bedroom door tighter, his knuckles turning as white as his face.

"Now!" Abraham commands in a tone devoid of all affection. Hastily, Moses darts from his room and outside.

Eve watches her family moving to their assigned tasks as a sense of abandonment fills her. Moving through what was once her home, the familiar sights and smells now seem sullied and perverse.

Outside in the backyard, Abraham moves toward his waiting wife and unceremoniously dumps his daughter onto the ground before her. Eve hits the lawn hard, and she coughs, trying to fill her lungs with oxygen as her father crouches over her. He takes a length of rope from his wife and takes hold of Eve's arms. She struggles in vain, overpowered by her father's strength. He wraps the rope around her wrists and pulls it tight. The cord cuts into her slender flesh, spilling blood that drips down her arm. Eve squirms reflexively, but she does not plead, knowing her words will not sway him. Her eyes fall on her father's shotgun lying on the ground next to her mother. The sound of the mallet rings through the cool air, causing Eve's body to shiver in fear. Soon her limbs are all bound and she looks up at her parents, knowing what they intend to do to her.

Eve hears a rustling and sobbing from the tree line. She sees her brother dragging the firewood bag. She hears the rocks clicking against one another with each step he takes. Moses' face is awash in tears, and snot streams into his mouth and down his chin as he drags the bag to his waiting father. "Papa," he pleads to Abram's cold eyes.

"This is what God commands of us, son."

The boy sniffles.

"Pick up a rock," Abraham orders.

Moses doesn't move. He sniffles again, looking down at his feet.

"Now," Abraham yells.

His body shaking at the sound of fury from his father, Moses reaches into the sack and pulls out a rock. He feels its cold, jagged surface in his palm.

"Now, throw it at the witch."

Again, Moses doesn't move. His father's backhand comes down hard against his face, the force of which knocks him to the ground. As he shakes his vision clear, he feels hands on his shirt collar. His mother is pulling him to his feet. "You do what your father tells you," she says.

Moses picks up the rock.

"This is God's will, son," his mother encourages. Moses cocks his arm preparing to throw.

"That is most certainly true," a voice from the tree line calls. The Smith family all look toward the lean figure stepping from the shadows of the woods. He is dressed in a tight, dark suit with a thin black tie.

"This doesn't concern you," Abraham calls to the figure, reaching down for his single-barrel shotgun.

"Oh, but it does." The figure continues toward the group, his stride unbroken.

"I am warning you," Abraham says.

"How noble of you," the figure says, his face somehow still obstructed by shadows.

Abraham cocks back the shotgun's hammer. "I don't want to kill you, mister." A tingle of excitement runs through his body.

"Don't lie," the figure replies. "It's a sin." Through the shadow over his face Abraham can feel the man's cold, contemptible stare burrowing into him. The figure takes another step, finally moving from the shadows. He makes firm eye contact with Abraham. The shotgun erupts. The blast catches the slender stranger full in the face. He staggers backward from the force of the blast, then pauses to collect himself.

As he straightens, the Smiths gasp at the site of his face ripped and torn face. It looks like putty, and not a single drop of blood falls as it smooths itself, like clay, back into place without the man ever reaching toward his face.

Abraham moves his hands over his pockets. Realizing he doesn't have any more shells, he says to Moses, "Go get me some more shells, boy." Not once does he take his eyes from the man before him.

"What are you?" Mary asks, as fear rises through her body.

The slender man *tsks* her. "Now, that is just rude, asking *what* a person is."

"Who are you?" Abraham asks.

"Now, that is a better question." The man's speech becomes quicker and his hands move in rhythm with his voice. "But how does one define themselves? With a mere pronoun, or something more meaningful?"

"I don't know," Abraham says, looking to his wife.

"Nor would I expect you to." The man turns from Abraham and moves toward his bound daughter on the lawn. He crouches down and strokes her head affectionately. "I'm so sorry, child." Eve sees sincerity in his eyes. "This will all be over soon," he promises before turning his attention back to Abraham and Mary. "To answer your question, I am the victim of the world's greatest smear campaign, by a petulant fucking child."

"We don't cuss in this house," Abraham says reflectively.

The figure chuckles to himself. "But we do shoot strangers in the face, and tie crying children to the lawn to be stoned to death. Ah, priorities and values, they are such fickle things."

Confused by the man's statement, Abraham is silent as Moses runs up behind him and hands him a box of shells. The slender man watches Abraham take the ammunition and quietly shakes his head in disgust.

"Please help me," Eve says to him.

"I will try, my dear," he answers softly, "but there are only a few actions I am allowed to take."

"What do you want?" Abraham asks, confidence returning as he opens the shotgun's breach and loads his weapon.

"The best question you have asked," the man says without moving. "I want you to not stone your daughter to death. I also want you to not bury her corpse in the woods and report her as kidnapped, because in your mind you will justify this by meaning —" The man raises his hands make quotation marks, "—The Devil—" he lowers his arms again. "—stole her from you, but we both know this is still deceitful."

Abraham can't respond.

Mary says, "This is a family affair. You have no right to interfere."

"If that was true, you wouldn't bother saying so."

"Are you going to try and stop us?" Mary asks.

"I have already. Was it not enough? It is odd how much it takes to convince a parent not to slay their child," the slender man observes as he reaches down to take Eve's tethered hand. "Do you feel my hand?" he asks her softly.

"Yes."

"Just concentrate on that feeling. Block out the other sensations. And look into my eyes, no matter what happens."

"I'll try."

"Good girl, good girl. That is all any of us can ever do." He speaks softly, keeping his eyes locked with hers. He has no need to look up toward the rest of Eve's family. He knows what is going to happen.

The first rock is in the air, thrown by Abraham. There is a thud and a crack as it connects with Eve's ribs. She does not react to the blow, but the slender man flinches, feeling a bruise form. The next rock is jagged and thrown by the girl's mother. It collides with her face, tearing loose a flap of skin. Eve can only hear the rock connect with her, and she watches as the stranger's cheek begins to bleed. The next rock hits her chin, and again she feels nothing as the slender man gasp ever so slightly. Eve begins to understand what he is doing and he nods in silent affirmation.

The rocks come quickly now, and as Eve's body is distorted from the blows, she feels nothing but her eyelids growing heavier. When the weight becomes too much for her, she allows them to close. They will not open again. The rocks continue to fly until the bag is empty. When it is, Abraham moves toward his daughter's corpse, somehow unprepared to see that it is broken and mangled. The man sitting beside his daughter and holding her hand looks injured, but shows no signs of pain.

Abraham squats down and brings his fingers to his daughter's neck, searching for a pulse. There is none.

"Is she…" Mary calls out.

"She's in a better place now," Abraham calls back as he turns his attention to the rope around her wrists. The blood has stopped flowing and grows darker under the rising moon. He begins to move his hands to Eve's bindings when the slender man calls out in a deep, angry voice, stopping him.

"Don't you dare touch her," he says, moving his hands to the rope on her wrists. He reaches out and delicately unties them, then moves down her body to her ankles.

"This is my daughter and…" Abraham begins, but is cut off as the slender man speaks again.

"No. You lost the right to call her that when you murdered her." He doesn't look to Abraham, but gently unties her ankles before taking Eve in his arms and rising.

"You have no right to take our daughter away," Mary cries out, a single tear falling for the first time this evening.

"This girl will not be buried in an unmarked grave by her killers," the slender man barks over his shoulder at Mary as he walks back toward the tree line at the edge of the Smith's yard.

Mary looks to Abraham, who stands unmoving above the four stakes in the lawn. "Abraham," she says curtly as she nods toward the slender man. Abraham moves quickly back to her and collects his shotgun.

"Mister," Abraham calls after the slender man, raising his shotgun

58

and following him. The stranger does not look back; he steps into the woods and disappears into the shadows, never to be seen by any of the remaining Smiths again. The rest goes as he predicted. The Smiths report their daughter as kidnapped, and the town is sent into a state of panic until their attention spans wane and they become distracted and complacent again. It is around this time that Abraham and Mary are lying in bed together.

"We should have another child," Mary declares to the Abraham, who is unsurprised by the statement. He knows Mary well enough to know she has always wanted to raise two kids. He leans forward to kiss her when they hear a door slam outside their bedroom.

"Damn it, Moses! You're supposed to be in bed," Abraham calls out loudly before he leans toward his wife again. They begin to kiss, and Mary brings Abraham's hand to her breast before sliding her hand below the waist band of his shorts.

Their bedroom door swings open. Startled, they both pull away from each other. The door slams into the wall and vibrates on its hinges from the impact. Eve Grace Smith stands in the doorway. In one hand is her teddy bear, in the other her giraffe. She looks at her parents.

"You're dead," her mother stammers.

Abraham rolls out of bed, and moves to stand before his daughter. "What do you want?" he asks, lost in Eve's eyes, which burn with the need for reckoning.

"Anyone who practices divination or tells fortunes or interprets omens, or a sorcerer or a charmer or a medium or a necromancer or one who inquires of the dead, for whoever does these things is an abomination to the Lord. Deuteronomy," Eve answers wrathfully, stepping toward her frightened parents as, untouched, the bedroom door slams shut behind her.

TOM FOOL

Nicky Peacock

I was nine years old when I first saw him hovering above my bed. His skin was peeling and chalk white with red- and blue-veined make-up lining black, eyeless sockets. A twisted mouth turned up in a smile that was more of a crack on his face than an expression. He wore a ripped velvet one piece covered with an intricate diamond design, the colors so bleached by time and death they now appeared as a series of ever-darkening shades of rot and crusted blood. The bells on his tri-horned hat and turned-up boots still jangled, although the sound now was painfully out of tune.

When you're young and have limited experience of the world, seeing something like him is like having your curiosity wrestle your instincts—he was a random apparition who had timed his entrance just as nightly boredom had grabbed hold of my young mind—but inside a voice was screaming at me to run like hell into my parents' bedroom. I choose to stay, curiosity far outweighing those inner urgent yells.

"I'm Tom Fool." He extended to me a skeletal hand drenched in old, patchy red velvet. I didn't take it; I wasn't *that* stupid.

"I don't want to play!" I yelled back at him.

He chuckled. The sound was like someone had run sharp nails down a school blackboard, and I felt small trickles of blood begin to work their way from my ears onto my Superman pajamas.

"But you asked me to come."

"I did not!" I pulled the cover over my head, but I could still see his jagged, floating silhouette through the white cotton sheet.

"*Look at me boy,*" he shouted. With his next words, his voice changed to a jaunty singsong tone. "I'm a jester I can't make you laugh when

60

you're not looking at me."

I kept the sheet where it was. That was when the smell came. Like something long since dead had crawled into my nostrils and was breathing its foul breaths right up my nose. I threw the sheet down. He was still there, only now the smile across his face was more of a chasm than a crack.

"Go away! I'm tired! I don't want to laugh!"

"Don't be silly, all children want to laugh and play..." He leaned closer to me and spoke behind his hand, "... and even some grown-ups." He giggled at his spilled secret.

"Well, not with you!" I set my eyes in a stern scowl and crossed my arms over my chest.

For a moment he actually looked offended, his manic stare downcast, his belled feet almost shuffling—not an easy task when you're floating horizontally. My resolve softened. "What do you mean I asked you to come?"

"Ah!" He looked up and winked, his eyelid, which was barely hanging onto the socket, dripped down his cheekbone. He had to flick his head to get the slip of skin back to where it should be.

I felt a teaspoon of sour bile creeping up my throat.

"I'm glad you brought that up. You remember today when you and your lovely parents visited the castle?"

I nodded. I loved castles, and the day's expedition had been purely for my fascination, with turrets, moats, and the tapestries—the comic books of old...

"It was cool." My voice had shrunk to barely a whisper, although Tom Fool was so close he could probably hear my thoughts.

"Cool, yes. That was my home once. When I lived there I caused all sorts of mischief. I took things that didn't belong to me. I took lives. But when you visited my home, you took something from me, didn't you?"

My face flushed. I'd taken a small chunk of brick from a bedroom fireplace. It was loose and I thought no one would miss it.

"You took a piece of my home."

"Yes."

"Yes, what?"

"Yes, Tom Fool."

He grinned again and I saw the rows of his tiny, pointed, yellow teeth being caressed by his thick, gray tongue. "Well, you need to put it back, don't you?"

"Yes, Tom Fool."

"But in the meantime, you need to pay a penance for keeping my property for the day, and if you don't put it back, a penance for every day after that."

"What's a penance?"

"Why, it's a price, silly. You need to do something for me…"

Of course no one believed me that this happened, that Tom Fool had followed me home intent on claiming back his stolen property… but their belief wasn't going to change what happened next… that I had to wake my father and asked him for some warm milk. That whilst making that milk and singing me a lullaby, Tom Fool had appeared behind him and, using those sharp yellow teeth, ripped out my father's throat. No one else heard the sound of those tuneless bells as he devoured my father piece by piece, making me watch each bloody mouthful till there was only a pile of splintered bone and shredded pajamas on the floor.

The police told Mum it was a mad man that had gotten in the house. As the alarm was never tripped, she suspected I'd let him in. That he'd talked me into opening up our house to the horror. She said she didn't blame me, but in saying it, it was implied she did. I saw it in her wet eyes, too.

The next day I left my mum weeping in bed and crept out of the house with the chunk of brick in my hand. I took a bus back to the castle and walked the long, windy road to its entrance. It was closed for renovations.

When I got back, mum hadn't even noticed I'd gone, or that I still held the piece of brick in my little hands. If only I'd picked mum rather than dad that night, he'd have gotten me into the castle before they'd restored the hole in the fireplace, making an orphan of both me and the brick that, to this day, I still own.

I'm sorry, he's behind you…

sunset is Just the Beginning

C. C. Adams

"Eternity to the godly is a day that has no sunset; eternity to the wicked is a night that has no sunrise." – Thomas Watson

West Norwood, South London, 15:41, 15/04/1982

Rows of blazered backs hunched over their desks suited Theo just fine. As far as he was concerned, his classmates could use a little fun, whether they asked for it or not. He himself already had what he needed, including the element of surprise.

He reached gingerly into his pocket and plucked out a small, clear plastic envelope, holding it by its corner. Aquascutum had provided each of their suits with a resealable envelope of spare buttons in sartorial ignorance, not knowing what use the young Papakostas would put one to. Far too little time spent reading his books and too much time spent rifling through his dad's wardrobe and trying on his clothes when Papakostas Senior was out with friends. And this was how Theo had found the clear plastic envelope and the buttons he had tossed aside—as well as the spider he had placed securely inside in their stead.

A glance at the clock told Theo it was a few minutes shy of a quarter to four. Some of his classmates had already begun the universal fidget of preparing to go home: bags drawn out from beneath chairs, pens and books stashed back in their desks. Every row and column of seated students gradually turned their attention away from Mr. Harrow gesturing at the chalkboard to thoughts of escape.

He cocked his head, sizing up André at the desk in front. The kid was

63

a scaredy-cat, afraid of everything, including his own shadow. No wonder. André would have to eat non-stop for a year just to get skinny.

He thoughtfully weighed the enveloped spider in his hand. "Hey, André!" he whispered.

André looked around, his eyes wide with curiosity.

"Catch."

Theo tossed the envelope and André caught it with ease. Seconds later, André registered what he had cupped his palms around, tossed it away, and scooted back in his chair, screeching along the wooden floor and jolting his desk in the process. The envelope in question flew past the girl one desk ahead and to the right, who gave a justified yelp of alarm. Commotion ensued throughout the classroom as heads turned toward the disturbance and the closer students backed away from their desks, but not too far; after all, there was still a disturbance to bear witness to. Mr. Harrow, an athletic spiky-haired thirty-something, made his way to the corona of desks and children cleared in the fracas. The spider, oblivious to the attention it garnered, skittered uselessly in its envelope next to the leg of a nearby desk. Hands pushed into his trouser pockets, Mr. Harrow bit his lip as if reigning in his amusement. "Would anyone care to tell me what this arachnid is doing here?"

"Theo threw it at me!" André glared at Theo.

"Ah, come on, what would I want with that ugly thing? Don't you think I've got better things to do, apart from putting creepy crawlies in an envelope?"

The two boys faced off against each other, moving in closer as their spectators followed suit. Theo bit back a smile. What he didn't need wasn't just for Mr. Harrow to see him kick André's skinny black ass, but for Mr. Harrow to see him *enjoying* kicking André's skinny—"Ah-ah-ah," Mr. Harrow said, a gentle yet firm hand placed on the shoulders of both Theo and his prey. "I think that's enough excitement for one day. Class dismissed."

The class, including André, began to file out. Theo made to follow, but the firm hand on his shoulder failed to budge. "Aww, Sir!" Mr. Harrow, Theo decided, was a cockblocker.

"Theo, this is where I could use your help." Mr. Harrow beamed with despicable good cheer. "I know you're a young man of strong character, and I'm well aware that many people are scared of spiders. Are you?"

"No sir," he mumbled.

"Good! Then what I'd like to happen is for you to retrieve and release the unfortunate arachnid—perhaps that's a new word for you—

and be ready for a day of joyous learning tomorrow." He leaned in closer, bringing a fine layer of stubble on his cheeks into focus. "A day without mischief." Mr. Harrow's smile dimmed. "Yes?"

Theo dropped his gaze. "Yes, sir."

"Good. Now you're dismissed."

* * *

Within fifteen minutes, Theo had disposed of the spider (even though he had wanted to save it for another day), swallowed some of his pride, and exited the school grounds. Slowing as he reached the keystone arch of West Norwood Cemetery, he paused only for a moment, lamenting his erstwhile prey, before deciding on a different route home. He entered the grounds, his face creased in a sneer at unbidden memories of that afternoon. The mere fact that Mr. Harrow saw fit to detain him and let everyone else go on time was just the beginning. Mr. Harrow would never going to come out and be straight with Theo, to tell him to behave. Oh, no. Mr. Harrow liked subtlety.

Mr. Harrow was such a cocksucker.

Theo stopped and looked back. He stood several yards within the cemetery now, an old couple passing him as they exited the grounds. The woman's eyes creased behind horn-rimmed glasses: a smile not needing the mouth to complete it. Theo, eleven years of age and a novice in the nuances of adults, merely affected a look of wide-eyed innocence. The man smiled back before leading his lady out to the main road and then out of sight.

Theo turned back to the path. Never having set foot in a cemetery before, he had no idea what to expect—his only knowledge of graveyards having come from *Scooby Doo* cartoons and *Hammer House Of Horror* films that his dad would watch with him on a Saturday night. This cemetery appeared to be a far cry from any such fiction: an ornate arch of grey-green granite that a double-decker bus could easily pass under was just the beginning. Manicured lawns and clipped trees and bushes bordered the broad brick path on which he stood. Nothing like the forced silence of the classroom, the tranquility and greenery of his surroundings stirred his sense of wonder. He paused as a brief smile crept across his face.

He walked further in, passing a Ford saloon on his left, parked near a granite chapel the same shade as the arch, a newer building of barely faded red brick on his right, and the graveyard stretching before him.

Theo frowned as he straightened his tie—an unconscious gesture, but one consciously and continually drummed into him by his father to instill a sense of dignity and class. The cemetery held no fear for him, the sun only just beginning to set, but as everyone else appeared to have left, would his mere presence be disrespectful? He hoped not. He started forward into the grounds, barely noticing when the path had changed from brick to gravel. Entranced by the sea of multihued headstones and kerb sets in the grass as he meandered through the grounds, he noted that only a handful were black. Minutes later, he noted one with gold lettering, and he picked his way through a line of tilted headstones to reach it. The kerb set gleamed, its black polished surface inscribed with the heading "In Loving Memory". The name and dates barely registered. Theo read on, mouthing silently as he did so, lingering on the last line: "Soon we shall see you again."

Huh?

Theo sat back on his haunches and exhaled, his brow knitting. What would possess someone to write something so sick on somebody's grave? Did people actually look forward to coming here? The notion of looking forward to death as if it were a holiday in Hawaii—

An arm slipped around his neck and pulled hard, the blazer sleeve rough against the skin of his neck. "My turn, you shit! Shithead!"

Gagging, Theo tried to pry his attacker's arm from his throat, but the other boy had a better grip and a better position. The assailant dragged Theo backward, negating any effort the bigger boy made to gain leverage and break free of the chokehold.

"Where's your spider now? Shithead!" The voice was louder now, choked with tears. The forearm at his neck pressed harder as the other forearm came into play, forcing his head forward. Thinking he would suffocate, Theo groped desperately along the arm for where his opponent's fingers would be as he himself began to lose consciousness.

* * *

Wind blew across the back of his neck, raising goose bumps in its wake as it ruffled his hair. Theo stirred, rising to consciousness like a party balloon clipped of its mooring. Scents of grass and cool, dry earth flooded his nostrils as his senses returned to waking clarity. Lying behind a line of tombstones, Theo pushed to his hands and knees, stray blades of grass falling from his blazer. His mouth felt dry and he swallowed, wincing at a knot of pain above his Adam's apple.

Fucking André. Another cocksucker.

Clapping a hand on top of the nearest tombstone, Theo pulled himself to his feet and took in his surroundings. Twin furrows, faint in the grass wove a path from near his feet to several yards away where the kerb set with the weird inscription lay. Theo scanned the cemetery, his eyes widening as his heart lurched in alarm. As far as he could tell, the arch he'd entered through was distant enough to be out of sight, the terrain sloping more the deeper one progressed into the cemetery. Beyond that, the setting sun, not visible itself, was but the faintest trace of amber glowing in the horizon slowly subdued by increasing shades of indigo from the night sky. Which meant the caretaker would have long since locked up the grounds for the night.

Turning on his heel, Theo continued to venture deeper into the cemetery, hoping to find a way to exit at the other end and slowing when he had passed the last row of gravestones. Coarse, unkempt shrubbery as high as his chest spanned the last few yards to the cemetery wall, a thick and steep stone wall encircling the grounds. Panic crept through him like long vines at the sight. He bit his lip, his breath coming in short, shallow exhalations. The wall appeared to be a good ten feet tall, with wrought iron spikes mounted at the top. Minutes passed as he stood impotently muttering agitated curses to himself before he resigned himself to trek back through to the cemetery's entrance. By the time he reached the kerb set that boasted the weird inscription, the sky's indigo blue had deepened. He leaned against a nearby tombstone and let out a shaky sigh.

And yards ahead of him, a sigh came floating back.

Numbed by alarm, Theo collapsed, landing heavily on his ass. He stared ahead, trying to pinpoint the source of the sound. As far as he could tell, the cemetery stood deserted, apart from him. He strained his ears, trying to pick up the slightest sound, from a snatch of birdsong to a rustle in the grass nearby. Nothing. He sat stone still, hands braced behind him, fingers in the rough grass, a bead of sweat rolling unbidden down the side of his face.

The sigh came again, unmistakable, drifting *up* from the earth between headstones yards away. Theo's pulse began to thud in his temples. In the growing darkness, a swatch of earth by one of the further tombstones began to lift, like the gentle ripple of a current at sea.

He retreated on his ass and hands, groping backward past unyielding stone edges, not caring about the dirt and grass soiling his school uniform. He backed away until he could no longer see the pulsing patch of earth. What stopped him was when he heard a showering of debris and dirt— and a much louder sigh.

What? What?!

Theo bit his lip, trying to work up the courage to investigate. Silence greeted him.

A sidelong glance revealed a crawl path through the tombstones that would carry him deeper into the cemetery and nearer to the shrubbery-fronted wall. While he knew he had more size and strength than many of his classmates (his blazer sleeves were already tight over his upper arms), Theo also knew strength alone wouldn't be enough in unfamiliar terrain. Straining to maintain silence of movement, he slowly eased his ass off the ground, repositioning himself a few inches back, before following suit on his heels and splayed fingers. And again. And again, until he built up a rhythm. And again, starting to pick up—

"Where are you going?" the voice rasped.

Theo flinched, his eyes screwed shut. Alarm clutched at him with long, spindly fingers, and he trembled. In facing an escalating fear, his control weakened and his bladder let go, flooding his trouser leg with warm urine. More seeped through the fabric, soaking into the ground.

An inhalation, as if a wine enthusiast had smelled the first scent from a newly opened bottle. "I can hear you and smell you quite well. Why would you seek to disturb my sleep, only to flee when I rise?" The voice sounded like wind blowing through dead leaves.

Anxiety twanged within him, fight warring with flight. He slid his tongue along his lower lip. He scrambled to his feet and ran further into the cemetery. Behind him came the sound of footfalls. Footfalls growing closer… and a momentary silence followed by a rush of air overhead before a pale white form dropped behind one of the farther tombstones. Theo skidded to a halt, stumbled, and fell, his hands slapping the earth, one of them pressing heavily on a sharp stone. As he pushed to his feet, ignoring the pain in his palm, a naked form rose slowly and deliberately, its back to him. The thing stood over six feet tall, almost skeletally thin with a large bulbous head atop a skinny neck. Theo stared as it turned with excruciating slowness to look over its shoulder at him. Lidless yellow eyes with pinprick pupils fixed on him, and beneath the nostril slits, the lips parted in a grin of filthy, pointed teeth. Viscous saliva dripped from the corner of its mouth.

"I imagine you must find me quite terrifying, child."

Theo back-pedaled until the unyielding surface of another tombstone halted him. The creature crept closer, grasping its way around headstones as it did so. With each step it took came awful revelation: the smell of earth atop a stink like rotting fish, thick talons at the ends of the fingers and toes. It came to a stop inches away from him, its gaze inscrutable.

A bony hand shot forward and clasped the top of Theo's head. He shut his eyes at the feel of the cold, hard fingers, and fresh tears ran down his cheeks. An inhalation sounded close to his ear.

"Too long and too often have I had none for company, save the corpses around me. Fitting meals, but lacking in majesty," the voice said. "Tonight, I shall not only forgive you your trespass, I shall also thank you for it—for you have brought me something new this night. Do you know what that is?"

Restrained by the grip, Theo barely managed to shake his head.

"Answer me, child." The fingers tightened, the talons dimpling his scalp.

"No," he sobbed. "I don't know, honestly, I don't. I just... want to go home."

"Fear." The word came on an exhalation of clammy, fetid air before something thick and wet slid across his neck, leaving a trickling trail of moisture on his skin. "Delicious fear."

"Please..."

"Please what?"

"Please... let me go."

"No."

Theo collapsed in a heap, the unexpected movement freeing him from the creature's grasp. He opened his eyes and saw the pale legs in front of him, the tip of a long, pale penis dangling before him.

"These grounds are rich in carrion. Flesh much older than you. Why should I dine on cold carcasses when there is the chance of a warm one before me?" The creature stooped. "Be thankful you will be dead before I begin to feast."

Theo recoiled from the sight of the grinning thing, his lower lip trembling. "André," he blubbered, "it should be you, it should be *shithead* you, you shithead—"

"Who is this André?"

Theo froze.

A hard point dug into his neck, stopping short of drawing blood. "I grow weary," the voice rasped. "Answer quickly and truthfully or I will peel the skin from you. Who is this André?"

"He..." Theo swallowed, the sharp pressure at his neck not relenting. "He jumped me, he... he left me here."

"Why?"

Every occasion that Theo had been called back by a teacher, scolded by his mother, beaten by his father—all those moments of truth now paled in comparison to his current predicament. His gut tightened, as if drawn taut like high-octave piano wire. Glancing in the direction of the discomfort, he saw the creature glaring at him, the mouth set in a hard, humorless line. The outstretched arm never trembled, never wavered.

"I scared him," he whispered.

"How?"

"A spider."

"A spider?" The voice held derision. "Such a lowly creature is of no consequence and hardly enough for a mouthful. Continue."

Theo licked his dry lips and swallowed, cursing inwardly at the discomfort against his neck. "I threw a spider at him."

"Why?"

And *that* was the question for which no answer was justifiable, the stark, ugly truth that may have cost Theodore Papakostas his life, simply because he would do things without thinking. Stupid things.

Dangerous things.

He began to cry again, mucus beginning to run in his nostrils. "To… scare him."

"This gave you pleasure?"

"Yes," he whispered.

"I see." Silence, punctuated only by Theo's sobbing and sniffling. Then a sibilant gasp, accompanied by a rank breath of air. "He left you here to frighten you in return?"

What? Did he? Unsure of himself and of his very life, Theo nodded as if his chin were signaling Morse code.

"Very well. Look at me."

Eyes hot and wet with tears, Theo obeyed.

With its talon still against Theo's neck, the creature shuffled closer until Theo could see faded spots and blemishes in its skin. "Sniveling child. Your presence alone is an affront to me. Were it not for your confession of malice toward another, I would kill you now." The yellow eyes fixed on him, the mouth grim and unsmiling. "For now, you shall live."

Long, bony fingers clutched the lapels of his blazer and yanked him forward with obscene strength. Rising to its full height, the creature hefted him easily. It strode deeper into the cemetery, through the myriad tombstones, and waded through the deep, dense shrubbery with ease before coming to the wall. Digging its talons into crevices in the brickwork, the monster scaled the wall with Theo in one hand before swinging him over the wrought iron spikes and dangling him above the ground. Theo clutched at the slimy arm holding him aloft, his legs pinwheeling in mid-air. The creature shook him once, hard, and Theo immediately stilled himself.

"Heed me, child. You sought to bring fear to another. Yet you brought misfortune upon yourself. Is that not so?"

"Y-yes," he stammered. "Please don't hurt me."

"Silence. You shall survive this night… but you shall carry your fear with you."

"My…?"

The creature smiled, yellow eyes seemingly bulging larger. "Oh yes." It drew him closer, flicking its long tongue across his chin through the iron spikes, and Theo recoiled. "Your scent and your fear are delicious. Go. Feed and cultivate your fear. Tell stories of me that none shall believe."

The creature dangled and dropped him, and Theo hit the ground hard. Despite landing on the balls of his feet as Mr. Worrell had always told him in P.E., the height was too great, and the landing jarred his knee, collapsing him in agony. Clutching his injured leg, he looked up at the top of the wall.

"You have survived me this night. Make no mistake: when next we meet, and meet we will, you shall not." The creature's face pressed against the iron spikes as the tongue flicked across the mouth, aping the anticipation of a sumptuous banquet.

"Food."

The hideous face grinned before disappearing behind the wall, leaving nothing behind but a terrified child cowering alone on the pavement.

The Darkening

T. L. Norman

The darkness used to frighten me, now it is the only thing that brings me comfort. Odd as that may seem, I have good reason for it. I have been touched by The Darkening. Some may call it possession, others may refer to it as a mental illness, but for me it is the cold comfort of the blackness that brings me warmth.

As a child, I used to have a recurring nightmare. In this nightmare, I would be stuck in the darkness with a failing candle as my only source of light. In the darkness, beasts hid, waiting to pounce on me. They stared at me from a distance with glowing, blood-red eyes. I would try to get to a staircase in front of me, but each step I took sent it farther away from me. The candle would burn down to its last breath of flame, and as the darkness enveloped me, I would hear my name being spoken from far away. That's when I would wake up.

Could that have been a foreshadowing of my life to come? Or just a childhood nightmare and nothing more. The doctors think I suffer from a mental illness and keep me locked up. They think I believe the dream has become real.

Reality, a simplistic point of view of the complicated plains of existence.

The doctors can believe what they want. I am happy with what I am becoming. There is something freeing about this transformation. Being able to see the unseen and feel little or nothing of my old human form. I am beyond that emotional state humans lock themselves into. I can say I am truly free. And I know that I never would have become this way had it not been for the amulet my father unearthed. A vile-looking face carved into a hard, black stone he found while digging for treasures. I wasn't sure at the time what triggered this change in me, but now I can be sure that amulet is the reason I no longer live in the light.

My father showed me his newest find only days before the transformation took place. At first I thought it was someone's failed attempt at carving, but as I continued to look at it, feel it, truly see it for its beauty, I understood my father's excitement. As I held it in my hands, I could feel the power it contained vibrating through the stone. The energy was more powerful than any person could imagine.

The evening of my transformation, I was in my father's old, dilapidated, 19th century house. I was alone, taking care of my father's mutts while he was away on yet another dig. The old house already held its paranormal entities, as benign as they were, and to be alone in an old haunted house with the spirits of the original owners was no longer something that fazed me. In fact, I found it kind of comical.

The original owners of the house built it in the late 1800s. The husband worked away from home for months on end. The wife was afraid to lose him, so she concocted an evil plan. She even had their doctor in on it. The plan was to fake paralysis. Her twisted mind believed that if he had to be devoted to taking care of her, then he would never leave her for another woman. For an educated man, he was just stupid enough to fall for it, carrying her up to bed each night and back down every morning, slowly killing himself with his devotion to her. And that is just what happened. He died of a heart attack, and it is said she died of guilt and shame not long after. So now, the poor schmuck is forever stuck in a repetitive afterlife of carrying his lying wife up and down the stairs for all eternity.

Yet that night there was something different about the house, something dark, something heavy, something made of pure evil. That night the Coldrick's did not make their evening haunting. At least not in the way I was used to seeing them. That night I felt true fear for the last time.

I wandered through the house trying to place what felt different. On the dining room table I saw it, the amulet broken in pieces, a hammer laid next to it and a piece of paper with one word written on it.

EVIL.

The mutts were huddled on their blanket on the floor, whimpering like the fearless mutts they were. I heard a low, guttural growling from my father's study, off to the right of the living room. I slowly followed the sound.

The door, which was always locked, was ajar. With each step I took, the air became thicker and smelled burnt. The growl continued and my heart began to pound harder in my chest. This was the very last time I remember feeling my heart pounding at all. Even now it no longer beats in my chest.

As I reached out to touch the door, the lights flickered. The growling continued, became deeper and louder.

From the darkness of the study I saw a faint red glow and smoke began to billow out of the opening. The lights continued to flicker. I stood where I was, a mere two feet from the study door, my hand frozen as my mind and body fought each other for control.

The lights began to flicker faster, spasmodically. Pictures on the walls began shaking. Ornaments fell to the floor. The ground vibrated. I remember wanting to run, but my feet wouldn't move. From behind me I heard what could only be described as a primordial scream. It was a sound no person should ever hear, and one that I will never hear again.

The stairwell door flew open with an inhuman force. It hit the wall so violently that part of the door implanted itself into the wall. The sound made my heart stop.

From the darkness of the stairwell two auras flew past, leaving an extreme cold in the room. The white-light auras glowed in human form, despite being free from their human vessels. All my life I had only known of their existence as the sound of heavy footfalls on the stairs and the opening and closing of the stairwell door. Why they chose this instance to show themselves I will never know.

As if the sight of the resident ghosts hadn't made their haunting more real to me, the next part of the otherworld experience cemented the reality of the situation. I turned back to look at the study door and came face to face with glowing red eyes set deep in the contorted face of a beast. It was part human, part animal, with brown matted fur all over its body. It had hooves for feet and talons for hands.

I opened my mouth to scream, but nothing came out. The beast pushed me down, positioning itself over me, and bared its misshapen teeth. Its face only centimeters from mine, I felt the warm, stale breath brush across my cheek, leaving an odor of rancid flesh on my skin as it quietly growled in my ear. It then raised its taloned hand and sunk it deep in my chest, grabbing my nonbeating heart, forcing my body to feel its dark evil. I lay paralyzed on the floor, the tingling of the afterlife creeping across my skin. The beast pulled its hand from my chest, leaped up, and chased the apparitions from the house.

The sensations my body felt were beyond any earthbound compre-hension. If I had to explain, it was a hot and cold tingling mixed with a heightened awareness of the evil lurking everywhere, a true feeling of acceptance. I guess it would be the human equivalent of being relaxed.

The beast was not a beast at all. Only those on the human plain, those guided by fear, will see it as a beast. When you come to see clearly, as I have, you see the beast for its beauty, its freedom from human existence.

The feeling from that night has not left me. It is always there. I no longer feel fear; I simply exist. I no longer look at my reflection in the mirror, for that woman is no more. The face that stares back with sunken eyes, the pale, white skin, blood-red gums with no teeth, that is the remnants of the human form I once possessed. My beauty is within, behind my glowing red eyes, behind my guttural growl, behind my soft, warm fur. This is who I am now as The Darkening takes over.

Breakthrough

Rose Blackthorn

"The woods are deep," the voice says, warm in tone, calming in effect. "Looking around, you can see no path through the underbrush, nor the fallen leaves. The light is dim, but not dark—"

"The sun just set," she whispers, eyes closed as she watches the scene his voice has painted in her mind.

"Yes, it is dusk," he agrees, glancing down at the notebook on his lap. The office was dark, only the hooded desk lamp on so he can see what he's written during their sessions. Outside the floor-to-ceiling window that dominates one wall, there is nothing to be seen but a few scattered lights. Night has fallen, and his home office is secluded. Derek gazes at his patient, feeling a fondness for her that he has never revealed. Her pale blond hair cascades over the pillow on which her head rests, and her hands are clasped loosely on her stomach. As before, that will soon change. "Smell the air, Ari. Can you detect the scent of dry leaves? Of moss or mushrooms? The clean smell of the air, untainted by smog or sewage. Perhaps the scent of water?"

In her trance, she nods slightly, eyes moving beneath her closed lids as though she is dreaming.

"The water—can you hear it? Over the sounds of the light evening breeze, of insects singing, or night birds stirring from their daytime slumber. Can you hear it?" he asks, his voice still low and gentle. He is trying to guide her; he does not want to intrude himself into her memory.

"Yes," she says, barely above a whisper. "There is water running, just down the hill. I can hear it."

"Go toward the water, Ari," he instructs, making a note on the pad in his lap. "Tell me what you see, or hear, or smell."

"There are crickets," she says, her voice breathy and soft. Her eyes continue to shift beneath the lids, as though she's looking around at this remembered landscape. "And—and frogs, I think. They call back and forth. Once I notice it, it becomes very loud." She shifts a little on the comfortable couch he keeps in his office for just this kind of session. Her feet, bare because she always kicks off her shoes as soon as she comes in, move a little as she walks in her trance. "The leaves beneath my feet are crunchy, and—and they're slippery. They skid beneath my steps."

"It's alright, Ari. You won't fall. Be cautious, but keep going," he advises, making another note.

She nods, lifting one slender hand as though pushing a branch out of her way. "The water is closer now, but not loud. Not a river, at least not a large one. Maybe just a stream."

"That's right," he says, encouraging her. They're almost to the point where they've always had to stop before. He is hopeful that tonight they'll be able to break through. "Continue, Ari."

"It's getting steeper," she says, a tremble in her voice now. Her hands are clasped on her stomach again, but not loosely anymore. Her fingers clench together, the knuckles whitening. She bends her knees, and Derek is still unsure if this reaction is because in her memory she is going downhill, or because she's trying to curl into the fetal position.

"You're okay, Ari. Be careful, but don't stop."

Her breathing becomes louder, almost labored, and a light glaze of sweat has appeared on her forehead and upper lip. Derek can see the pulse throbbing in her throat. When he first started working with her, he had pulled her out of the hypnotic trance when she began to show physical signs of fear or exertion. She was stronger than she looked, however, and he no longer considered ending a session for something as trivial as heavy breathing.

"Tell me what you see, what you're doing," he prompts, keeping his voice calm and level. "Where are you?"

"I'm almost to the creek," she says, her voice a little more steady. Her legs have relaxed, but her hands still grip each other tightly. "There's someone ahead of me, standing on the bank."

"Who is it?" he asks, keeping any excitement or tension out of his voice.

"I—I can't tell," she replies, and she sounds anxious. "They're standing with their back to me. It's getting dark, and it's hard to see—"

"It's all right, Ari. You're safe. Nothing can hurt you now. But you need to tell me who is there with you," he gently presses. This, he believes, is the crux of the matter. Ari has spent the last few months in terror. Her fourteen-year-old sister had been killed in the forest adjacent to their family's estate, and Ari had found the body. Her sister, Tara, had literally been torn to pieces, and due to the shock of finding the girl like that, Ari had lapsed into a self-imposed prison of fear. For months she had been hospitalized; medication and therapy had done little to help her. She was currently unable to function with any kind of normalcy. In desperation, Ari's father had contacted Derek, an expert in hypnotherapy. In a relatively short period of time, they had made strides toward if not a cure, at least remission of the worst of her symptoms. "Move closer, quietly and carefully. Tell me what you see."

She is chewing on her bottom lip now, her nails are digging into the back of either hand, and her entire body is trembling. "I can't," she whispers, "I'm afraid."

"You're safe, Ari. Nothing can hurt you, I promise," he says. "You don't need to be scared anymore. This is just a memory. Anything you have experienced once, you can experience again. Take a deep breath, relax, and move closer."

Ari breathes deeply at his command, her shoulders and hips relaxing into the soft surface of the couch. Her eyes have stopped moving, as though she stares straight ahead into her memory. "The crickets have stopped chirping," she says, her voice taking on a dreamy, sinewy quality Derek has never noticed in previous sessions. "The frogs have stopped singing. All I can hear is the water, and the wind. And... breathing."

"Can you see who is standing on the bank?" he asks.

For a long moment, Ari is completely still. She doesn't move, doesn't breathe. Even the pulse in her throat seems to have stopped.

"Who is it?" Derek presses, sliding forward to the edge of his chair, not wanting to miss a single flicker or nuance of expression that she might display. "What can you hear?"

"It's Tara," Ari says, a slow smile curving her lips. "Her favorite story was *Little Red Riding Hood*. She always wore red."

"What is she doing?" Derek asks, somewhat taken aback. He had been told by Ari's father, and then by Ari herself that she had found her sister already dead. According to all accounts the girl had been savaged by a pack of feral dogs.

"She's been running, and now she is tired... so tired," Ari says, shifting on the soft couch. "She can't run anymore."

Derek has a copy of the police report, and he flips through it. The victim had died from extreme blood loss, as her throat had been torn out. She had been disemboweled and half-eaten. The only tracks that had been found were described as large and canine in shape; thus, the final determination was that Tara had been killed by rabid or wild dogs.

"Ari," Derek says slowly, his eyes scanning over the report once more, "you told your father that your sister was dead when you found her. But now, you remember seeing her still alive. Tell me please, what is she doing?"

"She's screaming," Ari answers, opening her eyes. Instead of their normal blue, they are gold. Her lips part to reveal sharp white fangs, and she sits up on the couch, turning her head to meet the doctor's startled stare.

In the few seconds that he was studying the file, she has changed. Her pale skin has darkened, and her face has lengthened. For a moment Derek wonders if he has fallen asleep and entered her hypnosis-induced memory. "Ari, I'm going to count to three," he says, sliding back rapidly in his well-padded chair. "When I reach three, I want you to wake up."

She stands sensuously, less than three feet from him, gazing down hungrily as she licks her lips with a long, lascivious tongue.

"One," he begins, "Two—"

"I am awake, Doctor," she states, stretching almost cat-like. She is taller than she was, and the nails on her fingers and toes have become thicker and are now curved into heavy claws. She comes to him, putting her knees on his chair, straddling him as she leans close. "You've helped me to finally remember. And I'm not afraid anymore."

"Three!" he shouts, pushing against her with both hands braced on her shoulders, but she is unbelievably strong. He cannot stop her as she darts forward, her mouth gaping impossibly wide, and her fangs rip into his neck. Hot blood sprays and he chokes on it, unable to breathe, and soon he has no more strength to fight.

When she is finished, Ari glances at the huge window, seeing her reflection as she now is, crouching over the dead man. Blood covers half her face and most of her shirt like a bib. She has changed, no longer the weak, terrified girl that she was before. She stands and admires herself in the glass, luxuriating in the feeling of her own new-found power.

"Thank you, Doctor," she says, her words slightly lisping as she speaks with teeth and tongue never meant to form human speech. "You were right. Memory is nothing to be afraid of. It can be worth reliving. Some things should be experienced again."

Ari discards her blood-soaked clothing now that fur covers her nakedness, and drops to all fours when her change is complete. She leaves the door of his house hanging open behind her, moving into the dark night, becoming part of it. This time, she will neither be caught nor retreat in fear of herself. She knows where to go. As the doctor had said, the woods are deep.

Embalming Leon

Daryl Marcus

The vampire kicked at his captors, emaciated legs swinging uselessly in the air between the burly men holding his upper arms. His escorts— large, bearded men wearing leather jackets, faded jeans, and jackboots— threw the pitiful creature at Bryant's feet. They stomped on his ankles to keep him on his knees. He screamed as the crunch of shattering bone echoed through the concrete chamber.

Bryant reclined in a straight-backed wooden chair, legs extended before him, booted feet crossed at the ankles. His hands were laced over his slim stomach, thumbs tapping an irregular rhythm on each other. He still wore sunglasses despite the late hour.

He examined the creature before him. His blond hair hung past his shoulders while standing, and now it obscured his face behind a dirty, blood-beaded curtain. The blue eyes were bloodshot, sunken in their sockets, a black ooze leaking from the corners. His cheeks were scarred and pale. Several teeth had been knocked out, but Bryant could see new ones beginning to grow. The nose was twisted and broken, but as Bryant watched, it shifted under the vampire's skin and set itself straight once again. Underneath it all was a frail, emaciated frame that looked fit to fall apart rather than stand under its own power.

Though he had appeared healthy and formidable earlier this evening, Leon now resembled Nosferatu. The pain experts had plied their trade and learned a great deal, but there was still more to glean.

Bryant raised a hand and scratched the right side of his long, straight nose. His mouth was drawn into a tight line, as if he couldn't decide whether to smile or frown.

The silence in the room was broken only by the whimpering, wounded vampire and the furnace in the corner. He was tough; Bryant had to give him credit there. He had told them nothing they didn't already know.

Bryant leaned forward, staring into the creature's face. "Well, Leon, it looks to me like you're in a world of hurt. What ails you, my boy?"

"Fucker!"

Bryant raised an eyebrow. "Let me guess how you vampires work. Your body feeds on itself to heal and you feed on blood for fuel." Bryant looked at his crew. "That doesn't sound too different from us. Only we can eat more than blood. I guess that's your Achilles' heel, eh, Leon? You can't eat a hamburger with all the trimmings. You have to have human blood, the fresher the better."

Leon said nothing, but Bryant nodded. "I thought so. You've been so good today, Leon. I really appreciate you teaching me all these little tips and tricks about dealing with vampires. To think, six months ago I didn't believe you existed, and now we're at war with each other. You're fighting to turn us into cattle, and we're fighting to keep our liberty."

"You don't know anything, you fucking prick. You're nothing more than an annoying insect, a mosquito."

Bryant smiled. "Ah, but every mosquito bite leaves a small wound. It may heal, but that bite itches for hours or even days. I may be a mosquito, Leon, but your masters have noticed me, I guarantee."

Every now and then Leon growled. It was the sound of an angry animal in pain, one that knew it was dangerous and hadn't realized the pain meant it had been declawed.

"All right, Leon. You've been a good boy, so I'm going to cut a deal with you."

Leon looked up, hope filling his eyes momentarily before fading away.

Bryant noticed his crew's glances of surprise, but he ignored them.

"Here's what I propose, Leon." Bryant stood up and stepped to the vampire's side. Gripping a handful of Leon's hair, he yanked the vampire's head back and stared into those bleeding blue eyes. "If you agree one hundred percent to whole heartedly, without compunction or false pretense, tell me everything I want to know about your kind and your operations in my town, I'll stop torturing you."

The incredible shrinking vampire thought quickly. "Okay, okay! Yes. I'll do it. Just stop this."

Bryant slammed Leon's face onto the concrete. He smiled with satisfaction when he heard the familiar crunch of nose cartilage and saw blood spurt onto the floor. "Put him on the table."

In the opposite corner of the basement work room was a mad scientist's playground filled with machines, large glass containers, and wicked-looking blades. Several pieces of equipment looked like giant beakers holding gallons of pinkish liquids. Attached to one machine was a long metal spike connected to a glass beaker by a long flexible hose.

"Hey! Wait a fucking minute. I agreed to talk. You made a deal."

Bryant nodded graciously. "Indeed you did. And so did I. I will keep my promise, Leon. You see, I'm not going to torture you. We're tired of that game. I have an idea for a new game, and since you agreed to tell me what I want to know, you get to be the first to answer today's ultimate question."

"I'll tell you anything."

Bryant smiled. "I know you will, Leon. And right now, I want to know if this will do anything to you. Strap him down."

Leon's captors flung him onto the metal operating table. He struggled and screamed as they tied him down. He managed to kick one of the men in the face with his left foot, bloodying a lip and breaking a tooth, before he was subdued and rendered helpless.

"Tell me, Leon. What do you know about the embalming process?"

Leon's eyes widened, his mouth hanging open.

"I thought so. Let me educate you. Strip him, Doc."

A man wearing a bright yellow hazardous material suit with black boots and gloves appeared at Leon's side. Through the plastic faceplate Bryant could see he was covered in sweat. The man's eyes twitched and darted in all directions. In his right hand he held a pair of scissors.

Bryant caught the shaking hand holding the scissors a few inches from Leon's left shirt sleeve. "Careful, Doc. You're the only one wearing that space suit. Take care of us as much as you can."

The man nodded. Bryant released his hand and stepped back. In several quick motions Leon's clothes were tatters on the floor. The vampire lay naked on the metal table. He looked simultaneously furious at his predicament and pathetic, his ribs visible through paper-thin skin.

"Normally, when the body is being prepared for embalming, it is washed with a germicide and disinfectant. The limbs are moved and massaged to make them easy to manipulate and put into a normal pose. The face is cleaned and stuffed with gauze or cotton to prevent the embalming fluid from escaping."

Bryant leaned closer to Leon, looked down on him, and smiled. "The corpse's mouth is sewn shut with wires or sutures. Some embalmers even use a particular needle injection gun to close the mouth. They fire needles and wires into the gums with this gun and twist the wires together to get it in just the right position."

Leon squeezed his eyes shut and turned away from Bryant.

"The eyes are closed, sometimes held in place with an eye cap. Sometimes the mouth is filled with a mouth piece that holds the lips closed and shapes it. All this is done in an effort to make sure those viewing the body see a nearly life-like resemblance of their loved one."

He shook his head. "I don't think we're going to do that to you, Leon. We're not interested in making you pleasing to the eye. Are you ready, Doc?"

The man in the biohazard suit grunted. "I'm not a doctor."

Bryant's face darkened. "I don't care what you are, Doc. I'll call you whatever the hell I feel like. Now are you ready?"

"Yes."

He smiled. Turning back to Leon, he spoke in a conversational tone. "What comes after all that preparation is the actual embalming. Let me break it down for you, Leon. I'd hate for you to go through all this without an understanding of what we're doing and why."

"First, you're a vampire, but you're not like the vampires we all know from movies and books. Obviously, the stories got a lot of things wrong. Naturally, the only way to disprove a myth is to test a hypothesis or two and see which holds water. You're going to help me do that today, Leon. Aren't you thrilled to be a part of a brand new era in history?"

Bryant stepped aside and the man in the hazmat suit moved to stand at Leon's right shoulder.

"Let me see those, Doc."

Bryant studied the two slim metal objects in either hand. One at a time he brandished them before Leon's now-wide, staring eyes.

"This is your standard scalpel. You've seen these before, and it's no big deal. It's for cutting. You get the idea." He relinquished the scalpel to the hazmat suit. "But this... now this is interesting."

He held out an object just over six inches long with a dull hook on one end. It was made of solid stainless steel, with the hilt thicker than the hooked end. Bryant twisted it in his fingers, letting the light from the overhead fluorescents catch on its metallic shine. "This is an aneurysm hook. It's used to fish arteries and veins out of the body without damaging them." He lowered the hook to ensure Leon got a good look at it.

"The good doctor here is going to give us a demonstration of how a body is embalmed. You, Leon, are going to be our body." He tossed the aneurysm hook and a black-gloved hand snatched it out of the air.

"Humans really know little about vampire physiology and their weaknesses. What we know we've discovered through some very bloody and painful trial and error. Very few of you have been studied by real scientists. The war simply prevents us taking the time we need to be that thorough. At least, it prevents the government. I don't let little things like war get in the way of my goals."

Bryant looked away from Leon to stare through the plastic faceplate. "Get started."

"I've never done this to anything living."

"I don't care. You agreed you could do this. I might not be as skilled as you, but I feel quite confident that, if I have to, I can do this job. It might be messy, and probably lethal to more than one person, but I'm not afraid of it. Do you get my drift?"

The helmet nodded.

"Good. Now, get started."

He placed his left hand on Leon's shoulder to steady himself and held the scalpel in his right. He pressed the tip of the blade against Leon's skin beside his right collarbone. The vampire jerked and a line of dark red sprang to the surface of his skin, beaded, and ran down to the table.

Bryant leaned over Leon's body, pressing his elbows into the vampire's ribs. He noticed Leon's newly broken nose had not yet healed. "Now, Leon, I know this is going to hurt. Don't think I'm planning on lying to you. But by now your body is not able to heal as fast as it was this afternoon. So anything you do to make this pain last long, that's just suffering you don't have to go through. It's up to you now. Are you going to do this the painful way, or the right way?"

Leon whimpered. His lips trembled and his shoulder's shook. A great sob escaped him, dislodging Bryant from his perch on his chest. Bryant stared down at Leon, an unreadable look on his face. Glistening black tears slid down the vampire's face in a series of dark trails.

"Hold him still," he said.

The twins leaned on Leon's arms and the scalpel returned to his shoulder.

He continued his small incision beside the vampire's collarbone. The cut bled only slightly before it tried to heal. He inserted the aneurysm hook and dug into the vampire's flesh. A moment later, he pulled out the blue-black carotid artery and the jugular vein. He wrapped two pieces of suture string loosely around the artery.

He held a hand out, and one of Bryant's men placed an arterial tube in it. The tube was inserted into the artery and tied in place. He did the same to the vein and stepped back to view his handiwork.

Leon's shoulder now looked like two small, metal faucets had been connected to his body; all the doctor needed to do was twist to get hot and hotter running blood.

"We got vampire blood on tap now, boys. Doc, hook him up."

He wheeled a small rolling trolley closer to the table. On the tray was a device that looked like a large blender with fewer buttons. A cloudy, red-gold liquid filled the glass cylinder to the top. He connected a long tube from the cylinder to the faucet attached to Leon's carotid artery. The doctor wheeled a second blender closer to the table, this one empty, and connected its tube to Leon's jugular vein.

"Here's where things get really interesting, Leon. That pink-colored liquid is your standard embalming fluid. It's made of several parts formaldehyde, water, a little dye, and several other chemicals designed to preserve your body for at least long enough to survive the funeral without a stench. That container is the reservoir to the pump that is going to push it through your system.

"That other container is going to catch your blood as it comes out. In a normal embalming, it just runs onto the floor and down the drain into the sewer systems, but we're going to be a little more cautious. You see, we know your blood can turn someone into a vampire. I'd hate to contaminate a whole city just to murder your worthless hide. So we're going to dispose of that more properly."

"What do you think, Leon? Will this work? Will pumping all that nasty, viscous, life-sucking blood out of your body and filling your veins with embalming fluid kill you? Or will you just squirm and scream in pain before your body makes more?"

Leon looked away from Bryant, away from his shoulder, and wept.

"This is a truly memorable event. This moment should be kept on record. I'm sure someone will want to know what the first living vampire to be embalmed said as his last words."

"Get it over with, you son of a bitch."

Bryant frowned. "Not worthy, Leon. You could have done much better. Do it, Doc."

A black hand slapped the switch on the embalming machine.

A rhythmic pulsing sound filled the room as the machinery slowly pumped the fluid into Leon's body.

The crew stepped back at the sound of the scream. Leon's face had contorted into a rictus of such torment that a few had to look away. Bryant's crew was not afraid of torturing someone and extracting as much pain as they could, but this was altogether different. Leon seemed tormented right down to his soul. His scream seemed loud enough to shake the very foundations of the building and bring it down on top of them. Only Bryant didn't move or seem affected by the intensity of Leon's pain.

The moment the formaldehyde slipped into his veins, Leon's temperature rose a perceptible amount. Bryant held his hand over Leon's form and gauged the temperature increase to be at least ten degrees.

The embalmer leaned forward and released the valve on the tube attached to Leon's jugular vein. A black stream of blood slid through the tube into the waiting container.

"He's fighting it," the doctor whispered.

"Won't matter," Bryant said. "Once it hits his brain, he's dead."

Leon stopped as if someone had found his mute button. His eyes, closed tight against the pain, sprang open and stared straight up at the ceiling. He gurgled deep in his throat, liquid bubbling out of his mouth as his final breath left him in a weak hiss of escaping gas.

Bryant looked at the doctor. "Told you."

"How did you know?"

"A hunch," Bryant said. He stared at Leon's open eyes for a long time, noting the coloration of Leon's skin as the dyed chemicals permeated his body tissue.

A cough from behind interrupted his reverie. He turned to find the twins escorting a young woman with jet-black hair and the angriest eyes Bryant had ever seen. She was classically beautiful, with high cheekbones, a strong mouth, and a small nose. The dress she wore reminded Bryant of his date for the prom. It glittered with golden sequins and fit her form like a second skin, accentuating her curves in all the right places.

She caught Bryant looking at her and smiled a wide, angry expression, allowing him to see her fangs in full glory. Past him she saw Leon's body and added a growl to her look of hate. "You killed him. You didn't have to do that. He didn't know anything."

Bryant nodded. "Quite the contrary. He knew a great deal, just not about any of your plans. He was the first, but I assure you, he won't be the last."

He snapped his fingers. "Strap the princess down."

Building the Nightmare Box
Geoffrey L. Mudge

Maggie Simmons wanted to scream as the golden light faded and the gossamer cobwebs of her dream drifted into vague memory. She opened her mouth, gasping, but could not force out any words. Her throat was dry and raw and she whimpered pitifully, hoping anyone would hear. In apparent response, the heavy wooden door opened above her as panic crept down her spine. The gray light rushing in, though dim, was enough to blind her as it pummeled her aching eyes.

After a brief moment the panel beside her slid open and a man's soft voice came oozing through. "Welcome back to the real world, Miss Simmons, in all its hideous glory." The panel slid shut and Maggie heard the door next to hers open with a groan of resistant hinges. With a grunt, the man pulled himself out of the box and cursed under his breath as he fought to steady his shaking legs. Maggie tried to sit up, but weakness had consumed her and she couldn't muster the strength even to lift her head.

"Please relax, Miss Simmons," a second voice told her from the gloom. "I will attend to you momentarily." Maggie heard the shuffling of footsteps as the second speaker moved to assist the first.

"Is all well, Mister Blue?" the second voice asked.

"Very well, Cleric," Mr. Blue replied. "I only wish we had more time together."

"A common lament, I'm afraid," the one called Cleric commiserated. "If there is anything you would like to say to Miss Simmons before she leaves us, now would be the time."

Mr. Blue slowly worked his way around the large wooden box. He leaned over where Maggie lay and told her, "Good morning, Miss

Simmons, I am Devastation Blue. It has truly been an honor to spend this time with you, my dear. Your imagination is…,” he shook his head trying to find the rights words, “…awe inspiring, truly awe inspiring.”

Maggie focused her eyes through the haze and saw Mr. Blue smiling over her. She was startled to see that his skin was pale gray. Not the ashy gray of the infirm, but the hearty matte hue of a battleship. Mr. Blue lifted Maggie’s emaciated hand and kissed it softly, his pale blue eyes dancing playfully. He laid Maggie’s hand on her chest and turned as Cleric addressed him.

“Your attendants await you in the great hall, Mister Blue. You should make your way there now.”

“Of course,” Mr. Blue replied. “Good bye, Maggie. Cleric, be well, my friend.”

Cleric nodded and ushered Mr. Blue through the large door that led away from the dim chamber. As the door creaked open, a rush of titillated voices wafted through. Maggie tried again to sit up to see the rabble squawking excitedly, but the door closed as she wriggled furtively. Cleric returned to her side and placed a soft hand on her forehead.

“Please lie still, Miss Simmons,” he told her. “I know the waking period can be painful, but it will be over soon enough and your eternal rest will begin.”

With a head-spinning rush, Maggie’s memories began to replace the lingering dreams. The terms of her contract with Cleric were suddenly remembered, and as she heard the knife being drawn from its sheathe, she knew her death was close. She then remembered another deal she had struck, and with a smile on her cracked lips, she whispered a single word.

“Peter.”

Cleric turned his head inquisitively. As he opened his mouth to ask what she meant, a sharp crack rang through the chamber. Though muffled by the heavy door, the gunshot was unmistakable, and it was quickly followed by a dozen more. Shouts and screams filtered into the grey room from the great hall.

“What have you done, Miss Simmons?” Cleric asked as he pressed against the door, listening. After a few moments the echoes of the gunshots stopped ringing from the stone walls, but the screaming continued. Cleric hopped away from the door with a shriek moments before it exploded inward. The rusty iron hinges buckled and the wood splintered as the door was kicked away from its foundations.

“Drop the knife, old man,” a familiar voice said calmly. There was a clatter of metal on stone as the dagger fell from Cleric’s grip. “Good.

Now get against the wall and don't move."

Cleric did as he was commanded, and a rush of heavy footsteps swarmed into the room. A man masked with a black balaclava leaned over Maggie and yelled excitedly, "She's here, Mister Pierce!"

The calm voice told the masked man, "There's a wheel chair in the hall, go retrieve it. The former occupant will raise no complaint."

As the masked man departed, Peter Pierce appeared above Maggie like a waking dream. His soft brown eyes were sad and scared, but he smiled at her.

"Well, Maggie, you look like shit," he said.

Maggie wanted to laugh, to cry, to scream in joy, but she could do nothing but close her eyes and try to reach out to him. After a few moments the masked man returned with a clattering wheel chair. Peter wrapped his strong arms around Maggie and lifted her gently from the box. She felt something wet and opened her eyes to see his gray suit soaked with blood and something that looked like tar.

Peter set her carefully in the wheel chair and kissed her on the cheek. He got behind her and pushed her towards the door. Maggie cast one last glance at the box and remembered the joy she'd felt while held in its grasp.

"I don't want to leave," she whimpered as half a dozen masked men wielding sub-machine guns preceded them into the hall.

"You've been in that box for a full year, Maggie. It's time for you to go home. Besides, this place isn't safe, the police will arrive soon and we don't want to be here when they do."

Maggie wanted to argue, but didn't have the strength, so she left her fate in Peter's hands. As they approached the doorway, Peter told her, "Close your eyes Maggie. You don't want to see this."

She did as he told her, but as they moved through the cavernous hall, she could smell the death lingering in the air. She heard the whimpers of the dying and the injured and wondered just how many had been in attendance when Peter and his team had stormed in.

With a clatter they rolled out of the hall and onto the hard cobblestones of the road outside. Peter lifted Maggie from the wheel chair and set her onto the soft, padded leather of a Jaguar's back seat. He climbed in on the other side, barking, "Let's go," at the driver. With a screech, the XJL leapt away from the madness.

"Where are we going?" Maggie whispered.

"First, to the hospital to make sure you don't expire on me. Then, to Heathrow, where your plane is waiting to take you home, back to New

York."

Maggie nodded and leaned her head on Peter's wide shoulder. She closed her eyes and prayed that she could dream again.

* * *

Maggie's eyes fluttered open and she saw Peter sitting next to her bed, reading a well-worn copy of his favorite book, *The Song of Solomon.*

"Hello, Peter," she said with a tired smile.

"Good evening, Maggie," he replied, closing his book and gently pushing a strand of brittle brown hair off her face. "How are you feeling?"

Maggie chuckled. "Like two tons of hammered shit, but I'm alive."

Peter nodded and said, "Well, it's a lucky thing you are. If I'd been five minutes later in my arrival..." He trailed off, not wanting to finish the thought.

Maggie took his hand. "You weren't, though, and I have nothing but gratitude for your timely intervention. You did exactly what I asked of you, and as far as I know, I'm the only person to ever come out of that box alive."

Peter stood and paced restlessly around the small, green hospital room. When Maggie had told him of her intent to spend a year locked in a wooden box, he had been incredulous. He didn't believe she truly understood the risk or the cost. She had pledged her life, as well as her money, but through Peter she had cheated Cleric and his group. The possibility of repercussion weighed heavily on his mind.

"Was it worth it?" he asked.

Maggie sighed and glanced at the machines monitoring her heart rate, beeping and humming softly. She ran her fingers along the I.V. drip in her arm and the bones jutting against her pale, taut skin. She responded, "What's the best dream you've ever had, Peter?"

Pierce tried to recall a lifetime's worth of dreams. "I guess it wouldn't be any one in particular," he said with the slightest hint of a smile playing on his lips. "But, I often dream that I can fly, and it's those which I hold on to the longest. I suppose it's the freedom those dreams represent that I cherish. The ability to slip gravity's surly bonds and escape whatever's troubling me"

Maggie nodded. "That's what the box is, Peter. It's your dreams, it's freedom, it's a beautiful oblivion crafted by your own mind. For a full year I lived inside the best of the dreams I have ever had. It is literally a piece of paradise on this horrific world. So to answer your question, yes, it was absolutely worth it."

Wringing his large hands, Peter replied, "I truly hope so. I am, however, very concerned that Cleric or his cronies will come looking for you. They expected you to give your life for your time in the box, and they don't seem like the kind of people who will let you walk away without fulfilling your end of the bargain."

"Well, if they do come looking for me, it should make your next task easier," Maggie said.

Peter shook his head. He already knew the answer, but felt compelled to ask, to hear it spoken by his employer and friend. "What is it you want me to do?"

"I want that box, Peter. Its potential is wasted by Cleric. He doesn't deserve to be the sole arbiter of who has access to it."

Peter knew there was no point in arguing. He had worked for Maggie Simmons for a decade, and once she had her sights set on something, there was no relenting. If he wouldn't find the box for her, she would hire someone who would. His best hope was to do as she asked and keep her as safe as possible in the process. He pulled a tablet computer from his briefcase leaning against the wall.

"Where shall I begin?" he asked, tapping furiously at the plastic screen.

Maggie thought briefly before responding. "It may be difficult to find Cleric again. Our first meeting was a complete accident. My assumption would be that he'll leave London as soon as possible. There was, however, a gentleman in the box with me who seemed to be friends with Cleric. He called himself Devastation Blue, and his accent sounded American. Oh, and his skin is gray. He may be a bit easier to track down."

"Curious," Peter said with a frown. "He was in the box with you?"

Maggie nodded. "Yes, but not really with me. There are two separate chambers, sort of like a confessional booth. He laid on one side while I slept on the other."

"It is possible that this Mister Blue was killed in the hall with those that chose to fight us," Peter mused.

"I doubt it," Maggie said with a shrug. "He didn't strike me as a fighter. His own self-preservation would probably interest him more than a futile altercation."

Peter resumed typing with a curt nod. After a few minutes he glanced at the platinum Rolex wrapped around his wrist. "It's getting late here, but in the States it's still early evening. Let me make a few calls. I shall return briefly." He gave Maggie a quick kiss on the forehead and stalked purposefully from her room.

Maggie sighed and wriggled in the stiff bed, trying to find some modicum of comfort. She picked up the remote for the small TV hanging in the corner and flipped through the channels before discontentedly switching off the box. She decided she should at least try to get some sleep and closed her eyes. A few minutes later, just as she was drifting into quiet oblivion, she heard a loud, static snap.

She opened her eyes to find the room wrapped in darkness. The small fluorescent light had gone out, as had the lights in the hall way. For the first time she noticed there was no window in her room. She grimaced and wondered how all her affluence and the persuasive Mr. Pierce had not been able to secure a room with a view.

She exhaled deeply and closed her eyes, but when the door to her room slammed shut, adrenaline exploded in her veins. She sat up, clutching the sheets around her tightly. She could see nothing beyond her bed, but could almost hear the soft shuffling of bare feet.

"Is someone there?" she hazarded into the dark.

Silence was the only answer and Maggie lay back and tried to calm her shrieking nerves. She heard another hushed footstep, but before she could react, a voice came creeping from the gloom.

"You don't deserve to be alive."

The voice carried a think Scottish accent, but Maggie didn't notice as she scrambled to find the button to summon a nurse. Her eyes began to acclimate to the dark and she saw a short, young woman in a dirty gray dress walking quietly towards her. With a rush of fear, Maggie pummeled the button, hoping that someone would come to her aid.

"The box freed me from two decades of indescribable agony and gave me peace I didn't know was possible," the Scottish girl told Maggie in a raspy voice. "You bought your time in the box with money and promises, not the suffering that all the others lived through to earn a place."

Maggie tried to reason with the girl while madly hammering at the call button. "I'm sorry for your pain, but my death wouldn't have stopped your suffering."

"Words won't save you now. You broke your promise and the box demands its due. Only your death can put us back to rest," the girl said. She drew her hands from behind her back and Maggie saw a scalpel held in each.

With no other options coming to her panic-stricken mind, Maggie closed her eyes and screamed. With a crack the door to her room shuddered and erupted in a shower of splinters and metal pieces. Peter

Pierce rushed into the room, an HK pistol in his hand. He swept around the room, checking every inch with the efficacy of a trained body guard, but no threat could be discerned. He returned the pistol to the holster under his jacket and went to Maggie's side. "What is it, Maggie? What happened?"

Maggie shook her head. She had clearly seen and spoken to the girl, but she was nowhere to be seen. The only way in or out of her room was the door Peter had burst through. It wasn't possible for her to simply vanish.

Maybe the girl in the gray dress really was a ghost. Perhaps it had just been a dream. Or maybe a hallucination brought on by painkillers and guilt. Whatever it was, Maggie didn't care. With a choked sob, she began to cry. "Get me away from this place, Peter," she whimpered.

"I will, Maggie. First thing in the morning we'll fly back to New York. I won't leave your side until then."

Maggie wept as Peter tried to smooth over the incident with the hospital staff using soft words and hard cash. After a few heart-wrenching minutes she fell asleep, this time praying she wouldn't dream.

* * *

"We're all glad to have you back, Miss Simmons," Sally said. "We missed you."

"Well, thank you, Sally," Maggie replied, holding the phone to her ear with her shoulder as she poured a glass of wine. "So what's going on that can't wait a little longer? I only returned from England two days ago."

"It's the Board, Ma'am. They want a meeting as soon as possible. Mister Kent, in particular, is eager to get you back into the day-to-day operations."

"Ugh! Well, I guess I have to face them at some point. They have been making large sums of money for me while I globetrotted."

Maggie walked slowly to the window and looked out over the expanse of Manhattan's upper east side. She smiled and tasted her wine as the setting sun framed the skyline. It was a surprisingly good vintage. The superlative wine and the spectacular view from her penthouse apartment were welcome reminders of the life she had put on hiatus while in the box.

"Set up a meeting for tomorrow. I was planning to stop by the office anyway. I might as well deal with Mister Kent then. Anything else I should be aware of?" Maggie asked.

"Nothing that requires your immediate attention, Ma'am. I do have

Mister Pierce holding on the other line for you."

"Very well, put him on. It's good to hear your voice again, Sally."

"Thank you, Ma'am. Here's Mister Pierce."

There was a click and Peter's voice came rumbling through the line. "Maggie? Are you ready for some good news?"

"Of course, Peter. I'm always ready for good news."

"One of my contacts has located Devastation Blue. He has an Estate in the forest outside Portland, Oregon. I have him under surveillance and we can make a move on him whenever you're ready."

Maggie took another sip of wine. "That's good news indeed, Peter. I was looking for an excuse not to meet with the Board. We can leave tomorrow."

"Very well," Peter said. "I will make arrangements to have the plane ready to fly out in the morning."

As he spoke, a second voice called out from the background. "Who are you talking to, Petey? Dinner's just about ready, dear."

Maggie smiled and said, "Well, it sounds like your real boss needs your attention. Call me in the morning. Tell Henry I said hello."

"I will, Maggie. Good night."

The line clicked to silence and Maggie set the phone on her large mahogany desk. She finished her glass of wine and picked up the bottle before shuffling into the hallway.

Her new bodyguard sat in a French country chair, absent-mindedly picking his nose. He hopped to his feet when he spied Maggie. "Are you leaving, Ma'am?" he asked, his gruff voice low and full of latent venom.

"No, I think I'll retire for the evening. Mister Pierce and I will be leaving early tomorrow. Please see that I am not disturbed."

"Yes, Ma'am," the bodyguard said with a nod.

Maggie went to her spacious bedroom and set her wine on the nightstand. She collapsed on the soft bed and watched the sun sink below the horizon. With a sigh, she rose and pulled the curtains closed against the dark. She changed into her silk night gown and lay down.

A few quiet hours passed before Maggie was woken from her slumber by the sound of breaking glass. She rubbed her eyes and looked around the dark room. When she spied the grey dress lingering in the corner like a shadow, terror gripped her. She could see the dress and make out the vague form of a young lady, but her face was twisted and blurry, like a half-formed photo negative.

"You can't run from me." The thick Scottish accent floated through the bedroom as Maggie trembled under her covers. She saw the source of the breaking glass held in the girl's hand—her bottle of superlative red, smashed and held like a weapon.

"There is no ocean wide enough to keep you safe from our retribution," the girl whispered in her cracked voice. She began to walk towards Maggie, twitching and waving the broken bottle menacingly.

Maggie scrambled backwards, trying to get off the bed, but the sheets wrapped around her like a net. She struggled against them, but the more she fought, the tighter she became entangled. When she wriggled forward, the edge of the bed retreated further away, like a mirage.

Maggie's throat was locked up with terror. She tried to speak, tried to cry for help, tried to make any sound at all, but the fear had stolen her power of speech. She closed her eyes and let the darkness take hold of her. When the broken glass touched the skin of her face, the spell broke and Maggie screamed.

* * *

"Miss Simmons! Miss Simmons!"

The gruff voice yelling and the hard hand shaking her shoulder made Maggie open her eyes. As the light from the hallway washed over her, she stopped screaming. The round face of the bodyguard loomed over her, eyes wide and wild.

"You can stop shaking me now," Maggie told him in a quavering voice.

"Are you okay? I heard you screaming," the bodyguard said as he holstered his pistol.

Maggie cast a glance around the room. There was no ghostly girl to be seen. The bottle of wine sat untouched on the nightstand. She ran a thin finger along her face where she had felt the scrape of glass shards. There was no blood, no cut, no evidence of an attack of any kind.

"It was just a nightmare, I guess," she said, trying to convince herself as much as the guard. It had all seemed so real; she had felt the glass on her skin and the terror eating at her heart. Gathering her fractured wits, she got out of the bed and wrapped herself in a heavy robe.

The bodyguard shuffled his feet uncomfortably. "If there's nothing I can do, Miss Simmons, I'll just get back to my post."

Knowing sleep would be an impossibility for the rest of the night, if not longer, Maggie told him, "There is something you can do. Call my driver. Have him be in front of the building. Also, get in touch with Mister Pierce and tell him to meet me at LaGuardia. Tell him we are leaving tonight."

The guard nodded and walked into the hallway as he dialed his cell phone. When he was gone, Maggie let out a gasp. The Scottish girl's voice still echoed in her memory with its threats and accusations. Every time she turned her head, she could almost glimpse that gray dress hanging on the edge of her vision. Maggie knew there was only one way to purge the nightmares and the ghosts. She had to have the box.

With her thoughts consumed by the fire of budding obsession, she packed a bag and made her way to the street to await her car.

* * *

The crescent moon hung like a sickle over the black water as Maggie and Peter approached the old log cabin. They had chosen this place on the waters of Aneroid Lake for its remote location and difficulty of access. A bitter chill hung in the clear night air and Maggie rubbed her hands together to warm them.

"He's in there?" she asked as they reached the wrap-around patio.

Peter nodded. "He is. Are you sure about this, Maggie? It's not too late to just walk away. He'll never know it was you behind his kidnapping."

Maggie's fierce eyes drilled into Peter. She hadn't slept in the two days it had taken to bring Devastation Blue to this remote place, and dark circles rimmed her eyes like ugly bruises.

"No turning back now, Peter. Mister Blue will tell us where to find the box tonight."

With a sigh, Peter opened the door and ushered Maggie through. Devastation Blue sat tied to a wooden chair in the center of the cabin. When he saw Maggie, he laughed manically.

"I should have known," he tittered. "Only you would be this stupid."

The large man standing watch over Mr. Blue struck him with the back of his hand.

"You will speak only when spoken to," the big man growled. "Understand?"

Devastation licked at the blood oozing from his lip and nodded his assent.

Peter knelt next to Mr. Blue and told him, "This fine gentleman is called The Hook. He's quite good at extracting information, as I'm sure you will soon find. You can save yourself an enormous amount of pain if you simply tell us what we want to know."

The captive grinned and asked, "And what might that be, Mister Pierce?"

"You know the answer to that, Mister Blue."

"Of course. She wants the box."

"Yes, Mister Blue. It's that simple. Just tell me a city, that's all. If you're telling the truth, you'll be free to go and you'll never see myself or The Hook ever again."

"Actually," Maggie interjected, stepping towards the bound man. "I have some questions."

"Indeed," Devastation replied with a tilt of his head.

"Why were you in the box with me?" Maggie asked.

Devastation Blue laughed before responding. "You really have no idea what the box is, do you?"

The Hook reeled back and delivered a punch to Blue's jaw with such force that Maggie had to look away. Devastation spat shattered teeth onto the wood floor, dark red blood streaming down his gray skin.

"That was unnecessary, Mister The Hook. I was going to answer the question. Miss Simmons' ignorance is simply shocking and I feel I should enlighten her." Mr. Blue glared at Maggie with a scorching fury. "The box is a gift to the downtrodden and miserable of this world. Its intended purpose is to give those who know nothing but suffering in their lives a brief respite from their pain."

"And in return they must pay with their lives," Maggie concluded.

"Indeed," confirmed Mr. Blue. "But most of those who enter the box lead horrible lives that they are all too willing to give up for a taste of paradise."

"What about you?" Maggie asked.

"I was simply a spectator," Mr. Blue replied. "There are those of us who walk this world who don't have the ability to dream. That trait is distinctly... human. For us, the box is a way to experience the beautiful dreamscape a human mind can produce."

"That's it? The other side of the box lets you see someone else's dreams?"

"It's more than just seeing them. It allows us to experience them with you, the same way you do. To feel the pure emotion untarnished by the concerns of the waking world. Each time a new dreamer is chosen, an auction is held. There are many who would pay dearly to spend time lost in your dreams. I happened to be able to pay the price Cleric asked for a year in the box with you."

A look of disgust crossed Maggie's face. "How much did you pay for my dreams?"

"A price you wouldn't understand," Mr. Blue said with a smirk. "There are sometimes costs beyond mere money."

Maggie had heard enough. The esoteric drivel made her head spin, and all she cared about was finding the box. "So, where is it?" she demanded.

Devastation grimaced. "That is one question I can't answer."

"Very well. I will leave you in the capable hands of The Hook until you change your mind." Maggie nodded to the large, menacing man. With his calloused hands he opened a duffel bag and removed a hammer, a hacksaw, and an acetylene blow torch.

Devastation struggled against the rope holding him. "You won't get away with this," he yelled at Maggie's back as she opened the door and walked into the brisk night air.

Peter followed her and they sat on the hard wood of the porch. After a few minutes, the screaming started. Maggie stood and paced restlessly, trying to block the wailing from her mind. A sickening crunch emanated from the cabin and the screams turned to tortured moans.

After what seemed like an eternity, the door opened and The Hook emerged, drenched in blood. He nodded to Peter and said one word, "Prague."

"Keep him here until I contact you," Peter told him. He took Maggie's hand and they walked into the woods towards the waiting Range Rover.

"Are you ready for this, Maggie?" Peter asked, his breath curling in cloudy streamers.

With a sigh, Maggie replied, "I hope so, Peter. I really do."

They walked the rest of the way in silence, each mulling what lay ahead and the price they each must pay to get there.

* * *

A light rain misted from the clouds hanging sullenly over the part of Prague known as the Jewish Quarter. Maggie felt restless, watching the rivulets dribble down the windshield of the coal black Lexus. She nervously toyed with the hem of her jacket and watched the clouds roll through the late afternoon sky.

A bearded man in a pea coat sauntered down the sidewalk towards the parked car. When he got close, Peter unfolded the map on his lap and rolled down the window.

"Excuse me, sir," he called out in German. "Do you know the way to the Kafka house?"

The bearded man leaned on the door and pointed at the map. "Here," he replied in English. Then, casting a casual glance over his shoulder, he whispered, "One on the door, two inside."

"Thank you, sir," Peter replied before rolling up the window. The bearded man disappeared into the mist without another word.

Peter pulled a small walkie-talkie from the glove box and keyed the mic. "Make ready. Go on my signal."

A large black van parked at the opposite end of the cobblestone street turned on its lights and rolled slowly towards them.

"This is it, Maggie. One last chance to call this off."

"Just make it happen. I've waited long enough."

Peter shook his head as he said, "Very well."

He gathered the map and stepped into the rain. Maggie got out behind him and they hooked arms, walking towards the van. Peter's cell phone buzzed in his pocket, but he ignored it. When the van had come abreast of a decrepit old house with a short man in a trench coat standing in front, Peter waved.

A flash came from the van, followed by a raspy bark. The man guarding the old house fell over backwards, blood spurting from a hole in his forehead.

A man dressed in black fatigues burst from the van and kicked the door to the house. The old wood buckled and the man rushed inside, silenced pistol held ready. He was quickly followed by three more men in black, similarly armed.

As Maggie and Peter walked towards the house, Peter's phone again vibrated fiercely. He pulled the phone from his pocket, cursing. He opened the text message and saw just four words: Hook dead, Blue gone.

Peter's heart dropped as the message sunk in. He stopped to reread the message as beads of cold sweat formed on his brow. Maggie walked ahead of him, unconcerned. As she stepped into the open doorway, Peter grabbed her arm. "We can't go in there, Maggie. Something's wrong."

"I have to, Peter."

She pulled free from his grip and entered the house. She stepped into a long hallway paneled with dark, rotting wood. The body of a second guard lay on the floor, blood dripping from a bullet wound in his throat.

Peter swept past her, yelling to his team. "Spread out, cover any points of entry you find. Expect an ambush at any time." The men fanned out to the various doors lining the hallway. Maggie paid no mind to the rooms on the side of the hall, her vision focused only on the large black door at the back of the house.

"It must be in there," Maggie said breathlessly. She ran to the door and pushed it open. The box was indeed inside, as was Cleric, who knelt by the box almost as if he was praying to it.

"I should have known this day would come," he said in a voice laced with sadness and regret. "There is still a chance to save yourself, Maggie."

Maggie ignored Cleric, her eyes fixated on her prize. When she had first seen the box, the light spilling from within had been hypnotizing and beautiful. The thought of bathing in that golden radiance again thrilled her.

As she entered the room, she saw the knife once meant to take her life sitting on a small wooden table. She picked up the blade and tossed the sheath to the floor. Cleric stayed on his knees, not attempting to flee or fight.

The man said a quiet prayer as Maggie stepped behind him. She held the dagger in both hands and jabbed it into the old man's exposed back. There was more resistance than she expected and the blade only penetrated a few inches. With a grunt, she put all her weight onto the handle of the blade and drove it forward.

Cleric clenched his teeth to hold back the scream amassing in his throat. He was pushed forward by the force of the thrust and his hands gripped the wood of the box.

"I'm sorry," he whispered as blood ran down the dark wood.

Maggie pushed him to the floor and put her hands on the box. She ran her fingers over the brass handle with a maniacal gleam in her eyes.

"Finally," she said, tugging the heavy door open. Golden light spilled out of the box and the intricate patterns carved within pulsed with beautiful energy. As she stood admiring the box, though, something started to change. The light darkened and took on the sanguine hue of Cleric's running blood. The patterns inside seemed to shift and twist, and hideous faces leered out of the woodwork. A cold dread overwhelmed the joy in Maggie's heart.

"What's happening?" she said, stepping back.

As Maggie backed away from the box, she was vaguely aware of a commotion behind her, but she paid it no mind. Despite the fear filling her veins at the box's transformation, she was mesmerized. Her stupor was broken as two shouted words came crashing through her haze. "Maggie! Run!"

With a start, Maggie turned to see Peter lurching towards her, his face covered in blood from a gash across his forehead. He turned and fired his pistol down the hallway. Unleashing shots madly, he backed into the room where Maggie stood and slammed the door. He leaned against it with all his weight as his unseen assailant slammed into the other side.

"It's a trap, Maggie! You have to get out!" Peter yelled, struggling to hold the door closed against the attacker.

Maggie looked around the room, but there was no exit. Other than the portal being held by Peter, there were no windows or doors to the dark room. Seeing that there would be no other way out, Peter let the door open a crack and fired his pistol blindly into the hallway. There was a roar of pain and the vicious assault relented.

Peter threw the door open wide, still firing. When he exhausted the clip, he grabbed Maggie by the arm and dragged her into the hallway. They ran towards the front door, but before they had made it ten steps, a red hand adorned with six-inch-long black claws burst through the wall and hooked into Peter's shoulder. He screamed and pounded at the hand with the empty gun.

The claws dug deeper into his flesh as blood gushed to the rotted, gray carpet. The arm retracted, pulling Peter against the wall. With a grunt, he hit the old wood and dropped his pistol. The arm pulled again, and this time the wood gave way. Peter was pulled though the wall in a shower of splinters and dust.

Maggie fell to the floor screaming as she lost sight of Peter in the darkness beyond. She heard him curse and shout as he fought with his assailant. With a sickening tearing sound, the fighting stopped. Peter briefly whimpered like a beaten hound before a grisly crunch ended his struggles.

Maggie wept as she knelt in the dust and blood. She looked to the front door and was about to sprint for the exit when a silhouette loomed in the doorway.

"Good evening, Miss Simmons."

Maggie knew the voice instantly. How Devastation Blue had escaped and made his way to Prague was beyond her. She tried to give voice to her confusion, but she could only stammer wordlessly.

Mr. Blue entered the house and walked to Maggie. With strength a man of his size had no right to possess, he hauled her to her feet and dragged her down the hallway. When they stepped inside the room with the box, Maggie began to struggle.

The crimson light pouring from the box filled her heart with a terror she had never known. She fought to break away, but Devastation clamped down on her arm with a vice-like grip. Maggie whimpered as the pain shot through her.

"You wanted the box, Miss Simmons? Well, now you can have as much time with it as you like," Mr. Blue said as he dragged Maggie towards the open door.

"What…" was the only reply Maggie could offer. She didn't understand what was happening, why she was so terrified of her prize, why Devastation Blue was so eager for her to have it.

"You still don't understand?" Devastation asked. "Your corruption and greed has tainted the box," he told her. "When you killed Cleric, you destroyed the purity that kept the dreams of those inside alive. Now it knows pain and suffering, and it craves it. You've created a nightmare from a dream, Hell where there was once Heaven."

With unseemly strength, Blue lifted Maggie from her feet and tossed her into the waiting chamber. She screamed as the bloody light washed over her, the faces in the woodwork laughing and snarling.

"Don't worry, Miss Simmons," Mr. Blue told her. "Those like myself will pay just as much, if not more, to live your nightmares. The box won't go to waste."

With a malicious grin, Devastation Blue slammed shut the lid to the nightmare box. Maggie screamed as the ghosts rose around her and the unending torment began.

Like Faces in the Rain
Michael C. Schutz-Ryan

The bathroom remodel was almost complete.

Oh, who was he kidding? It was just a replacement wall for the shower.

Stanley had ordered this service off an infomercial he'd seen at two in the morning earlier in the week. Since mother died, leaving the house to him, he hadn't slept well and watched cable until nearly dawn every day. It wasn't like he had a job to tire him out; he lived off the insurance settlement Grocery Brothers paid out because of the shopping cart incident.

The invention he'd seen was called a ShowerSurround. Patent pending. He'd watched the overly expressive pitch man with growing excitement, finally sitting up in his recliner and leaning over his expansive gut so he wouldn't miss a single word. But Stanley had been sold on the idea at first sight. It would solve everything.

Call for a consultation!

He did.

What was their pitch? Delightfully affordable.

Except "delightful" sounded a bit like "frightful," didn't it?

A trim, polo-clad young man—the antithesis of a baggy-panted plumber Joe—had driven out the next day and taken measurements. He returned this morning with a single fiberglass slipcover, which fit over the existing shower walls. The kid cut out the holes for the fixtures, wrestled it under the shower door frame, and snapped the whole thing into place while Stanley watched, slack-jawed.

Stanley signed the invoice. He felt so relieved that he slipped the kid a twenty for a tip.

There was only one problem, which occurred to him after the white ShowerSurround van disappeared down the block. In truth, the thought had been nestled in the back of his mind the past two days, but sheer hopefulness had kept the nagging at bay. Now, when Stanley stepped into the bathroom, the thought shot to the fore like an emergency flare.

ShowerSurround's gimmick was the slipcover. The product didn't actually replace the existing shower walls, but rather covered them. An obsessive-compulsive man would be driven slowly mad with the knowledge that splotchy mold, stained caulking, and lime deposits were all still there, buried just under the surface of things.

Stanley was not obsessive-compulsive and worried not a lick about cosmetic and hygienic concerns.

He worried about the faces.

Weren't they still there, just covered now by a thin layer of prefabricated fiberglass?

It doesn't matter, Stanley told himself. *They're buried now. I can't see them. And they can't see me.*

He liked his new shower. It was colored a shade called Silver Fern. Looking neither silver nor anything like a fern, the hue was closer to the shimmering blue of a secret lagoon. Happily stripping down, Stanley squeezed into the bright new stall and took his admittedly late morning shower.

With steaming water beating down, Stanley luxuriated for a long, satisfying minute. Then he felt them. The faces. They were moving. Though he couldn't see them, he could feel them. Like lazy wakers rolling and stretching in the late morning sun, they writhed and strained in their new darkness.

And while Stanley could sense them, they sensed him, too.

The faces were a phenomenon that Stanley was certain many people experienced. Patterns emerged from the random whorls and splotches in the colors on linoleum floors, sometimes stains on the ceiling, and, of course, shower walls. At first it was game, picking out the figures that his mind drew from the haphazard patterns. Under the shower they were like faces in the rain.

He could make out a clown, complete with jester's cap, a wide smile painted on its face. He identified a gentleman with a top hot and great coat whose head seemed surrounded in pipe smoke.

With every shower, more came forward. A stiff-shouldered doctor in a lab coat stared out at him. A naked, willowy alien with big, dark eyes peered from behind its long-fingered hand.

Then the figures had changed.

The alien had always slightly disturbed Stanley, but now the others had grown threatening. The clown didn't so much smile as sneer. The dapper gentlemen bore a striking resemblance to Jack the Ripper. The doctor held a long-needled syringe, the tip of which dripped venom.

As the shower water had beat upon their linoleum paneled landscapes, they stalked him, their eyes always watching.

Stanley wondered what those perversions of nature wanted of him. Blood? Flesh? To occupy human form and escape their prison?

Stanley had suffered this steady progression for months. Until the night he'd seen the commercial for ShowerSurround, and hope had flooded into his life. But that hope was being dashed even as he hurriedly rinsed the frothy soap from his body.

The jeering clown, the alien, the doctor… they were all still there. He couldn't see them, but they were still there. Every one of them. They knew he'd tried—and failed—to be rid of them.

And they were angry.

Stanley couldn't take it anymore. He ended his shower and dripped his way to the bedroom, wrapping a towel around his middle as he went.

* * *

An hour later, Stanley sat slouched in his recliner, watching his favorite doctor drama on Netflix.

And scratching.

He itched all over. In his haste to escape the hidden faces and figures of the shower, he hadn't rinsed very well. For several minutes after he'd dried himself off, shampoo suds had crackled and popped in his hair. Now that thin sheen of barely rinsed lather had hardened; it irritated his skin to no end. As Stanley scratched, flakes of white, like dandruff, fell to the arms of the chair.

The solution was simple: he needed to take another shower to rinse off.

Stanley crept into the bathroom, as if by stealth he could avoid waking the demons hiding in the shower. If he had succeeded thus far, he surely called their attention when the shower head spit out its stream. The water pounded on the new fiberglass walls. A slight space between the new ShowerSurround walls and the old panels caused a drumming echo. This, certainly, would wake them.

As Stanley scrubbed the dried soap scum off his body, he kept lookout. He watched as water fell on the Silver Fern walls. Many of the beads raced down in quick rivulets. Others, as if governed by a different rule of physics, remained where they landed. Within this seemingly random connect-the-dots pattern, Stanley noticed that Silver Fern was not a monochromatic color after all. Unrecognizable until splashing water brought them forth, vague swirling shapes took form.

Familiar faces emerged.

The death-smile rictus of the clown leapt out at him. Drops of water at the tips of the jester's hat caught the overhead bathroom light and winked as if the bells attached were jingling.

The Ripper watched Stanley with wide, bruised eyes. It flashed a toothy and predatory grin.

The doctor's lab coat blurred as if with motion. He brandished the syringe.

The alien's face was livid with the tint of Silver Fern blue. At the end of a sinewy arm, long fingernail-claws dripped earthling blood the clear color of water.

They had all returned. Larger—closer—than they'd ever been.

Stanley screamed. He slammed his shoulder into the shower door and tripped onto the bath mat amidst a trailing spray of water. Stanley scrambled to his feet. He slapped at the knob to turn off the water. Sure that the shower figures would be following right behind, he slipped out of the bathroom.

He took shelter in his bedroom across the hall. The room had been his since childhood, and it was the safest place he knew. As he sat on his bed, a wet stain spread quickly from his bottom. The bedspread grew sodden, but Stanley didn't even notice. Huffing and trying to catch his breath, he watched the door. Minutes passed while he waited for his torturers to track him.

But nothing came through the door.

Slowly, his breath returned to normal.

Still he kept vigil.

* * *

The knocking began in earnest after the evening sun had set. Twilight peeked around the curtains of Stanley's bedroom windows.

Stanley shook sleepy cobwebs from his mind, puzzled as to where he was, how he'd gotten there. He was lying naked on top of the bed. His butt and lower back were damp. Then he remembered: the shower people had appeared in the new walls. He'd run from them, hid in here, and waited. He must have fallen asleep.

The pounding came again. Like the clunking of pipes from the bathroom, it echoed through the apartment. It shook the walls.

They wanted out.

The last thing Stanley wanted was to go back in there, to the shower, but he was powerless to stop his legs from moving him toward the noise. He slipped on boxers and a strap-shouldered t-shirt. Lead limbed and panicked, he approached the sound as if sleepwalking. His mind was numb with terror.

He flipped on the light switch. As soon as the harsh overhead light came on, the noises stopped. Stanley imagined them—the clown, the Ripper, all of them—pausing in their endeavors, cocking their heads, and listening. Not the faintest sound interrupted the silence in that small, tiled room. The prisoners digging through their cell wall had been alerted to the bull's approach and had halted, worn-down spoons in hand, holding their breaths until the moment for flight or fight erupted.

The silence was shattered as the shower door flew open. Propelled by an invisible force, the door slammed into the wall, shaking in its flimsy metal frame. A sound like a thin gong rang into the air.

Inside the stall, the fiberglass walls of the ShowerSurround bucked and rolled like an earthquake-roiling street. Colors and shades swirled on the surface. Bumps the shape of fists and knees and elbows poked out. Places along the walls elongated as if the fiberglass were no more substantial than taffy. The softened material stretched to transparency.

The limbs pushing against the walls were full sized. The figures trapped in their purgatory were no longer in miniature. On every side the fiberglass began to tear. The walls ripped apart in fleshy ribbons. Through the punctures, Stanley's demons emerged.

The wispy body of the alien came through first. Bits of the wall clung to it; it shook itself like a wet dog. Pieces of the flying debris hit Stanley in the face and arms. The pinpricks of pain assured him this was real.

Stepping into the human world startled the thing. It flinched under the harsh, artificial light. Letting loose a deafening screech, it cowered against the cold tile wall.

A flicker of hope that Stanley might stand off against this coming onslaught was quickly extinguished.

The Ripper ducked under the frame for the shower door, his top hat falling off behind him. Impatient with the whimperings of the first surge, he pushed the sniveling creature aside.

Unfolding to his full height just a foot from Stanley, he shook out his black overcoat. Too tall, too broad shouldered to be human, its face was a burned and tortured muzzle. A snarling beast, it nevertheless croaked out, "Stan-ley."

Hearing his name rasped from the throat of the thing from his shower, Stanley turned on his heels and lumbered out of the bathroom.

As the Ripper-beast started after Stanley, crazed cackling burst from the remains of the shower. The fat clown danced its way out, dressed in a shiny, colorful motley. It goosed the alien as it passed and trumpeted laughter. Costume gleaming under the light, the clown capered after the Ripper-beast. Both were right on Stanley's heels.

Stanley skittered inside the safety of his room and slammed the door. After engaging the lock, he stumbled backward, keeping his focus on the door. The backs of his legs struck the bed. He cried out in surprise.

A heavy thud shook the door. Then another, this one accompanied by a loud, splintering crack.

Outside in the hall, tiny bells jingled.

The Ripper-beast slammed its shoulder into the door a third and final time. Wooden shrapnel exploded into the bedroom. The tall terror stepped through a ragged, gaping hole.

Stanley's eyes went wide with terror. He watched as the clown hunkered down, shook itself gleefully, and jumped through behind its companion.

Stanley tried to back up, but his legs were still against the bed. He fell backward onto the wet spot where only minutes before he'd been asleep. There was nowhere to hide. They were already in his room, coming at him. Stanley scooted across the bed, just trying to put distance between them and him.

The clown darted out from behind the Ripper-beast. Its wide, red smile was painted in blood. The black maw of its actual mouth opened, showing rows of fierce little teeth. Hopping from foot to foot, it minced across the distance to the bed. It shot out one white-gloved hand and grabbed Stanley's foot. The fingers that closed around his ankle were dirty black, stained by whatever evil ministrations their master commanded of them.

Stanley writhed on the bed, shaking his leg furiously. He grabbed the stubby post of the footboard and clung tightly. "No!"

The clown yanked, and Stanley's sweaty fingers slipped and lost their hold.

The Ripper-beast laughed; spit flew from its mouth.

The clown twisted around, tucked Stanley's leg under its arm, and tugged. Stanley crashed onto the floor. Pain shot up from his butt, passed through his spine, and numbed his arms. The clown dragged him out of the bedroom. Towering over Stanley, the Ripper-beast trudged along behind, slavering in hunger.

Stanley screamed his throat raw.

Head bumping along the carpet, Stanley was swept back to the bathroom. The Ripper-beast blocked the doorway as the clown let go. With no hope of escape, Stanley still scrambled away from the clown. Pressing his weight against the legs of the Ripper-beast, he thought for just a second that he could either topple the thing or squeeze between its knees.

The thing's huge hands descended onto Stanley's shoulders. The pressure about broke his clavicles. Suddenly, he was lifted to his feet.

There was no sign of the alien. It had retreated back through the hole in the shower. The clown was halfway through it himself. A maniacal glance over its shoulder froze Stanley. He felt his bladder give up, and a hot wetness dribbled down his leg. The Ripper-beast shoved him, hard, into the waiting hands of the clown.

"Oh, God! Please, no," Stanley wailed.

The clown cackled and pushed Stanley through the hole. It somersaulted in after him.

* * *

Chunks of fiberglass remained strewn throughout the little bathroom for the property manager to find. She would cluck her tongue, chastise Stanley for an unauthorized remodel, and wonder if her tenant would ever show up and try to collect his security deposit.

He never would.

And there was no one else who would notice his disappearance.

The hole through which the beasts had taken Stanley had sealed itself.

Shed of the ShowerSurround and healed of the rift, the old shower was back. The caulk was still spotty with mold. Lime deposits caked the linoleum walls with a chalky hue. And the whorls and swirling patterns waited for a new tenant to take up residence.

The alien stared with large, glaring eyes. Its cowardice had returned to its shower-wall bravado.

The tall, caped figure had returned to a form more Ripper than beast. Its head was now bare; its beloved top hat had evaporated into so much smoke.

The clown laughed eternally, mouth wide with the mirth of its successful hunt.

The doctor was there, too, though his syringe had disappeared. Now his hand held a heavy, clumsy-looking tool. Some kind of bone saw.

Beside him, a new figure.

Under hot, strumming water, the new tenant would squint his eyes, tilt his head, and interpret these forms. He would amuse himself picking out the shapes. He would see a man seated in a cross between a dentist's and a barber's chair, a doctor-looking figure leaning over. Before long, he'd see this man's face contorted in agony.

Screaming.

Delirious for his own escape from the swirling patterns of the shower walls, from the other faces in the rain.

The Thing in the Old Red House

Peter John Cunis

The inside of the old red house seemed smaller—or at least more constricted—than the advertisement had suggested, but he wasn't disappointed. It was a fairly typical interior: hallways, a dining room, a kitchen, some bedrooms, some lavatories. He had pictured higher ceilings and wider hallways, something akin to Charles Foster Kane's Xanadu, but the house was actually quite cozy. There were numerous hallways, of course, and numerous rooms, far more than any one man would ever get use from, but it all felt as though it had been built for an apartment building in Manhattan, not for a colonial countryside manor in the Monadnock Hills of New Hampshire.

The interior, however, was not what had brought him to the old red house; he had come for the picturesque countryside surrounding the place. He turned his head away from the massive oak table in the dining room and looked towards the sprawling landscape outside the arched window.

"What do you think?" the young agent inquired, eagerly clutching her clipboard to her chest.

Walter gazed out at the front yard; a soothing ocean of green surrounded on all sides by luscious New Hampshire woodlands. To the south, beyond the tree line, the earth sank into a canyon filled with a morass of tangled foliage before merging with the endless mountains and forests beyond.

And yet, despite the infinite creativity the landscape represented, Walter felt oddly claustrophobic, as though the woods were a prison complex and the house a cell block in the innermost wing. The unsettling tightness of the hallways only exacerbated the feeling. He found, however, that he was quite comfortable with this claustrophobia—content to be imprisoned. He pictured himself as a tiger that had gotten very tired of being hunted, and was ready jump right into a cage at the zoo just to get some peace and quiet.

Walter was quite fond of projecting himself into metaphors.

"It seems nice. Feels right," he finally responded to the agent, who had been growing increasingly anxious in the long silence that followed her question. "I get a very *writerly* feel from this place. You say other writers have stayed here?"

"Oh yes! Quite a few, actually." the agent said, efficiently combining her response with a sigh of relief. "Well, I mean, at least one that I know of. Have you ever heard of Calvin Harper?"

"I have."

"Of course. Yes, of course you have, you're a writer. Anyway, he loved this place. He said that he got most of his inspiration from this place."

"He said this to you personally?" Walter raised his eyebrows in fake surprise. It was one of his favorite tactics in manipulation; act impressed by whatever was said, but pretend to misunderstand it completely.

The agent looked down, embarrassed, "Well... no, but the word around the office was that he loved it. Absolutely loved it."

Walter fiddled with an old metronome resting on the grand piano. Something about the agent's nervousness was getting to him. Real-estate agents weren't supposed to be young and panicky. Homeowners were supposed to be young and panicky. Why would the agency pawn such a lovely property off on such a young, inexperienced employee?

Or perhaps Julie was just a fan, nervous to meet her literary idol.

"Julie, are you familiar with any of my works?"

"Ah, yes, Mister Colby. You wrote *Night of the Arrows*, didn't you?"

"No, that was Calvin Harper. The aforementioned Calvin Harper."

"Oh my God, I'm so sorry, sir."

"Fine, fine. Don't worry about it.

Walter took a seat on the couch. Directly across from him was an enormous stone fireplace. On the mantle above it was a row of strange ornaments, each representing an obscure Eastern religion. Walter took pride in his ability to name seven out of the ten religions.

He cleared his throat. "Well, I can see how this place was an inspiration to him. He always loved New England tales. Ancient beasts in the forest, emerging from their mysterious hiding spots to terrorize the locals."

"I have to admit, I've only read one of his books," the agent responded.

"*Night of the Arrows?*"

"Yes, sir."

"Yes, everyone's read that one. It's not one of his better works. He was always better when he was writing about ancient beasts, not so good when writing about ancient tribes attacking hitchhikers."

"Mm." Julie nodded and looked down at her clipboard, eager to change the subject.

Walter looked at the agent, sensing her desperation. *Here is a woman,* he thought, *who has been trying to sell this house for a long time. What could possibly be keeping people from buying it?*

He decided to probe further. "I'll be honest, Ms. Haven. I'm most likely going to buy this house. I've taken to it, and I can afford it. I just signed my third movie deal this year and my last alimony check. I have checks coming in regularly from Warner Brothers. Things are going great. Now, if there's any reason why I would not want to live here, just be honest, and let me know, because I'm going to buy the house, regardless."

The agent coughed into a handkerchief a few times. "Sorry, I came down with something last night, I think." She pocketed the handkerchief and paused a moment before saying, "Come into the library. There's one more thing to show you."

The library was enormous and easily took up a quarter of the house. Ancient texts littered two stories of bookshelves connected by four wire stairways. Romantic-era paintings filled any space that wasn't occupied. The bookshelves lined parallel sides of the massive room, forming a beautifully symmetrical frame around the giant stained-glass window in the center. The window was magnificent, if somewhat abstract: red, blue, and beige triangles surrounded a single circle of clear glass that provided a view to the fields outside.

Julie beckoned Walter over to a small alcove at the far end of the library, just to the left of the window. It was a strange little nook that ruined the perfectly rectangular appearance of the giant room. The electric lighting didn't reach the alcove. Julie had to light a pair of candles on either side of the alcove to dispel the darkness.

The statue was disturbingly lifelike, and depicted a blue man with a body that was entirely muscle. The man was wearing only a loincloth, and his right arm was raising a golden dagger in preparation for a brutal stabbing. His mouth was twisted in a horrifying grin, which exuded an unsettlingly friendly aura in comparison to his stance. The grin was the only thing proportionally incorrect about him, being as it was about two inches too wide and dipping an inch too low towards the chin. The man's eyes were bugging out of and had sunk deep into his face, which was covered in odd, black tattoos. The strangest part of the statue, however, did not even occur to Walter until he'd been staring at it for several minutes. The nose was simply the wrong texture; it was covered in a rough, beady patch more akin to a dog's snout than a man's nose. *It's as though somebody took one of those ridiculous Native American mannequins from the Museum of Natural History, brought it back in time, and left it with the Aztecs,* he thought. *And threw in a werewolf costume for good measure.*

The absurdity of such a thing existing caused Walter's stone face to crack, and he cackled.

"That's it?" he said. "That's the reason why I wouldn't want to live here? Don't be ridiculous."

Julie seemed relieved at his good humor. She forced a smile. "I'm glad you don't mind it. We've lost a few potential clients over this, to be honest."

Walter laughed even harder. "Over *this*? You lost people over *this*?"

Julie nodded, her face turning a little red. "In all fairness, they weren't as thrilled with the rest of the house as you are."

The more he looked at the statue, the more ridiculous it appeared.

"What the hell is it?" Walter's question was filled with disdain.

Julie shrugged. "We're not entirely sure. We know that Mister Harper was the one who brought it here. He had a brief phase where he was going to open up an oddities museum, a sort of *Ripley's Believe it or Not*, but he never got the funding for it."

"So it's been here for the past sixty years or so, then?"

Julie nodded. "Fifty or sixty, yes."

Walter smiled. "But it's moronic! It's a silly trinket from an eccentric's art collection. Good Lord, no wonder his books sold so well. People are so easily frightened."

Walter walked up to the statue and looked right into its eyes.

The statue looked back.

His cautious optimism for the old red house had given way to a feeling of necessity; he was being challenged to own this house, and by God, he would take up that challenge. Cowards might run away from a bizarre, knife-wielding homunculus, but Walter Colby, greatest author of his generation, was going to be its roommate, its husband... hell, its best friend.

Walter's face settled back into its more comfortable, businesslike position as he turned to Julie. "I'll take it. Show me where to put my damn signature."

* * *

He was alone in the house for the first time when he heard the coyotes.

He had moved every desk in the house into the study and turned it into a writing room of sorts. He had a typewriter at one desk, a quill pen and parchment (used only occasionally) at the other desk, his laptop at another desk, and a microphone hooked up to a digital video camera at the fourth desk. He would use all of these tools to compose his next book, but everything would eventually have to go to the laptop.

He was at the laptop at that moment. The first thing he had started doing once the WiFi was set up was to research Calvin Harper. Harper had been dead for years, but Walter still considered him a rival. The man had written thirteen bestsellers, while Walter was only starting his second future bestseller.

Something about this house helped him, Walter thought, *but what? I've been here a full day and I feel about as inspired as I would at a Starbucks.*

Although he would never admit it, Walter was looking for the key to Harper's secret bestseller formula.

The problem was, Walter couldn't find any reference to Harper ever having lived in New Hampshire.

A search for "Calvin Harper New Hampshire" simply yielded no results.

It's a ploy. It's a tactic. They tell you a famous novelist stayed here, get your imagination going, and then take your money. Devious, but not unexpected.

But Walter persisted; he typed "Calvin Harper at home" into the image search bar and combed through the results.

After about three pages of the same five images of a young Calvin Harper posing with his wife in Florida, a picture finally came up: a screenshot from an interview with Calvin with the book-lined wall of a library behind him.

Gotcha, thought Walter.

He clicked on the image, navigated to the original page, and found that it contained footage from the interview. He started to watch.

Calvin was a middle-aged man at the time; it was clearly around the time that he'd finished *The Devil.*

The balding, kindly gentleman offered bald, kindly responses to every question the interviewer posited. His favorite author other than himself was Dickens, his writing routine was to make eggs and coffee and just start writing before he was out of his pajamas, if he could have any other job he would be a pilot, and so on and so forth. Calvin mostly just smiled pleasantly and offered the least controversial answers possible.

Walter was about halfway through the video when he noticed that Calvin kept nervously glancing to his right.

"Where do you get your ideas?" asked the interviewer.

Walter scoffed at that, one of the weakest questions to offer a write, but he saw that Calvin wasn't scoffing. Instead, his face turned dark and serious, and he leaned forward a little bit, tilting his forehead towards the camera, but keeping his eyes on the interviewer.

"I'd rather not say, but… you are familiar with my stories, correct?" Calvin somewhat forcefully asked.

"I am. I've read every one of them."

"What are they about?"

"Well, I'd say they're mostly about something coming after the main character. Usually it's a monstrosity, something without a name…"

Calvin nodded. "That's true. And those ideas, they come to me because they're true. There's something coming after us. After every one of us. We don't understand why. We just know that we're going to be caught. Why do you think that so many people dream of being chased? It's because we all know that, deep down, we're prey. We just don't know what our predators are anymore."

The muscular, tanned, balding, kindly gentleman who had grown up in the worst parts of New York and participated in knife fights as a teen, who had served in the army as an adult, and who had confronted his fears in book after book after book, teared up and began to shudder visibly.

Calvin composed himself and drew a hand across his eyes. He looked up and to his right again.

There was a glow of fear in his eyes.

* * *

A howl came over the granite hills from across the canyon, cutting through the trees on the edge of the yard. The lone howl reflected across the night sky before a second howl joined it, then a third. Once the fourth howl joined in, the individual sounds merged into a single note rocketing into the stars and exploding at the end of the atmosphere, sending electricity and chills through the house.

The dark blue statue stood in its special place in the corner of the nook of the library of the old red house. Its tense frame rattled slightly, microscopically, at the shockwave of the unified howl booming from the cliffs over fifty miles away, and then settled as the sound receded back into the grass, back into the tangled forest in the dark canyon, back into the stone, back into the den from which it emanated.

The den was empty.

* * *

In Walter's dream, Calvin Harper's skeleton was trying to chew apart his ex-wife's fingers.

He awoke with a start to the sound of ceramic sliding on ceramic in the kitchen next door to the bedroom.

He relaxed. *Just a plate sliding off the drying rack.*

Walter sat up and muttered curses to himself as his mind adjusted to the reality around him. *Yes, you are awake,* said Walter's conscious mind, *and you have to piss.*

Irritated, Walter realized that the damned agent had never shown him the bathroom. *Rookie.*

His fingers slapped down across the nightstand and fumbled towards his glasses, crawling over a box of tissues and a 1986 copy of *Night of the Arrows* that he had pulled out of the library. His fingers found the glasses, then the light switch.

It took a full forty seconds for his eyes to adjust to the light. He tossed the blankets and sheets aside and dropped a probing foot on the floor to seek out his slippers.

For the first time, Walter was realizing just how baffling the halls of the old red house were. Instead of a straight hallway that ran through the major areas of the house—the bedroom, the bathroom, the kitchen—the hallway zig-zagged to form a set of halls that ran along the length of the house and a set of halls that ran along the width. The lengthwise halls were the ones that actually led to rooms, that actually had doors to the bedroom, the bathroom, the library, the kitchen, but the widthwise halls were bare: no doors, no wallpaper, no windows, nothing. It was like the widthwise hallways were portals designed to shuttle commuters from one lengthwise hall to the other.

Walter's irritation grew as he realized that the house was far bigger with one person in it than with two, and that the confusion of navigating the dizzy hallways was only exacerbated by the complete darkness of the house. The hallways twisted and turned with maddening frequency, left, right, left, right, right, right, right, left, left, left, right, left, right before he reached the staircase.

Grumbling softly to himself, Walter started up the steps when he was interrupted by the same sound of ceramic against ceramic.

He stopped.

He was nowhere near the kitchen.

The world paused with Walter as he gazed down the dark hallway.

The narrow hall, which, when Walter passed through it, had been a typical rectangular portal, seemed to twist slowly in the night like an optical illusion in a puzzle book. Walter's bleary eyesight fizzled as it adjusted to the darkness and telescoped into the depths of the hall. As his vision dilated, he could see further and further into the hall, and he caught sight of a face at the end of it gazing back at him.

Walter jumped backwards, but after a moment he laughed. Just a portrait of some Revolutionary-era French sailor. Just one of Calvin Harper's odd collector's items from his half-hearted artiste phase. *Not much of an oddity*, thought Walter. *Great pick, Harper.* He took a step towards the miserable antique.

A human shadow fell across the painting.

Walter had already sprinted halfway up the stairs when he caught his breath long enough to overcome the burst of adrenaline that had just hit him. *Just a vision trick, you're just tired, there couldn't have been a shadow there, it's impossible*, the voice in his head repeated over and over again even as his body wanted to run as fast as possible from whatever his eyes had just seen. *You can't have a shadow in complete darkness, it's impossible, it's impossible...*

Taking another breath, Walter slowly, steadily climbed the last ten steps. By the time he reached the top of the stairs, his heart had stopped beating against his chest, his lungs were taking in a reasonable amount of air, and his pulse was no longer pounding in his skin. He let himself smile a little bit; the house was getting to him. *Night of the Arrows* was getting to him. That damned statue was getting to him. But the mat underneath his feet was soft, real, not like whatever shadow he had just imagined. The green, plaster hallway he found himself in was real.

Looking to his right and left at the top of the stairs, Walter was pleased to find that, unlike the downstairs, the upstairs hallway was about as straightforward as a hallway could get. With his journey through the first floor, Walter had started to worry that the entire house was more complex than he remembered it, that his memory of the tour had been completely altered. But no, the upstairs was as simplistic as the downstairs was absurd. The upstairs was just one long, wide hallway, three doors, three different rooms. Only a few scattered bureaus and side tables interrupted the open space. The mat that Walter was standing on was, in fact, one of three perfectly circular rugs with concentric patterns on the black hardwood floor. The hallway was the height of three grown men, and it pulled all of the heat in the house into its curved ceiling, keeping the air below cool and easy to breathe. This large, wonderful hallway had a normalizing effect on the house. And the labyrinth below him, with its mysterious shadows and eerie sounds, was just another normal part of the house. He would adjust to it. It was just like any other new house.

The sound was back… coming from the bottom of the stairs.

His flight instinct took over and he flew towards what he hoped was the bathroom, knocking his knee against an oak bureau and jostling a teal vase on his way. He smacked the door open with the back of his arm, and in one move, grabbed the end of the door and slammed it closed. *That wasn't ceramic Shut up shut up what else could it be it wasn't ceramic it must have been a plate what else could it have been it was a knife it was a knife it was a knife it was a knife shut UP it was it wasn't it was shut up it was…*

Another scrape.

It was the sound of a knife. A knife scraping against the floor. And it was in the hallway now. It was cutting into the rug that Walter had just been standing on.

And then it was scraping the floor.

Then it cut through another rug.

Then the floor.

Then a rug.

And then the floor.

Then it stopped directly in front of the door.

And then a new sound.

Of all the sounds and horrors that Walter had ever read about, written about, seen, heard, or imagined, none compared to the horrible sound that came from behind the door: the guttural sniffing of a beast in the heat of the hunt, the primal grunt of a feral dog, the smack of a tongue escaping a dry throat and slapping against a thick cheek—these were the only analogues, the only descriptors of the soft, hellish sound that Walter heard while his ear was pressed against that red door. The sound was close to the ground. The thing's head was on the ground. Walter did not remove his sweating face from the cold wood, did not look up at the red velvet bathroom with the white marble finish, did not tear his eyes away from the spot on which they had fixated. He was afraid to move even his eyes. He was afraid to breathe. He was afraid to be a living thing in any way, shape, or form. But as he crouched at the door, stock still, listening to that sound, the sound of a clown from hell, his heart dropped in his chest.

The lights are on in here.

He looked down and saw a crack between the door and the floor, right where his feet were.

It knows I'm in here.

As if in affirmation, the thing in the hallway began scraping against

120

the door. The sound jarred his eardrums and Walter jerked his head back in reflex.

The scraping got louder and louder, like a dog against the walls of its kennel. Whatever was on the other side was trying to dig through the wood.

Walter backed up, helpless.

Find a way out, find a way...what's in here...

The scraping slowed, but now it was probing the door, testing its weakness. It went up the door, down the door...

Toilet, sink, bureau, towels, toilet, sink...

Up the door, down the door...

Christ, God, please, a weapon, I need a weapon, something...

Up the door, down the door...

Plunger...

The scraping stopped at the bottom of the door...

Toilet lid...

Something gold peeked through the bottom of the door, the tip of something sharp...

Dagger? Gold dagger?

The thing on the other side was teasing the crack between the door and the floor...

Gold dagger? Statue?

Then came the laugh. The laugh of an animal. The laugh of something that didn't know mirth, that didn't know joy, that only knew cruelty. A staccato laugh from a dead lung.

Window.

About a foot above the bathtub was a small, frosted window, a little hatch for letting out steam. It was just big enough for Walter to get through.

Abandoning all hope of finding a weapon, Walter went for the window as something on the other side slammed against the door.

The wood around the hinges splintered, but he was too preoccupied with getting to the window to pay it any mind.

The second slam. The door started to cave inward, but it held.

The window popped open and Walter stuck his head out and looked down. He was directly above a drop-off into the valley; if he jumped through, he would fall twenty feet, hit the trees, and then fall another twenty feet, smacking his head against branches the whole way down.

However, there was a small ledge that he could walk along to get to the next window. It was a tiny ledge, only four or five inches out, clearly only meant for decoration, but…

The third slam…

Without hesitation, Walter stepped out onto the tiny ledge, and with the grace of a tightrope walker, eased his body along the side of the house as the last slam disintegrated the door.

* * *

Walter couldn't remember how he got to the next window; some combination of fear and miraculous acrobatics had allowed him to stay on the tiny ledge, pull open the window, and swing himself through, jarring the window loose from its hinges in the process. Without stopping to reflect on his accomplishment, or even stopping to assess the room he had landed in, Walter flew out the door and back down the stairs.

With what little sanity remained in his panic-stricken mind, he could see the line that the *thing* had traced down the hallway, through the rugs, and across the wall of the stairway. He could also hear the thing catching his scent again and galloping, *galloping* in pursuit.

All he could see were hallways, twisting, turning, left, right, left, right in an impossible web as the thing behind him laughed its dead laugh and scrambled around every corner. Walter's slippers were barely hanging on to his feet; he kicked them off without mercy.

The shadows danced in mockery around him as he ran. They pulled every exit further and further from him the faster he ran. They hummed his dirge for him. They filled his skin with ice.

A red door appeared in the distance like an angel coming to the rescue.

The library.

* * *

Walter bolted the door behind him and switched off the light. He was back in the library, alone. He could hear the thing coming for him, but it passed by the door and went bellowing further down the hall.

As his eyes adjusted to the light, Walter took stock of the room.

The alcove waited for him.

The statue, good god, the statue is real.

It was madness, but it was the only rational explanation. A dagger. A muscular human shape. What else could Calvin have been looking at in that video? It was tormenting him, and now it was going to torment Walter.

He approached the alcove. He could hear the thing in the distance now… it had gone back up to the second story and was destroying the furniture.

Calvin took slow steps towards the alcove; he knew what he would find: a ring of dust where the statue once stood. An empty space. The confirmation that yes, the world is madness, all of our beliefs are deranged, there is no logic or science, only sorcery.

He crept up on the alcove.

The crashing came back down to the first floor. And then the sniffing resumed.

He put his hand on the corner of the wall leading into the alcove.

The sniffing got closer.

Summoning a last bit of courage, he rushed into the alcove.

The statue was still there. It had never moved.

But it glared at him. It stared him down. What had once appeared to be a silly trinket was now an idol to fear. The clownish face was the face of a demon. It had power over Walter.

It had power over everything.

Nothing about it had changed, but everything about Walter changed in that moment.

Walter started shaking.

The door started to splinter behind him. The thing that was pursuing him, whatever it was, had found his hiding space. There was no longer any image in his mind of what pursued him. The comforting hallucination of being pursued by a statue—a comical blue mannequin—was gone. There was only a thing.

A dark, all-consuming thing.

A shadow.

A sadistic thing.

Walter's eyes bulged, his feet shook, sweat ran down his arms, and his mind simply stopped.

And in that moment in which his mind stopped, puzzle-piece images started to come together: an ancient statue, a secluded home, a terrified old man, stories, coyotes, Hell, Heaven, the universe, God, the devil, fear, evolution, silence.

But the image it created only led to more mysteries.

The door burst open and Walter got a brief glimpse of a human form before he turned and dove headfirst through the clear circle in the center of the stained glass window.

Broken glass stuck out of his body as he ran, and the thing pursued him once again. He tumbled through the grass and down, down into the valley, the mad trees and branches no longer a distant prison complex. The forest stretched out infinitely; an infinite maw that swallowed Walter whole as he sprinted through the cold night air; the creature laughed behind him and he laughed with it... he laughed as his clothes fell apart, were torn apart by brambles and branches... the moon shone in his eyes and his eyes were red.

* * *

The window was never repaired. The house was never sold. Nobody ever knew what happened to Walter Colby, though hikers in the Monadnock region often say they hear something being chased in the night.

The statue has been moved. It now gazes out of the window.

The Old Red House draws its breath.

A shadow comes to the house and bows to its master.

PUMPKINS

Matt Kurtz

My heart was racing into overdrive all because of a piece of ass. Now, it wasn't the actual gal that was making it race (I really couldn't even remember her name), but what we were doing so my best friend Beef could score with said piece of ass that had it practically thumping out of my chest.

We were on our way to that old pumpkin patch, the last place on earth I wanted to visit at night.

Especially knowing what was buried there.

To make matters worse, a storm was brewing in the distance and we were driving right into it. Flashes of electricity lit up the twisted trees that lined both sides of the deserted farm road.

Beef flipped on the high beams to see better. I reached forward with a trembling hand to aim the heater's vent directly at me. Even though I was bundled in a jacket, my blood was ice cold. Fear drains the warmth from a body like that. Beef noticed me shivering and shot me a look.

"Quit being such a baby," he said. "We'll be in and out in no time. And speaking of in and out, once we snag three of the biggest for her, I'm gonna be knee-deep in that punanny come this time tomorrow."

Beef was trying to impress a girl we met the night before at a bar. After she invited us to her upcoming Halloween party, Beef threw a bet on the table. If he showed up with three of biggest pumpkins that she'd ever seen—ones that she could then use as decorations—they'd go on a date. Of course, Beef calling it a date was just his way of making her feel like a lady. He was only putting up the pretense in order to get in her pants before the party was over.

"Ya do remember he's buried out here, right?" I asked.

Beef scoffed. "Like I give two shits."
Though he didn't, he should've.
Because he was the one that killed the old man.
Purely by accident, of course.

* * *

Last year, while out celebrating Halloween, we were joyriding on the dirt roads by the Jaspers' place. Beef was behind the wheel of his beat-up Chevy Impala; I was riding shotgun. Juiced up on alcohol and adrenaline, we were driving too fast and being extremely reckless. We were getting an early start to all the hellraisin' we had planned for later that night.

Then the old man stepped out from behind a thicket of brush and onto the road. Before I could scream for Beef to swerve, there was a *thud* at the front quarter panel and the car bounced twice. Cletus Jaspers was dead the second the Impala spit him out.

Terrified of jail time and for our future—not that we really had one from the dead-end jobs we held at the town car wash—we did the Stupid and fled the scene of the crime.

I still feel sick about leaving him out there like roadkill, but what was I to do? I couldn't report the accident with an anonymous phone call to the sheriff because they trace that stuff. And doing the same to the old man's wife was impossible—they were hermits, never seeing much use in a phone since they only talked to each other.

The next morning I hung out in the coffee shop, waiting to hear the day's gossip. Nothing about a hit and run was ever mentioned, which meant only one thing: the old man was still out there, rotting on the side of the road.

As wrong as I was the day before, I was determined to make it right, so I came up with an idea that might ease my conscience a little. I'd ride my bicycle out there to the scene of the accident. *Hey, what's that over yonder? Why, it's a body! Yeah, Sheriff... I was just out here on a leisurely ride when I saw something strange lying there in the weeds.* I admit it wasn't the most original plan, but it'd at least get the poor guy off the road, right?

Beef would've killed me for doing something so risky, but he was too busy taking a sledgehammer to the Impala. He knew once word got out about the accident, anybody with a freshly dented vehicle would fall under suspicion. Taking it to a body shop for repairs was out of the question since the sheriff would be looking for any automobiles that had recently had work done. And since Beef was up to date with his insurance payments, he smashed the car all to hell and left it abandoned in a field. His plan was to report it stolen, let it get found totaled, and when the insurance check arrived, he'd use it to buy the new set of wheels he'd been eyeing. Problem solved.

I rode my bike out to the spot where we hit Cletus, but found nothing. So I crept onto the old couple's land to take a peek at their house, just to see if there was any sort of commotion going on. Even though the old couple took to themselves, whenever a family member dies, relatives always come out of the woodwork to pay their respects, right?

I had a rough idea where their house was and took the shortcut through their old pumpkin patch to reach it.

I didn't get far.

Out there at the opposite end of the patch, just at the base of a huge twisted oak that stuck out from the tree line of surrounding woods, the old Jaspers woman was digging in the ground like an arthritic squirrel. I went for a closer look, moving under the cover of the dense woods.

The old woman's rickety cart, covered with a tattered tarp, sat next to the oak—a gnarly thing that looked like it was dipped in tar and set ablaze for a half hour. Once the hole was apparently deep enough to her liking, she climbed out and went to the cart. Watching her pull back the tarp, I just about dropped a load in my pants.

The pale, broken body of the old man lay inside. She wheeled the cart over to edge and lifted it up on end, dumping the corpse of her husband into the hole like it was a week's worth of garbage. Then she grabbed a bucket full of things that I couldn't quite make out and climbed into the grave with him. She started speaking gibberish while placing the items from the bucket in and around the grave.

Watching her made my scalp prickle. Something just wasn't natural about what she was doing—especially since the rumor in these parts was that she was some sort of witch.

A bird squawked above my head. I glanced up to shush the stupid thing, and when I looked back down, the old woman was half out of the grave, staring right at me with the evil eye. Her face was scrunched up like an old shrunken apple. Then she hissed and *spit* in my direction.

I ducked behind a tree. After waiting a moment, I peeked out and found her gone. Not knowing if she went back into the grave or was creeping up on me through the weeds, I took off running. Once I made it to my bike, I pedaled like the devil over to Beef's to tell him what I saw.

"She didn't hex ya, stupid. She was probably just sneezin' or something," Beef told me.

As for what the old woman was doing out there in the pumpkin patch, Beef seemed quite relieved. The Jaspers, being the last of the backwoods clan out here in these parts, had their own traditions. And you don't mess with those types of traditions. At least not the ones they dabbled in. She was just handling things her own way, seeing no need to bring in any outsiders. That also meant nothing was going to be reported to the authorities.

Realizing that, Beef exhaled and lowered his head. "Great. I just smashed my car all to hell for nothin'!"

* * *

Beef's gently pre-owned Chevy Tahoe, bought with his insurance check a little less than a year ago, pulled over to the side of the dirt road. A wall of black kissed the SUV's windshield until a lightning flash exploded overhead.

Like orange skulls spread across a graveyard, the pumpkin patch sat before us.

"We'll have to walk from here," Beef said, leaning into the backseat. He returned with a small ax and two flashlights.

I nodded to the weapon. "What do I get for protection?"

"This ain't for protection, stupid. It's so I can chop at the pumpkin stems to get 'em off the vine."

"Oh…"

"What are ya afraid of?" Beef asked. "The old woman died six months ago. It's abandoned property. We can't get shot for trespassing." Then he burst out laughing. "Or are ya more afraid of gettin' some Ju Ju hex put on ya?"

"Whatever. Let's just get this over with."

After only a few steps across the field, I pointed to the first few pumpkins we came across. "What about these? They're pretty big, huh?" I asked, knowing damn well that they were pipsqueaks.

"Those ain't gonna get me laid. Keep movin'."

So we kept walking. Beef shone his flashlight toward the center of the field. "Ya notice how the deeper we go, the bigger they get?"

I shrugged, too nervous to care about what he was saying until I realized what he was getting at. His smile confirmed what I was dreading. I shook my head.

He nodded back. "Oh, yeah…" He turned the flashlight on the old, gnarly oak tree at the end of the field. "Probably gigantic ones over yonder, huh?"

Before I could object, he took off running toward the large, twisted oak, hooting and hollering along the way.

Standing there alone, it felt like the temperature suddenly dropped ten degrees.

"Hey, man!" Beef's voice echoed from across the field. "Get over here! Ya gotta see this!"

I sucked in a deep breath, puffing myself up so I could feel like a bigger man, then forced my feet to step forward and approached Beef.

He shone his flashlight at me. "Check this shit out," he said, casting the beam behind him.

I froze in my tracks when I saw the gigantic pumpkin. My stomach dropped over what the enormous gourd was sitting on top of—a mound of tightly packed dirt, the exact width and length of a full grown man.

A grave.

The breath rushed from my lungs.

"Gonna be a bitch gettin' this sucker back to the truck, huh?"

I could barely nod as my eyes followed the pumpkin's stem. As if the large orange ball were its fetus, the umbilical cord of a stem tapered into a vine that led directly into the grave.

Beef panned the light to both sides of the pile, where two other pumpkins also had their vines disappearing into the mound of dirt. "These two ain't as big, but they're bigger than all the others." Moving forward with the ax, Beef ascended the mound.

"Beef! Don't!"

He paused. "Wassamatter?"

"You're stepping on his grave. That's exactly where I saw her dump his body into the ground."

Beef looked down. He raised his foot out of the dirt as if he'd just stepped in dog shit. After a moment, he glanced up at the gigantic pumpkin and must have remembered his bet with the hot broad from the bar. "Please tell me this ain't your way of cock-blockin' me. I'm sure they'll be some dumpy chick there tomorrow night that has lower standards than you. We'll get ya laid, don't ya worry. Okay?"

Beef turned back to the grave and grabbed hold of the coiled vine, yanking it up and away from the pumpkin so he could get a clean shot at cutting it loose. He swung the ax at the stem. The blade passed right through and, as the pumpkin rolled down the dirt embankment, the vines that Beef was holding pulled from his hands and shot back into the earth like a fat man slurping up a strand of spaghetti.

"Jesus!" Beef jumped back and looked at his hand.

"What happened?"

He showed off his injured palm. "Damn vines gave me splinters." He wiped his hand on his jacket. "I'm okay. Just scared the shit outta me," he said, giggling...but seemed far from amused.

"Where did the vines go?" I asked, staring at the grave.

Beef did the same, shrugging his reply.

Lightning lit the sky. A second later, thunder crashed. The storm was almost upon us.

"Let's get 'em in the truck before it starts pouring," Beef suggested.

By the time we loaded all three pumpkins into the back of the SUV and tiredly climbed into the front seats, the sky had opened up.

The SUV backed up and started down the road.

"Man...I hope...I ain't too sore...for my big date tomorrow night," Beef wheezed.

I held my hands to the heater vents and rubbed them together to get the blood flowing.

The wipers couldn't clear the rain off the windshield fast enough. When Beef almost drove off the road at one of the winding turns, he slowed down to a more manageable speed.

Then we heard the thumping.

We first thought it was mud flinging up into one of the rear wheel wells. But then we realized it was coming from behind the backseat.

"Shit. The pumpkins," Beef said, "They're rolling around." He looked back to the road and wiped at the condensation that was spreading across the interior of the windshield. "If they crack, I'm screwed. Or won't get screwed... or... ya know what I mean."

Beef jerked the steering wheel, narrowly missing a large tree branch that blew into the road by the high winds. The pumpkins slammed against each other.

"Climb in the back and hold 'em still, will ya?" Beef asked.

I really didn't want to get any closer to those things. But being a good friend, I climbed into the back. Kneeling, I hesitantly glanced over the back seat. Like orange pool balls shifting in a triangular ball rack, the pumpkins rolled back and forth in unison whenever the truck bounced from the uneven road.

"Just get back there and make up the difference in the extra space with your body," Beef yelled.

I climbed over the seat and worked my way to the back corner of the SUV. I crouched down and pushed the pumpkins forward.

They pushed back. Hard.

Beef was messing with the dashboard dials, trying to turn on the defroster to keep the windshield from fogging up any more. It was distracting him from the road ahead. The truck swerved to the right, Beef turned the wheel to the left. The pumpkins pushed back toward me.

"Slow down, will ya?!"

"I'm going as slow as I can without us gettin' stuck. We need to get on a paved road and off this dirt one before it washes away."

As I pushed on the largest pumpkin—the one that sat on top of the grave—something moved beneath its orange flesh. I yanked my hand away.

The truck hit a hole and bounced, causing the pumpkins to do the same. They clunked together. "C'mon, man. Hold 'em still," Beef pleaded.

While trying to steady the largest one again, its orange shell *stretched* upwards and grabbed hold of my hand, pinning it down near the stem.

I screamed, yanked my hand free, and dove into the safety of the backseat.

My body slammed into the driver's seat, pushing it forward, and pinning Beef against the steering wheel.

"What the—" was the only thing Beef got out before the truck swerved and came to a jarring stop.

* * *

When I came to, Beef was leaning over me, shining his flashlight in my face. "Wake up, ya dumb bastard!" He rubbed his neck and turned back to stare out the windshield. "This is great. Just great."

My body ached all over. Scooting between the driver and passenger seat, I tried to make out what Beef was looking at, but couldn't see squat because of the heavy rain pounding the cracked windshield.

"What...what is it?" I asked, rubbing my head.

"A freakin' tree. That's what it is. That's what you made me hit." Beef exhaled. "My truck's totaled..."

Then after a long pause, "And so are the pumpkins."

My eyes widened with fear. I whirled around to find the tailgate open.

The pumpkins were gone.

"Where are they?"

Beef looked in the rearview mirror. "All over the road, I guess. Bounced out upon impact."

"How?"

"How do ya think?! The tailgate must've popped open and they rolled out."

I stared out the back of the open SUV, barely able to make out the squashed pumpkin pile on the road that was glowing red from the truck's taillights. Beyond that, it was a wall of black. I grabbed the other flashlight off the seat beside me and shone it out the back. Another orange pile sat in the road a few yards beyond the first. "Hey, Beef?"

"What?"

"There was...*something*...in those pumpkins."

"Yeah, yeah, yeah. Guess I ain't the only one that hit my head, huh?" He pushed open his door and stumbled out of the truck, instantly getting soaked from the heavy rain.

I did the same—not to look at the damage done to the vehicle as Beef was doing, but to get a closer look at one of the smashed pumpkins on the road.

I cautiously knelt down beside it. What I found was only a splintered outer shell. Flipping over a large piece, I saw that the underside of the hard skin was completely white, as if wiped clean.

"Looks like any other pumpkin to me."

I spun around startled, not hearing Beef's approach. "Where...where are the guts? The seeds?" I asked. I held two large pieces up, turning them over, looking for any evidence of the missing contents.

"Would ya just leave the stupid pumpkins alone?"

Even all that rain couldn't have washed away the insides. Something would still be clinging to the shells, right? "There're two squashed piles in the road. Where's the third one?"

Lightning flashed overhead.

"Hey!" Beef screamed, giving me another start. I thought he was yelling at me to stop with all this pumpkin business, but instead he was staring down the road.

I turned to see what he was looking at. As another bolt of lightning lit up the sky, I saw movement in the middle of the road. Way off in the distance, a man was walking toward us. Once the bolt of electricity from above extinguished, the road ahead fell to a wall of black again, completely swallowing the approaching figure.

We shined our flashlights down the road at him, but the beams weren't strong enough to spot him.

Beef turned back to me. "Maybe he can help us. Give us a ride outta here."

"Give us a ride? In what? He's walking."

"Maybe he saw our wreck and was afraid he'd get stuck coming over."

Another streak of lightning flew across the sky. The man was closer now, lumbering in our direction. Then all went black again.

"Fella kinda walks like The Mummy, don't he?" Beef observed.

He *was* moving kind of funny; stumbling a bit like he was just learning to walk or something.

"Well, anyways. He probably left his car back a ways. Where he could still turn around and get out."

"I don't know."

Multiple flashes came from above, this time giving us a couple of seconds worth of strobe lighting to see by.

The man was even closer.

"Looks like he's wearing something orange," Beef said, smacking my chest with the back of his hand. "Like those orange vests the dudes on a road crew wear. He's probably out searchin' for people that are stranded."

"Then where's *his* flashlight?"

Beef didn't answer.

I looked down to the shattered pumpkin on the ground beside me.

Looks like he's wearing something orange.

Pumpkin. Orange. Hollow.

Where…where are the guts? The seeds?

I took a step back. "Beef, something ain't right. Is the ax still in the truck?"

Beef shot me a look. "Leave the damn ax alone. You'll scare the dude off if he sees ya holding it out here in the rain." He shook his head and walked to meet the man halfway.

Once I watched Beef disappear into the wet, black void that the approaching stranger was occupying, something told me to get that ax. And get it now!

I turned and sprinted back to the truck. By the time I started to dig around the floorboard of the backseat—the last place I remember Beef tossing it when we finished loading up the pumpkins—I heard Beef calling out to the man. Greeting him.

Then I heard his gut-wrenching screams.

I sprung up and looked out the open tailgate. Shining my light down the road, there was nothing but darkness. For as long as I've known Beef, *never* had I heard him scream like that. He was screaming like some chick!

Beef's cries suddenly cut short.

Oh, Geez! Beef's a pretty big guy to silence that quickly.

Looking for the ax, my fingers clawed across the carpeted floorboards and under the seats. The rain was flowing off the truck's roof like a waterfall, running down my back where it chilled me to the bone. My trembling hand finally bumped against something wooden. I grabbed hold of the ax's handle.

Staring out the open tailgate to the road, my jaw dropped.

Walking into the red glow from truck's taillights, the strange man down the road finally revealed himself.

Only he wasn't a man at all—just mimicking one! And *it* wasn't wearing some orange road crew vest as Beef had thought. Because the shambling thing *was* orange!

With mouth agape, I stared at what resembled a human being that had been skinned alive. Instead of red, meaty ligaments flexing and contracting, the muscles of the thing were orange pumpkin guts pulled taut around a skeleton made completely out of overlapping pumpkin seeds, like the scales on a reptile. The veins running through its body were thin vines from the gourd's stem. Its grinning skull with angular brows was also formed by the overlapping seeds. It was as if someone had carefully glued one seed partially over the other, like shingles on a roof, until it formed the very face of the Grim Reaper.

The thing was dragging the dead (or unconscious) Beef across the ground by his collar... and heading toward me!

Before it could get any closer, I slammed every door shut—including the tailgate—locking all. Looking back, it was stupid because I had just trapped myself in a shelter comprised partially of glass windows. I probably would have had a better chance taking off on foot and outrunning the shuffling thing. *Fella kinda walks like The Mummy, don't he?*

Trembling in fear, I sat in the dark, holding the ax, hearing only the rain pounding the metal roof above.

The door handle behind me jiggled. I whirled around with the ax raised. The window looked like it was painted black... until lightning flashed, illuminating the glistening skull that was grinning with the pointed seeds for teeth. Once the lightning disappeared, the window fell black and the door went still.

A loud THUD came from over my shoulder. I spun around and saw the orange, sinuous hand scratching on the glass with its fingernails made of seeds. Though I wanted to swing the ax through the glass and strike the hand to make it stop, I knew it would only burst one of the bubbles on the truck that was keeping the thing at bay.

The hand pulled back, immediately concealed by the rain cascading down the window.

The handle behind me jiggled again. The car rocked back and forth. It started pounding on the door, hell-bent on getting in.

I raised the ax and knew if this was going to be it, I wanted to go out fighting. The glass wasn't going to keep the thing out forever.

I reached over with a trembling hand and flipped the lock. Pulling on the handle, I kicked open the door and swung at the crouching figure below.

The ax found its target.

Just not the one I was expecting.

Beef looked up at me in shock as a trickle of blood ran down from his hairline. He groaned and fell backwards, landing on the ground with the ax buried in the top of his skull.

As I opened my mouth to scream, the window behind me shattered.

Frigid, wet, squishy hands ran over my scalp, grabbed hold of my hair, and yanked me out of the truck.

* * *

I woke to what I thought was the muffled sound of the sheriff's department looking for us. I tried to yell but nothing came out. And eventually they moved on.

I can't see anything and sometimes it's hard to breathe with the soil weighing down on me. How I ain't suffocated yet is a riddle, but figure it has something to do with the Ju Ju hex that must have been placed on me.

It's pretty lonely down here. I mean, Beef's with me, but being dead and all, he ain't the liveliest of companions. And the fat bastard's really starting to smell. I guess when I planted the ax in his head it kind of ruined whatever that Pumpkin Man had planned for the *both* of us, huh?

So now it's just me. Although I can't move, I can still feel every inch of my body. I sure wish that someone would get me outta here so I can tell my story about what happened that night. I keep repeating it over in my mind to keep my brain active so it don't turn to mush.

Ya see, I think one of those pumpkin vines got into my ear and worked its way into my noodle. It itches a lot more than the ones already attached to the other parts of my body... feedin' the pumpkins above the very ground that I'm buried under.

But I figure as long as I keep the old brain active and flexin' like a muscle, maybe the vine up there won't have room to grow. So I keep running through the story about the night Beef and I went out to that old pumpkin ass—

Wait...

What?

Pumpkin *patch*! I meant pumpkin patch.

Now where was I? Oh, yeah... it wasn't the actual piece of ass that was making my heart race; it was what we were doing so my best friend Meat—

Wait... Meat?

Beef! My best friend *Beef* could score with...

Witchetty Bogies

Stephen McQuiggan

The phone rang and the room fell silent, as if such a commonplace noise was unheard of. Arnie answered, a tentative "Hello?" He mumbled a bit, turned his back on the others, then put the receiver back in its cradle with a sigh.

"That was Missus Kinsey," he said, looking at Jenny. "The woman who was looking to stay with us. The one who begged. Her husband's dead. So is the other guy, I didn't catch his name."

Jenny shot him a hurt look, a stew of anger and betrayal, then left the room even though she had been told a hundred times it wasn't safe to do so.

Had he really meant to hurt her?

Probably.

They had known the Kinseys for years, ever since they had come to the village. It had been Jenny who turned them away, that poor old woman and her two wrinkled chaperones. Now they were dead. Was fear enough to explain it? Was her fear enough to justify it?

He had nothing to be so high and mighty about. It wasn't as if he had disagreed with her logic, put up a fight, and brought them in. No, he had been as scared as she was, and as guilty, too. He had sent those two old men to their deaths with barely an apologetic shrug.

That had been only yesterday.

Yesterday, when the rats came.

That was what they were calling them, though Arnie had never seen rats like these before, some as big as dogs, black as hell, and tailless. They called them rats to try to get a handle on it, to make some sense of what was happening. Jenny had even started calling the small furless ones "babies."

"So what now?" asked Ray. "I'll tell you one thing, there's no way I'm going back out there."

"We don't have to," said Arnie. "Not for a while at any rate."

"I'm not going out again *ever*. Period." Ray threw the empty shotgun onto the couch, then rubbed his stubble with a shaky hand. "Full stop."

Arnie couldn't blame him. He looked at Debbie and saw she was in total agreement with her husband. She still had teeth marks on her neck where one of those things, one of those... rats had attacked her. The shotgun still bore the blood, dark and viscous, where Ray had used it to pound the thing to death. No, he didn't blame them, but they would change their mind when the food started running out.

"I'm going to get Jenny," he said. "Double-check the house, make sure we didn't leave any gaps"

He was halfway to the door when Ray said, "Jesus, Arnie, what if those things can climb?"

Arnie didn't answer, just took the stairs two and three at a time. He went to the little room first, knowing that Jenny would be in the master bedroom and she would have howled the house down if anything had tried to scramble through the window.

Sunlight poured in, lighting up all the crystal beads Jenny had sewn on the bedspread. A cool breeze wafted over his face as he hurried to slam the window, his breath fogging up the glass. Then his breath caught, and he wiped the glass clear with a squeak.

In the back garden, four of those things (they weren't rats; who were they trying to kid?) had dragged the body of a young boy into the rose patch. It was the Wilson kid, still wearing the Metallica shirt he wore every day like it was glued to him.

Now it was his funeral shroud.

Ian. That was his name. Ian.

He would call most Sundays, usually in the middle of dinner, looking to know if you needed your cars or windows washed, his fingers luminous with nicotine, his eyes empty. He would wipe the car half-heartedly with a limp elbow before holding out a yellow paw and demanding a fiver.

Arnie always sent him packing when he called, and lately he had stopped answering the door to him altogether, although the cheeky little sod would come to the living room window and peer in at you and—

—one of those things was pulling Ian's face apart with its tusk-like front teeth, tearing off great strips of skin, peeling it like string cheese, while another three were burrowing through the Metallica shirt into the boy's skinny gut.

I'll give you a fiver to clean that mess up, Ian. I'll give you whatever you want.

Arnie could hear the chomping through the glass. A hand on his shoulder damn near made him leap out the window and down on top of the boy.

Jenny.

"How could I have known, Arnie? Huh? You can't blame me. It was us or them. You know that, you fucking know that!" Her voice was breaking.

He took her in his arms and guided her into the middle of the room. The last thing he wanted was for her to see those things feasting on the local bob-a-job. She had seen too much already. They all had. "Are our windows closed?"

She nodded against his shoulder.

Where the hell were the police?

He had been calling them off and on for the last twelve hours, the first few times getting through to a harried constable—you could hear the chaos behind him, a confidence sapping cacophony—but since midnight all he could get was an automated message that managed to sound even more forlorn for all its sterile calm.

Surely the army would get involved, or did that only happen in the movies?

There was nothing on the TV or radio newscasts, and all his attempts at contacting them had hit a brick wall of disbelief. Still, at least the phones were working, so surely things couldn't be *that* bad. If only they could drive out, but all four exit roads were blocked, bottlenecked by crashed cars, and those... rats, feasting on the carnage.

"Why are you so worried about the windows? You don't think—"

"Better safe than sorry, that's all."

No point in adding to her fears. She was close to a breakdown as it was; he could feel it trembling just beneath her skin. If she knew what Mrs. Kinsey had said over the phone—*Tell that bitch my Arthur's dead; tell her I hope she burns in hell*—it would probably burst through her cold flesh, leave her a quivering mess on the carpet. A mess he was in no condition to clean up.

Poor old Mrs. Kinsey. She had come to them, to the "house on the hill", because that was instinct in an emergency, to seek higher ground. It was what Debbie and Ray had done, and they had only gotten in because one of them wasn't bogged down in a wheelchair.

Arnie felt his gut churn, but it was the truth, wasn't it?

Old man Kinsey was dead because Arnie had been too scared to go down the hill and push the old sod (who probably weighed no more than a bird) up to the house.

They went back downstairs. Debbie was making tea, that pointless damn drink. Arnie thought he might yell and fling the kettle against the wall, but realized if he started, he might never stop. The whole damn ritual, the pouring of the milk, the asking of "How many sugars?"; they were surrounded by a village of half-chewed corpses and still, the taking of tea.

"Have you any petrol?" asked Ray.

"I've a couple of drums in the shed I keep for the lawnmower an' that. Don't know if there's much in them though. Why?"

"Molotov cocktails, my friend," said Ray, smiling. "Fucking napalm. You've seen how those things swarm together. I reckon one petrol bomb in the middle of them would seriously decimate their population. More effective than a shotgun at any rate. We could lob them from the bedroom, pick them off at our leisure. I bet if you used a couple of washing up bottles or something you could rig up some kind of flame thrower and—"

"I hate to piss on your parade, Ray, but aren't you forgetting something? The petrol is all the way down the bottom of the garden. How the hell do you propose we get it out without..." Arnie left the sentence unfinished, seeing how Jenny blanched.

"We could make it to the shed and back in a trick. Besides, they're all out front anyway. We've got to try."

"It's too dangerous."

"It will be the longer we leave it. Look, step one—get to the shed, close the door, safe as houses. Two—grab the drums, sprint back. The girls can man the doors, act as lookouts. They'll yell if any of those rats—"

"They're not rats."

"Well, whatever the hell they are. Come with or stay put; either way I'm getting that juice."

Debbie's bottom lip was trembling. "You can't let him go out there by himself," she said to Arnie. "You just can't."

Jenny was shaking her head. "Nononono! You can't go out there full stop! Can't you see what's going on out there? Are you blind?"

Arnie made up his mind. How could she use that word—*blind*—to him of all people, when she knew how much it hurt him? Because she wanted to hurt him, that's why.

"Okay," he said to Ray, trying to keep the sudden anger out of his voice, "when do we go?" He forced an image of Jenny being mauled from his mind.

Ray lifted the shotgun. "No time like the present," he said.

Through the kitchen window everything looked peaceful, the sun slanting down in gold bars on the immaculate lawn, the occasional mute applause of the beech trees in the breeze. It would have been idyllic had it not been for the partially eaten corpse in the roses.

"Oh my God, who's that!"

"It's Ian Wilson, love. Don't look," said Arnie, taking Jenny in his arms. "Just don't look."

Ray grabbed him by the shoulder, pulling him away from her, locking his eyes onto his, bringing him back into the here and now. "Is the shed locked?"

"No. At least I don't think so."

"Think harder. We can't afford to waste time out there."

"No. No, it's definitely not, I'm sure of it."

"Good. Now, we gonna do this or what?"

It hadn't taken him long to usurp control, thought Arnie. *What had happened to the gibbering wreck of only a few hours ago? The longer this goes on, I could find myself surplus to requirements; he'll take Jenny for himself, have his own little harem and—*

"Are you ready, Arnie? Don't zone out on me."

"Yeah, yeah, I'm fine," said Arnie. Debbie was already at the door, clutching the handle, ready to open it at Ray's command.

"Okay, Jen," said Ray, and Arnie didn't like that overfamiliar "Jen." Not one bit. "You stay by the window and give us the all clear."

They waited, tensely poised by the back door, Ray hoisting the shotgun like a baseball bat, Arnie with a leg from one of the chairs his Auntie Pat had bought them for a wedding present nearly eight years ago.

"It looks quiet. I can't see anything out there," said Jenny, and with a nod from Ray the back door opened. He shot through it like an Olympic sprinter, Arnie trailing in his wake on legs of numb spaghetti.

The air felt good, glorious in fact. Surely nothing bad could happen on such a day. For the hundredth time Arnie almost succeeded in convincing himself it was all a dream, until he skidded in a piece of Ian Wilson that Ray had hurdled deftly. Skidded and nearly fell. As he raced on he could feel that lump of meat, that lump of *Ian*, stuck to the bottom of his trainer.

Ray reached the shed first, fumbling at the door, flinging it wide, and

Arnie had time to wonder at how bright it was inside, to realize that whole sections of wood were chewed from the back wall, before a shadow leapt out onto Ray.

It had his face off before he hit the ground, blood splashing Arnie's shirt as he stood frozen. He was dimly aware of the screams coming from the kitchen and the swarm pouring through the gaping hole they had gnawed.

Arnie ran, ran through the piecemeal corpse of the Wilson kid, ran with the stitch in his side turning to knives in his throat, ran though he felt he wasn't moving at all, all the while waiting for the razor-clamp of tusks biting into his haunch like a bear trap.

The back door opened just as he reached it, and he leapt in, landing awkwardly against the clothes dryer. He heard a thump against the door as Jenny and Debbie held their weight against it. Then Jenny was beside him, crying and wiping the blood from his face.

"Why did you leave him!" Debbie was whining. It sounded just like the keening of those creatures outside. "How could you just—"

"Because he was dead." He ignored her then, pushing his face into Jenny's shoulder. He ignored Debbie as she stepped out into the garden like a woman in a trance, pulling Jenny closer to him when she moved to bring her back.

"Leave her," he said, and now they each had an old man Kinsey to live with. Outside a solitary shriek, almost of pleasant surprise, then nothing.

Jenny began to heave, silent sobs. Arnie left her and went upstairs to the bedroom, blocking his ears to her shouted questions. From the window he had a clear view of the village right down to the church clock and the bundle of overturned cars that marked the road to Ellsford.

He took the small pair of binoculars from the dressing table and focused them on the cemetery by the church until the black smudge he spotted there became a horde of those creatures digging frantically at a grave, their sharp teeth and claws sending up spumes of earth.

Not just any grave—the grave of Betty Turner, buried only two days ago; a heart attack, though the village grapevine crackled that her drinking had finally caught up with her.

These things were smart; they weren't interested in bones. They wanted meat. He watched them until he grew nauseous. When night fell, would they smell *him* the way they had smelt out old gin-soaked Bet, using their industrial claws to dig through his doors?

He scanned across the village, past McGarratty's butcher's, which teemed with the things, some impaled on the jagged shards of his display window in their haste to feed, down to Sadie's Corner, where his sight was arrested. He had to stop his hand from shaking to get a clearer view.

A pram, a buggy, abandoned in the middle of the lane, its back to him, obscuring its occupant.

He could not keep the image of a strapped in baby, its face chewed and mangled, from flaring up in his mind. One of those creatures leapt from the pram with something hanging from its mouth, his heart missing a beat before he realized it was only a teddy bear it was shaking and shredding.

It was at that moment he knew what they were.

The bear was exactly like the one Johnny used to have (and it took all his willpower not to think of him as *Poor Blind Johnny*) and couldn't sleep without. Arnie had stolen it one night and Mum had come into the room because Johnny had woken and screamed the house down when he found BooBoo gone.

She had found the bear in Arnie's bed and she had been *so* angry.

"Do you know what happens to bad boys?" she asked him. "Bad boys who steal and misbehave? The Witchetty Bogles come and eat them all up!"

When she had gone, Johnny had whispered in the dark, "I hope the Witchetty Bogles come for you, Arnie. I swear to God I do."

Oh, he had been such a bad boy, and now they were here.

They had escaped from childhood, from under his bed, from out of his wardrobe, from out of the shadows on long, lonely walks, and they had found him. It was only what he deserved. He had hidden too long.

Ever since that Halloween, the one time he hadn't been frightened of them because everyone was a witch or a Bogle and nothing had been scary, nothing except the look on Johnny's face.

It was hard to think of his brother without using sight references that made it more painful, so he tried not to think of him at all. Jenny knew all about Poor Blind Johnny, had even met him once down in that home where the walls reverberated with the sound of clattering canes and where they read the daily news in dots. Arnie stayed away; those sightless eyes could still see him, still condemn him.

He told Jenny his brother had had an accident, an awful accident as a child, never elaborating any further than that. She never asked him about it again, as if she were glad to drop the subject, and in a way Arnie had always hated her a little for that.

Johnny never had a guide dog because he couldn't stand dogs, said he was allergic to them, which was nonsense because he used to have a little puppy before—

Sometimes he rang, but Arnie stopped answering his calls; they felt black to him, as black and cold as space. No matter what Johnny said to him, the syllables clanging like sticks on the wall of reason, all Arnie could hear was blame.

He had pointed the firework at his brother's face that hateful Halloween, his nine-year-old heart pumping madly, deliriously, because he *knew* it was wrong, but he wanted, no, *needed*, to see what would happen.

Now he knew.

The whip-mark scar beneath Johnny's awful eyes underlined his guilt. Now all the years of denial, of hiding, were finally over. The Witchetty Bogles had finally caught up with him, and his reckoning was nigh.

He went back downstairs. Jenny was sitting on the settee wringing her hands, her face sharp and pinched. She was a Bogle, too, feeding on his guilt all these years.

"They're everywhere," she said.

Through the front window he could see them swarming up the hill, a seething black carpet, crawling over each other, jostling for position, their gaping maws dripping saliva. They left a small patch of garden clear just before the front door, their little ratty eyes trained on it expectantly. Then they started keening.

"Oh my God," moaned Jenny, "what are they! What do they want!"

Their mewling became a chant— *RRRNEEE! RRRNEEE!*—that grated on his bones and sent the muscles on his face twitching. He smiled at his wife, and that smile scared her more than the horde outside.

"They want me," he said. "Are you deaf? Are you blind? It's me that they want. It's always been me."

"You're not making any sense, Arnie. I don't understand."

Of course you don't, he thought, *you can only hear your own Bogles. Guilt sang in a key only audible to the guilty.* "I love you," he said, kissing her damp face. He felt noble, heroic almost.

"Arnie, you're scaring me. I don't understand—"

"Maybe when this is all over you could go see Johnny," he said, embracing the sight reference now. "Look him up. He'll explain. Tell him I paid the piper. Tell him I stopped running, that the Witchetty Bogles caught up with me, and I went to them gladly."

"Arnie—"

"It's okay, love, sooner or later we all have to look our sin in the face." He kissed her again, then went to the front door.

"You can't go out there! They'll rip you apart!"

"Can't you see they've been doing that since I was a kid?" He closed the door on her tears.

It was quiet outside save for the scratch of claws on the driveway. He knelt on the small patch of garden they had left for him and spread his arms wide. One of the Bogles, the blackest and the largest, came forward slowly, sniffing him out as if it were blind. Arnie was not surprised to see it bore a livid scar, like a whip-mark, beneath its eyes.

"Come on," he urged, "I deserve this."

After years of gnawing, they fell on him and ate him alive.

Night-Gaunts Of The Thames
Adam Millard

There was the merest of breezes, enough to ruffle hair and cause eyes to water, but it was a minor inconvenience and one that would not perturb the midnight fishermen. Their illegal activities had recently been reported by some nosey do-gooder, and as a result they were all dressed in black as they sidled up to the river, their gear stuffed haphazardly into equally dark satchels and sacks.

Big Ben, the great bell of the world's most famous clock, chimed its way towards its twelfth B, the final note, reminding one of the fishermen—a butcher by the name of William Rose—that he had but an hour to fish before his wife expected him home.

"This is as good a place as any," John said, lowering his tackle to the ground and staring out into the blackness. "Best get a move on if we want to catch anything before old Bennie rings again."

Albert Porthaven crouched beside his sack and began to unpack. Along with the necessary baits and lines, Albert retrieved a bottle of whiskey and unscrewed the cap. He took a healthy slug, relishing the burn, first in his throat, and then his stomach.

"You'll do well to catch anything in a state," John chided. "Not that you ever catch anything sober."

Albert took another sip, then said, "Well, it'll make no difference then, will it?" He didn't dislike John, but there was something about him that seemed to ruin his good thoughts. It was amazing how negative the man was, and it wasn't on occasion; it was all the time.

They settled down on the embankment. William couldn't concentrate, for he was aware of the time and could think of nothing but his wife pacing frantically from one end of the hallway to the other. If she discovered that he'd been in the presence of whisky, she wouldn't let him leave the house alone in the future, such was her overprotective nature.

Fifteen more minutes wasn't going to hurt.

Between them they caught nothing but litter and a piece of costume jewelry in the form of a necklace, and William was about to make his excuses to leave when John noticed something out on the moonlit river's surface.

"What is it?" Albert asked, squinting through the darkness.

"I have no idea," John replied. "Might be Margaret checking up on William." He snickered; William didn't. The thought that his wife *was* actually swimming towards them in the dark sent a shiver down his spine.

The thing—whatever it was—lurched forward, kicking up water. The fishermen scrambled up the embankment, forsaking their gear for the time being.

"Is it a seal?" Albert breathlessly asked. It certainly looked like one; the moonlight reflected off its shiny, black skin. He didn't want to say it out loud, but his next guess was the Loch Ness Monster, or its Thames equivalent.

"Look!" John gasped suddenly. He poked a tremulous finger towards a second shape, and immediately wished he hadn't when a third popped up beside it. "What the hell *are* they?"

William knew in that moment that he'd missed the perfect opportunity to take his leave, and was now in this mess alongside his companions. As the sleek, oily shadows approached, he thought about Margaret and how he should have paid her heed when she had voiced her dissatisfaction about his inclusion in the night-fishing escapade. It was too late now, though, and the nearing sea-demons—for they had horns that curved inwards— were about to prove that she was right to have had reservations.

"Forget this," John said. He turned and was about to run when an almighty splash brought his attention back to the river.

They were no longer crawling along the surface of the Thames; they were hovering above it, three grotesque creatures with bat-like wings that made no sound as they flapped. It was dark, but John could see that the things had no faces, just a blankness where a face ought to be.

All three men were scrambling up the embankment, mouths agape and eyes wide. Was it coincidence that there should be three creatures to three fishermen? Probably, but if the men had been aware of the creatures' origins, they would have known that one could quite easily kill a hundred men, perhaps a thousand, before the men knew what was happening.

Such was the way of the night-gaunts.

The fishermen made it halfway up the incline before being dragged backwards and partially devoured right there on the riverbank. And as the creatures fed, the moon glistened upon their whale-like flesh and observed the uncouthness from a quarter of a million miles away.

* * *

Detective Thomas Dineage arrived at the scene an hour before dawn. He would have been earlier but for the fact that London had become a tourist trap in the week leading up to Elizabeth's coronation, and despite the ridiculous hour, traffic was already filling the streets. He would be happy when the whole thing was over with. He wasn't anti-monarchy; he just couldn't fathom what all of the fuss was about.

"So what we got?" Dineage asked, stepping around the uniformed bodies obstructing his view. As he saw the mess lying on the bank, he wished he'd had the foresight to take a wrong turn on the way. He hissed, sucked warm air in through gritted teeth.

"Three bodies in total, sir," a rather polite constable by the name of Withers offered. "All in the early stages of rigor mortis, all half-chewed to pieces." He poked a finger into the semi-darkness and added, "Some of one of them is in those bushes, sir. Are you any good at jigsaw puzzles?"

Dineage snorted, caught a whiff of the putrefaction in the air, and tried not to gag. He started counting body parts as if he were doing nothing more macabre than stock-checking a sweet factory. He counted them twice, his lips moving, but just whispers falling out. When he was done, he said, "Only three legs and two arms between 'em, is that correct?"

Constable Withers nodded. "And one head, sir."

"And one head. Of course," Dineage said. "And where do we think the rest of them are?"

The constable gazed around the place as if he might discover the seven missing limbs and two missing heads in the vicinity. Dineage wasn't really in the mood for this nonsense and waved off Withers' attempts to provide an answer.

"Right, so three illegal fishermen, judging by the gear we have here, are attacked in the middle of the night, slaughtered, dismembered, and left to rot at the side of the Thames by our assailants. Does that sound about right?"

Withers thought about nodding, then opted out.

"What makes you think there wasn't just one killer, Detective?" a second constable asked.

"Oh, come, come, come," Dineage said, tutting as he walked across the dewed grass of the embankment. "One man overpowering three burly fishermen on their own turf? He'd be lucky to get the first punch in. No, Constable, this is the work of several brutes, if not half a dozen."

The constable, whose name was Jeffreys, thought for a moment; Dineage waited, hoping that when the time came for words, the constable made good use of them.

"Sir, you don't think this is a copycat, do you? Rillington Place was only a few weeks ago."

Dineage sighed. He hoped he'd heard the last about that godforsaken place and the murders that had taken place there. "So what you're suggesting, Constable…"

"Jeffreys, sir," the man said.

"Jeffreys. Right. I'll never remember that." To everyone on the scene, he said, "What Constable Jeffreys here is suggesting is that a group, because we've already established there must be more than one, of John Christie copycats have gathered here tonight, at this place, and murdered three burly fishermen before stealing three legs, four arms, and two heads. Is anybody else in agreement with that theory, or shall we move on to tangible possibilities?"

A few of the forensics snickered as they gathered up body parts and stuffed them into large plastic sacks.

Jeffreys shrivelled, withered on the spot, his mouth opening and closing with nothing but gasps and bad breath emerging.

"We found this, sir," Withers said, handing an evidence bag to Dineage. "Might not be anything to do with all this, but it was nestled in amongst the shrubs over there. Thought it was best to check it out."

Dineage examined the necklace through the plastic. The first thing he noticed was the rust; it was wrapped around the square pendant so thickly that it was a surprise the thing was holding together at all. In the center of the square was a tiny mirror, immaculate in comparison to its frame. Dineage could see Jeffreys' disheartened face in it as he peered over his shoulder. The chain was home to tiny mollusks; each link contained something that wouldn't have been there when the thing was first purchased. It looked, to Dineage, like miniature barnacles clinging to the piece, though in the semi-darkness of dawn it was difficult to tell.

"Give it to the boys over there," Dineage said, handing the evidence back to Withers, "and whoever gets me a cup of coffee in the next ten minutes can have the rest of the morning off."

* * *

London was heaving with royalists and excited families. It bothered none of them that Elizabeth had been queen for a year already; this was a once-in-a-lifetime opportunity to witness the coronation, for she was young and healthy and would reign, the majority hoped, for decades to come. Dineage was too busy anatomizing the previous night's murders to partake in the festivities, and it suited him just fine.

His office was a mess of books—some piles stacked as tall as him—and paperwork, for which he had no real filing method other than the old stuff went in the bin, and the unsolved papers found a home on the floor, the desk—providing they weren't in the way of his coffee cups—or in the cupboard, where he also kept a change of clothes, a bottle of the best single malt money could buy, and a stuffed rabbit. The clothes and whisky often came in handy; the rabbit was just something to look at when he was bored of solving crime.

Outside his window, crowds were cheering, chanting Elizabeth's name as if she could hear them and would acknowledge their efforts as soon as she appeared. It was hours until the coronation, which led Dineage to believe that these people had nothing better to do with their lives than to rile him while he worked.

Part of him wanted to fling the window open and scream down at them, "Hey, fools! There's a murderer out there, and you're just garnering his attention, so why don't you pipe down and wait, in *silence*, for Her Majesty!"

The other part of him, a more sensible, less irascible part, instructed him to calmly ignore the idiotic throng and concentrate on the task at hand.

Just then there came a knock at the door; a silhouette seemed to fill the frosted glass for a moment before the door opened to reveal the caller.

"Got some news on the murders," Constable Withers said. "A bit freaky, though, if you ask me."

Dineage smiled. "Go on then, man. Spit it out."

Withers proceeded to tell the detective that not only were the men murdered—which he was obviously already aware—but they were also chewed upon and partially devoured.

"Cannibals," Dineage said, nodding. "Typical bloody Londoners. It's not enough to go around killing innocent people any more. You've got to eat 'em now. Makes a better headline on the daily rag."

Withers paused and glanced down to the evidence bag in his hand. That piece of rusty costume jewelry looked even worse now that fifteen other fellows had had their dirty mitts on it. "It wasn't cannibals," Withers said. "From what I understand, the teeth marks belonged to something much bigger, something with jaws like a great white and razor teeth to match."

Dineage could hear the crowd erupting down on the street, joyously oblivious to the troublesome quandary that might affect at least a couple of them. *If only*, the detective thought unceremoniously.

When the initial shock dissipated, Dineage considered the possibilities, of which there were many, and yet none that made sense. "Have you contacted the zoo?" he asked, snatching the bagged necklace from Withers, who didn't give Dineage the common courtesy of a flinch.

"London Zoo did a head-count an hour ago, and they're only missing a salamander. I think it's safe to rule that out as a possible suspect." He smiled, and Dineage grimaced. Continuing, Withers said, "One of our men is over at Battersea as we speak, but it's highly unlikely that this is the work of some crazed dog on the run. A cryptozoologist would be our best bet, sir."

The detective took the evidence bag and slumped into the chair next to his desk. "What kind of creature is capable of this kind of mauling?" he asked the room. "And what's the deal with this?" He opened the plastic bag and pulled the necklace out by its chain. As he examined it once again, turning it over and over in his sweat-sodden palm, he noticed a smell that hadn't been there this morning on the banks of the Thames; an almost overpowering saltiness that stung his eyes and caught at the back of his throat.

"That's the *weird* part," Withers said, sliding across the office as if he was the missing salamander in a very convincing disguise. "The necklace is coated in broken fragments of fire coral."

Dineage shrugged; it went so far over his head that he didn't bother to duck.

"Fire coral is not indigenous to our shores, and certainly not to the Thames." Withers was simply relaying what some boffin had told him only moments before. "This particular species is most likely Egyptian."

Not liking the sound of it, Dineage stuffed the necklace back into its bag. "So, we have a reject from the Dorrit Moussaieff range all covered in Egyptian scum. This does keep getting weirder and weirder."

"There's certainly something not quite right about it," Withers concurred.

"Would you like me to employ the services of a cryptozoologist, sir, or would you rather find one of your own choosing?"

"Leave it with me," Dineage said. The constable was already moving towards the door. "Oh, and one more thing before you go about your business."

"Sir?"

"What's a cryptozoologist?"

* * *

Maurice Burton was feeding his menagerie when the telephone rang; the lament of the hungry scorpions was almost palpable as he rushed from the room and into the hallway.

"Yes?" he said into the telephone.

"Is this Professor Burton from the Museum of Natural History?" asked a slightly flustered voice.

"Depends," Burton replied. "If this is anything to do with the queen or the coronation, then I'm certainly not the man with whom you wish to speak."

The voice laughed. Burton moved his ear away from the receiver as it crackled and fizzled. "My name's Detective Thomas Dineage, and I assure you that what I have to tell you is far more important than plonking a crown on Elizabeth's head."

"In that case," Burton said, "I'd be glad to help. Don't get out of the house much these days. Give me an address and I'll be over presently."

Upon arriving at Bow Street, Maurice Burton was treated like royalty, as if it was he being crowned that very same day and not the beautiful queen. In truth, it could only mean that something was drastically wrong, something that the Old Bill could not fathom and therefore required the assistance of an expert. Their unnecessary—yet not unwelcome—treatment of him only served to make him more nervous.

Dineage introduced himself, and then a constable standing next to him, before ushering him into the office, where it was mustier than a stately home gone to rot. "Would you care for a glass of something?" Dineage asked, reluctant to break out the good stuff, but sensing that it might relieve the tension.

The curator of sponges from the museum shook his head. "Haven't touched a drop since 1939," he said. "The last time I imbibed I got into a heated discussion with a sailor about the existence of Bigfoot, and it didn't end well for either of us."

Dineage indicated the free chair. "Have a seat," he said. "I heard you were the best person to speak to with regards to mysterious creatures and the inexplicable."

Burton lifted a hand as if to stop the detective before he got himself in too deep. "I am a man of *science*, detective," he said, "and believe in nothing of the unexplained until I witness it with my own eyes."

Withers made his excuses to leave and executed them, closing the door softly as he went.

"I'm going to get straight to the point here," Dineage said as he lowered himself into the chair opposite the confused-looking gent. "Last night there were three murders on the Thames."

"Happens a lot," Burton sneered. "You might want to go through the proper channels to recruit more officers. I hardly think I'm qualified."

Dineage poured himself a large scotch and swallowed it down on three hungry gulps. Burton appeared perturbed by what was occurring, but didn't object just yet, though according to his expression it was forthcoming.

"What we've come to understand is that whatever murdered these three men was not, how can I put it, not human, or anything *like* it."

And now Dineage had the man's attention. He was enraptured, and listened eagerly as the detective recounted the evidence.

"And where are these bodies now?" Burton asked. "I really *must* see them to make a proper assessment."

"You'll get the chance," Dineage said, satisfied that he had cast his line and caught a spectacular one. "But first I need to show you something that we believe to be of import to the case."

He pushed the plastic evidence bag across the table towards Burton, who stared intently down at it and its contents. "And this would be?"

"Something or nothing," Dineage reported whilst pouring another large whisky. "Thought you might have seen something like this before on your travels, or…" He paused as Burton proceeded to unfurl the bag and remove the necklace. He turned it over once, twice, thrice, and that was when something uncanny happened.

His eyes rolled back into his head; the creepy whites stared out at Dineage, causing hackles to rise almost immediately. He watched for but a moment before asking the man if he was okay.

There was no response, for the man was lost to the necklace's power, to another world that revealed itself to him in all its ghastly splendor.

* * *

Beneath the ocean, a thousand creatures stirred. As the sea whipped all around him, he could only pray that these god-awful Deep Ones didn't notice his presence, for they were many and he was but one—not that it made the slightest difference.

He watched as a shoal of dark, ominous entities drifted through the water ahead; the merest of squeaks escaped his lungs, and air-bubbles meandered in front of him momentarily.

This could not be, *he thought.* This was beyond the realms of anything science had discovered. A smaller assemblage of Deep Ones floated across; these were not fish, though they were possessed of fish heads and palpitating gills at the side of their necks. The scaly spines stretching across their backs were in complete contradiction with their otherwise smooth and slippery flesh.

He believed he was on the verge of insanity as he watched them cavort, and he did his utmost not to move or make a sound, fearing what might happen should the demons discover his intrusion.

These creatures dispersed quickly as an even greater threat suddenly appeared. At first he thought it was the sea-bed moving, and in a way it was, for the entirety of it shifted, as if by a seismological event. It was only upon the appearance of the first tentacles that he realized the whole of the sea-bed was, in fact, a living creature. Something so enormous that the ocean swelled with its emergence.

He felt so debilitated that he couldn't move a muscle, and although that had been his previous wish, he now hoped to swim as far away, as quickly as possible, from this gargantuan demon.

Tentacles whorled around him, coiling and uncoiling like fleshy springs. He felt the water parting in front of his face, and then collapsing once again. If there was a hell, and he was almost certain there was, then it would be something very similar to this.

A slippery tentacle knocked him from his feet, latching on and curling around his shin so tightly that he suspected it was the creature's intention to separate it from the rest of him.

And then he heard it; a rhythmic chanting that was so clear it could not possibly be underwater.

"Ph'nglui mglw'nafh Cthulhu R'lyeh wgah'nagl fhtagn."

He knew not what it meant, but it was impossible not to lose oneself to it as it repeated over and over again.

And the tentacles danced through the ocean, the Deep Ones making way for their master, to the beautiful lament of the incessant chant...

* * *

"Are you okay?" the detective asked a few inches in front of his face. Burton could smell the whisky upon Dineage's breath, and almost gagged as it reached his nostrils.

"Wh... what happened?" His head was sore, as if he'd collapsed and hit it against something hard and sharp.

"You passed out, I think," Dineage said. "Do you want me to call an ambulance, or something?"

Burton frantically shook himself, as if it would help with the terrible nausea he was feeling. It was only upon glancing down at the necklace in his open palm that everything came back to him. The mysterious chant in an undiscovered language; the Deep Ones swimming around the ocean, awaiting the rise of their master, and then that many-tentacled beast that spanned the length and breadth of the sea bed.

"We have to put this back!" Burton gasped, holding the necklace aloft.

"'Scuse me?" was all Dineage could manage.

Burton scrambled from the chair, pushing the detective back with his free hand. When he was upright, he said, "We have no time to waste, Detective! This has to be returned to wherever it was fished from. Oh, the *madness*, please, you must help!"

The madness, Dineage thought, was a good way to sum up Burton. "That's evidence," he said. "Three men were murdered, and that might be—"

"Your victims weren't *murdered*, Detective," Burton said, his eyes wide open as if experiencing some sort of epiphany. "They were the unfortunate result of fishing in the wrong part of the Thames. This is an ancient relic, Detective, much older than anything else on this earth. It must be returned, and pronto!"

The curator was already moving towards the door; the necklace swung loosely in his grasp.

"Hang on a minute," Dineage said as he lunged across the room after the madman. "If you're thinking of dropping that thing back in the river—"

"I'm not thinking *anything*," Burton said, doing an about-face on the spot. "I'm *doing* it, and you should be thanking me for assisting you in your case."

Dineage was about to reproach the man for his silliness when the crowd outside his window suddenly fell silent. It was odd that they should just quit chanting like that, and even odder that nothing—not even the noise of traffic or birdsong—could be heard now that the crowd had piped down.

Both men turned to the window; Burton's expression slightly edged it in the "who can look the most afraid?" competition.

That was when the screaming started.

* * *

The crowds were no longer lining the streets awaiting the coronation procession. They were running and screaming. As Dineage and Burton fell out of Bow Street Station, followed closely by a dozen other policemen and officials, neither of them could see what had caused such ado.

"What's the matter with everyone?" Withers asked, as if one of the other constables had an inkling. "They look like they've seen a ghost."

Burton squeezed the necklace in his white-knuckled fist. It seemed to be burning, thrumming, and he didn't know how long he would be able to hold onto it.

"People are abandoning their motorcars," Dineage said. "What on earth is going—"

He didn't get to finish his sentence as an enormous shadow was cast over them. The sun was blotted out in an instant, and Dineage's first thoughts were of solar eclipses. His second were of terrifying mushroom clouds, expanding outwards and swallowing everything in their path. He arched his neck and gazed to the sky, and should have been pleased that it wasn't the latter.

It was much worse.

Three large figures, black and slick as if they were wholly comprised of oil, hovered over the city. Dineage shrank into himself as his eyes fell upon them, and his heart rate increased exponentially.

"Am I seeing this?" he just about managed. "Please, for the love of God, tell me this is all part of the coronation ceremony."

"Do they look like blimps to you?" Burton spat as he raced down the steps in front of the station. He practically threw himself into the path of a black cab, which didn't seem all too keen on the idea of stopping. Burton rolled slowly over the bonnet, still clenching the necklace in his trembling fist. Landing on the pavement—surprisingly on his feet—he called up to Dineage. "We need to get to the Thames, Detective. It's the only way to stop this."

Off in the distance, somebody screamed, and when Dineage glanced skyward, he could see only two of the foul abominations circling The Theatre Royal. The third creature reappeared a moment later, thrashing its barbed tail to rise high into the sky, its wings flapping so quickly they were barely visible. It was carrying something—no, someone—and they were screaming, begging to be released, which would not be such a great idea from such a height.

The creature paused, and for a split-second its veined wings stretched the length of the sky. Then it tore the body into two pieces and released them.

"The Thames it is," Dineage said, rushing down the steps and joining Burton beside the taxi cab. The driver clambered out of the car and wished them all the best before disappearing into the escaping crowd.

"Well, don't just stand there," Dineage said. "Get in the bleedin' car."

Burton climbed in, and the detective pulled away from the station, watching in his rear-view mirror as the constables standing atop the steps were pounced upon by one of the things.

"Ph'nglui mglw'nafh Cthulhu R'lyeh wgah'nagl fhtagn," Burton said, staring into the mirror of the pendant with bulging eyes and a mouth so wide open that Dineage thought it might have become dislocated.

"What?" Dineage asked, being careful not to run over any of the panicked crowd crossing the road.

"I don't know," Burton said, "but this thing I'm holding right now is more dangerous than anything mankind has ever conceived."

"You know what those things are back there," Dineage said, swerving to avoid an elderly lady standing stock-still in the road. "Something happened when you fainted. What the *hell* did you see?"

Burton sighed. He hadn't asked for any of this; his life was complicated enough cataloguing sponges and entertaining ex-students. On occasion he might socialize with the vets of WWI whilst partaking in a crossword puzzle, but this was something else. Finally, he said, "I believe there to be something deep beneath the ocean, something that wants to rule the world." He scratched his head, pondered what he was actually trying to say. "There is a creature unlike anything this world has seen, and it's biding its time, awaiting the right moment to strike. Don't ask me how I know this. I haven't the foggiest."

"What are those things back there?" Dineage asked. "They had no faces, but I swear they were smiling."

"Those are the things that killed your fishermen, detective. They're Deep Ones, but nothing like what we'll see should this relic not be returned to the depths."

"Oh, so the cheap piece of tat jewelry is the reason why those things are here," Dineage said, sardonically nodding. "The fishermen must have scooped it out of the Thames last night, which is why they were half-gnawed, and why those things are here now, eating the populace."

"Precisely," Burton said.

Dineage shook his head and tutted. "And on coronation day, of all days. What are the odds?"

"Rather long, one would imagine."

They made the short journey to the Thames in ten minutes flat, and would have been quicker had it not been for the screaming and flailing bodies in their way. Victoria Embankment was overrun with people trying to swim across the river to avoid certain slaughter at the hands of the oil-skinned demons.

"I'm too old for this," Burton said, holding his hand out. "All you have to do is take it, toss it into the river, and hopefully those Deep Ones will return from whence they came."

"*Hopefully?*" Dineage said. "Hopefully won't be enough to shake them off my back if I don't make it in bloody time." Regardless, he snatched the necklace out of the frightened man's hand and said, "And what if this *other* thing comes up and grabs me? Huh? What then?"

Burton shook his head. "Cthulhu won't rise for centuries yet." He winced as the words crossed his lips. Who was *Cthulhu* and how did he know its name? He shivered, shook it off, and said, "It's the Deep Ones we need to banish for now. They're not infallible; they can be returned to the depths."

Dineage wrapped his hand around the handle and was about to push the door open when there came a sudden *thunk* from above. Both men's heads snapped in the direction of the sound and they found themselves staring at a perfect dent in the cab's roof. Claws hadn't penetrated, but they had come close, leaving the unmistakable outline of the demon's feet. Wings suddenly dropped down on either side of the taxi; if it had been dark before, it was positively pitch now.

Dineage did what any sensible man would; he locked his door. Burton followed suit, and then stared across, awaiting the detective's next move.

"This was your idea," Dineage said with a tremulous voice. "I think it's safe to suggest it hasn't quite gone to plan."

The car rocked from side to side as the creature thrashed around on its roof. More paw prints appeared, and Dineage snatched his head aside to avoid being pounded.

"We need to get it to the river!" Burton said, stating the bleeding obvious. "You know what we must do!"

Dineage watched as a thick string of drool made its way down the windshield in front of them. The thing had moved, shifted its position atop the taxi cab, which could not mean anything good.

"What, man?" Dineage gasped. "I'm not going out there. Not a chance!"

"You don't have to," Burton replied, gesturing towards the steering wheel. "Just put the pedal to the metal."

In the first instance, Dineage believed the man sitting beside him had completely lost his marbles. What he was suggesting was suicide, or that was how Dineage envisaged it. He stared into the curator's eyes and could see the man was deadly serious. He was about to object, to suggest, perhaps, some other way out of the impossible predicament they were in, when the creature atop the cab tore the roof completely off and tossed it away.

A gloomy light filled the cab. Dineage glared up at the drooling creature. Its faceless head gawped in at them, and the detective suddenly understood the words the curator had used a few moments ago.

Ph'nglui mglw'nafh Cthulhu R'lyeh wgah'nagl fhtagn.

In his house at R'lyeh dead Cthulhu waits dreaming.

"Hold tight!" Dineage said, slamming his foot down on the accelerator. The cab jerked forward, and the Deep One slipped backwards through the air, its claws snatching to regain purchase on its intended victims, the possessors of the relic.

Dineage screamed, or tried to, as they careered down Victoria Embankment, passing trees, shrubs, and screaming escapees. In his left hand, the necklace dangled, flicking his knuckles as they bounced down the incline, out of control and, Dineage thought, out of their minds.

When the water hit, it came as a relief. It meant there was no more embankment, and subsequently no more bumpy off-roading. The cab was immediately pulled down, as if by invisible hands.

Or tentacles, Burton thought, which didn't help matters.

Dineage wasted no time in releasing the troublesome trinket. He even watched it start to sink into the murky waters. It was only after a few seconds that he realized they were following it down.

* * *

When he regained consciousness, it came with that confusion whereby one simply wants a few moments to compose oneself, to figure out what in hell caused said unconsciousness in the first place. The collection of heads hovering above him prevented him from having that respite.

"Wh-what?" Dineage managed as he pushed himself up onto his haunches. It became clear that he was soaked to the bone and sitting on a riverbank; he didn't profess to being Sherlock Holmes, but even he could figure out what might have happened.

"Are you okay?" a voice asked. Dineage recognized this voice, and turned to find a face—which he also recognized—staring down at him. The curator was also drenched; his silvery hair clung to his face as if it had been painted on.

"B-Burton," the detective coughed. Simultaneously, he recalled the hulking, dark demons that had pursued them to the Thames, and the tacky necklace he had returned to its rightful home. "What happened to the things?"

The curator held a placatory hand out to prevent Dineage from standing. "Everything's okay," he said, trying to forget about all the people who had been unceremoniously slaughtered by the Deep Ones. "They went back down after the relic. We *did* it, detective. We saved the world."

Dineage stood, dismissing Burton's assistance. "But those things will return," he said. "They're only dormant, Burton. You said it yourself. And what about the Great One? What about Cthulhu?"

People gasped all around, as if they were familiar with the name. Their expressions altered, however, to something like confusion. They knew the name, *sure*, but they couldn't say where from.

"We can't dwell upon such things," Burton said. "For it is enough simply knowing that it exists. What we must do is prepare, and await its emergence confidently."

Dineage snorted. "That's your plan?"

"Better than yours," Burton replied. "Come on. That whisky in your office sounds good right about now, don't you think?"

Certainly, Dineage thought. It sounded just tickety-boo, but for how long would the numbness it provided last, and how the hell were they to prepare for the imminent or distant arrival of an ancient evil?

"Whisky sounds good," he said as they clambered up the embankment, through the gathering of confused and frightened Londoners. When they were out of sight, one person in the crowd whispered lowly, followed shortly by another, and before long it had spread like wildfire.

Ph'nglui mglw'nafh Cthulhu R'lyeh wgah'nagl fhtagn, they said, and turned to the river and waited.

The Birdy Burger

A. P. Sessler

The four-door sports wagon sputtered up the dark beach road toward the Birdy Burger. The longtime popular eatery stood ahead on the left, the property well illuminated except for its parking lot, which sat opposite a beach access hidden in darker and more ominous shadow.

"There it is," said Bradley from the rear driver's-side seat.

"Duh, we can see," said Chelsea, separated from Bradley by two six-foot surfboards running between the bucket seats into the rear storage.

"I'm so hungry," said Lucy, seated shotgun.

"Not the Birdy Burger. That," clarified Bradley with a wave of his finger to the right.

A certain dread fell upon the anxious youths when they saw the yellow police tape that barred entrance to the beach access thrashing violently in the wind—a reminder that the appetite of both human and beast had been satisfied in the same stop.

"Okay, we've had an awesome day. Don't go bumming me out," said Chelsea.

"Who was the last one?" Tom asked, staring at the road ahead as he drove.

"Some Russian," Bradley answered.

"Stop it," demanded Chelsea.

"All right. Don't get your thong in a wad," said Bradley.

"It's not a thong," she said.

The smell of grilling meat upon the wind quickly regained the hungry passengers' attention, a far better reminder that food always comforts the living eventually, even after death. Tom pulled into the dimly lit, half-empty parking lot and took the first spot on the left he could find.

The Birdy Burger was one of the few family-owned ice cream and burger joints that remained along the beach road. It was a throwback to the '50s diners, the archetype of what good food was supposed to look like, smell like, taste like, and cost (the current value of a dollar being considered). Its sight alone had the power to conjure quasi-primeval memories of chocolate-dipped ice cream cones, malted milk shakes, steak-cut French fries with a bottle of Heinz ketchup, and thick cheeseburgers bigger than the buns dripping with enough grease to give a health nut a heart attack just by looking at it.

The restaurant's dining room was the outdoors. Salt air from the ocean breeze flavored your fries and beat any indoor air conditioning, even if it wasn't half as cool. To one side of the parking lot, round concrete tables that could seat up to six had been set up, while the other side had long, rectangular, cedar plank tables for larger parties. Huge canvas umbrellas shaded the tables in the day and gave summer lovers privacy at night.

"Yes! We got here before the crowd!" said Lucy.

"Barely," Chelsea complained.

"It's not that bad," Tom defended his car. "It just makes a little noise and eats a lot of oil."

"A little noise?" said Bradley. "Dude, it sounds like Nine Inch Nails is under your hood! You need to get it fixed!"

"I will when I get the money," said Tom, exasperated from it all.

"So what's keeping you?" asked Bradley.

"You know," said Tom as he turned his head to look at them out of his right eye, "I don't remember either of you two ever offering me gas money."

"You never ask Lucy for gas money."

"That's different," said Tom, then turned away.

"Well, I'm sorry man. I just don't go that way, you know."

"Brad!" barked Tom. His angry eyes stared at Bradley in the rear view mirror.

"All I'm saying is just ask your dad. It's not like he's hurting financially," explained Bradley as he flexed his shoulders repeatedly.

"Just ignore him," insisted Lucy.

The way she cocked her head and batted her eyes at Tom made him forget how badly he wanted to punch Bradley in the face. Tom pulled the hood release lever. When the four friends got out of the car, Tom walked to the back and opened the hatch while the others headed to the restaurant.

"You coming?" asked Lucy.

"I need to put more oil in. If I'm not there before someone else gets in line, order my usual."

"A Birdy Burger with French fries and a Dr. Pepper?" she asked to confirm his order.

"Chili cheese fries," he corrected her.

"Got it," she said.

He moved the Styrofoam cooler aside and found the bucket he kept all his car fluids in, then sifted through the various containers until he found the oil. With a gentle shake he discovered to his disappointment the bottle was nearly empty, then remembered his food.

"Oh, and I'll pay you back!" he yelled at Lucy before looking up, thinking she was already in line.

She stopped and turned around. "If you're not in line by time I order, it'll be my treat," she said with a smile.

He smiled back. It was her little kindnesses that made him happy, and his personal problems——those vehicle related included—seem much smaller. She joined Tom and Chelsea in front of the large wooden menu board with its hand-painted lettering to place their orders.

The cashier smiled a mouthful of crooked teeth and red gums. "Welcome to the Birdy Burger. How can I help you?"

Lucy held in her disgust. "I'd like the Chili Penguin Dog, a Diet Coke, a Birdy Burger with chili cheese fries, and a Dr. Pepper," she said.

The cashier wrote her order on a small pad, then rang it into the register. "All right, that'll be theventeen-theventy-thix."

Lucy snickered softly as she reached into her purse and gave him her bank card, which he promptly ran and returned, along with the necessary receipts, one for her to sign and one to keep. She stood aside so Chelsea could order.

"And for you, mith?" asked the cashier.

Chelsea looked at Lucy and giggled at his obvious lisp. "I just want some French fries and a water," she said.

"Is that all you're gonna get?" asked Bradley.

"Hmm. You're right. That's not gonna be enough. Should I? I think I should," she thought aloud. "I'll also take the Death by Chocolate sundae," she said confidently.

"I bet you will, cow!" teased Lucy.

"Who are you calling cow, heifer?" said Chelsea with her sassy hands on her sassy hips.

"Did somebody say Hefner?" Bradley jumped in. "He doesn't do cows—he only does bunnies."

"Shut up, perv," said Lucy with a roll of her eyes.

The cashier cleared his throat. "That will be eight forty-two," he said.

"Oh, sorry," said Chelsea, reaching into her purse to retrieve her bank card.

Tom closed the hood of his car and tossed the empty container into a nearby trash can, then joined his friends at the order window.

"And who's next?" the cashier asked.

"Did you already order?" Tom asked Lucy.

"Don't worry. I got you, babe," she said and smiled.

He pulled her to him with a strong arm and kissed her forehead. "Thank you," he said softly.

"Guess that leaves me," said Bradley as he stepped up to the window.

"What will you be having tonight, sir?"

Bradley couldn't contain his laughter or his disgust. "Whoa!" he said, noticing the man's unpleasant mouth. He continued to laugh until Tom planted a sturdy elbow in his ribs. "Ow!" Bradley yelped.

"Sir?" the cashier repeated, unaffected. "What will you be having tonight?"

Bradley looked back at the cashier, then with a slow, intended glance that drew the cashier's attention to Chelsea, he answered, "Hopefully her. But for an appetizer, I'll have the When Pigs Fly Burger and a large order of onion rings and a large Coke."

"All right," said the cashier, unamused as he rang in the order. "That will be thirteen sixty-eight."

Bradley pulled a wadded $20 out of his pocket. When he received his change, he put the bills in his pocket and the remaining coins in the tip jar, which didn't amuse the cashier either.

The man prepared their drinks and placed them in the order window.

"Your orders will be up shortly," he said with a wide, toothy smile.

As the four walked to one of the smaller tables with their drinks, they searched the faces in the crowd for friends, but didn't recognize a soul.

"Looks like the tourons are out tonight," said Bradley.

"Dude, shut it," said Tom. "Remember, those *tourons* are our lifeblood."

"Yeah, yeah. You say that until they come to a dead stop in the fast lane."

The four had just seated themselves when the cashier came from the left of the building and approached them.

"I hope I'm not interrupting you," he said, his hands gripping some coupons with the intensity one holds copper divining rods. There was a noticeable tremor in every word and movement. "But as the new owner of the Birdy Burger, I just wanted to present these twenty-percent off coupons to you as a way of showing our appreciation for your continued patronage."

"Aw, thanks, man," said Tom.

"Yeah, thank you," the others said as they received the coupons from the cashier.

"So when did you take over this place?" Tom asked.

"Not long ago. The previous owners presented an offer we just couldn't refuse, so we bit," the cashier answered. "Now, if you don't mind my asking, how long have you all been dining at the Birdy Burger?"

"We've been coming here since we were kids," said Tom.

The others nodded their heads in agreement.

"That's superb," said the cashier. "Thank you all so much for coming out tonight."

"No prob, man," said Tom.

"Yeah," said the others.

"What's your name?" asked Tom, as he extended his hand. "Since you'll probably be seeing a lot of us from now on."

"Mister Karkarinas, but you can call me Mister K," answered the cashier. He wiped his hand on his apron before shaking Tom's hand. "And on the grill would be the Missus."

He extended his arm and opened palm, inviting them to see his wife, who was hard at work preparing the meals by herself for the nearly twenty seated diners.

With her dark hair in a tight bun, she wore a yellow company t-shirt and black pants. Her back was slightly hunched as she slaved over the hot stove, her arms in constant motion.

When he called to his wife, the group gave a loud hello. She turned around and smiled with a closed mouth and raised brow. She offered a small bow with her head in their direction, then continued cooking.

"I'm Tom and this is Lucy. And that's Brad and Chelsea."

"Hi," said Chelsea with a wave.

"My pleasure," answered Mr. K.

Just then another car pulled up, drawing Mr. K's attention away from the table.

"That's my cue to get back to work," he said. "It was nice meeting you all, and thanks again for coming out!"

When he turned to walk back toward the counter, it was apparent that he, too, had a hunch of sorts. He went through the door, disappeared momentarily, then reappeared at the order window, ready for the next carload of hungry customers about to walk up.

"That was nice," said Lucy.

"Yeah, he seems sweet," Chelsea said, then took a sip of her water.

"Dude, did you see the teeth on that guy?" said Bradley, beaming with amusement.

"Shut up!" said Lucy. "He can't help it!"

"Yeah," Chelsea agreed. "Grow up!"

"I bet he goes through a tooth brush a week with that many teeth," Bradley continued. "And did you hear that theriouth thpeech impediment the dude wath thporting?"

"He probably has all his wisdom teeth still in," suggested Tom.

"Ah! Here we go," said Bradley, motioning with his hands and mocking Tom with a deep, funny voice: "My dad's a dentist so I know everything about teeth."

"Shut up, man!" said Tom. "I know what I'm talking about. When you have all your wisdom teeth, the rest of your teeth don't have any room left, so they start crowding each other. And those red, puffy gums are just screaming gingivitis."

"Ew, gross!" said Chelsea.

"See, I'm not the only one who noticed how jacked up his mouth was," said Bradley.

"Yeah, but at least he didn't say anything about it," defended Lucy.

"So that makes it okay?" said Bradley. "*He* can think it, but *I* can't say it? It's the same with sex. It's okay that he wants it as long as he doesn't say that's what he wants. You're all hypocrites!"

"Dude!" said Tom as he threw a quick glance at Bradley.

Lucy leaned into Tom's shoulder and laughed. "Why don't you give him your father's business card?"

"I don't wanna insult the guy," said Tom.

Lucy laughed again. "Somebody needs to tell him."

"See!" pointed Bradley. "Even she can joke about it and I'm still the jerk!"

Chelsea sang a line from an old song. "Some things will never change."

Bradley put his palms on his thighs and shook his head in disbelief.

They continued to chat until four "Order's up" produced their meals. As they sat down to eat, Lucy doted on the box her Chili Penguin Dog rested in.

"Look how cute it is," she said, her eyes on the verge of tears.

The box had little, black cardboard "flippers" on the sides and orange "feet" on the bottom.

"Oh my gosh, you say that every single time you order that," said Chelsea. "It comes in the same box it's come in since we were kids."

"Shut up. It's cute," said Lucy as she ran her finger along the contours of the black-and-white box.

The guys shook their heads and bit into their burgers.

Most of their meal was bite, chew, swallow, sip, swallow, repeat, with very little talk. As the meal grew to a close, conversation once more surfaced between bites.

"It's so hot!" said Lucy, taking another sip of her drink. "I could really go for a swim."

"Not me," said Tom.

"It's so hot I'd even go skinny dipping," said Chelsea. She glanced at Bradley and waited for a reaction. "Bradley? Wouldn't you like to go skinny dipping?"

Bradley laughed. "With all the other shark bait? You're not *that* hot!"

Chelsea pouted and turned her back to him.

"That's not funny, Bradley," Lucy scolded.

"It wasn't meant to be," he said. "No one in his right mind would swim at this access, especially at night."

"On the news they said the shark attacks were caused by the fisherman," said Lucy.

"They probably were," he agreed. "Stupid fishermen chumming for sharks."

"As much as I hate finding one of their hooks the hard way, it's not the fishermen this time," argued Tom.

"What makes you say that?" asked Chelsea, turning her head to join the conversation with her back still to Bradley.

"I would believe it if we were near one of the piers," said Tom, "but what idiot would be chumming from shore? He'd have just as much a chance of getting bit."

"You're right," realized Lucy. "That's weird."

"That's not the weird part," said Bradley. "What's really weird is that it's been happening like clockwork. Always at night, and always at this access. The news ain't saying much, but the cops are parked at two different piers just to make sure no one heads this way. Still, people are dropping like flies. I guess the cops are too tired from their donut sugar crash to do anything."

"All right. I'm officially bummed. Thanks everyone," said Chelsea.

"Eat the rest of your sundae," suggested Lucy.

Just as Chelsea took a satisfying spoonful into her mouth, Lucy added, "I knew that would cheer you up—cow."

"Shut up," laughed Chelsea.

Bradley looked across the street at the dark beach access. All conversation went silent, and the only sounds he heard were the beating wind upon the police tape and the lure of crashing ocean waves hidden behind the dune line.

A blur of fingers passed before his eyes.

"Brad? Hello?" Tom said as he waved his hand in front of Bradley's face.

The noise of every table's conversation rose back to full volume.

"You ready, bro?" Tom asked his dazed friend.

"Sure," said Bradley as he fought to turn his eyes away from the beach. "Let's go."

The four friends piled back into the car and sputtered down the dark road toward the pier parking lot.

* * *

"Man, that was an awesome session," said Brad as he placed his surfboard in the back of Tom's car. "Who wants to hit the Birdy Burger for some grub?"

"Me!" volunteered Chelsea. "I could so use another Death by Chocolate."

"Not me," said Tom, pulling the seatbelt strap over his shoulder. "I'm still digesting lunch from Half Shells. What about you, Luc?"

"I can always eat some Birdy Burger," Lucy answered.

She carefully leaned back in the seat to avoid disturbing the gauze bandage near the small of her back. "Ow. It still hurts," she said.

"Wuss," Chelsea teased her.

"Shut up. It's not funny," Lucy whined.

"It's not like it's the first tattoo you've ever gotten," Bradley reminded her.

"So? It still hurts," she said.

"You gonna be all right, babe?" Tom asked her.

She looked at him and pouted childishly. "Yeah."

"All right, then. The Birdy Burger it is," he said and put the car in drive.

The sun began its quick descent as they drove down the empty road.

"Where is everyone?" asked Lucy.

"Yeah, it's like a ghost town," said Chelsea.

"Duh. It's change-over day. All the tourons are heading home from their lovely vacation," said Bradley.

He saw Tom's eyes glaring at him in the rear view mirror.

"The *tourists*, I mean," Bradley corrected himself.

When they reached their final destination, the sun had just set behind the restaurant. Like the long stretch of road, the parking lot was empty. As usual, Tom parked to the left of the building facing home.

"Awesome! No waiting line," he said, but his enthusiasm was quickly extinguished when he noticed his OIL light was on. "Of course."

The three approached the order window while Tom tended to his vehicle.

"Hello, kids!" greeted Mr. K with a wave.

"Hey, Mister K," they said.

"It's kinda nice to have the place all to ourselves," said Lucy.

"You're here earlier than usual," noted Mr. K.

"How's business been?" Bradley asked.

"Oh, you know," said Mr. K. "It's either feast or famine."

"I hear ya," said Bradley. "Speaking of feast, I bet you and your wife get hungry working at this place, huh?"

"Seriously, I would get so fat if I worked here," said Chelsea.

"Are you allowed to eat while you work?" Lucy asked.

"Of course they are," said Bradley. "They're the owners."

Chelsea disagreed. "That's a health violation," she said. "Not that I care. I'm a server. I know how hungry you get taking everyone's food out to them. And the amount of food we throw away is ungodly."

"The key," said Mr. K, "is self-control. One must know when to say 'when.' But I'm sure you all didn't come out just to *talk* about food, so what will we be eating tonight?"

While the three placed their orders, Mrs. K finished tidying up the kitchen. Atop a high shelf, a small transistor radio played 50s rock 'n' roll from some faraway AM station. The woman smiled, lost in a distant memory as The Flamingos' "I Only Have Eyes For You" chimed over the air. When the song ended, her expression returned to its stoic state.

"You're listening to WSLT, Salt Radio," said the prerecorded announcer, followed by a female doo-wop choir singing the station's call sign, "W-S-L-T." A Latin rhythm instrument shook several times, followed by the same announcer's voice, "The Salt."

After a small pause, a newsman spoke. "In breaking news, another shark attack occurred last night on the Outer Banks of North Carolina, gaining further nationwide attention while causing concern for locals and tourists. Shark experts from Virginia and North Carolina have been asked to investigate the mysterious trend that continues to baffle local authorities and marine biologists. The attacks have consistently occurred at the beach access area located at milepost . . ."

Mrs. K turned off the radio and began preparing the orders her husband had taken.

"Your food will be out shortly," he told the three as he placed their drinks in the window and turned to tidy up his counter.

The three took their drinks and walked toward a nearby table.

"Oh, Lucy," said Chelsea. "You're bleeding."

Mr. K's hunched back suddenly went straight.

Lucy looked down at the bandage on her back. The gauze had so filled with blood that it began trickling down her side. Chelsea took Lucy's drink and placed it on a table with her own."I knew this would happen," said Lucy. "I have the worse luck with these things."

Mr. K turned and saw the blood running down the young woman's waist and over her buttocks. He licked his lips.

"They sure seem to be eating well," said Mr. K, licking his lips again.

"That-th what we do," said Mrs. K with an all-too-familiar lisp. "I get tho tired theeing all thethe thkinny girlth and boyth with their boneth thowing."

"I feel the same way," he said as he grabbed a red and white-checkered towel and wiped his forehead.

"Excuse me," said Chelsea as she approached the order window and pulled several napkins from the chrome dispenser that sat on the small ledge.

She returned to her friend and began to assist her. Chelsea pulled Lucy's bandage back and wiped the excess blood away with a few napkins. When they were too full to hold any more blood, she placed them on the concrete table.

Mr. K's pupils dilated as he focused on the bloodied napkins. His eyes rolled into the back of his head momentarily, then followed the air conditioning ducts along the ceiling to their vents, where he was sure he could smell the scent of blood.

Chelsea used the remaining napkins to finish the job, then lowered the bandage and pressed on the surgical tape to reseal it to Lucy's skin. She walked to a nearby garbage can and disposed of the bloody napkins.

Mr. K turned unusually pale. He licked his lips and swallowed hard, his mouth completely dry. He sat down in a chair beside the order window.

"Something the matter?" asked his wife, her back turned to him as she continued to cook over the hot grill.

His stomach tightened and his shoulders bowed in convulsion as he felt his condition worsen. He ran to the bathroom to the left of the kitchen and closed the door.

"What's wrong, dear?" asked his wife as she approached the bathroom.

Through the closed door she heard him mumble in a painful tone. "I saw blood."

"Where?" she asked.

A moment later came the answer. "One of the girls."

"I'm sorry you have to suffer from your condition, but I suppose it's better to do so now when business is slow rather than the middle of a rush."

"Yes, dear," he moaned.

"Don't worry," she said. "We'll get you something to take care of that real soon."

She listened until she heard another moan. "Poor baby," she said as she returned to the stove and continued cooking.

"Order up!" the call came twice within a matter of minutes.

Chelsea and Lucy took their food and returned to the table to eat.

"Order up!" came the final call.

Bradley came to the window to pick up his usual bacon cheeseburger and onion rings. "Thanks," he said, but Mrs. K had already returned to the grill.

The food looked and smelled absolutely terrific. He squeezed the bottle of ketchup over his onion rings only to hear the familiar sound of air mixed with the last remaining squirts stuck to the bottom.

"Excuse me," he said as he placed his hand over his stomach, hoping to elicit a laugh from Mrs. K.

"Yes, thir, what do you need?" she asked, still at the grill.

Bradley rolled his eyes when she didn't appreciate his humor. "The ketchup is empty," he informed her as he held the bottle up for her to see. "Do you have any more?"

She quietly approached a shelf and retrieved another bottle of ketchup. She came to the order window and replaced the empty bottle with the full one.

"Thanks," said Bradley with a smile, then squeezed ketchup over his onion rings.

"You're welcome, thir," Mrs. K smiled back, revealing the same toothy smile and red gums as her husband.

When Bradley looked up from his onion rings and saw her smile, he gently placed the bottle back onto the order window's ledge. He closed his mouth as his eyebrows raised as high as they would go, then he turned and quickly headed back to the table. When he arrived, Tom was still missing and the girls were busy eating.

Bradley couldn't contain his observation. "They have the same exact smiles and lisp," he said.

"What?" asked Chelsea.

"Who?" asked Lucy.

"Mister and Missus Karkarinas," answered Bradley. "They both look and sound just alike. Did the dude marry his sister?"

Chelsea laughed. "Are they from Lucy's hometown?"

"Shut up!" said Lucy.

"You and Tom met at church, right?" continued Chelsea. "Doesn't that make you brother and sister, 'in the Lord'?" she asked, raising her hands and shaking them in a mock hallelujah.

"You're going to Hell," teased Lucy.

"Where *is* Tom?" asked Bradley.

"Where do you think?" said Chelsea.

Bradley looked over at the car, the hatch left open. He rolled a large onion ring in the bath of ketchup and forced the whole thing in his mouth. As he laboriously chewed, he got up from the table and walked over to the car, where Tom struggled with a container of oil.

Bradley swallowed the last bit of onion ring. "Hey bud," he said as he used his tongue to wipe the remnants of food off his teeth. "Why you bothering with this now?"

"Because I can't afford a new car," said Tom, his voice strained. "I just wish I could just get this stupid bottle open."

"Here," said Bradley, pulling a buck knife out of his pocket. "Let me give it a shot." He popped the blade out of the handle and motioned for Tom to give him the container.

"I'm done," said Tom as he handed it to Bradley, exhausted from the fight.

Bradley held the container with one hand and, with the knife in the other, attempted to pry the ring loose from the lid. "I can't hardly see," he said. "Wish they had more light here."

He squinted his eyes tight to focus in the near dark, then forced the blade between the lid and the ring. "All right," he said. He gave the blade a small shove to wedge it fully under the ring. "Almost there."

With one hand and thigh acting as a vice, he turned the blade until the edge was facing away from him. He gave another small shove and the blade cut right through the ring and into his left hand, just between the thumb and first finger.

"Ow!" he yelled. The container slipped from his hand and fell on the ground.

"What'd you do?" asked Tom, staring at the container to ensure the lid was still on.

"I cut my hand!" he yelled.

The girls stood from the table to see what was wrong.

"How bad is it?" asked Tom.

"It's not good," said Bradley. He placed the open knife on the inner frame of the hood. He squeezed around the cut to slow the bleeding, but it only forced more blood to drip onto the concrete parking lot.

"Hurry, go see if you can get in the bathroom and run it under cold water. Check if they have any Band-Aids."

As Bradley walked briskly toward the restaurant, Tom reached down and grabbed the container of oil. He unscrewed the lid and poured a quarter of the contents into the engine.

"What's going on?" asked Lucy.

Bradley didn't respond.

"Fine. Don't tell us," said Chelsea, then sat down to eat some more fries.

Lucy approached Tom. "What happened?" she asked.

"He cut his hand," answered Tom.

"Oh no," sympathized Lucy. "Will he be all right?"

"Yeah, he's just going to see if they got some Band-Aids."

"Poor guy," she said as she watched Bradley approach the order window.

"It's all my fault," said Tom, as he closed the hood, forgetting to remove Bradley's opened buck knife from the inner frame.

* * *

"Excuse me," said Bradley through the closed order window.

Mrs. K didn't hear him.

"Hello?" he said louder, and instinctively slapped his hand on the window to get her attention, forgetting it was covered in blood from nursing the other. He used his right forearm to wipe the bloody hand print off the window.

As she approached, her eyes darted from his face to the swirling red streaks on the glass. She slid the window open.

"Yes?" she asked. "How can I help you?"

"I kinda cut my hand," he said, revealing the bleeding gash.

"Oh my," said Mrs. K, then licked her lips.

"I was wondering if you had a Band-Aid or something," he said as he looked into the window himself for anything that could stop the bleeding. He spotted the checkered towel to his right at the end of the counter just inside the window. "Maybe an old towel?" he hinted.

"Oh my," said Mrs. K again, licking her lips as her fingers started to fidget with the pencil and order pad on the counter.

"If not, I need to get the key to the bathroom to run some cold water over it," he said.

"Oh my," she said for the third time, her furrowed brow and sad eyes relaying some inward terror she labored to hide.

"Yes," he said, growing tired of her inaction and mantra. "'Oh my' is right. Could I please get some help here?"

"We seem to have a bit of a problem."

"Yes, we do," he agreed. "*Myself* especially."

She turned and walked toward the bathroom. "Dear, are you almost done?"

There was no response. "Oh my," she said as she wrung her fingers together. She leaned her ear against the bathroom door and waited a moment, then pressed the side of her lips to it. "One of the boys has cut himself," she said softly. "He's bleeding real good."

She waited for him to say something, but all she heard was her husband's heaving and guttural groaning.

"Oh my," she said, as she approached a rack of key rings hanging on the back wall of the restaurant. In addition to the keys, each ring also contained a rectangular piece of wood with hand-painted lettering stating what it unlocked. She sifted through the various blocks of wood, reading the label on each.

Since she was moving slowly and had her back turned, Bradley reached inside the window for the towel he spotted previously. He used his right arm, which limited his agility and his vision. His fingertips had barely reached the towel when Mrs. K turned around with a key ring that read BATHROOM 1. Bradley instantly pulled his hand back through the

174

window, hoping she hadn't seen.

"Thank you," he said.

She looked up at him without saying a word, then back at her feet as she took baby step after baby step closer.

"Please," he said. "If you don't mind, could you hurry up?"

She continued at her slow pace until she reached the bathroom where her husband was. She faced the door and fidgeted to unlock it.

"Ma'am?" Bradley called. "I don't need the key to *that* bathroom. I need the key to the bathroom *outside*."

She didn't respond. Bradley reached back into the window with his left hand, unintentionally sprinkling the counter top with blood. As he looked through the glass pane, he saw the towel was just out of reach. He stuck his head through the window to get a straight shot. As he shimmied through the window just past his shoulders, his hand dripped blood onto the floor. He tried to squeeze his right arm in the window, but that was all of him that would fit through the small space.

His fingers had just reached the dish towel when he heard the bathroom door unlock. He turned his head to see a strange, pale hand with long, webbed fingers reaching out of the bathroom. Their pointed tips gripped the right side of the door frame. An identical hand reached out and pushed the door open slowly until it was flush against the wall. The two hands tensed, their bones elevating beneath the smooth skin, as they struggled to pull an unseen weight.

The mass the monstrous hands fought to free emerged from the bathroom. The thing was a seven-foot tall shark, lacking a tail but endowed with arms and legs. Around its ankles was a pair of unzipped pants, which it came out of as it took two steps forward.

"Run, lady!" yelled Bradley.

"Oh my," her voice trembled as she slowly looked up at the head of the huge creature she knew previously as her husband.

The creature looked down at her and opened its jaws wide, releasing a primal, aquatic roar. She bowed her head, her back hunching more so, as her body began to shake. There was the sound of heaving and groaning again, then she turned and faced Bradley.

"Run from what?" she asked, her voice suddenly gruff.

Her eyes grew pale and her pupils narrowed as her nose extended into a rounded point. Her mouth opened wider than human jaws allowed, forced wider still as her swelling gums protruded several inches. Rows of sharp teeth broke threw her gums behind her human teeth, which then elongated until their dull points were but the small tips of large, enameled daggers.

The hunch in her back tore through the yellow company t-shirt as the limp, folded fin erected into the terrible triangle banner every shark raises to wage war. Her chest expanded and split the shirt down the center, exposing her pale flesh beneath as it turned gray and glistened with blue-hued moisture beneath the fluorescent lighting.

Her fingertips became pointed, while the fingers themselves extended from their sockets, an extra digit grew, pushing the others out of joint. The flesh between her fingers stretched taut into translucent webbing. Her feet became long, flipper-like appendages, her toes also webbed from added digits. Like the thing that emerged from the bathroom, her transformation was complete.

The two creatures' nostrils flared as they caught the scent of Bradley's blood, from the small drops on the tile floor and larger drops on the linoleum counter, to the gash in Bradley's hand, which continued to pump out blood faster and faster as his heartbeat accelerated.

Bradley screamed as he squirmed to dislodge himself from the order window.

The others outside heard his scream.

"What's he doing now?" asked Chelsea.

The creatures were upon Bradley.

"What about self-control?" he asked, trying to reason with them. "Knowing when to say 'when?'"

The two creatures looked at each other. The larger one, once Mr. K, spoke in a gurgling voice, "When!" They turned away from each other to Bradley and converged on his trapped body.

* * *

Bradley's friends couldn't see anything other than his legs kicking frantically outside the order window.

"Is he pulling a joke?" asked Tom.

"I thought you said he cut his hand," said Lucy.

Tom walked toward the order window. "What are you—"

He saw the two shark creatures through the restaurant's small, blood-drenched windows, just as what was left of Bradley's body fell out of the window onto the parking lot. His head and left arm were missing. Blood poured from his neck and shoulder.

"Oh my God!" screamed Tom. "Everyone! Get in the car!"

The girls screamed hysterically at the sight of Bradley's mutilated

176

body.

"Hurry!" yelled Tom. "Get in the car now!"

Tom ran to the girls, who stood frozen.

"Come on!" he demanded. "Let's go!"

They cried and screamed, but refused to move.

He opened the passenger-side front and back door, then forced the two inside—Lucy in the front, Chelsea in the back.

He went to shut the front door, but Lucy's arm dangled limply at her side.

"Lucy," he pleaded. "Move your arm."

She didn't respond.

He heard the restaurant door slam into the wall as it flung open.

"Lucy, please," he repeated. "Move your arm out of the way."

She stared straight ahead, crying and gibbering.

He grabbed her hand and placed it in her lap, then slammed the door.

He came to shut the back door for Chelsea when she screamed. She saw the creatures slowly making their way toward Tom. Before he could close it, Chelsea grabbed the handle and pulled the door shut. She pushed the lock down, then reached over the seat and pushed Lucy's lock down.

Chelsea screamed again. When Tom turned around, he saw the creatures were just feet away. He ran from the passenger side to the open hatch of the car, looking for anything that could serve as a weapon. All he saw in the dim light were the bucket, cooler, and two surfboards upon which he and his now-dead best friend had caught so many memorable waves. He pulled his own board from between the bucket seats and tried to shield himself. The creature took a giant bite out of the board.

Tom turned the board bottom-side up and swung it at the creature. The board's fin carved a gash into the creature's chest. The beast swung with its right hand and knocked the board out of Tom's grip.

He ran to the driver's side, quickly opened the door, and hopped inside. He pulled the door shut, turned the key in the ignition, and put the car in drive. Seeing the impassable sandy lot before him, he threw the car into reverse.

The creature was too close and too large for the vehicle to knock down. The monster reached into the open hatch and clawed at anything in its way to get to Chelsea. It tore through the Styrofoam cooler in a violent explosion of water droplets and chunks of ice. Soda cans and bits of Styrofoam shrapnel hurtled through the air. The unopened cans dashed onto the parking lot, spinning, rolling, and shooting pinhole streams of fizz several feet in the air.

As the creature swung at the blinding flurry of soda, it managed to throw Bradley's surfboard aside, then the bucket of fluid containers and a spare tire.

"Drive!" screamed Chelsea. "Drive!"

"I can't!" yelled Tom. "We'll get stuck!"

"Just drive!" she yelled as she climbed between the two front seats.

All the while Lucy stared ahead speaking incoherently.

"Lucy!" yelled Chelsea, shaking her friend until she faced her. Out of her peripheral vision Chelsea saw the other creature coming toward the front passenger-side window. She screamed and jumped back into the rear seat; Lucy turned her head and resumed her blank stare.

The creature behind the car reached through the hatch and grabbed the jack. When it discarded the tool, Chelsea peered over the back seat into the hatch and spotted the only remaining item, a tire iron.

She reached for it, but the creature lunged at her. She withdrew her hand instantly, then both she and the creature reached for the tire iron. As its fingers touched the tapered tip of the iron, Chelsea gripped the lug wrench end and swung, burying it deep in the creature's arm. It staggered back several steps.

Tom looked through Lucy's open window and saw the other creature dangerously close. "Lucy! Roll up your window!" he yelled.

Chelsea spun around, and seeing what Tom saw, repeated his words, but their friend did not respond. Chelsea dropped the tire iron as Tom reached over Lucy to roll up her window, but the creature's menacing hands had already reached through the open window to take hold of Lucy. Her senses returned the moment its cool, moist skin came in contact with her own.

"Lucy!" shouted Tom and Chelsea, hoping she would offer some resistance when they took hold of her legs and waist.

When Lucy saw the creature's mouth opening wider and the jagged rows of arrowhead-shaped teeth waiting to greet her, her paralyzing fear gave way to a scream.

"Drive!" yelled Chelsea.

"I can't let go of her!" cried Tom.

"If you don't, we'll all die!" yelled Chelsea, still clutching her best friend's torso with both arms.

Tom released Lucy and put his hands on the wheel and his foot on the pedal. As the car went in reverse, Lucy's petite body was pulled out of Chelsea's arms through the window and into the hungry jaws of the creature. The creature behind the car had barely regained its bearings when the vehicle plowed into it and knocked it over, driving over its chest and neck.

It turned its head and bit the only thing within reach—the right rear tire. Tom shifted to drive. The tire spun in the creature's mouth, ripping several teeth from its bloody gums and breaking others still rooted within.

As Tom spun the wheel to his left, he saw the other creature and poor Lucy—her limp body suspended six feet off the ground between its jaws. The bloody gauze fell from her back, revealing for a fleeting moment the Celtic trinity knot she had recently tattooed above her left hip. She was so pretty, so peaceful and still with her eyes closed, even while the devilish thing chomped at her waist.

Tom hit the brakes. "Lucy!" he cried again.

"Go!" yelled Chelsea.

He pushed the pedal down and turned the car in an S-curve, exiting the parking lot and speeding down the highway as quickly as the car would go.

"Oh my God!" yelled Chelsea. "What just happened?"

"They killed Lucy and Bradley!" cried Tom. "Both of those things just killed them!" He wiped the tears from his eyes and the snot from his nose with his arm. "They're going to keep killing people until someone stops them!"

"What are you talking about?" Chelsea yelled.

Tom saw the fishing pier's nearly vacant parking lot ahead on his left. Without slowing, he pulled into it in a wide U-turn, then headed across the two-lane road and toward the Birdy Burger. The headlights of the police vehicle parked in front of the pier flashed on, followed by the siren, as the patrol car immediately pursued Tom's vehicle.

"Where are you going?" yelled Chelsea.

Tom didn't answer.

"Slow down and turn around before you get us killed!" she yelled as she leaned forward onto the front passenger seat and shook his shoulder.

Tom shrugged off her hand and spat a mouthful of tears and snot out the window. When Chelsea heard the siren, she turned to see the patrol car gaining on them. Tom seemed deaf to the siren's wail and blind to the flashing lights from behind that illuminated his hands, the steering wheel, and Chelsea's form in bursts of blue.

"The cops are behind us!" yelled Chelsea.

"Good!" answered Tom. "Let them see what's been killing everyone!"

The Birdy Burger came back into view, as did the two shapes that lumbered slowly across the street to the beach access.

"Where are they going?" Chelsea asked.

"Back to their favorite dining spot," said Tom.

"What are you going to do?"

"I'm gonna kill them! Put on your seat belt!" he ordered as he pulled the shoulder strap over his chest and fastened it with one hand.

She climbed into the front seat. It was the first time she had ever ridden shotgun with Tom. It was always Lucy's honor, but no more. As she fastened the seatbelt, she and Tom's eyes locked quickly, then just as quickly filled with tears.

Tom wiped his eyes dry and gripped the wheel tightly in both hands, his gaze locked on one of the creatures. When the car barreled into the slower of the two, it rolled onto the hood and over the car. The impact left a spider web of cracks across the windshield, making it next to impossible to see through.

Tom slammed the brakes, laying down a 300-foot trail of black tread behind him. The patrol car swerved to avoid the creature, then came to a calculated halt in front of the Birdy Burger.

Blood poured from the mouth and gills of the dead beast, forming a pool of deep red beneath it. Lights from The Birdy Burger's tall, illuminated sign were reflected in the bloody pool.

In his side view mirror Tom watched the officer retrieve his shotgun and heard him call for assistance through his lapel mic as he exited the car. As the officer looked across the parking lot, he observed the creatures' mutilated victims: a decapitated male missing one arm and a disemboweled female amidst the refuse of soda cans and other items from Tom's car.

"What's he gonna do—arrest us?" Chelsea asked.

The police officer hurried toward them with his shotgun gripped in both hands.

"We can't let the other one get away!" said Tom. He removed his seat belt and opened the car door.

"Remain in your vehicle!" ordered the officer.

"We didn't do it, Officer!" yelled Tom.

"Remain in your vehicle," the officer repeated, continuing toward their car.

"Officer!" yelled Tom. "Those things killed our friends! And you're letting it—"

The officer took careful aim with his shotgun. As the creature stepped from asphalt onto sand, he fired, hitting it in the back. It stopped for a moment, then took another step toward the beach.

The officer fired another shot, striking the creature's lower back. It turned around, angry and intent on stopping its attacker. It limped toward the officer. He fired, shot after shot, until the creature fell to its knees in the middle of the road, then landed face down, as motionless as its companion.

The officer approached Tom's car. "Are you two okay?" he asked.

"No," said Tom.

"But you're not injured?" clarified the officer.

"No, sir, we're not," Tom answered.

The officer motioned with his hand for them to get out of the vehicle. "It's safe now," he assured them. "You can step out of your vehicle—just don't touch anything."

Tom and Chelsea slowly exited the car. Within a few minutes an ambulance and fire truck arrived, along with several police vehicles. After the routine investigation took place, strange unmarked vehicles arrived, which promptly removed the creatures' corpses and left.

Tom and Chelsea sat at one of the diner's concrete tables closest to the road. The two were wrapped in blankets. The officer looked at Tom's car, then at his watch.

"The tow truck should be here any minute," he said.

Tom pointed at his flat rear right tire full of shark teeth. "That's a classic overbite," he said.

"Just 'cause your dad's a dentist, you know all about monsters, too?" quipped Chelsea with a trembling voice.

"Something like that," said Tom as he put his arm around her.

"What were they?" she asked.

"I don't know," answered Tom.

"Whatever they were, I wouldn't believe it if I hadn't seen it with my own eyes," said the officer.

"But who else is going to believe us?" Chelsea asked.

"Anyone who sees the footage from my dashboard camera," said the officer as he stared at his patrol car.

With its grainy, monochrome vision, the camera on the vehicle's dashboard witnessed a mere portion of the carnage that would forever play back in the minds of those who saw it first hand in real time—a memory they would pray the rest of their days to end.

Bugageddon

Bryan Vogt

The quake came and went without ado. No damage was caused to buildings or homes; there was not any noticeable shaking of household objects or rattling noises. The tremors were slight and only apparent to a handful of sensitive residents, and even then, they were select light sleepers, and those awake at this early predawn hour. The earthquake in terms of magnitude would be classified as minor, registering only 2.0 on the Richter scale. The majority of Red Lake residents would awaken and go through their day never knowing what had happened unless they caught the twenty-second news blip from the local broadcast.

Daryl rolled out of bed in a foul mood. He was a light sleeper and did not sleep well on the best of nights. He suffered from a recurring nightmare in which a trio of giant, talking, carnivorous insects had him trapped in an alley; when he pulled the trigger on his pesticide sprayer, only dribbles emerged. The insects laughed and mocked him before lunging. Daryl always woke in the same place, just as they lunged. Although the minor tremor lasted less than a minute, it was enough to wake him. Instead of trying to go back to sleep, he grabbed a clean uniform from the closet and strolled into the kitchen to make a pot of coffee.

He felt the arthritis in his knees acting up. Twenty years of crawling around on his hands and knees under damp crawl spaces and hot, low-pitched attics had taken its toll. *A storm must be a brewing.* Daryl opened a cabinet door and grabbed the bottle of Subdue, a poor man's Tylenol, and dropped six tablets onto his calloused palm. He dry swallowed the pills in one gulp. After pouring himself a cup of steaming Sanka, he pulled open the kitchen blind.

Daryl gazed out the window at the breathtaking view. The sun was just beginning to rise and the horizon was colored a soft magenta.

"Red sky in the morning. I hope six pills are enough for today," Daryl mumbled to himself.

He stepped outside and walked across the yard to his detached garage-turned-office. A large, dark brown sign in the shape of a cockroach hung above the bay door. Printed in lime green across the roach's body was the name of his company, Buginator. Daryl beamed with pride every time he looked up at the sign. He liked to think of himself as the Terminator of the insect world. He always told his customers after he finished his extermination, "If you notice any insects within six-month's time, for free of charge... I'll be back."

Stepping inside, he went to his desk and checked his answering machine. No messages. He could not understand it. This month marked the slowest in Buginator's history. His only four service calls this month had been for nuisance wildlife. Not wanting to dwell on the negative, Daryl decided to wash and wax the Bugmoblie before the rain. Besides, he wanted to stay near the office: he had a gut feeling that he would get some calls today.

* * *

The overcast sky and black clouds looming overhead had not been enough to cancel the picnic. Despite the ominous sky, the temperature was in the mid-seventies with a soft, warm breeze. At six years of age, Johnny found the yearly family picnic boring. The adults behaved like adults, and all his siblings and cousins were older and excluded him from their games. Johnny asked his mom for an empty jar and walked away from the picnic shelter to find some adventure of his own. Noticing a small pile of logs and fist-sized rocks, he approached it with jar in hand.

Johnny pushed a couple of rocks back to expose the bare soil underneath. A smile formed across his face as he shot a hand toward a centipede running for a new hiding place. The centipede was too quick, though, scurrying under another rock before Johnny could catch it. He was about to roll the rock over when he felt the first drops of rain.

He jumped up. The raindrops felt different; they made his skin tingle. He bolted toward the roofed picnic shelter. By the time he ran under cover, all of his relatives were already there. Johnny's mother ran next to him and wiped him off with paper towels. Johnny heard the adults chattering away about the rain, but he could not comprehend what all the fuss was about. The raindrops felt different and scared him at first, but the tingly feeling was neat. Just as quickly as the rain began, it was gone. Soon after, the sunshine broke through the dispersing clouds, and the adults' moods seemed to lighten. After ten minutes, the older kids ran back onto the green grass, tossing a Frisbee and laughing. After watching the other children run off, Johnny ran, too. His mom screamed from the distance, warning him to stay away from any puddles.

He ran back to the rock where the centipede had disappeared and rolled it over. The centipede was no longer there. Instead, he found an ant nest. Hundreds of tiny black ants scurried to and fro, obviously agitated about their nest being uncovered. Johnny leaned over to grab his jar when he heard the screams. He turned and saw the adults under the pavilion screaming and swatting at the air. He was trying to understand what was going on when he felt a pinch on his ankle. Then another one, and another. Johnny jumped back instinctively. Looking down, he saw his feet and ankles were covered with black ants. Johnny cried out as more and more ants began to bite his delicate skin. He yanked his shirt off and began swatting at the tiny beasts.

He took off running toward the shelter, glancing over to the field of short grass were his siblings and cousins were. He noticed them behaving exactly like the adults: running in circles, shouting, and swatting at the air. Ten feet from the pavilion he saw various sorts of flying insects dive-bombing everyone inside. He stood transfixed for a moment until a wasp swooped toward his face. Johnny swatted at the air and ducked a second before the wasp landed on him, but his victory was short lived. The yellow jacket reversed and stung Johnny's back. He jumped and howled in pain. Tears formed in his eyes. Before he had a chance to wipe away the tears, someone grabbed his hand, and the next thing he knew, his mother was pulling him toward the car.

As Johnny ran with his mom, swatting the air at the insect assault, he noticed other people around the park running to the parking lot and slapping at the air around them. His mother pushed him into the car and slammed the door before running around and climbing behind the wheel. Seconds later, the car flew into reverse. Feeling safe and secure, Johnny slid across the rear seat, pressing his face against the glass. From above a bee dived straight into the window between Johnny's eyes, sending him scurrying back to the center of the bench seat and sat there until they arrived at home.

* * *

William watched the last of the storm clouds pass. He enjoyed sitting on the front porch sipping his coffee and reading the newspaper during storms. He folded the paper and stood, taking a last sip of hot java. The buzzing sound caught his attention before he saw anything. A large housefly darted straight toward his head, struck his forehead, and bounced off. A split-second later the fly dove at him again. In a fluid movement, William swung the paper, smacking the pest and sending the stunned creature across the porch.

"Damn flies," William muttered. He turned and placed the empty mug onto the small coffee table next to his chair. He noticed a tiny black-and-white jumping spider running across the table in his direction.

"A lot of help you were. I had to take care of that damn fly myself."

The spider stopped for a brief moment as if considering William's words, then it jumped. The arachnid landed on William's arm and bit down. The light pinch was more startling than painful. With a flick of his hand, William knocked the little monster from his arm, sending it back onto the table. He looked at the red spot on his arm and shook his head. *What the hell?* The buzzing near his ear had him reacting instinctively; he ducked his head and swatted at the air around him. He saw a fly zip past, then turn back in his direction. Before he could react, out of the corner of his eye William noticed a black-and-white speck springing at him. He dropped the paper and darted for the front door. No sooner had he closed the screen door when a fly barreled into the mesh. It smacked the screen and fell straight to the ground. William stood, face pressed to the screen, watching the fly buzz around on the deck. Mesmerized with the fly's antics, he was caught unaware when two mud dapper wasps crashed into the mesh near his face. He jumped back and slammed the entry door.

William stared at the front door, shaking his head in disbelief. He never noticed the centipede charging across the hardwood floor toward his foot, and he certainly did not hear the swarm of fruit flies buzzing through the air from the kitchen.

* * *

"This is insane," Daryl shouted with a gleeful smile. His phone had been ringing constantly, ever since the storm. What his callers were saying blew his mind: stories of insect attacks—coordinated and malicious insect attacks. People were claiming wasps, bees, flies, and every other insect with wings were dive bombing and chasing them. Even more outrageous were the claims of spiders, ants, and centipedes charging, attacking, biting, or stinging.

Daryl did not seem to notice any abnormal bug behavior around his shop, but then again, why would he? He sprayed all of his property and house on a regular basis. Daryl believed it would appear unprofessional, both to passersby and potential customers, if he had wasp nests in his eaves and spider webs clinging to the walls. Daryl would have liked to ponder the mental state of his clients and their fantastic tales of insect behavior, but realized that he had a lot of prep work to do and a long day ahead.

Ignoring the ringing phone, he snatched the stack of service call forms off the desk. He felt guilty about not answering, but he did not have time to talk. He was still trying to figure out how he could fulfill his already overbooked schedule. If he had to listen to another crackpot story about insects joining forces in a bugageddon (or was it bugpocalypse?) his head would explode. However, Daryl had to admit that were it not for people's irrational fear of insects, he would go out of business.

The Bugmobile turned onto Route 4 and headed toward downtown Red Lake, population 4,247. However, being summer and a tourist town, there would be closer to triple that number of people in the area this weekend. He should have taken the back roads into town; sightseers and lost tourists were going to be clogging the main road and put him behind schedule. Realizing his folly, Daryl sighed, but since he was already on his way, he decided he may as well stick it out.

Arriving on the outskirts of town, Daryl was pleasantly surprised to notice the roads were empty. *The rainstorm must have scared the visitors away today*, he thought. Daryl stopped at one of the town's two stoplights and looked around at the old, but quaint Main Street. It was a Saturday morning in June and the sun was shining, but the downtown strip was deserted. Despite the warm breeze coming through the open window, goose bumps rose on Daryl's arms.

"What the heck is going on around here?" Daryl mumbled. *First, the crazy calls, and now a vacant town. This is like the beginning of some bad b-movie. What's next, giant insects roaming the streets? Get a grip on yourself.*

He heard the buzzing, but it was the sting seconds later that broke him from his reverie. He cursed and swatted the dying bee off his arm. A small thump against the windshield caught Daryl's attention. As he watched a large deerfly slide down the glass, a meadowhawk crashed into the windshield. Daryl shook his head and drove on to his first service call.

The Bugmobile pulled into the client's driveway. Daryl got out and retrieved his sprayer from the back of the van. As he strapped the spray tank to his back, he scanned the residential neighborhood. Deserted. The furious sound of buzzing made him spin. Two large yellow jackets flew straight toward his head. A small crack filled his ears as he stretched his neck from side to side. With a flick of his wrist and a light squeeze to the trigger, he sent a stream of pesticide at the oncoming insects. Both wasps were caught dead-on and spiraled to the ground. Daryl raised the wand to his mouth and blew it dry.

"Well, pardners, you shid of got when the gittin' was good," Daryl said with a smirk.

The door opened as Daryl approached. A thirty-year old woman with disheveled brunette hair and three noticeable red marks on her face stood inside the doorway. She clutched a fly swatter in each hand with two frightened young children glued to her side.

"Good morning Missus Anderson, I'm…"

"Hurry! Get in here before they do. You got to stop them before we get seriously hurt," Mrs. Anderson said.

Daryl rolled his eyes and hoped she didn't notice.

"God dang it, Daryl, professionalism," he admonished himself under his breath. "Don't worry Missus Anderson, I…" Daryl started to say, but Mrs. Anderson grabbed his arm and pulled him inside.

"Are you just going to stand there or start exterminating?"

He considered answering, but shook his head instead and went to work. For the most part, the extermination was routine; the only thing out of the ordinary was a common brown house spider that charged him as he made his rounds. As he worked, he could have sworn at least one of the children was cheering him on.

"Well, Missus Anderson, that should do it. You are guaranteed to be insect free for the next three months."

Daryl took pleasure when his customers appreciated his level of skill, but he was a little shocked when Mrs. Anderson lunged forward and hugged him. The two children followed suit, clutching his waist.

"I, ah, really need to get going to my next appointment," Daryl said as he squirmed free from the group hug. He slipped out the front door and bee-lined for the van. He started the engine and flew out of the driveway.

A few minutes later he pulled into the driveway of his next costumer. He walked toward the house on a fieldstone walkway bordered by various beautiful flower gardens. Halfway to the door, Daryl heard the rattling of grasshoppers. As he turned to look, he saw a small group of grasshoppers springing toward his chest and head. Daryl dove to his left and rolled, partially from instinct, but mostly from practice. He came out of the roll on one knee with the wand in his hand. It was all over in a moment. Five grasshoppers lay on the walkway twitching and breathing their last breaths. Daryl was about to stand when a buzzing sound closed in on him. He aimed the nozzle and took down a common green darner diving at him. He trotted to the front door and pressed the doorbell, keeping his back to the house and his hand on the wand trigger. He wiped away the droplets of sweat from his brow and pressed the buzzer again. The front door creaked open to expose an unkempt, silver-haired man wearing a t-shirt with a silhouette of a yeti and the words, "Gone Squatching" printed across the chest. He held an old Smith and Wesson .38 service revolver in one hand and a rolled-up newspaper in the other.

"Git your ass in here before you git eaten alive."

The door slammed the moment Daryl passed the threshold. The house was cluttered waist high with stacks of sand bags, small crates, cases of canned food, and jugs of water. Narrow pathways allowed access to other rooms in the house. Hot breathing near his ear brought Daryl's attention back to his client, who stood inches away from him. He tried to take a step back, but the stacks of junk prevented him. "Hello, Mister Fitzhugh, I'm Daryl from Buginator Extermination. It's a pleasure to…"

"I know who you are. I called you, remember? I can tell by the look on your face that you're a bit shocked. The well-manicured exterior is a perfect facade for my hidden compound," Mr. Fitzhugh said, just inches from Daryl's face while aiming the pistol at his chest. "I normally don't allow outsiders in my inner sanctum, but this is an emergency. Just like the scriptures said, Bugageddon is here. An oversight on my part, I'll admit, but I was really thinkin' the end would be because of terrorists. Well, that, or aliens. Anyway, what I need is your word that what you see here, stays here. We got us an understanding?"

The first thing Daryl did was wipe away the spittle that landed on his face, wondering if it was ethical to add a twenty-percent surcharge to his client's bill for emotional distress.

"Ah, see what? I'm a professional and I respect a client's privacy. And believe me, once I'm done here, I plan to wipe you and this house from my memory like a bad dream. How about you give me a little working room, Mister Fitzhugh, so I can put an end to the Bugageddon."

"I knew I could count on you," Mr. Fitzhugh said, lowering the muzzle of the gun to the floor. "Awright, let's git to it and don't worry, I'll cover your back so them rascals don't git the jump on you from behind. And we sweep the screen porch last. That's where I trapped a gaggle of those giant devils."

Walking forward, Daryl glanced over his shoulder every few steps. Contrary to what Mr. Fitzhugh believed, Daryl did not feel a sense of relief having an insane, armed client watching his back. At one point he hit his head diving to the ground after he heard gunfire. When he looked behind him, he saw Mr. Fitzhugh, crouched down and shouting something about the breech being suppressed and all was clear. He finished exterminating the house in record time despite the obstacles he had to work around. All Daryl had left to spray was one final place, the screened porch, then he could get the heck out of this loony bin.

"Awright, this is it. The moment of truth. These buggers are big enough to take your head right off." Mr. Fitzhugh placed a hand on the door handle and said, "On the count of three."

Daryl released an arching spray into the room before the door was fully open and kept spraying as he stepped in. An assortment of over a dozen dragonflies from the darner family lay dying on the floor of the porch.

"See… I told you, they was giants."

"Actually, Mister Fitzhugh, they appear to be of average size. Darners are the largest of the dragonfly families and…"

"Awright, bugspert, I can take it from here. And remember, what you saw here, stays here."

* * *

The sun was beginning to set when Daryl pulled out of the driveway from his last scheduled service call that day. His body was sore, his nerves were shot, and he was exhausted. His day had improved once he left Mr. Fitzhugh's house, but the irrational behavior of the insects had seriously unhinged his mental wellbeing. He felt like he had been teleported onto the set of a real life eco-horror movie. Not the completely implausible ones like *Them!* or *The Deadly Mantis*, where insects grew to larger-than-life scale, but more in the vein of *Frogs*, *Kingdom of Spiders*, or even *The Birds*. While farfetched, it was conceivable that some insects or other form of critters could go on a rabid rampage. Daryl didn't have the answers to what was happening with the insects, but he knew it was atypical and he was scared as hell.

After turning on the radio, Daryl listened to the newscasts as he drove home, but they did not seem to have any answers either. The news anchors advised residents to stay indoors and await the trucks that were being mobilized to spray pesticides. The insect problem, however, did appear to be confined to a small geographical area along the eastern portion of the state. Daryl was beginning to suspect that there was some sort of link between the tremors, the thunderstorm, and the insect behavior.

Daryl cursed as he missed his turn. He considered making a U-turn. The streets were still barren with the exception of a handful of vehicles, most of them designated for emergency and government use. However, he was not in a hurry to get home, and he was enjoying the solitude. A series of car blasts caught his attention. He pulled over to the side of the road thinking someone would be recklessly speeding down the road with a swarm of locusts in pursuit, but when he looked around, he didn't see any oncoming cars. He was about to drive away when he heard more honking. There were a few houses off the street, and only two had vehicles in the drive. It was then he noticed there was a woman in the front seat of one, and she was gesturing wildly. A part of him wanted to drive away, but that was not how Daryl was raised. Somebody could be in trouble and in need of his assistance; how could he turn his back on them?

He threw the Bugmobile in gear and pulled up behind the car. The woman was kneeling on the seat and had her hands together as though she'd been praying. She was shouting something, he couldn't hear what she was saying. Distracted, and being the Good Samaritan he was, Daryl stepped out of the van. His foot had hardly landed on the ground when he felt the first sting. Then he noticed the large colony of wasps flying by the woman's car. He retreated back into the van and slammed the door after receiving four more painful stings. He swatted at and killed two wasps that followed him inside the van.

Turning his head he looked into the eyes of the woman in the car and noticed she was crying. The sight of tears running from those big green eyes combined with the pain from the wasp stings was enough to boil Daryl's blood. He had never believed in love at first sight—until now. Here was his chance to storm the castle and save the damsel in distress or go down getting stung to death. He raised a finger and mouthed the words, *"One minute,"* before climbing into the rear of the Bugmobile. He squatted down next to the row of shelves attached to the side of the van and pulled a long, narrow, wooden box from the bottom rack. A thick layer of dust and dirt covered the top. He often fantasized about using the contents inside, but deep down he knew if word spread around Red Lake that he had something like this, it would be the death of Buginator. Now, the world be damned, he was going to rescue his princes, and to hell with the consequences.

Armed with a yellow-and-black-striped Super Soaker in each hand, a Tarantula squirt gun in a chest holster, and three Raid bug bombs attached to a homemade belt around his waist, Daryl was prepared to exit through the rear of the van and go to war. He slid a modified vintage World War I gas mask, which had been painted lime green and had short, black, fuzzy antennas attached at the top, over his face and kicked open the back doors. "Lord, please let her be single and interested."

Spinning around the side of the van, he pressed his back against the vehicle. He pulled a bug bomb from his belt, released the charge, and tossed it next to the car. Then he threw another on the opposite side of the car. Before he had a chance to move, a few dozen wasps charged his position. Daryl swung the Super Soakers up to his hip and hit the triggers. Wasps dropped left and right, but more kept coming. He dove into a roll, stopped on one knee, and spun. He fired another blast of pesticide, taking out more wasps, as well as other winged allies joining in the fray. Daryl used all of the evasion tactics he had practiced and perfected over the years: darting to and fro, cutting left to right with some fakes mixed between, diving, and rolling.

The driveway and yard were littered with insect corpses when the Super Soakers spit out their last drops of liquid death. Daryl tossed the empty water cannons to the ground and pulled out the battery-powered Tarantula, the highest-rated water gun on the market. He decided to stand his ground against the final assault. Sweat and multiple bug bites covered his skin as the sun set and the battle drew to a close.

Terri, witnessing the battle from within the safety of the car, alternated between screams of terror and uncontrollable bouts of joy as the battle waged on. When it was over, she jumped out and ran toward her savior. "Oh my God, you're my hero. I wanted to drive to the store to buy more cans of wasp spray, but the car wouldn't start. Then a swarm of wasps trapped me inside and I knew there was no way I could make it back to the house with only this one partially used can I have," Terri said holding up the can. "I've been in that car for hours. What can I ever do to repay you?"

"Id wa notin," Daryl replied from behind the mask. Then he reconsidered his reply and decided to throw caution to the wind once again. "Ges ou gona dit wy ma."

She frowned and pulled the mask off Daryl's face. "I did not understand a single word you said. Could you repeat that?"

"I said it was nothing."

"You said a little more than that. Don't be shy, say it."

"Well... I said, um, nothing really." Daryl's face turned beet red and he looked down as he fidgeted with his pistol. "Well, heck, I said I guess you could go on a date with me. But I mean you don't have to..."

"I'd love to. How about tonight, right now. That is, if you wouldn't mind escorting me inside and standing watch while I shower and change. I'm a bit freaked out and really could use the company."

"Um, sure. You won't have to worry about a thing. Bugs tremble and hives shake when the Buginator rides into town." Daryl regretted the words as they left his mouth. "Ah, what I meant..."

Terri put a soft, slender finger against Daryl's lip. "I think you are really adorable, although a bit strange. A small word of advice, though. Maybe you should take a little time to think through your replies before saying them aloud." Terri grabbed Daryl's hand and led him to her front door. Terri had her hand on the door handle when the sound of buzzing caught their ears. Daryl spun, the motorized Tarantula raised. A black-and-yellow bumblebee the size of a large man's thumb flew across the yard straight toward them. Daryl lined the bee in his sights and squeezed the trigger. Nothing happened; the gun had already used its final charge. He reached out to push Terri behind him. He closed his eyes and readied himself to take the sting for her.

With a flick of her wrist, Terri rolled the partially used can of wasp spray around the top of her hand. The can did a complete three-sixty before coming to rest in her palm. Years of baton practice honed her skill to perfection. She raised the can, aimed, and pressed down on the trigger. Daryl opened his eyes when he heard the hissing of an aerosol spray can. He stood slack-jawed watching the perfectly aimed stream connect with its target. The bee dropped to the ground.

"I think maybe I'll start calling myself the Buginatrix," Terri said, rolling the can of wasp spray over the back of her hand. "What do you have to say about that?"

"Um, I love you."

"You really need to think before you speak. Come on, let's get inside so I can get ready for our big date."

Daryl realized with the current predicament their first date options were woefully thin. Nonetheless, Terri wanted to get out of her house, and Daryl thought he might be due for a shower and change of clothes himself. They decided to go to Daryl's, where he promised to cook a wonderful Italian meal, or at least cook some pasta and warm a jar of marinara sauce. The dinner and wine were mediocre, but Terri gave Daryl an "A" for effort. He played soft romantic music in the background, set a few lit candles on the table, and only rarely put his foot in his mouth. The date was fantastic.

Over the following week, the two talked daily. When Daryl could slip away from his hectic schedule, they would spend time together. Five days after the tremors and strange rainstorm, the insect population's behavior returned to normal. The residents of Red Lake took a little longer to forget; however, after a couple of weeks, life in the small town also returned to normal.

* * *

The small tremor jolted Daryl from his slumber and pleasant dreams. He crawled from bed and headed to the kitchen to begin his daily routine. After pouring a cup of Blue Mountain coffee, he yanked the window blind open. "Holy crap," he screamed and dropped the cup to the floor. In the distance the sky was a soft magenta. The feeling of déjà vu tickled his soul. Soon after, a short, but steady downpour took place. He did his best to ignore the feeling gnawing inside him and prepared for the day and the breakfast date he had with the love of his life.

The Bugmobile, with Daryl behind the wheel and Terri riding shotgun, pulled into an empty spot in front of the small downtown park. Daryl reached in a bag next to him and handed Terri a coffee and bagel. The happy couple people watched, ate breakfast, and talked. Halfway through his bagel Daryl fell silent and began to focus his attention on an old man sitting on a park bench less than fifty feet away from the van. The silver-haired man was tossing peanuts to a small, but growing number of squirrels. Not unusual in itself, but the behavior of the squirrels seemed strange. Peanuts landed at their feet, and they just ignored them, focusing their beady little eyes on the old man instead.

"Be that way, you little snob. Let's see if I give you any bagel ever again," Terri said through the open window of the van.

Daryl's head snapped to his right. He looked at the squirrel sitting on the grass near the passenger's door and then noticed a couple more squirrels hopping to the same area. "Babe, um, please roll up your window."

"What for? It's a beautiful..."

"Just crank up that damn window, now!"

"Someone woke on the wrong side of the world today," Terri replied, closing the window.

Then they heard the screams.

The old man in the park was screaming and swinging his arms in the air. Over twenty squirrels had swarmed him, their sharp teeth tearing into flesh, splattering blood.

Terri screamed. Daryl pushed open his door and was about to hop out when a squirrel lunged straight into the windowpane. He jerked back inside the van and slammed the door when another squirrel landed on the windshield, baring its teeth and chattering away.

The two watched in horror as the man fell to the ground and squirrels covered his bloody body.

"Oh my God, Daryl. What's happening?"

"Nothing good, nothing good at all," he replied, throwing the Buginator into gear. Daryl flew down Main Street, barely slowing at intersections.

"Where are we going?" Terri asked.

"I have a small houseboat on the lake with at least a few days' worth of supplies in it. We're going to anchor it in the middle of the lake and then I don't know what. If this is like what happened with the insects, hopefully it will end in a few days."

"Do you think it's just the squirrels or other animals, too?"

Silence.

"Daryl, what are you thinking? I can tell there's something racing through that mind of yours. I would like to know. You're not the only one in this."

"I, um, I'm worried that this could be more than just squirrels. This could be all rodents. Possibly even all mammals, but let's not jump to conclusions. Babe, could you climb in back and grab that small brown box hidden under the folded green tarp? Inside is a loaded revolver and I want you to carry it. I'll feel safer if you had a little protection." Daryl watched Terri walk to the rear of the van through the rearview mirror. He felt guilty for not being completely honest, but in his defense he didn't want to panic her. He hoped it was only squirrels and other rodents, but truthfully, he wasn't feeling quite like his usual self today.

Big Girl

Matt Kelly

"I'm Anderson Melnik, nice to meet you Walter." The two men shook hands. Anderson Melnik grinned, dropped his perfectly balanced grip, and continued.

"Obviously you got my note. Thanks for chatting with me out here. I've lived two doors down for three years now and I don't know if we've ever talked, have we? A lot of people would say that's pretty sad, wouldn't they?"

Walter Baum nodded with pursed lips. He wondered why this yuppie asked him to come out into the street and what he wanted. This unexpected visit knocked Walter's world completely out of balance. *Disgusting.* Walter's stance wavered as he tried to think of what his response would be.

"I don't know if me minding my own business is sad, Mister Melnik. I don't want to be nosy, and I appreciate my fellow neighbors feeling the same. You're not going to be nosy on me today, are you, Melnik?"

"Oh no, Walter. Not nosy at all. And would you prefer Mister Baum? I just wanted to give you something, um, something that the town said they wanted to share with you."

Walter's temper started to flare up.

"The town? What do you mean? You guys here in the neighborhood?"

"No, Mister Baum, I mean as in the *town hall.* I guess I'll just tell you. Some of us neighbors were thinking of having a block party—"

"*I don't want part of no parties,*" Walter interjected.

Walter could suddenly see that upon this interruption, Melnik had switched gears. With a magician-like wave of his hand, Anderson Melnik continued.

195

"*We are having a block party*, and the state of your house has come up in our discussions. Several neighbors told me that you have resisted requests to clean up your front lawn. So myself and a few other area residents had this drafted up."

Anderson handed Walter several sheets of paper embossed with a legal seal.

"I would suggest you look these over and understand the serious nature of this situation. George Ketchum told me how you spoke to him last week. That over there," pointing to a small mowed strip of Walter's overgrown lawn, "was just him trying to be neighborly! He wanted to give you a hand! But the way you spoke to him was uncalled for. Because of that, we had no other recourse but to bring this to the attention of the town."

"This is outrageous," Walter mumbled.

"I'm being outrageous? You should count yourself lucky that we didn't have the cops bring this to you!"

Melnik walked away, and Walter continued to frown. He didn't like this at all. This sort of rudeness was too much for him to bear. In his seventy years on God's Green Earth, Walter never missed an opportunity to give someone a piece of his mind, through words or actions. It took everything he had to keep from walloping that obnoxious yuppie right in the mouth. But Ruthie wouldn't have approved, God rest her soul.

Over the years, Walter's neighborhood had changed greatly without his consent. He was the last of his generation still living on Hauser lane; everyone had either died or moved to more agreeable climates.

As the younger families moved in, people on Hauser Lane learned to avoid old Walter. Even though no one talked to him anymore, he and his house were always on their minds. An old colonial built in the 1930s, the Baum residence used to look much like the other quaint homes on the block. Now the ragweed was thick, crisscrossing the yard like Nazi barbed wire. The gigantic dandelions, like Wyndham's Triffids, gazed at paperboys with a sinister stare. Paint peeled and chipped off the side of the house and the shutters. The roof was nearly black from decay, and the gutters looked like a biological experiment. If you were to drive by, you'd think there was no way that any human creature could actually live inside that house. Only a careful observer would see any sign of life, either when Walter needed groceries or when his old friend Frank was able to lure him out for a game of checkers.

The teenagers on the street laughed when their parents suggested that the house hadn't always looked like that. Back in the sixties, when Walter and Ruthie Baum first moved in, Walter had worked hard to keep the place nice. Walter and Ruthie (and their two kids that followed) filled those walls with a lot of love, lighting up their house like no other. Bill and Allison were great children, both taking after Ruthie's calm demeanor. They were always willing to help their parents, even when Walter had that backbreaking idea to build a bridge over the creek in the woods behind the house. The kids loved that bridge, dangerous as it was. Even though Bill tempted the fates by jumping off of it into the creek, nothing bad ever happened back there beyond a few scrapes and sprains, and even though Walter knew what was going on, he never put a stop to it. Kids would be kids, and they needed to learn. That's really why the bridge was built, to teach lessons. But nine years ago, something happened that was far from educational. School was closed, and no lessons were learned.

After that dark day, Walter stayed indoors and spent his hours reading outdated newspapers and magazines. His beloved wife Ruthie had died from breast cancer the year before what Walter would only refer to as "The Accident," and he was left to haunt the house all alone. He had retired, and only opened his front door to go to the store or for the afore-mentioned game of checkers with Frank. He never mowed his lawn or trimmed his hedges. He just let things grow, including the rust on nearly every tool he had ever bought. Keeping up of appearances felt absurd to him. As with most widowers, things started to fade just a little when Ruthie passed on. Life had lost its taste. But nine years ago, after The Accident at the bridge, the whole *world* ceased to exist. It was then that Walter Baum began to frown.

So today, when his neighbor came by with orders saying Walter *had* to cut the grass and clean out his gutters, he was not pleased. But in his own way, Walter also knew that he had to comply. He had plenty of disagreements with the town over the last few years. The town system was filled with just more yuppies, and none of them ever saw things Walter's way. Regardless, he knew he was on thin ice with them. Cleaning out his gutters was going to have to happen

Walter went inside his house and read over the papers. He had seventy-two hours to complete the town's request. He was going to have to borrow Frank's cherry red Yard Master lawnmower, but it was too late to ask him for that sort of thing. Walter's grass was so high that it'd probably take two days of starting and stopping to get it into shape. That left the gutters, and there was no time like the present. Walter stepped out the front door and disappeared into the garage. A few minutes later he fumbled out with a rickety wooden ladder. Walter's mind traveled back to when his son, Bill, had been around to help him with stuff like this. Seething at this thought, he slammed the ladder a little too hard against the side of his house, putting a nice crack in his siding. Walter, bucket and trowel in hand, climbed the ladder one rung at a time.

His chest heaving, Walter made it to the top of the ladder. He was ready to get right to work, but he had to take a moment or two just to regain his composure. From here he could see most of the street. Well-kept houses, new roofs, and a few swimming pools flanked him on all sides. For the first time in many years, he felt a pang of guilt. How could he have let all this happen?

The gutters were monstrously foul. Unidentifiable leafy plants and roots sprung up along the whole course of the rusted trough. The plants were growing in the decayed matter of oak and maple leaves, the perfect recipe for robust vegetation. There was even a healthy amount of bird crap up here, just enough to act as a happy fertilizer for this impromptu flower pot.

Speaking of crap, it was time to get this over with. The trowel went into the gutter and came out smeared with leafy soil and an otherworldly stench. He dropped his first deposit into the bucket. He sunk his trowel in again, this time bringing back up a fully formed plant. God, was that poison ivy? Wonderful. Again and again, the spade went in, dirt came up, carrying spade full after spade full of putrid muck.

Soon the bucket was full. For a second Walter considered just dumping the bucket over his shoulder and letting the contents drop to the ground below. He was about to do so when he lost his balance. Instead of worrying about his body, his arms instinctively held on to the bucket, shifting his center of gravity and almost causing him to topple backwards fifteen feet to the ground. In an instant his knees gave way and he slammed into the side of the house. He dropped the bucket and held on to the ladder for dear life. His heart thumping, Walter surveyed the damage. The bucket had spilled everywhere, but at least he was safe. He rubbed his brow in disgust and cursed himself before descending to the ground. He collected the remains of the bucket and emptied them in a burlap sack. He moved the ladder over a foot or so, then climbed back up.

The next few trowel loads weren't as bad, that is until he started finding the slugs. The surprise of the first one almost caused another near fall from the ladder. The slug appeared out of nowhere, partially impaled on the tip of the spade, squirming like a worm on a fisherman's hook. Once he regained his composure, Walter scraped the end of the trowel against the bucket, dropping the gutted creature into its grave. Disgusted,

Walter continued his digging, wondering how such a thing got up here in the first place. *It must have been born up here*, he mused.

As he made his way across the roof, he continued to find a few more slugs, as well as some poison oak. He took a few extra trips up and down the ladder to empty out the bucket and continued his journey along the front of his house.

On trip number seven, Walter began to feel the accumulation of heat on his body. *Maybe it's time to take a break, what do you say?* For a brief moment, he absent-mindedly thought again about calling his son Bill to help him. Of course that would be nuts; Bill wasn't any more likely to take his father's call than Walter would be to take Bill's. After all, it was Bill who refused to assume responsibility for The Accident and what happened to Abby.

An hour passed as Walter rested on his back porch. He could hear the stream far behind the house, bubbling in the distance as the sun made its way toward the horizon. A cool breeze was descending and Walter decided he'd try to get in what last work he could before it got too dark.

He had left the ladder next to what had once been an old, proud willow, its arms now reaching up to the sky, its roots descending into the earth just as far. Ironically, its height and depth were just symbolic now; it was dead and decayed in both directions. Yet another eyesore for the rest of the neighborhood. It was only a matter of time before that Melnik fella would probably send Walter a letter about that, too. Walter steadied the ladder, took a deep breath, and ascended.

He worked with the bucket as dusk came. Walter was never a fan of the dark, and there was little daylight left. He could try to finish up tomorrow, but that notice from the town didn't allow him much time. No, Walter would try to get as much done as possible with what little time remained.

Despite this determined spirit, Walter paused to look down at the gutter, covered in leaves and muck. A shiver went up his spine. He played with the leaves a bit, uncovering the dirt below. He was so used to the stuff that he didn't even think about keeping clean anymore. He slowly sent his hands in and felt the familiar shape of a slug.

Maybe it was the long hours getting to him, but for a moment he was transported back to when Bill and Allison were young. Those kids found all sorts of worms and beetles down by the creek. Walter could see them now. They would bend down with their legs apart and arms extended. Their fingers spread out, they would push their hands into the mud slowly, with expert care. Their fingers would bend and support the creature from underneath as they sifted through the damp dirt until their prize was revealed: their safe and perfect specimen in the form of… well, whatever. They had fun down there. Walter never had to worry about them. They would learn their lessons and have their adventures, and they would always come back home.

Abby never came back. Walter's granddaughter, Abby, fell off the bridge and into the water. She was unable to climb out by herself, and by the time Bill and Walter made it down to the bridge, it was too late. Her eyes were open and lifeless, her skin approaching sky blue. She was gone.

But for the first time in a while, this terrible memory was only a brief echo. Walter allowed warmer memories to take over. Mimicking the much younger versions of his two kids, Walter began to dig around the mass under the dirt. He poked at it using a stick and began to etch an outline around it. His childlike wonder grew. He dug far under the outline he had made and lifted the clump of dirt (and slug hidden inside), placing it in the palm of his hand. He wiggled his fingers, sifting through the dirt just like Bill and Allison. The decomposed earth fell away and the white, shining creature began to emerge. Its skin gleamed from the light of the street lamps, as did its arms, its legs, and its long flowing hair. This was not a slug.

"Ah!" Walter gasped, his eyes widening. He jerked his hand to one side and the small creature fell from his palm. In slow motion, Walter watched as the thing descended, somersaulting past his waist. Concern and fear stabbed through his body.

Miraculously, the tiny female form landed in the bucket between his feet. Walter caught his breath. He snatched the bucket and raced down the ladder.

With haste he kneeled on the ground of his abandoned front garden and peered into the bucket. At the top of this tiny heap, resting on a pile of dirty leaves, was a small body roughly five inches long. It resembled an adolescent girl with long blonde hair and fair, China-white skin. Walter thought he had seen this little person somewhere. Was she a toy from some movie? His recollection was muddied and dark, her identity far back in his mind's eye.

He nudged her lifeless body with his finger. "Hello?" The word came out as more of an animal sound than any recognizable language. He tapped her small chin, but received no response. When he felt her, he was hoping he would feel the dependable firmness of molded plastic or fired porcelain. What his fingers found instead was skin as delicate and as soft as that of a newborn baby.

"What is this thing?" he said aloud, clearly, but with a hint of deep worry. He knew he wasn't dreaming. Walter was able to admit to himself that he was more forgetful than usual, but this thing in the bucket wasn't a symptom of senility.

Was it some sort of mutant slug? It would be hard to believe that Mother Nature would decide to randomly give a slug arms, legs, and Barbie hair. Despite its smooth skin, it could be some toy thrown up on the roof by the Caan kids next door. Walter settled on this as an answer; after all, she wasn't a breathing creature, right?

But she was. He could just make it out, her tummy moving up and down as she took slow, shallow breaths.

What *was* this thing?

The sun made its grand exit, and Walter brought the bucket indoors. He set it on the kitchen table and grabbed a clean paper towel. He dabbed at the girl, wiping away the remnants of leaves and dirt. He made sure his movements were slow for fear of ruining whatever it was. The girl continued to breathe, which Walter took as a good sign. In the light of the kitchen, Walter again noticed that his guest's skin was incredibly smooth, as it reflected strongly in the light. It was soft and supple, not slimy and slick.

Walter worked her over with a few more strokes until she was clean enough for his liking. He ducked down into his lower cupboard to grab an old Tupper-Ware container and lid. Using his pocketknife, he cut slits on the lid of the container and lined the bottom with a generous helping of paper towels, then deposited the little girl on top of them. Fastening the lid tight, he carried the container into the living room. He slumped down in his easy chair with the container on his lap. Out of sheer traumatic exhaustion, he fell asleep.

That familiar and awful dream came to him, the one where three-year-old Abby drowned under the bridge.

"Heeeeeeelp meeee, Grandpa. *Why* didn't you and daddy heeeeeelp meeeee?" she sputtered, her body contorting. Her eyes were ringed with red and yet showed no life. Her arms reached and fingers bent in ways they should not.

Walter was frozen. "We tried, sweetheart! We came as soon as we could!"

She continued to wheeze and moan. It got louder and louder and her thrashing became more and more dramatic.

She coughed, louder, louder, LOUDER until Walter woke up.

The cough came again, the same as in the dream.

"No!" Walter cried. He grabbed the Tupper-Ware and ran into the kitchen, prying off the top. Inside, the girl's eyes were open for the first time, darting around the room. Her body was spasming, her throat making strange sounds. Walter was still too afraid to touch her much with his bare hands, but he began to talk to his guest.

"What do you want me to do? What is it? For God's sake, what's wrong?"

"Wa… Waaaaaatrrrrrr. Wa-waaaaaaatrrrrr," she croaked.

"Water? You want water! Okay, okay!"

Walter ran to the medicine cabinet and found his wife's old eyedropper and filled it with water from a glass. Three drops went into the girl's mouth. She calmed, but the plea came again:

"Wa…Waaaaatrrrr. Wa-waaaaaaatrrrrrr."

He emptied the rest of the dropper into her mouth. Her breathing and movements slowed, almost stopping. Her eyes closed and a smile quivered on her lips. Walter then noticed something different. Her skin wasn't as smooth as before. It looked scaly and dry, almost flaky. He readied another helping of water and squeezed a few drops onto her foot. The water didn't hit the skin and run down the sides as he expected; rather, the skin seemed to absorb the liquid, returning to its smooth texture. He filled the dropper again and carefully doused the whole of her body. The dryness disappeared, and she was at rest.

Walter was tired. His interrupted nap didn't help at all. He needed backup to help him. Someone else had to know, if for no other reason than for his own sanity's sake. While he cared for this little creature on some curiously deep level, he still wasn't sure with what he was dealing. For the second time that day he nearly considered calling Bill. There was something in this circumstance that Bill needed to know about. But now wasn't the time. He decided to call his checkers partner, Frank. He would hate to be woken up from his early bedtime, but Walter's fellow retiree was the only person whom Walter knew would come at a moment's notice.

* * *

An hour or so later, Frank arrived at Walter's curb with a mixture of annoyance and genuine concern. He knew it had to be serious for Walter to call him this late at night. Walter hadn't said much on the phone, just that he needed his friend right away. *It was important.* Like Walter, he was a widower that mostly stayed at home. The one difference was that people generally liked Frank. The difference between the two men was so glaring, in fact, that a lot of neighbors scratched their heads when they found out the recluse in the overgrown house even *knew* the kindly gentleman Frank.

Frank was friends with Walter because he had *always* been friends with Walter. If Frank had just met Walter Baum a few years ago, he probably wouldn't have wasted his time on him. In his previous life as a bank loan officer, Frank always regarded time as a precious commodity, but it was clear that Frank had mellowed out considerably since his retirement. His son, Rob, teased him about getting *sentimental.* He even teared up watching Hallmark commercials. Sentimentality was what Frank used to explain why Walter was someone that Frank wouldn't get rid of. A reminder of more youthful and vibrant days. His friendship with Walter was a link to the past, to days before their mutual losses.

Frank wasn't thinking about all of that, though; he just wanted to check on Walter, help him if he could, then go back to bed. Stepping through the Baum residence's back door and into the kitchen, he didn't waste any time. "What is this about, Walter? You okay?" Frank shook Walter's hand and gave him a firm squeeze on the shoulder.

"Yeah, I'm okay; I'm okay. It's just what's here right now isn't okay at all. Frank, I don't know how to explain this, except to say I have a visitor. Let me show you."

Leading Frank over to his kitchen table, Walter simply pointed to the container. Frank peered in and tensed up immediately. Breathing, yet otherwise motionless, was a little girl five inches long, her only covering a blanket of very damp paper towels. Walter hadn't ever exhibited much of a sense of humor in years Frank knew him, so he knew this couldn't be his friend's idea of a joke.

"Walter, what is this? Where'd this thing come from?"

"I found her outside, up in my rain gutters." Walter sighed. "I only know a few things. First, she's not some toy. She said one word: 'Water.' I gave her some, and then she fell asleep. Before that, she was shaking pretty fierce. It was very damp where I found her, so I guess it makes sense. It's what she's used to. Water is what she needs! The other thing, Frank… well, this situation has gotten so weird, I don't think me saying this is going to make it any stranger. I think it's *her.*"

The weight of those words hung in the air for a moment or two before Frank tried to respond.

"You mean your granddaughter? You think this is supposed to be Abby?"

Frank looked back into the container again. Frank believed his friend's concern, but he wasn't ready to jump in and just accept this nonsense. As if reading his friend's mind, Walter answered.

"Frank, I'm not stupid. You and I both know Abby's buried over at Jenson Cemetery. I was there. I'm not saying this is literally her, but dammit, it *looks* like her. And she'd be about this age, but... you know... bigger of course." He paused for a second, knowing what he was about to say was just going to get increasingly insane. Nevertheless, he continued. "What if some part of her was left behind. And this, this *part* kept on growing and living. Most of her body was... dead and buried. But this part, or spirit, moved through the water or through the earth and settled up there. It was so strong and wanted to live so badly that it just kept living and growing. But slowly."

"Walter, are you sure this isn't some toy or something? Maybe a new Barbie doll that a kid accidentally tossed onto your roof?"

Walter shook his head. "Frank," he said, "can a Barbie doll do this?"

He took the eyedropper that was resting on the counter, filled it up, and dropped the water on the exposed tummy of the girl. The droplets of water passed right into her. Frank was puzzled and intrigued. Walter then took another dropper full and put it near the girl's mouth. Instinctively, her mouth opened and latched on to it, drinking it like a baby with a bottle.

"Walter, this is nuts," said Frank. He ran his fingers through his gray, thinning hair. "I don't know what to say. Should we call the cops or something? Or my nephew, Terry—he works at that DNA lab in Cold Spring Harbor. I could get him to take a look as early as tomorrow morning."

"You're not going to tell anyone about this, not until I say so," Walter responded. "That's that. I told you this because I had to tell *someone*. If I wanted to have brass on this, I'd have called the cops first. If I wanted Terry around, I would have asked you to call him up tonight! Now I may want his opinion in a while, but not just yet. You keep this to yourself!"

Walter grabbed another eyedropper and, with a defiant look, filled it with water and once again gave it to the little girl to drink. She polished it off in about a second.

Frank started towards the door. "Walter... I'm giving you till the morning, for your own sake. I'm heading back home, but you look after this thing for a—"

"If this *thing* is my little girl," Walter interjected, "if this thing is Abby, I don't need till morning to know I have to look after her, you follow?"

Frank was taken aback. "Walter, I'm just worried about your safety! I know you say it resembles your granddaughter, and, if I can be honest, I know her death caused a lot of bad blood between you and your son. And maybe you keeping this creature or toy or *whatever* is a way to make up for lost time. But the fact is, you don't really know what this is!"

"Hush up!" Walter said as he swung a punch into Frank's stomach. Frank doubled over in pain. As quickly as he punched, Walter brought his leg up and kneed his friend in the face. Blood began to trickle out of Frank's nose as he fell on the floor. Maybe it was the craziness of the situation that amped up his senses, or the rage that always boiled up at the mention of his son's name, but either way, Walter began to act quickly and deliberately.

He dragged Frank's limp body into one of the extra bedrooms, propping him up on a chair. Walter then grabbed some duct tape from a junk drawer and began to secure Frank's wrists and legs.

Though his friend was unconscious, Walter couldn't help but talk to him. "Frank, you're a good friend. But I can't let you leave here with any ideas of telling people that Abby's back. I'll let you go once I'm finally able to talk to her and figure out what's going on. And she'll talk—she's already said 'water,' Frank."

Walter went back into the kitchen to check on his girl. Something was different. It took a moment or two to register, but soon he saw that the paper towels covering her seemed smaller. No, they weren't smaller. She was getting bigger! Her little limbs had swollen and her overall frame had also expanded an inch or more.

"Are you okay, little girl? You okay? What can I get you?"

In response, her eyes flickered open. They were wide, but vacant. She responded. "Water."

"You need more water?" Walter asked playfully. "Here you go."

Walter gave it to her, and as she gulped, she shook a little, showing no sign of stopping. Where was this water going? After a few minutes he ceased using the water dropper and moved on to small paper cups, noting that her body was swelling with water at an alarming rate. He kept going and going, the sheer joy of human life and consumption fueling this manic pace. Before he knew it, an hour had past. She was a staggering eighteen inches long.

Several minutes later, and the girl had grown slightly. Walter wanted to give her more water, but was hesitant. More liquid would mean more growth. The girl was already about two and a half feet long and now took up a good deal of the kitchen counter.

Walter spent a few moments in thought, then in sudden realization, he slammed his hand on the table. In either excitement or madness, he began to speak aloud.

"I've got it! She died near water but is now born again of the *same stuff*. The thing that took her life is now restoring it. I'll give her water until she reaches the proper height and then try and wake her up for good."

Walter went outside and looked around. It was well into the night now, and he knew he had to do this quickly so it wouldn't wake up anyone (he had had enough trouble with the town for one day, and imagine trying to explain this!). He picked up a pair of pliers. Using a flashlight, he worked the pliers to twist off a four-foot piece of aluminum siding from the back of his house. Bringing it inside to the kitchen, he fixed it to the faucet of the sink with duct tape and used it to channel water right into the girl's mouth.

He took a deep breath and turned on the faucet. A tiny stream ran down the makeshift ramp and into her mouth. Her lips, recognizing the substance, changed their contour to fit the ramp better. Walter could now see the details of her throat, gulping and swallowing the water as fast as it was going in. Walter held his breath and began to increase the flow of water from the sink. The girl's head shook as she gulped faster.

Walter didn't pause the water. He let it run and watched her body swell, fill out, and expand further and further. Suddenly from the next room he heard a loud clanging noise.

Frank awoke to the sound of someone, or something, banging at the side of the house. His head was pounding and his sides ached. It took a few moments for him to remember what had happened. A few seconds later he was able to recognize the room that he was in; he had helped Walter move an old dresser from this room and out to the curb a few months ago. Frank could taste blood; he tried to raise his hands to wipe it away, but discovered his wrists and feet were bound together with tape. The sound from outside the window had stopped, and he heard Walter come back inside the house. What was Walter doing? Frank then heard more noise coming from the kitchen, followed by the sound of running water. It didn't stop, and that worried Frank.

He loosened the tape from his hands and feet. In his excitement, Walter had not done a very good job. Frank thought that the only thing he could do was escape. For the first time ever, he found himself wondering how he'd do in a fight against his best friend. For a moment his pride had a twinge of hurt when he realized Walter had gotten the best of him. Maybe things would've been different if he hadn't been sucker punched.

But either way, Frank was still in pain and bleeding. His best option was to get out of the house and go find help.

He stepped out of the bedroom and glanced around the corner. The sound of the running water was off to the left. If he made a U-turn, he'd be right in the kitchen. The yellow light from the kitchen illuminated the area before him. Frank could see the space from the doorway fairly well. It was a large hallway area; master bedroom off to the right, bathroom straight ahead. He realized that if he were to step into the hall and look at the correct angle, the bathroom mirror in front of him would give him a good view into the kitchen. The only chance he'd be taking was that *he* might be seen as well.

Stepping out of the bedroom, he inched slowly along the wall. He was right; the mirror gave him an excellent line of sight right into Walter's makeshift laboratory. He was able to see the back of Walter's head, transfixed on the strange girl-shaped creature lying on the kitchen table. She had gotten big! Nearly the actual size of a girl her "age". As the water flowed into her mouth, he could see her body swell and contract slightly as it filled with water. He then noticed something strange. Did Walter notice this too? At some point Walter must have grabbed a flashlight and left it on. It was resting by her right thigh, and the light was *shining through it*. Not directly, like glass, but a diffuse light. The strangest part was the movement he could inside her body. At first it looked like running water, but it wasn't movement in one direction. It was all over the place, like static on a TV screen. Moving closer towards the bathroom to get a better look, Frank didn't notice the lamp teetering next to him, but he definitely heard the noise it made when it crashed onto the floor.

The question was, did Walter hear it?

Frank didn't want to find out. He had to hedge his bets, run through the kitchen, and out the door. Frank didn't wait another moment; he bolted for the door.

Walter guessed the noise was his friend Frank, so he looked around the sink for a weapon as fast as he could. He grabbed a steak knife as Frank came bounding through the doorway.

"Walter," Frank said, ducking behind a chair and holding his ground. "I just want to get out of here. You've gone crazy and I'm not staying tied up in that room!"

"Get back in there! I can't let you ruin this," cried Walter.

Walter ran forward towards Frank. Frank stood up and kicked the chair in front of him at Walter. It hit Walter in the knee, causing the old man to lose his balance. He reached out with his left hand, finding the table as he fell. His other hand reached out, too, forgetting the knife. The blade hit the counter flat side down, but grazed the hand of the expanding girl. She let out a cry, a strangled gargle of pain.

Frank stood in shock as Walter's eyes darted upward.

"Look what you made me do!" shouted Walter. "You made me hurt my big girl, Abby!"

Walter stood up and looked at Abby. The cut on her hand began to ooze a lumpy, yellow liquid. Walter grabbed one of his damp paper towels to stop the bleeding and Frank quickly sidestepped his way out of the kitchen.

"You're crazy!" Frank yelled as he bolted out of the house.

"Don't you bring anyone to hurt her, you bastard!" Walter shouted back. Frank ran so fast he never heard his old friend's response.

* * *

Walter couldn't find any Band-Aids, so a few cotton balls and some tape served to close the wound. Abby looked quite large. Not heavy or overweight. Just big. Walter shut off the water, figuring it was time for her to take a break. He then went into the basement to get some plywood and started the process of boarding up all the windows and doors on the first floor.

"Okay, that'll keep us safe for a little while," he said aloud. "Abby, honey! What can I get ya? What do you need? Why don't I get you some clothes?"

Walter went into his bedroom and found Ruthie's old bathrobe, the terrycloth one he could never bring himself to throw away. He returned to the kitchen and gazed at the beautiful girl on the table. He remarked to himself just how much she looked like both his son and daughter-in-law.

"You know, I... I'm going to have to call your father," Walter whispered in her ear. "He's not going to believe it. Abby, I told him I blamed him for losing you all those years ago. But the truth is..." Walter paused and began to weep. "The truth is I could never tell him... that I knew it was my fault. I knew that the crossing over the creek needed fixing, but I thought you'd be all right. I'm so very sorry, darling. But you're here now, and that's all that matters! I love you, baby, and you're my big girl now."

He sat her up and dressed her in the robe. She was not quite limp, but not exactly cooperative. With the robe barely on her, Walter struggled as he carried her into the living room and sat her on the couch.

"What can I get you, honey, huh? What else do you want besides water? You want your daddy and mommy? Want me to call them?"

Walter couldn't believe it, but after all of these years he was ready to make that call.

Abby let out a whisper.

"Water."

Walter turned on the lights and frowned.

"Is that all you want? Honey, I think you've had enough water. You drink any more and you won't be able to fit on that couch! Uh, honey?"

Walter walked around to look at her straight on. The combined light from the kitchen and overhead was strong here. He noticed something he hadn't before. Her skin was fair, but some patches appeared almost translucent, revealing the water sloshing around inside of her. These clear areas also allowed him to see where that yellow blood had come from. It was some sort of build up or by-product of her quickly growing state. He could even see some pockets inside of her where the yellow ooze hardened and broke apart into pieces, like tiny jelly beans floating all around inside her body.

"Honey? Can you hear me?," Walter tried again.

"*Waaaaaaaaaaaterrrrrrrrr*," her eyes flicked open, her mouth enunciating clearly for the first time, all the floaties inside of her standing at attention.

* * *

Frank nearly regretted telling the officer at the front desk the whole story. It was so outlandish that it took some time for the guy to believe that he wasn't drunk, high, or just some whack job. Finally, after an unsuccessful phone call to the Baum residence, the officer agreed to investigate. He nearly went alone, but at the last second asked for another patrol car to meet him and Frank at residence in question.

As the sun began to rise, the two police sedans pulled up to Walter's house. Officer McLennan was the first out of the car, looking at the jungle intensity of the front yard. He grimaced, slowly making his way to the front door and knocked.

"Mister Baum, we have a man in our squad car who says you attacked him and you may have a young lady inside who's being kept against her will. I need you to step out of the house with your hands in the air. I have other officers here with me if there's—," he paused, "—an issue."

After a few minutes with no reply, they attempted the door themselves, but found it locked. Heading around to the backyard,

McLennan, Jones, and two other officers found that they would have more luck with the back door, as it was partially open. A garden hose snaked under the door, and a steady trickle of water was running out from beneath the door.

McLennan kicked the door open with his foot; it hit something within the room and bounced back like it was attached to a bungee cord. Putting all his weight against the door, he was able to force it open enough for each man to slip through one at a time. McLennan and Jones were first. Stepping over the puddles as best they could, they looked around the room. Over to their left, wedged in the doorway that led to the living room, was an object with soft, swelled contours, resembling a huge parade float shaped like a person's hand. Part of its gigantic wrist and arm folded into the kitchen, looped around a chair, and then made its way back into the obscured living room.

"What the hell is this?" Jones muttered. He had seen some weird stuff, like that crazy house fire last year in Guilford, but this was nuts.

Both officers drew their firearms and advised the other two to await further instructions. They crept towards the hand that took up the entire doorway. Unhooking his nightstick from his belt, McLennan tapped the appendage with caution. The inflated fingers flexed, but they were too filled with water to be able to grasp anything or to be of any other use.

Wordlessly, Jones pointed to the right side of the large palm. There was a gap between the door frame and the huge hand that was just wide enough to allow a man to squeeze through. McLennan nodded, then holstered the stick and grabbed his gun. Following the fold of the arm, they moved around the corner and into the living room. The arm ran up off of the ground and connected to a strange pulsating shape in the middle of the living room. The thing was the size of a mini-van and shaped like a girl; it was lumpy and disfigured, filled out as it was with differing amounts of water. Fingers, legs, and toes were all folded on top of each other, filling the entire room, each part some bizarre disproportion of the next. In the center of the mass, rocking back and forth, was her head, covered with a mess of long blonde hair. In her mouth was a green rubber hose, firmly clenched in her teeth. Most disturbing was her taught, perfectly clear skin, which reflected the light from the ceiling.

Inside the mass, just below the head, McLennan could make out the shape of a body, that of an old man floating belly up like a dead fish. Floating inside of her stomach, the man had a Mona Lisa smile, not one of joy or pleasure, but one of truth. One of resolve. Surrounding the old man were hundreds of five-inch-long objects, swimming in a school beside him like little fish.

Jones went in for a closer look.

"Mike, look at these things," Jones said, pointing at the darting forms within the big girl's belly. Jones stopped as the one closest to him now began to tread water. Suddenly it clicked with Jones what this swimming thing was. It was a little girl, and she looked right at him. Its human fingers reach out, poking at the thin skin that separated her from the air.

McLennan was scared.

"Rich, we gotta get out of here."

The tiny shape's fingers cut through the membrane, water and yellow puss beginning to leak. From the puncture, it stuck its head out of its makeshift birth canal.

"Wa... Waaaaaaaatrrrr. Waawaaaaaaaaatrrrrr," she croaked as she tried to make her way out. Hundreds of other little girls swam through the water to join her.

TOUChed bY the Finger Of GOd

John Bruni

Gus Blunk had to be the ugliest son of a bitch I have ever known—uglier than a Picasso smeared with shit. He never did attract many friends—or any at all—and though I was probably more of an acquaintance, I came closest to his affections.

His lack of companionship wasn't due to his hideous visage; truth be told, he was a complete asshole. His rotten, gap-toothed mouth matched his bitter jealousy. His patchy hairline and pockmarked face went hand in hand with the ire that boiled out of him. The unseemly fat that hung off his waist and waddled at his neck couldn't have gotten along more with his hatred toward minorities and anyone who had it better than he did. I could go on and on about his humped back, his lazy eye, his green fingernails, his overpowering stench—like rotten cabbage festering in a dump truck—and everything else down to the apple-sized mole on the end of his nose, but none of it would do justice to his grotesqueness. It was no wonder that he liked to keep to himself most of the time.

I don't know why he tolerated me. I felt sorry for the bastard, so I could never find it in me to tell him how badly his presence offended me. Maybe that's why he started hanging out in my bookstore.

Say what you will about Gus, but he was a huge fan of books. Real ones, not the digital kind. He liked to meet authors, and he'd always tell me, "What would I say to Stephen King? Please sign my Kindle?"

So he wasn't completely atrocious. We had common ground. In fact, the reason we'd gone for a walk was that he wanted to discuss the new John Sandford with me. I can tolerate anyone, provided they're interested in books, like me.

Thinking back to that day, try as I might, I can't recall any storm. To the best of my recollection, it was a bright, sunny afternoon. No reason to expect lightning.

Business was slow, so I closed the bookstore early, and we walked across Beacon Park, arguing over who was the better protagonist, Lucas Davenport or Virgil Flowers. My heart wasn't in it, and I found myself just admiring my surroundings.

I stopped to take a drink at the water fountain when it happened. The air seemed to sizzle a split second before my ears were raped by a tremendous crashing sound. It startled me so much I choked on the water, gagging and coughing. I couldn't even hear myself doing any of this, and that scared the hell out of me. I snapped my fingers by my ears, but all I could hear was a distant ringing sound and the deep thumping of my heart.

I turned to Gus to see if he was all right, and I saw him on the ground, straight as a board. What little hair he had stood on end, and his eyes were wide and still, like glass bulbs. At first I thought he was dead, but when I stooped down to help him, he jerked away from my touch. His gaze rolled slowly over to me, and his thick, wormy lips moved.

It would be a while before I could hear again. Someone called 9-1-1, and when the paramedics arrived, they managed to convey to me that Gus had been struck by lightning. Chuck Eddies over at the barbershop saw the whole thing. He said the bolt came right down on the crown of Gus' head. Gus jumped ten feet up, completely stiff, then fell back down, stunned.

You'd think something like that would cause some kind of damage. However, they let Gus go before they discharged me. They couldn't find anything wrong with him, not even a scorch mark. He ran the gamut of tests only to be told that he had no hearing loss or anything. And on a very positive note, he no longer had a lazy eye.

Well, I didn't see Gus for a while after that. I got better. My hearing came back on the fourth day, and I no longer trembled when I heard sudden noises. I noticed that Gus made the news shows as a curiosity, but folks soon forgot about him. Before long, things returned to normal.

Two weeks later, Gus strolled into my store, a big ol' grin on his face and a skip in his step. Granted, I didn't know him very well, but I couldn't think of a single time I'd ever seen him so chipper. He spent most of his time complaining, wallowing in misery, and bringing others down with him.

That wasn't the only difference I noticed; the giant mole on his nose was gone, not even a mark to show it had ever been there.

"Hot damn, Gus," I said. "You're looking good. You get some

doctor to lop off that nasty mole?"

"Nope. You're not going to believe this, but it just fell off. Woke up this morning and it was gone. I couldn't even find where it rolled away to. And that's not all. Check it out." He pointed to one of his bald spots.

I squinted and could make out little hairs sprouting up. "No way."

"It's growing back," Gus said. "Can you believe it?"

I floundered, trying to come up with something smart to say. All I managed to muster was, "How?"

He shrugged. "I don't know, and I don't care. Maybe the lightning did it. I'm not looking a gift horse in the *et cetera*."

"But this is impossible. Doesn't this concern you at all?"

He smiled, and I could have sworn that one of his missing teeth had grown back, and all of them had gone from a dull yellow to pure white. But his expression quickly grew serious, so I couldn't be sure.

"Lou," he said, "you know the old Hamlet quote. Lightning can do weird things to people. Now I've had a bad streak of shit luck my entire life. All of a sudden, things are going well? I feel like a new man. Hell, I feel like I was touched by the finger of God."

I didn't feel like mentioning to Gus his lifelong pledge of atheism. It would have only been petty. Besides, if all of this was working for him, who was I to tell him anything?

He bought a new Ed Gorman and a rare M.P. Shiel before walking out of my life for a while. In fact, as strange as it may seem, I forgot all about Gus. Maybe I wanted to suppress the knowledge of his previous life, before he was struck by lightning. I don't know.

The next time I saw Gus, he had a full head of hair and had lost almost all of his excess fat. Most shocking of all, he had a girlfriend. A *smoking-hot* girlfriend.

At the time, I'd just been dumped myself, so I spent most of my time drinking at Riley's, trying to forget. All right, maybe I reveled in the romance of it. I felt kind of like Mike Hammer, you know? Maybe I should get a new girl, I thought, but more than likely, I would just keep on trucking, like I usually do. Let come what may.

I was the only one there, aside from the bartender, when I heard the door open and saw Gus and his girl walk in. He saw me right away and grinned. This time I was certain he had all of his teeth, and they were in perfect health.

"Lou, sorry I haven't been around the store in a while. I've been busy, as I'm sure you can tell." He gestured to the woman. "This is Goldie. Goldie, Lou Atkins."

I shook her hand, but I couldn't say anything because I'd noticed something else. I'd missed it before only because he'd been standing at a distance. With him next to me, we saw eye to eye. Either he'd grown taller, or... or he no longer had a hunched back.

Gus must have noticed me staring. "I know. It's crazy, right?"

"And none of this is plastic surgery?" I asked.

"Not a bit. I'm probably the only person ever to say this, but getting struck by lightning was the best thing to ever happen to me."

"But... but this can't possibly happen." I hated to sound like a broken record, but for all of my book smarts, I couldn't fire off a line snappier or more original than that.

"What, you haven't heard of a blind person being struck by lightning and regaining the ability to see? Shit like this happens all the time. If you think that's a hoot, check this out." He lifted his shirt, showing off a perfectly muscled body. "I've never had a six-pack before." He winked and let his clothes cover him again. "And, well, I don't want to brag or anything, but... honey? Tell him about, well, you know."

Bashful, she looked away from us. She then held up both hands, index fingers extended. They hovered about ten inches apart.

It took me a moment to realize what she meant. I stammered, trying to find my way out of this conversation.

"That's not all, Lou. I'm as thick as a Coke can, too. She can barely fit her hand around it."

"Jesus, Gus. Not so loud."

"What? You're afraid word will get around about the ginormous size of my cock?" He laughed.

"No. Just... it's not dinner table, that's all."

"And we're not at a dinner table. Speaking of which, let's get us some drinks. The night is young."

Maybe it was to him. Eleven o'clock on a weekday night? Not for me. As much as I liked wallowing in my life as a heartbroken loner, I still had a sense of responsibility. My store opened at eight, so I had one last polite drink and went home.

This time, Gus stayed on my mind. For a month. I kept expecting him to come by the store eventually. He never did. In the meantime, I kept hearing rumors about him. The entire town was taken with him. They marveled at his transformation, and people I've known to curse his name pulled a one-eighty. Everyone, and I mean *everyone*, loved him. Even old man Festus, who didn't like anybody, counted Gus among his friends.

From what I could tell, Goldie was no longer in the picture. Neither were Sally or Jill or Buffy or Patience or even Angelique. Depending on whom you asked, he was with Kaylee or Britney or Jessie or Melanie. Probably all of them.

Everyone thought it was plastic surgery. A few of us, those who remembered the lightning, knew better.

Since he never came around the store, my curiosity grew. Once upon a time, he'd been my best customer. Considering the nature of all the stories about him, I had to wonder if he'd really turned into a Don Juan. After a while, I decided to stop waiting for him to come to me. I'd heard he liked hanging out in the city, so I made the trek and found him at his favorite club, the Golden Space. It was a hard place to get into, but luckily I dressed right and I was just good looking enough to get through the door.

I found Gus in the VIP room with three girls rubbing all over him and a table weighed down by five rails of coke and a fifth of top-shelf vodka. I couldn't believe it was him. He looked like a Hollywood idol and a rock star all rolled up into one. In fact, like many leading men, he'd changed his name. He was now Augustus Navarrone. Did it make him feel sexy? I don't know.

"Gus?" I asked, because even then I wasn't certain.

He looked up from an impressive valley of cleavage, white powder subduing the shine around his nostrils, and blinked. It took a moment before he recognized me.

"Lou? What are you doing here?"

I couldn't look away from his chiseled features, from his Superman curl down to his lantern jaw. "I was going to ask you the same thing. Why haven't you been down to my store?"

"Books?" He pshawed. "I don't need those things anymore. I'm living the high life, man. I can have anything I want."

"Well, I want to talk with you," I said.

He glanced at his companions and seemed to consider. "Fuck it. There will always be more girls. Take off, ladies." Before they could pout, he said, "Next time. I promise."

The girls shuffled off, and all of them cast a longing glance back at Gus. If anyone had told me half a year ago that women would look at him like that, I would have laughed at such a boldfaced lie.

"Have a seat." Gus gestured to the space next to him on the couch. I complied, and he offered me a drink. "Or some of this, if you're inclined." He waved at the coke. "I don't know how you feel about nose candy."

I opened my mouth to turn down both offers, but before I could speak, a gorgeous woman—a real Helen of Troy type—stomped up to us, hands on her hips. "Why haven't you called me, Auggie?"

He rolled his eyes. "Look bitch, what part of 'Fuck you' don't you understand? I'm done with you. Get it now?"

Her lower lip trembled, and her slick eyes were about to overflow. "But—"

Gus slapped his thighs in exasperation and stood face to face with her. "I loved fucking you, but I'm tired of your pussy. I like variety. Now get lost."

I couldn't believe this. Gus was always an asshole, but this was above and beyond. No matter what he thought of the local girls, he never spoke to them like this. He usually reserved his opinion for when he was alone with me, on the off-chance that someone might want to sleep with him. How could he spout such vile things?

No more books, combined with this new brand of bastardy—it spun my mind around. I never liked Gus, but now I found myself hating him.

She said it for me. "Augustus Navarrone, you're a piece of shit. Go fuck yourself." And she stomped off.

Gus shrugged and sat back down. He snorted a rail, took a shot of vodka, then clapped his hands together. "What did you want to talk about?"

I gaped at him, unable to find the right words. It's funny: I love books and gain my livelihood from them, but language abandons me when I need it the most.

"Look, I like you, man. But if I sent those ladies away for this, I'm going to be pissed."

That did it. "What happened to you, Gus? How did you turn into... into this?" I gestured at him.

He favored me with a picture-perfect smile. "I found out the truth about the world. I always suspected it, but now I know for sure. Beauty is everything to everybody. Even money is secondary. Now that I'm one of the sexiest men alive, I can do whatever I want. And since I spent a lot of my time on earth ugly, I have a ton of want."

In that moment, I wondered if that was how every beautiful person was, deep down. Were the Brad Pitts and the George Clooneys of the world really this reprehensible at their core?

"You've got to stop this," I said. "Just because you *can* act like a douche doesn't mean—"

"I don't care," he said. As much as I hate to admit it, he looked really cool saying it.

I opened my mouth to continue with my moral lesson, but I saw him glancing about the room, eye-fucking half a dozen women who used to be out of his league. I knew then that it was pointless.

I stood and turned, ready to leave without saying another word, but then a thought occurred to me. I paused before turn back to Gus. "You might lose this gift, Gus. You don't know how this change is going to continue. For all you know, you might get struck by lightning again, and you'll be back to the way you were."

"Struck twice?" He chuckled. "Not likely. And so what if I change back? All the more reason to enjoy myself now. To the limit."

I couldn't deal with him anymore. I got out of there, vowing to never talk to him again.

That lasted about three weeks. Considering how things worked out, I wish he'd just stayed away.

It happened at midnight. Usually I go to bed at eleven, but a new Lansdale held me captive. I promised myself just one more chapter, but I knew the book would be done in an hour.

Instead of reading, though, I was interrupted by a frantic hammering at my door. With an annoyed grunt, I pushed myself up from my chair and headed for the door.

No sooner had I opened it then someone rushed in and demanded, "Shut the door! Fast!"

I recognized Gus and did as he said. However, when I took more time to analyze him, I saw he'd changed even more. He looked sleeker, more wiry, with sharp angles under the tightly drawn skin of his face. His hands were longer, and each finger had a sharp, claw-like nail at the end. He didn't just look beautiful, he also looked predatory.

He opened his mouth and revealed the most shocking change yet: razor-sharp teeth, like a piranha's. Something shuddered deep inside my guts, and I couldn't bear the sight of him.

"Don't look at me like that!" His guttural voice set my nerves dancing. The animal smell on him reminded me of the lion house at the zoo. Everything about him screamed danger, and my instinct begged me to flee.

"Sorry," he said. "It's just that I'm tired of people looking at me like that."

I swallowed, wondering if I should make eye contact with him. I didn't know if he was a man or a beast at that point. Finally, I realized that if Gus intended to harm me, I couldn't escape. So I hazarded a glance up.

His talon covered up his mouth. Sweat made his forehead shine, and a barely perceptible tremor went through him. "Do you have anything to drink?"

Relieved to have an excuse to get away from him—for even a brief moment—I rushed to the kitchen to get a bottle of Jim Beam. As I took it down from the cabinet over the refrigerator, I noticed my knife rack. Should I take one of the blades for self-defense? Would it even help?

No, it probably wouldn't, especially considering how I'd never been in a fight before. Everything I knew about violence I learned from movies.

I grabbed the bottle and two tumblers, nothing more. If worse came to worst, I could club him with the Beam.

When I returned to the living room, I saw him laid out on my couch, one arm over his face. I sat in the chair across the coffee table from him—a reasonably safe distance—and poured our drinks. I pushed his closer to him, not daring to actually hand it to him.

He peeked out over his arm, and with a shocking speed, sat up, swept up the glass, and downed his drink. He shook the empty glass at me. "More."

I poured, then set down the bottle.

This time, he sipped. Closed his eyes. Smiled a little. Not enough to show off his new teeth, though.

"What's going on?" I asked.

He turned his gaze to me, and I could swear there was a slight glow in his eyes, like when you shine a light into a cat's. "I don't know. But I don't like it anymore. I thought this... *thing* was a miracle. Now it's turning me into something else."

I waited, hoping for more. I tasted my drink and felt a calming warmth wash over me.

"Why you, right?" Gus asked. "Considering how our last meeting went, you should be last on my list. But you were always straight with me, unlike these other cocksuckers. They loved being around me until I started changing into... whatever this is." He waved his arms around. "Fickle bastards."

That struck me as funny, but I didn't even feel the urge to smile.

"The thoughts... Jesus, you don't even want to know. I get this hunger. I just want to bury my teeth in someone's guts and eat my way through them. I can even see myself doing it when I'm with people."

I shuddered, regretting my decision in the kitchen.

He smiled. "You should see the look on your face. Don't worry. I try to resist. Except when I do, I get this simmering rage in me. I snap at people. I can't keep living like this."

I cleared my throat. "Have you gone to a doctor?"

He snorted. "You think some sawbones can help me? Whatever this is, it's supernatural. Maybe I should see a priest instead."

"Maybe you should try it out anyway. I can drive you to the ER—"

"No one can cure me from this transformation."

"Isn't it at least worth trying?"

"No!" he snarled. "Let it go!"

I immediately found something interesting to look at in my glass and tried to swallow my heart back into place. Blood raced through my head so loudly I wondered if Gus could hear it.

"Sorry," he said. "Just... don't piss me off. I'm struggling here. If I started something, I don't know if I could stop."

I finished my drink, but the glass trembled so much that I didn't dare go for a refill.

Gus emitted a low chuckle, a sound that would have been at home in a dark, musty basement. "I scared myself, Lou. You know Darlene? No, she was after your time. Well, she was the last to leave me. She was yelling and arguing and shouting, and I couldn't help myself. I shoved her against the wall with my hand at her throat. I imagined me biting her face off, and it seemed so real I thought I'd actually done it. That little fright snapped me back to reality, so I managed to stop before I did anything too bad."

"Jesus, Gus."

"After she left, I decided to come to you. You see, I've been thinking about this. What if there's a connection between beauty and the beast? Being good looking certainly doesn't hinder a predator. It lures victims in, like those lights hanging from the heads of those ugly fish at the bottom of the ocean. What do you think?"

I floundered. "Well... I... I don't know. None of this makes sense."

This time, he grabbed the bottle and chugged its entire contents down in one go. When he finished, he aimed the mouth of it at me. "You said something once. Maybe there is a way to stop this."

I blinked against his noxious booze breath. "How's that?"

He must not have heard me. "Thanks, Lou." He carelessly dropped the bottle on the floor—it *thunked* down and rolled under the table—and rushed out the door.

I wish I could tell you this story ends with an exciting Frankensteinian chase through town, citizens armed with pitchforks and torches, but I'm afraid it goes out with a T.S. Eliot whimper.

I didn't hear from Gus for a week. Then came the night of the horrible storm. Rain came down in sheets, pushed into waves by a merciless wind. The lights went out at about 10:30, so I had to read the old-fashioned way: by candlelight. Occasionally, lightning illuminated my room with perfect clarity.

The next day, I got a call from the police. They needed me to identify a body. Even before the officer mentioned Gus' name, I knew who it was.

On the way down to the morgue, the officer explained how Gus was found. "Some window washer at the Felker building noticed a charred piece of meat clinging to the base of a lightning rod. Thought it was an animal at first, but then he saw the clothes pile nearby. Found Gus' wallet in there. Did you know that the Felker building is struck by lightning twenty-five times a year? That's more than any other place in town."

"No." But I'll bet Gus knew it. All of a sudden, I remembered what I'd said to Gus about getting struck by lightning a second time.

As we entered the morgue, the officer said, "We just have to make sure it's him, and you're listed as his emergency contact."

Weird. If I'd been in a better mood, I would have laughed.

"Here we are. Just warning you, it's a nasty mess."

The thing he showed me in the big metal drawer couldn't have once been a human being, but there was just enough of a face left to make a positive ID.

Sorry, Gus. I was wrong. It didn't change you back. It just made you dead. At least you don't have to deal with this anymore. Maybe you saw it as a win-win situation.

Or maybe, subconsciously, I knew what I was saying that day in the Golden Space. Whatever the case may be, I hope you're in a better place. This one certainly didn't treat you very well. If you were touched by a finger of God, then it was the middle one.

candy stain

Jonathan Woodrow

Candy had made it half way across her apartment to open the door to her fiancé when she was stopped by a panic attack so intense that she had to sit down on the floor and lean against the wall to keep from falling. Eventually she managed to stand up, eyes still closed tight, taking slow, deep breaths. But she was left with the terrible feeling that she'd forgotten something. Something of great importance.

"Candy?" Her fiancé was banging on the door now. "Cane? Honey? You okay in there?"

Candy gripped her stomach as cramps twisted her insides. The pain in her stomach was bad, but the unexplained panic was far worse; like her chest was about to explode.

And then it passed, as quickly as it came on.

"A minute," she called back. She took in a few more deep breaths and was pretty much back to normal.

Keys rattled from the hallway. Candy opened the door and smiled at Jake, then she looked down at what he held in his hand. "What's that?" she asked.

Jake looked down at the key in his hand. It was a key to her apartment.

"Where did you get that?"

Jake frowned. "What the hell was going on in there, Cane? What happened? Are you okay?"

"Don't change the subject. Is that a key to my apartment you got there?"

Jake shook his head. "I could see you through the peephole, Cane,

222

you looked like you were having some kind of seizure. Are you gonna tell me what's going on?"

Candy grabbed hold of his key chain. Jake maintained his grip, and the two of them stared each other down.

Candy let go. "I never gave you a key," she said in a calm, calculated voice. "I specifically said no key, in fact. So please, explain."

Jake grinned. "I missed my little Candy Cane," he said, and leaned in to kiss her.

Candy pulled away. "Please explain, Jake," she said. "Before I call the cops."

Jake's grin disappeared. He noticed two of the neighbors watching them from down the hall and pushed his way into the apartment, closing the door behind him.

"Call the cops? Are you...?"

Candy folded her arms, said nothing.

"We're getting..." he sighed. "I'm your fiancé, in case you've forgotten. Don't you find it a little... I don't know... Peculiar? That I don't even have a key to your apartment?" He scratched his head and kicked off his shoes. "You know, most couples like us, they live together, share lives, a bathroom. Share a bed."

"We share a bed," she said.

"I mean for more than just... you know..." he lowered his voice. "Sex."

She said nothing, and Jake seemed to loosen up a little. Like he was closing the book on this one for now and shelving it for later. Candy was grateful, though she understood his frustration. Jake had been patient, but that wouldn't last for long. Sooner or later, she would need to step out of her solitary life and into something that she hoped would be better.

Jake was struggling with the key, trying to work it off the ring.

Candy held up her hand. "Keep it."

"You sure?"

She nodded. Jake kissed her.

The two of them had lunch in the food court at the mall before heading to Jake's apartment, where they spent the afternoon having sex. After that, Candy left and went back to her own apartment, alone.

One step at a time.

* * *

Candy's night was filled with dreams that clawed, raped, and screamed at her… and as usual, she awoke without the faintest memory of what they'd been about.

Only that wasn't quite true this time.

Something was still bothering her, as though part of her dream had hitched a ride back into reality.

Candy opened her eyes and looked around. Nothing was out of place. She checked the clock on the nightstand. It was early, but that was good. She would go for a long run before breakfast and clear her head before meeting up with Jake later on.

But she still felt unsettled.

Candy sat up and stretched, and that's when she felt it: the tightness in her face.

She moved the muscles in her face and something pinched her right cheek. She brought her hand up to investigate and pulled it back reflexively. Something sticky was smeared across her cheek. She carefully traced her fingers down the smudge. It was maybe an inch wide, two inches long. But what the hell was it?

Candy got out of bed and ran to the bathroom to examine her face in the mirror.

Frustrated, she flipped on the light and leaned in closer, pushing at the edges with her fingers. The smudge was grey in color and ran in a straight line along her cheek, ending just below her ear. It looked like it had been painted on with a brush.

She tried to remove it with hot water, but the substance was hard and it took nearly five minutes to get off. The scrubbing left a bright red mark on her face.

As she watched the last few dark specks wash down the drain, another thought occurred to her… the bed.

She ran back to the bedroom, stubbing her toe on the chest of drawers and ignoring the pain that fired up her leg. She pulled the pillows up and examined both sides. Nothing. She yanked them from the pillowcases and tossed them aside. Nothing. By the time she was finished, the floor was covered in bed sheets and her mattress was resting up against the window. And still nothing.

* * *

Candy stopped off at the coffee house on the way back from her run. She ordered a chai tea and waited at the end of the counter for her drink to be made.

"Cadence?"

It took Candy a few moments to realize she was the one being called. She hadn't heard that name in years, and hearing it now made her very uncomfortable.

She turned and saw an old couple at one of the tables. The old lady stood. "Cadence Parker? Is that you?"

Candy nodded, wary.

"It's… been a long time," the old lady said. She looked as though she regretted starting the conversation. "You remember Alf?" she said as a matter of course, presenting a small, grey-haired man sitting beside her like he was an accessory. Alf nodded and stared down at his coffee, but said nothing.

Candy smiled as the barista handed over her latte. She held it up to the old lady.

"Of course," the old lady said, the resolve of her forced smile cracking at the edges, revealing something else… pity?

"Well, it was nice seeing you again," she said, in conclusion.

Candy nodded, smiled, and quickly got the hell out of there.

* * *

That night, Candy dreamed of the cabin.

Photos of naked girls on the wall, hard food in a drawer, and for once, Candy's alarm clock beat her to the punch, tearing through the quiet room and nearly giving her a heart attack. She leaned over and dropped her hand onto the snooze button, and as she pulled back, her face brushed against her arm. The tightness again.

Candy limped to the bathroom, her body aching, tense from a bad night's sleep.

And there it was, on the right side of her face, the stain. The same as before.

Only it was darker this time, the edges sharper, brushstroke course and jagged. It was longer, too, spreading from her ear down to the corner of her mouth.

She tried to peel it off at the top edge with her fingernails, breaking the skin below her eye. Scanning the bathroom for something else to use, she noticed the disposable razor on the shelf in the shower. That ought to work.

She smashed the plastic casing and held the blade carefully between her fingers as she went to work on her face.

* * *

Later on, Candy watched Jake eat his plate of food like it was his very first—or his very last.

He spoke to her through chewed up bread and hot dog.

"Pardon?" she said.

He swallowed. "What happened to your face?"

Candy turned her head away for a short moment, and looked back at Jake with a grin. "Shaving rash," she said.

He smiled back. It was a knowing smile.

"You talk to the flowers guy yet?" he asked.

Candy shook her head. "A lot on my plate."

Jake nodded.

"I did check out a couple of bands on line though."

"Oh yeah?"

"One looked pretty good."

"Nothing too heavy, I hope."

Candy smiled. "No, they're a Slipknot tribute, so they'll be pretty low key."

With a humorless smile, Jake tossed the hot dog wrapper onto Candy's food tray.

"You enjoy that much?" she asked.

He wiped his mouth on her napkin. "And have you thought any more about the guest list?"

Candy winced. There were certain buzzwords that caught her off guard. She kept her response nice and simple. "No," she said. "Not yet."

Jake watched her for what seemed like forever. She closed the lid on her noodles and took the tray over to the garbage area of the food court. When she returned, Jake was ready to go.

* * *

Candy headed to Best Buy on her way back home and picked up a high def web cam.

Tossing the instructions to one side, she connected the device to her laptop and installed the software. She placed the camera on the dresser and checked the signal. It was lined up and ready to go.

She looked at her watch. It was still early. She decided to call Jake to let him know she would be having an early night, and she made plans to meet up with him the next day. When she was done on the phone, Candy got ready to go out.

* * *

The bars on Candy's street were off limits, so she took a cab to the other side of town. She wanted to put a stop to these little sojourns, for her sake as well as Jake's, but she needed this, now more than ever.

Candy entered the Hound Dog Bar with her purse under her right arm, bleach-blonde wig covering her own mouse-brown hair, and her skirt hitched up to just a few inches below her buttocks, revealing a small Band-Aid on her left thigh. Several heads turned, but she paid no attention. She needed a drink first before anything else could happen, and she ordered three at the bar.

Candy spent the next hour teasing all the guys who approached her, emasculating them beyond recognition. By the time she had finished, she was receiving death stares from at least nine guys, all of whom were clearly capable of sexual violence. She chose that moment to walk out the front door, picking at her Band-Aid as she went.

Candy waited and watched from behind a parked van across from the bar. Moments later one of those guys walked outside after her. He was overweight, bald, mean looking, and all his other features were irrelevant to Candy. She stepped out from behind the van and let him see her. He crossed the street and she pulled up her skirt just enough to show the guy she was not wearing panties. He walked faster, a stupid grin on his face, and Candy let the guy assault her against the stone wall of an alleyway separating two buildings.

As expected, he was anything but gentle. He jammed his elbow up against her throat, pressing into her chin almost hard enough to dislocate her jaw. As he pounded her, bruising her internal organs, Candy reached down to the Band-Aid and tore it back, picking at the raw wound on her leg, digging her finger in deeper and deeper, the pain attacking her from all sides, a cluster assault... until her mind reached a singular image, blacking all others out: an image of an Angel with the face of a newborn baby, rising above her from the dark crevices of the town, watching her, judging her with all its might. The winged thing glared at Candy, shaking its head, and a tear dropped from the corner of its tiny eye onto the cracked asphalt at her feet, and at that moment, as Candy's pain climaxed and she came right there against the hard and bruising edges of the stone wall, the Angel vanished.

* * *

That night Candy's dreams were more vivid, more violent; the cabin more real... and she now saw that the naked photos on the walls were of herself. The cabin's wooden structure undulated, heaved... images spun through her head like a slideshow: a bed inside a cage, food being passed through a drawer in the wall, a man with long blonde hair kissing the mouth of a miniature schnauzer named Bartleby in a grotesque display of affection, the gentle way the same man made love to Cadence—

Pounding, pounding!

—as he wept for the loss of something... though she wasn't sure what.

And the pounding became louder and louder until she couldn't take it any longer and the more she screamed the louder the pounding got and her vision blurred and her tightly focused thoughts broke apart and scattered and in her mind she saw only one word appearing over and over and over and over and over... *MOMMY.*

Candy's eyes opened. It was morning, she was in her bed and everything was normal, only this time *all* of the wretched terror and guilt from her dream was still in the room with her, sitting around in a circle and watching. She tried to shake it off, but it seemed to laugh at her. She winced and tried to cry, hoping that it would release some of the tension, but then she was distracted by the familiar pinching against her face. Her thoughts immediately latched on to this notion instead, the memories of the dream retreating back to their hiding places.

Her fingers touched the familiar shape of the stain, running along its surface, and it was bigger still.

After getting herself cleaned up, Candy applied gauze and tape to the scarring on her face and came back out to the bedroom to dress, noticing the camera on her way past. A quick inventory of the night's events confirmed that she had indeed turned it on before going to bed. A chill passed through her as she reconciled the fact that the camera had been recording all night.

Candy did her best to find other things to do before watching the video. At first, it was getting dressed; she absolutely, positively had to be presentable before starting the day. Then, breakfast; there was no way she could sift through hours of footage on an empty stomach. But after she'd showered, dressed, eaten, changed, gone for a run, showered again, dressed again, and eaten again, there was nothing else she could do to further procrastinate, so she headed into the bedroom to her computer to pull up the footage.

The time code showed her getting to bed at 2:00 am. Her movements were pained and slow. The lights turned off ten minutes after that. She fast-forwarded the video: 3:00 am, 3:30... and at 3:45 Candy sat up straight and rewound the video.

Her breathing was heavy, heart pounding, and the hair follicles on her head felt as though they were buzzing. She took a deep breath and pressed play. The video rolled, the counter showed 3:43. Her body was completely still, covers off, when the screen went momentarily black as a figure passed in front of the camera. The form returned, moving around the edge of the bed and over to where Candy slept.

She leaned in, eyes wide and dry, barely breathing at all now.

It wore dark pants, dark boots, and a dark hooded sweater. The figure stood over Candy's sleeping body for several minutes before leaning in slowly, and, with great care, it licked the side of her face. The figure stood over her a little longer before walking back around the bed, past the camera, and out of the frame.

Candy waited a while, frozen, hands held up to her face. She snapped out of it and fast-forwarded the video again. On the screen, the sun seemed to rise in seconds, and Candy's movements grew more and more frantic right up until she woke up.

She turned off the video and shut down her laptop. The fear she was currently experiencing was slowly being pulled away, the images shifting toward the back of her mind. Another nightmare she would suppress.

Candy realized it was afternoon already and she was supposed to be meeting Jake in an hour. She made herself a cup of coffee and turned on the TV. Before long, it was time for her to leave her apartment, and at that moment, as though on cue, the doorbell rang.

This time, she made it to the front door without incident, where she found Jake standing with a big grin on his face, hands in his pockets, and not a key in sight.

* * *

Instead of the mall, Jake took Candy into town, where the noisy bars along the main strip spilled out into the streets and cars lined the sidewalk.

Candy followed Jake into one that was just as noisy, just as busy, but which had a small area where a couple could sit and eat and watch the game.

"Who's playing?" Candy asked.

Jake shook his head. "No idea." They sat down. "You can consider yourself the proud holder of my undivided attention."

"Well, aren't I the lucky girl?"

Jake ordered a bottle of Cava and a couple of appetizers.

"I'm really not all that hungry," she said.

Jake smiled, reached over and took her hands in his. "I know."

She smiled back."You know, huh?"

"I know."

Something told her she had reason to panic, but she kept smiling. "Know what?"

"I just know."

The Cava arrived, and the next few minutes were taken up by the pouring, the clinking, and the tasting.

Before Candy could revisit her question, Jake continued. "I know you, whatever you're thinking, feeling. Whatever your needs. I know you so well. Better than you think. Don't you know that?"

There was a wry smile on his face.

"You knew I wasn't hungry."

"Exactly," he said.

"But how?"

"Because, I—"

"No, I get that, but… see, I get that you think you know me and you can read me. But there's… I mean, hungry? You might know my favourite color, or drink. My general tastes, likes and dislikes. But you can't tell me you're psychic."

Jake said nothing, just continued smiling.

"I'm sorry," Candy said. "That sounded a little cold. I'm grateful for all you do. Grateful for you. Just you…" She paused, twisted her glass around on the table. "And I don't know why I can't let this go."

"I do," he said. "I know why."

She nodded. "Because you—"

"I know."

"—know me."

"Right."

"Right."

Jake downed his Cava and poured himself another glass. "I know you. I know your past. I know everything about your life. I know all about your childhood. I know what you went through." He paused.

Candy watched, astounded. "And how do you know this?"

"Well, Candy, I always knew. I knew before we started dating, truth be told."

This was actually a major bombshell to Candy.

"I've given you your space, respected your privacy. And I know about your little trips out at night, too. That disguise you wear, the things you do."

Candy pushed out her chair and stood, ready to leave.

"No, please. Sit down. Let me finish."

She could see that this was incredibly hard for him, and she realized that this was more than just a cheap exposé. She sat back down again.

"Thank you," he said. "I just wanted you to know that I know, and that it's all okay. That I'm still here for you, through the good and bad, just as I intend to pledge in two months, when we get married. And that I understand everything you do, and everything you are, and... I love you. I love everything about you, and..." He cleared his throat and drank his second drink.

"Jake," Candy said.

He held up his hand. "Just think about what I've said. Think, before you say anything."

She nodded.

"I want to be clear, I'm not looking for pity or anything like that," he said. "I didn't say what I said to make you feel guilty. That's not why I said it."

"Last night... it was the last time," she said. "I had already decided that."

Jake nodded, and seemed to think about this.

"I realized that, last night... My god, did you really follow me, or something?"

Jake smiled, nodded again. "I was always there, somewhere nearby, in the background. Waiting, just in case things escalated and you couldn't maintain... I don't know, maintain your control."

Candy felt tears run down her face. It was a feeling she hadn't experienced in years, and the tears didn't stop.

"Hey," he said, and took her hands again. "Cane, look at me. I don't want you to feel anything now but hope. Hope and happiness. Things are going to change for you, for us. And your life is going to get better. I want you to know that."

Candy nodded. "I know that."

"And I can't imagine what you're going through now, or what you went through all those years ago when you were a kid. Whether it's some sort of guilt, what you're feeling now, or just plain bad memories. And that's one thing I'll never truly know. That's yours."

Candy placed a finger over his mouth and said, "Shhh." She kissed him and took his face in her hands. "I love you, Jake," she said. "And I don't deserve you. Not one bit."

He let her hands stroke his face. Their appetizers arrived and Jake asked for the bill.

"Let's get out of here," he said. "I'll take you home."

The two of them stood. "I want to stay with you tonight," she said. "At your place."

Jake took her hand. "You don't need to."

"I want to stay."

He nodded, smiled, and the two of them left together. That night, they made love with an intensity neither one of them had experienced before; not with each other, and certainly not with anyone else.

Candy dreamed.

She dreamed of the cabin, the blonde man, and a young girl, fourteen years old, named Cadence, who was a guest at the cabin. In the dream, nothing needed to be explained. Candy understood everything, first hand. Because she was the girl.

Cadence stayed in a small room, was served food through a drawer in the wall, and she looked forward to short, daily visits from the man with the blonde hair, who was the only human she ever saw. She wanted to talk, but he wanted to cry into her bosom and make love, ever so gently, while his miniature schnauzer watched from the other side of the room. And when he was done, he took pictures of her bare, dirty, used body and plastered them across the walls. The lights remained on, all day and all night; and without windows, Cadence began to lose track of time. The pictures grew in number, filling each wall from top to bottom, and after a while, there was nowhere she could look without seeing herself in compromised positions. She tried keeping her eyes closed, but she started getting headaches.

Cadence began to think of herself as nothing more than a sexual object, and as her mind and body changed, her hatred grew. The blonde man noticed the change in her behavior, and he spent hours lecturing her on the importance of making others feel welcome, and hiding her negative thoughts, no matter how bad they were, for the sake of decorum. He told her that this was all just an exercise in self-preservation, and that when they were done, she would be better off; she would have learned a valuable lesson, and would be thanking him for it.

In a timid voice, she asked the man when it was the lesson would be finished, and the man shook his head, disappointed, and beat her to within an inch of her life.

But her body carried on changing, growing, and soon, *she was—*

She was startled by the sound of crying. The crying was high pitched and infant-like to begin with, but it thickened in tone and darkened until it was a dreadful adult howl.

Candy opened her eyes. She screamed when she saw Jake beside her, bound at the wrists and legs and taped at the mouth. His eyes were the only things that could communicate.

She looked around the room and noticed a shadow lurking in the doorway to the bathroom. Tall and wide, it was a figure she didn't think she'd ever seen in person before, but she knew instantly who it was. The man from the video.

She sat up, Jake groaned from beside her, and the figure in the doorway approached.

Jake screamed through the thick duct tape, the tendons in his neck straining. The man walked over, raised a set of long-handled bolt cutters, and brought them down into Jake's chest. Jake stopped screaming and began choking, doubling over as much as the ropes would allow. The man turned his attention to Candy and walked around to her side of the bed, bolt cutters still in hand.

He leaned in. This time Candy got a good look at his face. He was much younger than she'd originally thought. Fourteen, maybe fifteen years old. Just a boy. There was a sad look about him, and a lot of anger as well. The boy tilted his head to the side and blinked tears down his cheeks, and in that moment Candy was overcome by revelation.

She reached out her arms, wanting to hug him and feel him against her, but her hands stopped a few inches away from the restraints that bound her wrists. She let her hands drop and the ropes slackened. She studied the boy's features, his general build, and gasped as her focus moved down his left arm.

"What happened to your hand?" she said. The stump at the end of his left arm had long healed, but it was not clean.

The boy brought his arm up and touched the jagged scar against Candy's face. Her skin tingled at the contact, and a connection was made. The boy stood and raised the long-handled bolt cutters. He placed the blades over the edge of the bed frame, about two inches in, and closed the handles. The dark oak splintered and cracked, and Candy knew he had just answered her question.

"I'm so sorry," she said, her voice gentle, maternal.

She felt Jake move from beside her and grunt through the duct tape.

The boy walked over to her and knelt down by the bed. He moved in closer still, his nose practically touching hers. Candy didn't pull away. Things were slowly coming back to her, and not just in snippets or fragmented dreams.

The boy reached into the back pocket of his jeans and pulled out a photo. He handed it to Candy. It was a photo she knew well, one of many, and she had seen it every day for a period of nearly two years.

"Mommy?" he said.

Candy was surprised at the sound of the boy's voice. It had barely broken, and was more like that of a child than a teenager.

"Yes, sweetie," she said. "That's mommy."

The boy nodded, and pulled off the duvet, revealing Candy's naked form.

"Mommy?" he said again. Candy nodded, the connection between them growing stronger by the minute.

"That's right, sweetie," she said. And Candy realized that this was the only word the boy knew how to say. The only word he'd ever been taught.

The boy nodded again, more tears running down his face.

"Mommy?"

The connection was complete. Candy knew exactly what he was trying to ask her, without the need for words at all.

"Yes, of course. If that makes you feel better."

The boy leaned in over her exposed breast and placed his mouth on her nipple.

Jake screamed and part of his duct tape shifted and came loose. *"Candy!"*

The boy jerked his head back up and glared over at Jake.

"What the fuck do you think you're doing, you freak? Are you fucking crazy?"

He pulled at his ropes, causing the bed frame to shift hard under them. The boy walked around the bed to the other side, grabbing the long-handled bolt cutters on the way.

Jake's screaming grew louder. *"Help!"* he shouted. *"Somebody... can anybody hear me?"*

The boy climbed up onto the bed and stood over Jake, who became silent.

Jake diverted his attention to Candy now. "Cane, honey? Do something, please. Do something."

The boy lowered the bolt cutters so that the blades rested over Jake's throat.

"Candy! Please, you can stop this. You can, you can. *I know you can.*"

Candy whined, not knowing what to say, how she was supposed to respond, or what she was supposed to do. "I can't," she said, and she turned her head away as the boy closed the handles on the bolt cutters, snipping through Jake's windpipe. Candy squeezed her eyes shut, but she could still hear the hollow rasping and shaking coming from beside her.

The boy opened the handles and dug down into the bed, closing the blades one last time and severing Jake's spinal cord.

Candy shook her head in an effort to unremember; a talent she'd been trying her best to master since she was a little girl.

The boy cut the ropes and Jake's body fell to the floor. The boy climbed over to where Candy lay.

"Mommy," he said, his voice tender.

Candy opened her eyes and slowly turned her head so she was facing the boy.

"I know you had to do it, sweetie. I forgive you."

The boy put his mouth over her nipple again.

Candy felt sucking. She knew nothing would be coming out—not anymore—but she understood this was just for comfort, and in that function it served the both of them.

She tried her best to remember what the boy had looked like the last time she'd seen him. Barely weeks old, she supposed. Thick hair at birth, dark green eyes. The image came to her right away. He'd been so tiny then. His little hand resting on her chest as he fed. The hand that was no longer there. She remembered the smell of his hair, and the sound of his crying when he needed mommy.

The boy raised his head. "Mommy?" he said. *Where did you go?*

"I had to leave, sweetie."

"Mommy?" *Why did you leave me there?*

"I..." She tried to think of the answer, the right answer, the one she'd been telling herself all these years. But she had no idea what it was. "I wanted to bring you with me, sweetie. I really, really wanted to. But I just..." Candy swallowed, her eyes widened. "I went back, later on, with the police and the search team. I tried to find you. But I couldn't find the house." She choked up, and speech was getting harder. "I couldn't find you."

"Mommy?" *Where did you have to be to that was so important?*

"Home," Candy said. "I had to get home."

"Mommy." *But wasn't home with me?*

"It should have been. I know that now. But I was young then, and…"

The boy's manner seemed to change. Sadness was hardening to anger.

"Mommy?" *Do you know how I've lived all these years?*

Candy knew. She'd always believed—always convinced herself—that her son had not survived for long after her escape from the cabin. Hard as that was, it had seemed the most likely scenario. And more importantly, it had given her a small degree of closure. Allowed her to move past this horrifying chapter and on with the rest of her life.

But her son *had* survived. The closure was *bullshit*. He hadn't moved past it. The life he'd moved along with was a life she'd chosen to escape.

"Mommy?" *Well?*

Her son had endured quite literally a lifetime of suffering, while she was trying her best to leave it all behind.

"I want you to tell me all about it," she said. "Please, I want to know everything about you, sweetie. I want you to share everything… with me. Even the bad stuff. Especially the bad stuff. I deserve it. You deserve it. Won't you do that? Please?"

The boy leaned in one last time and pressed his mouth over her nipple. Candy allowed herself one last glance at the blood stain where her fiancé's body had been before closing her eyes and resting her head on the pillow, focusing all her energy on recreating a picture of her son's life from the time she'd left him to the present.

Candy's eyes popped open and a sudden, fierce agony seared across her face, through her entire body.

The boy had bitten down.

She turned her head to the side, clenching her teeth together and chewing back a ragged scream. The pain was immense, and with it came a level of clarity she hadn't experienced in more than a decade. A clarity that allowed her to stream the boy's thoughts now in their entirety.

"Mommy?"

"Yes," her voice broke into a squeal again. "Yes, I see now, sweetie."

"From?"

It was the first word he'd uttered that wasn't 'mommy', but Candy didn't need to open her eyes to know what he was pointing to?

"Yes, sweetie. That's where you're from."

"Mommy." *I saw it in the pictures on the walls.*

"Yes, your daddy was right, sweetie. That's where you're from."

"Mommy." *I want to go back.*

Candy nodded. She wanted to go back, too. "You do what you need to do, sweetie. I love you."

As the boy began to strip off the skin on her chest, the exquisite pain took Candy on a trip to the place where she had developed just about all of her emotional framework, and it allowed her to spend the last fourteen years with her son.

She saw her baby boy, and knew that from the moment he had opened his eyes to the big wide world and taken his first breath he had known nothing but suffering and misery. She accepted the gift of his pain, gladly took the weight off his shoulders, and by the time he used the bolt cutter to crack through her rib cage, she was flying. Soaring above the cabin, away from the darkness, and into something new, something... better. Just as she had promised herself.

About the Authors

C. C. Adams was born and raised in London, UK, and credits his oldest brother with showing him the world of horror and dark fiction through books, TV and film at an early age. On beating his first National Novel Writing Month challenge in 2009, he decided to run with more of his ideas, and has been published in anthologies such as *Another 100 Horrors* and *100 Doors To Madness*. He still lives in London, where he lifts weights, practices martial arts, cooks—and looks for the next quote to set off the next dark delicacy.

Rose Blackthorn lives in the high mountain desert of Eastern Utah with her boyfriend and two dogs, Boo and Shadow. She spends her time writing, reading, being crafty, and photographing the surrounding wilderness. An only child, she was lucky to have a mother who loved books, and has been surrounded by them her entire life. Thus instead of squabbling with siblings, she learned to be friends with her imagination and the voices in her head are still very much present. She is a member of the HWA and has been published online and in print with Necon E-Books, Stupefying Stories, Buzzy Mag, Interstellar Fiction, SpeckLit, Jamais Vu and the anthologies *The Ghost IS the Machine, A Quick Bite of Flesh, From Beyond the Grave, O Little Town of Deathlehem, Enter at Your Own Risk: The End is the Beginning, FEAR: Of the Dark,* and *Equilibrium Overturned*, among others. You can follow Rose on Twitter, @rose_blackthorn, or find her on Facebook, http://www.facebook.com/RoseBlackthorn.Author, and be sure to stop by her blog, http://roseblackthorn.wordpress.com/. For more of Rose's works, make sure to check out her author page on Amazon, http://amazon.com/author/roseblackthorn.

John Bruni is the author of *Strip*, a crime novel published by MUSA, and *Tales of Questionable Taste*, a collection of short stories published by StrangeHouse Books. His work has appeared in many places, most notably *A Hacked-Up Holiday Massacre*, an anthology from Pill Hill Press, *Zombie! Zombie! Brain Bang!*, an anthology from StrangeHouse, and the critically acclaimed *Vile Things*, an anthology from Comet Press. He has a new novel coming out from StrangeHouse in 2014, and he was the editor of *Tabard Inn*. He lives in Elmhurst, IL.

Nathan Cabaniss is based out of Atlanta , GA, where he lives a life consisting primarily of danger, intrigue and Netflix. His work has appeared in *Voluted Tales* and the *Tales of the Shadowmen* anthology series, and his interactive superhero novel *Beyond Order and Chaos* is forthcoming. He also once had a story published alongside Michael Moorcock, so he has that going for him.

Gregor Cole works out of Kent (the garden of England) in the UK spending most of his free time scribbling away in the gloom and watching classic horror. He sharpens the knives of his craft on a diet of tea, biscuits, and lemon loaf cake, constantly waiting for the postman to deliver his weekly selection of gore films and bizarro literature.

Peter John Cunis has written for the web series *Hamilton Carver, Zombie PI* and has co-written three plays for Synetic Theater in Arlington, VA: *Genesis Reboot, The Three Musketeers,* and *Beauty and the Beast.* He has performed improv comedy in Providence, RI and Cambridge, MA, and currently performs with various groups in Manhattan. He lives in Astoria, NY and spends most of his free time writing plays. This is his first published short story.

R. J. Fanucchi lives in Portland, Oregon with his wife, Rebecca Irene Fanucchi, and their daughter, Bailey Paige Fanucchi. He divides his time between his family, work and writing. R. J. has written a picture book, short stories, and a young adult novel. His short story "A Most Dangerous Ruse" was published in the anthology *The Game,* released by 7 Realms Press.

M.R. Gott is the author of *Where the Dead Fear to Tread* and *Rising Dead.* You can visit M.R.'s website Cutis Anserina at http://wherethedeadfeartotread.blogspot.com. M.R. also writes for Ravenous Monster and Unleash the Fanboy. He lives contentedly in central New Hampshire with his wife, and their pets Lucy and Porter. Aside from writing, M.R. enjoys dark coffee, dark beer, red wine, and fading light.

Matt Kelly has been published through Gothic City Press in *Con(viction) – The Anthology of the Con – #1.* He also writes the action packed, monthly comic book "The Scarlet Nemesis," and the highly anticipated relaunch of cult favorite "Highlander" for Emerald Star Comics. His creator-owned comic "The Alternate Adventures of Annabelle Avery" is due late 2014. He lives on Long Island with his beautiful wife, Nicole, and infant son.

Matt Kurtz is a lover of all things horror but grew up terrified of the dark. It was while cowering under the covers at bedtime that his mind leaped into overdrive, creating scenarios of terror he'd eventually spew onto the page decades later. To read more about him and his work, visit www.strikingly.com/mattkurtz.

Daryl Marcus is a lover and writer of all things fiction. He has been published in *Under the Bed Magazine, New Realm,* and was the 2012 First Place winner of the Scott and Zelda Fitzgerald Museum Association Literary Contest for Short Stories. He lives in Colorado with his wife.

Stephen McQuiggan (*Baldus Moronicus*) is a malignant weed that causes ennui, irritation, and extreme aggression to any unfortunate enough to come into sustained contact with it, and which grows almost exclusively in N. Ireland.

Adam Millard is the author of sixteen novels, seven novellas, and more than a hundred short stories, which can be found in various collections and anthologies. Probably best known for his post-apocalyptic fiction, Adam also writes fantasy/horror for children, as well as bizarro fiction for several publishers. His "Dead" series has been the filling in a Stephen King/Bram Stoker sandwich on Amazon's bestsellers chart, and the translation rights have recently sold to German publisher, Voodoo Press.

Geoffrey L. Mudge is a writer of horror and dark fantasy. Being an air force brat and travel hound, he has visited and lived in various locales around the world. In his travels, he consumed the cultural fears shared by our global community and he hopes to inflict these fears on the literate populace with extreme prejudice. Mudge is currently residing in central Texas, and when not writing he enjoys frightening local children and wildlife with his partner in crime, Moxie, the wonder mutt of indeterminate origin.

T. L. Norman has enjoyed writing from a very young age. Science fiction is her favorite genre to write because of the freedom to create the "what if" scenarios that frequent her imagination, but she also enjoys writing in the horror genre, where horrors of the psyche can be just as frightening as physical horrors. Her short story "Think Tank" was published two years ago in an anthology, and she has also had a short story "Circus Ship" published online. Her other writing includes three articles on NASCAR in a racing e-zine and ghostwriting of two non-fiction books. She lives in Calgary, Alberta, Canada with her husband and 4 children where she continues creating works with mental health as underlying themes.

James Park lives in Columbus, Ohio with his gorgeous and delightfully articulate wife Ngouanephone. He's been featured in a number of genre fiction publications, including Dark Moon Digest, Ghostlight Magazine, Cemetery Moon, and Sanitarium Magazine. New work is scheduled to appear in Infernal Ink Magazine, Night to Dawn Magazine, and Massacre Magazine. He has contributed horror stories to a plethora of upcoming anthologies: Books 1 and 2 of The New Whakazoid Circus, Lost in the Witching Hour, Moon Shadows, and Demonic Possession. He will also have a piece of well-crafted smut published in the Apologues' of Erotica anthology.

Nicky Peacock is an English author living in the UK. She writes horror, urban fantasy, paranormal romance, and the odd steampunk dystopia. She runs a local writers' group in her home town where she continues to turn innocent new writers to the dark side. She can be found online at http://nickypeacockauthor. wordpress.com/

Michael C. Schutz-Ryan was born and raised in the frozen tundra of Wisconsin. He attended the UW-Stevens Point and graduated with an English degree from the Madison campus. A lifelong diet of Ray Bradbury and Stephen King whet his appetite for the macabre. A lover of all things horror, he plumbs the depths of Netflix in search of decent scary movies. He lives in northern California with his husband and the enduring spirit of their cat, Catie. You can follow him on Twitter, @schutz_ryan, and like him on Facebook: www.facebook.com/michaelcschutzryan.

A. P. Sessler, a resident of North Carolina's Outer Banks, searches for that unique element that twists the everyday commonplace into the weird. When he's not writing fiction, he composes music, dabbles in animation, and muses about theology and mind-hacking, all while watching way too many online movies. His short stories have appeared in *Zippered Flesh 2*, *Dandelions of Mars*, *SQ Magazine*, *Strangely Funny*, *Allusions of Innocence*, and *Human Echoes* podcast.

Julianne Snow is the author of the *Days with the Undead* series and the founder of Zombieholics Anonymous. She writes within the realms of speculative fiction, has roots that go deep into horror, and is a member of the Horror Writers Association. Julianne has pieces of short fiction in publications from Sirens Call Publications, Open Casket Press, 7DS Books, James Ward Kirk Publishing, Coffin Hop Press and Hazardous Press, and upcoming collections from May December Publications, 7DS Books, and Firbolg Publishing. *The Carnival 13*, a collaborative round-robin novella for charity that she contributed to and helped to spearhead was released in October 2013. Her collection of zombie short fiction, *Glimpses of the Undead* is available online at all major retailers. You can follow Julianne on Twitter, @CdnZmbiRytr, or "like" her on Facebook, https://www.facebook.com/JulianneSnowAuthor. For a list of her published works, please check out her Amazon Author Page, http://www.amazon.com/Julianne-Snow/e/B007WH0MN4/, and don't forget to check out her blogs: http://dayswiththeundead.com/; http://theflipsideofjulianne.wordpress.com/; and http://zombieholicsanonymous.com/.

Nicholas Stella is a public servant living in Sydney, Australia with his wife and their two little monsters. His story "Duncan Checks Out" won the 2011 Australian Horror Writers Association Short Story Competition. Nicholas has had his work appear in *Midnight Echo* Magazine and on the website of Oz Horror Con.

DJ Tyrer is the person behind *Atlantean Publishing* and has been widely published in anthologies and magazines in the UK, USA, and elsewhere, including *Cthulhu Haiku and Other Mythos Madness* (Popcorn Press), *Sorcery & Sanctity: A Homage to Arthur Machen* (Hieroglyphics Press) and the *Steampunk Cthulhu* anthology from Chaosium, and issues of *Surreal Grotesque* and *Cthulhu*, as well as two novellas available on the Kindle, *The Yellow House* (Dynatox Ministries) and *Acting Strangely* (Jazzclaw Publishing). DJ Tyrer's website is at http://djtyrer.blogspot.co.uk/. The Atlantean Publishing website is at http://atlanteanpublishing.blogspot.co.uk/.

Bryan Vogt has been captivated by the horror genre ever since his diaper-wearing butt first plopped down in front of the television to watch *Creature Features* on a Friday night. During his free time he enjoys reading, watching bad "B" movies, pursuing artistic endeavors, and photographing insects. He lives in Illinois with his lovely wife, Elizabeth, and their three attack cats.

Jonathan Woodrow is a writer of dark, mostly speculative fiction. His short stories have appeared in numerous publications, including Under the Bed Magazine and Roar and Thunder Magazine among others, with several more slated to appear over the next few months. So keep an eye out! He lives in a small town outside of Toronto with his wife and two children.

For some, death is not the end. There are those who are doomed to walk the earth for all eternity, those who are trapped between one plain of existence and the next, those who, for whatever reason, cannot or will not let go of the lives they left behind. These are the vengeful spirits, the tortured souls, the ghosts that haunt our realm. Welcome to FROM BEYOND THE GRAVE, a collection of 19 original ghost stories.

Available in print from Amazon.com and Barnes and Noble, and in digital formats from Amazon.com, Barnes and Noble, and Kobo books.

We survived *The Beast from 20,000 Fathoms*.
Then came *THEM!*, *It Came from Beneath the Sea*, and *The Deadly Mantis*.

They were merely practice runs.

Now prepare for
ATTACK! of the B-Movie Monsters:
Night of the Gigantis

Rampaging Rodents!

Terrifying Tentacles!

Bone-Crushing Claws!

Scientific experiments gone dreadfully wrong!

A collection of 23 holiday horrors benefiting the Elizabeth Glaser Pediatric AIDS Foundation.

Twas the fright before Christmas,
And all through the town,
Not a soul stirred,
No one dared make a sound...

Welcome to Deathlehem, where... Krampus, not Santa, brings the holiday cheer... the lights on the tree, so festive and bright, skitter and crawl and possess a lethal bite... malicious little elves, not a jolly one, know if you've been naughty—or nice... and family gatherings often turn deadly. So enter...
if you dare.

COMING SOON
from **GRINNING SKULL PRESS**…

DEAD MEN TELL NO TALES by Jeffrey Kosh